Orb and Arrow

Book I:
Exploration

Second Edition

V. L. Stuart

Orb and Arrow: Exploration – Book 1

Published by Pen It! Publications, LLC in the U.S.A.
812-371-4128 www.penitpublications.com

ISBN: 978-1-63984-249-0
Edited by Marla Williams VanHoy

Dedication

For 'Crowe' – you know who you are.

Pronunciation Guide

Brillar: brĭ-LAHR
Garnelden: gar-NEL-den
Harrolen: HÅ-row-len
Rodenis: row-DEN-ĭs
Darwallen: dahr-WĂLL-ĕn
Prendar: PREN-dar

Uthalef: oo-THAL-ef
Yarell: YA-rĕl
Wa'olle: wah-O-lay
Ǣdhahren: ǣd-HAH-ren
Ǣlethee: ǢL-eth-ee
K'ish: K'īsh

Ǣlfair Language

Ǣlfain/ǣlfain: ǢL-ain (as in 'gain')
the people of the southern forests also the –ish suffix

Ǣlfair: ǢL-fair; the language
Ǣlfi/ǣlfi: ǢL-fī; child (either sex)
Ǣlfen/ǣlfen: ǢL-fĕn; female
Ǣlfe/ǣlfe: ǢL-fā; male
Ǣlfa/ǣlfa: ǢL-fă; of the ǣlfain people
For plurals, add 'c' or 'ec' as: ǣlfec or ǣlfenec
(ǣ: as in **cat** but longer)

Table of Contents

Prologue

Lord Celbex stood well back from the battle lines, tense with excitement. "My mages," he said as he pointed them out to his advisor. "Look at them. I told you recruiting them was a good idea."

Behind a shield wall, fully protected from the advancing orcs, his warrior mages were firing wall after wall of spells, splitting the advancing ranks. One was ripping orcs apart with whirling blades, sending grey-green blood spurting from mortal wounds; the other was concentrating fists of stone on the orcs, pushing them back into their oncoming ranks, toppling two sets of orcs with one thrown spell.

Above the growls and cries of the men in the front line protecting the mages, Celbex could hear Harrolen's screams of glee as blood flew everywhere.

"That's my man." Celbex pointed again. "That one there." He licked his lips, listening to him. "He glories in their blood, in ripping them apart."

"And married to that fair wench, the one big with child." Nelin, his adviser, was an older man, keen-eyed and well tested in battle. Mages, he had advised his lord, could be dangerous and needed to be controlled. Harrolen loved his wife dearly. Control her, Nelin had told his lord, and he would be easily managed.

"We'll tie him to us with her and the child when it's born; he's ours." Celbex stood and cheered encouragement.

The other mage was grim as he mowed down row after row of orcs on the field, keeping them from the line of men in from of him. They were there to keep the orcs from reaching him with axe and club; he wanted them safe. He could sidestep the boulders orcs threw when they were close enough, but if they broke the line, he was vulnerable, and he knew it. He battered them, keeping them from the men protecting him. Blood from Harrolen's kills splattered his mouth and he spat it out.

At the rich tent above the field, there was wine as the lord and his advisor watched the battle, enjoying the flow of orc blood. A man came up behind them. "My lord?"

Lord Celbex stood and turned, giving the man a slight bow. It was always appropriate to be courteous to a Master of the K'ish. The man was robed and cowled, but they could see his pale face and watery eyes as he turned to watch the battle.

"Ah, Master, please take a seat and enjoy some wine." The K'ish shook his head.

"How soon? The blood must be fresh from a wound." The hushed voice was dry and breathless.

"The mages I recruited should be finished with them shortly. As soon as the rest turn, you can have your choice from the ones on the field and men to guard you." The K'ish nodded and stepped away into the shadows.

Nelin shuddered as the man faded away

"I still don't like it, m'lord. Consorting with K'ish." He kept his voice low.

His concern was waved away. "The potions he promised will amaze you." Celbex jumped up and pointed. "Look, they're driving them from the field!"

Harrolen was screaming as his shield barrier pushed forward. He was drenched in the blood of orcs and the red blood of some of his own wounded protectors. He didn't seem to care about either as he pushed them forward over the dead and dying on the field.

Near him, the other mage was pressing forward as well, tossing bolts of lightning at them, following the bolts with flame then of stone and thunder that decimated the enemy but drew no blood.

"My lord? That other mage? How do we hold him? A wench he fancies? Gold?"

"They both came for gold. It's a strong enough tie. And his friend, Harrolen, ties him. They are Brothers of the same Great House, together for years and pledged, on their honor, to defend each other when they agreed to join us here. No, he'll never break his oath or leave his honored Brother. We have them both." His smile was covetous. He stood and cheered as he watched the retreating orcs fall and die under the onslaught of the mages. He barely noticed when the K'ish began to move among the dying to collect their blood, their tongues, their eyes, but his advisor, Nelin, turned away, sickened by the sight.

***

"Let my mages come forward!" Lord Celbex commanded at the feast after the battle. The tents were bright with lanterns, full of music; servants with wine and food made sure that cups and plates were always full. Harrolen had been sitting with his wife, enjoying the night and the honors that were being given him, but his friend was lounging with two lovelies, stroking the neck and half-exposed breast of one, kissing her, then turning to take wine from a cup held to his lips by another woman. Both stood at their lord's command.

"My good men, my fine men, my warrior mages," Celbex extolled them as they came forward, one a bit unsteady with drink, Harrolen's arm under his, to kneel before their lord.

"The gold that was promised!" Celbex held the pouches high to cheers and then handed one to each of his warrior mages. "More wine for everyone," he called. There was more cheering.

"Now, a private word with you." He turned, motioning his mages to follow, taking them into a private tent where advisors waited. Celbex lounged on a soft chair and set his glass on a table. "I have another task for you and more gold to follow."

"As our lord wills," Harrolen answered with a greedy smile, dragging his drunken friend into a bow.

"That gold I gave you so freely comes from the taxes I collect from my tenants. Fine people, most of them, good farmers and herders who live under my protection. Now that the orcs have been driven back, with your fine aid, they will enjoy more of that protection and more land." He waved to Nelin, who spread a map on the table.

"Not all my lord's tenants have been so quick to pay their taxes. These small settlements here?" He pointed on the map. "Three houses in one, five in the other. My lord wishes to send a message to the rest of the small holders that taxes are to be paid when due."

"Tomorrow," Celbex smiled and leaned forward, "*you* will give them a lesson in obedience. A lesson that will have the rest… biddable? I could send soldiers out to punish them, but they could defend against soldiers, and a lesson from you will be so much stronger." He held out his arms. "You, with your spells of fire; I think fire would be best and lightning to strike them if they try to run from you? Yes, when they have been punished, I think it will ensure that the rest understand their duty to their liege lord." He leaned back, waiting.

"To our liege lord." Harrolen held up his goblet, laughing greedily, nudging his friend.

"Our liege lord." The man joined in the laughter, then downed his drink and swayed. "If my liege lord wills," he gave a drunken bow, "I left a wench or two alone and I think they need tending." He made a crude gesture and even Nelin laughed.

Celbex waved a hand and he stumbled out, hearing more laughter behind him as the rest leaned over the map. He took the arm of a drunken wench, tugging on her clothes, kissing her roughly his hand on her breast. Then he pulled her out toward his own tent, shouting, "Celebrations for everyone." Course laughter and nudges followed him.

In private, he urged the woman to drink again and spoke a brief spell to rid himself of the effects of the wine. When she was soundly asleep, he lifted the rear of the tent and crept out into the night to warn the local farmers. That done, he fled to a port and used gold to buy passage on a ship that was sailing at dawn. Safely away, he tried to forget Harrolen, occupying himself with learning what sailors had to teach, but in private, he wept for his Brother.

When he finally returned to the Great House, he wrapped himself in new studies and buried the past and his Brother. It would be more than a decade before he thought about him again.

Part I

The dimlock cannot be removed but by him who holds the key.
Elder Lore

Symbol of the Brotherhood
Teachers of War, Item and Creature Magic

*** 1 ***

Fourteen years later

A young woman came out of the forest track and stopped, still sheltered by the trees, to survey the land ahead. She had come several miles through the woods on the Riven Road that ran through them and had enjoyed the cool darkness under the trees. Now she gave a small sigh as she looked down the track to the crossroad. The area was wide and deep. From the grass and flowers, she could see that these fields had been fallowed for at least six months. A good sign. Game was scarce in the forests and it would be easier to find a meal in the open area ahead of her, perhaps even some tubers to roast in a small fire. Her mouth began to water.

She took a step into the open and stopped, remembering her training. Reaching out with far-sight, she looked for echoes of darkness and found none. "Move to near the limit of sight, then reach out again," the Sisterhood had taught her. At the time, she had found the lessons tiresome, but now, at two and twenty, her years of walk-about, even in the settled lands, had taught her their wisdom.

The crossroad was only a dozen paces beyond her, but her path lay directly ahead. As there was no sign of current traffic, Brillar stepped into the open and continued on her way. She was dressed for the road. Sturdy wellisboots, soft leggings of poda hide, and a light tunic. Her aresh wood short bow, as always, over her shoulder and quiver at her side. Her cloak and other necessities were in the foldbox at her belt. *No need for them yet*, she thought, running fingers along the braid of dark red-brown hair at her shoulder.

Amazingly, the sign at the crossroad was well-maintained. Eafel to the left, Ikenlo to the right, and Foringil ahead through the next woods and beyond. *A few carts and some horses*, she thought as a breeze rippled the green grasses and flowers. An easy walk in the direction she needed to travel. She took a few steps toward Foringil and stopped to finger some droppings near a cart track. *Still a bit warm, perhaps two hours.* Horsemen and carters stopped early to make camp and let the horses feed. *I may reach them tonight.*

She picked up her pace, easy to do on this wide road. Traffic among the three towns here and the farther Denwis was behind her must be as steady as the innkeeper had told her when he came out to the road to bid her goodbye and thank her for the healing she had performed in the village. "Was good of ye to stay a while, as we have no healer of our own." He had thanked her, then became cautious. "Nae bandits be oft'n on these roads," he had said with his deep brogue. "We be a peaceful folk for the most, and the sheriff keeps good watch. Bad for business, bandits be." He had looked at her with some concern. "Still, a woman alone."

At his caution, Brillar had grinned and, in a smooth movement, plucked an arrow from her hip quiver, dropped to her knee and let fly. The fluid motion was over in the blink of an eye and the arrow lodged in a tree stump across from the inn.

Staring, the innkeeper looked to the arrow and back to its mistress and her bow. Brillar stood and clapped him on the shoulder as he stood dumbfounded before she went to the stump to retrieve her arrow. She had pulled lightly and the arrow was easy to remove.

"Forgi' me, lass. I think you equal to this road, or any." He scratched his head. "A fine shot there, a fine shot," he added as she crossed back to him.

"Thank you, good host," she had returned, shaking his rough hand, "and a fine day to you." The inn stood at the edge of the forest road and was soon behind her, lost among the trees. *A fine day for a walk through the woods*, she had thought as she entered the forest. Far-sight had shown her no danger there.

Now she stood at the crossroad and scanned the fields. In the distance, a cwel's head popped up above the grasses. *Too long for my bow, but where there's one, there are others.* Cwel, the flop-eared root grubbers were good eating, and where cwel dined there could be roots and tubers for her as well, although some of their diet was inedible for her.

She had lingered long enough. The sun was warm and the sky held no hint of rain. The track was wide and dry. It was a good day for walking and her stride ate up the distance easily. A few paces later, an unwary cwel raised its head, one paw holding a tuber hanging to its jaw, an easy target. With the same ease and grace that had amazed the innkeeper, Brill had an arrow loosed and the cwel was downed.

As she picked up her kill, Brillar spotted some of the tubers she had been hoping for. Taking out her belt knife, she quickly extracted them from the rich soil. She sniffed them, admiring their deep earthy scent and, shaking off some of the earth, stowed them in a belt pouch. Then she turned her attention to the cwel, deftly cleaning and skinning it. She wrapped the meat in its pelt, securing it by tying the legs together, then used the long furry tail to tie the bundle to her belt. Satisfied, she returned to the road.

I dine well tonight, she thought and lengthened her stride to make up some time, thinking back to the inn. The innkeeper's wife had made a fine, savory stew, rich and well-simmered last night and sent her off with a breakfast of eggs, fresh bread, and churned butter. Brillar often traveled on trail rations; today, she had been lucky. While there was plenty of large game around, killing a deer for one person was a waste and might deprive a family of food. She preferred to hunt small game when alone. 'Kill as you must for food,' was her father's early lesson to her and her siblings. 'There must be food on the table or your mother will howl at me.' They had all laughed at that. Theirs was a rich farm.

Thoughts of those days took her to the forest edge and she reached out into the twilight. *Two men, horses, a cart, something else, something dark?* She strained a bit. *Another animal?* She knew that carters sometimes had strange animals with them, using them to amuse and attract town folk so it was easier to sell their wares. *Seems safe enough.*

The air under the trees was a bit chilly, but she decided not to bring out her cloak until she had taken the measure of what lie ahead. Cwel over a fire with tubers was fine, but perhaps the men had a stew pot—carters often did—and they could add the meat. *If*, she remembered, *I am welcome at their fire.*

About a half-mile into the woods, she could smell their fire and the heavy scent of horses; she kept on. At fifty paces, she could see the fire off to the right in what appeared to be a small clearing off the road. Thirty paces more, and she called the standard greeting, "Ho, travelers," and waited for a response.

There was some undefined movement near the fire, a rustling, then, "The traveler is welcome," came the response.

Relaxing a bit, Brillar walked forward. A lone man, hatted and wrapped in a cloak, sat on a log near the fire, with what appeared to be a cwel roasted on a spit over it. "Welcome," he said again and gestured to a second log. "Sit, sit, the night can be damp."

Brillar's senses tingled just as a hoarse croak came from the right, "B'ware."

She leaped to the left, instantly fitting an arrow to her bow as a large man carrying a knife and rope jumped from behind a tree near where she had stood. Missing his quarry, he stumbled and fell to one knee.

"Damn you, Trog," shouted the first man, leaping to his feet and pulling the sword he had hidden under his cloak. The steel flashed in the firelight. He took a step toward Brillar.

"Drop the sword or die there." Her voice was steady, steadier than she felt. No bandits on the road? So much for that advice.

"Wot, a lass?" He raised the sword in threat and took another step, his last before he fell forward, her arrow lodged in his chest.

Another arrow was in her bow at once. "Your choice, Trog. Stand and let me see you." The big man rose slowly, wary of her bow.

"Drop the rope and knife." He did so. "Better drop the belt as well, just to be sure." She gestured slightly with the bow.

"If I drops me belt, me pants will fall," he whined. Although he had some size to him, he sounded like a child.

"Then they'll fall. Or do you care to join your friend?" Now there was steel in Brillar's voice. "One death here should be enough."

Trog untied his belt slowly. His hide pants, which were indeed tied up by the belt around his shirt, slid to the ground leaving him in his long shirt.

"Now put out your hands, step to the log and kneel."

Trog did as he was told and she moved to his belt. It was well-worn with no buckle, just leather straps to tie it around the waist.

Brillar slung her bow and slid out her knife quickly, warning, "Mind you, my knife is as fast as my bow," as she knelt to examine the belt. He nodded warily.

She noted that her fingers were trembling as she reached for the belt and took a deep, calming breath.

Two years on the trail? Have I changed so much? Whose lessons do I follow now? She shook her head to clear it and reached for Trog's belt pouch.

The pouches held a few coins and some trail rations. Evidently, the knife was his only weapon and she tucked it into her belt then kicked the belt over to him and threw him his pants, keeping the purse.

"We can't have you standing there in such an undignified state. Tie up your pants, then sit down." He did as he was told and she could smell the acrid scent of fear from him.

Am I still a healer? She dismissed the thought. The man had threatened her life twice; there had been no time to wound and heal, not with a second threat in Trog. She wrinkled her nose in distaste. No healer ever meant to instill fear.

Brillar untied the cwel from her belt and tossed it toward the edge of the fire. No sense being encumbered. She moved to the dead man. He was better dressed than Trog, a true belt with buckle, a belt knife, solid brown boots, and his clothes were made of good cloth, not homespun.

"My friend, he was," said Trog. "Named Pilik." He didn't move from his place, only watched her with round eyes.

She nodded, keeping one eye on Trog and one on the dead man. She rolled him over, removed the broken part of her arrow with its distinctive fletching and threw it on the fire. She tugged his belt from him.

"A heavy purse, this," she said, looking at Trog, who hung his head. "So he was your friend, but all you have is coppers while he has," she dumped the contents on the ground next to her, "silver and, yes, some gold in with his coppers. Perhaps he was not the best of friends?"

Trog shook his head and seemed on the edge of tears. "Good enough."

Brillar picked up the gold coins and some of the silver and set them aside, the rest she put back into Trog's purse and tossed it to him. Pilik's cloak, she threw to one side of the fire; the sword and Pilik's knife were tossed into the woods. Wary eyes stared at the now heavy purse and Trog licked his lips.

"Take the purse," she told him, bent to pick it up, keeping his eyes on her as she stood. "You'll need a story. You were out gathering firewood. You heard your friend yell for help, but when you got closer, you saw three men and knew your friend was already dead. There were too many so you didn't go any farther. You waited until the men rode off, then you searched the camp, but you were afraid the men would be back. You carried the body to the open ground—that is what you are going to do—and buried him with that broken shovel. You will do that too. It will be too dark to go on, so you will go to sleep in the open. In the morning, you will stumble toward Denwis. Do they know you in Denwis?"

"I've a cousin there." He was fingering the heavy purse. He had never had silvers.

"Then that will give you good reason. So, do you understand what you're to do?"

She had Trog repeat it, although she had her suspicions that with Pilik dead and silver in his pouch, Trog would say little to anyone. As he was told, he picked up Pilik's body and a broken handled shovel the men had been using to soften the ground for sleeping and headed toward the fields.

Most likely, she thought, *he will stop several times. All should go well.* Then she remembered the hoarse warning and turned toward the cart.

What she found, made her wish she hadn't been so lenient with Trog. There was a man, cut, bruised, half-clothed, and half-starved, tied to a post on the cart. The odor said he hadn't seen water in some time. Flies settled on him, were twitched off and returned. Even in the dim light, she could see the worst of it, a dimlock collar partly sunk in his flesh.

She stood back, shuddering; there had been lessons on dimlock lore when she was a student. A dimlock collar, made in mocking imitation of a great chain of office, was used to keep a mage from casting a spell or reaching out for mana. Its medallions were raised disks connected by short links, each disk active with a dark spell. With its sinister power, it made the wearer separate from mana and the world around him. A dimlock was used to bind, to punish, to transport a mage whose deeds were so horrible that only execution awaited him. Still, standing there, reaching out with all her power, Brillar found none of the evil that was said to radiate from such a mage, even when trapped by a dimlock. Nothing came from the man but anguish, grief, pain, and behind it... Behind it, Light? Dim, diffused, a weak shadow only, but Light. She made her decision.

First things first. The rough cart was two-wheeled, a style used by ordinary traders. Moving forward, Brillar cut through the leather thongs that held the man, grabbing at him with her other arm as he slumped toward the ground. Lowering him gently, she took out her flask and held it to his lips, tipping his head up so he could drink. He gulped gratefully.

"Thank... thank..." The voice was parched, weary, frightened.

"I should thank you, mage, for your warning. It must have cost you some strength."

From under dirty, matted hair, quizzical brown eyes met hers. "The dimlock collar has only one use. I can try to remove it, but there are risks. Pilik had no key." He nodded slowly and reached feebly for the flask.

"Yes, drink first. I hear a spring nearby and there's a jug on the cart. I'll get enough water to clean some of these wounds."

Better to use water for cleaning and save her strength for whatever was to come. If the dimlock had been used justly, she might have to strike quickly to avoid being overcome. What did she know of the dimlock besides its use? A key needed to unlock it. She had some skill with locks and smiled, remembering how easy it had become to sneak into locked doors and cabinets at the farm. *Unlocking this thing,* she thought, *might be easy, but removing it?* Each of the medallions was sunk into his flesh and they would have to be removed one by one. The spells on them would resist their removal if the lock was opened without the key. She wondered how long he had been secured.

Brillar propped him against the wheel and took the jug for water. When she returned, she found he had emptied the flask and refilled it from the jug. Checking in the cart, she found a cup, took it to the fire and filled it with water. "I need more light. Can you lean on me as far as the fire?"

A nod was the only answer.

The fire was only a few paces away, but Brillar almost lost her grip on him twice, he was so slippery with blood and fluids.

"Rest a moment while I prepare." Again, a short nod as she settled him gently on Pilik's cloak, folding its edges over him.

Brillar moved out of the man's view and pressed her fingers to the lock on her foldbox. Her mother, under the guidance of an Item Grand Master, had made it with all her skill and, although it looked common enough, it was far from ordinary. As it responded to her touch, the box opened, and opened again, folding outward with a faint glow. Brillar took several types of herbs and powders, cloth, a lock pick, and a small knife, plus other things she thought she needed.

What else do I know about the dimlock? She bit her lip in concentration, looking from the contents of the foldbox to the man at the fire. *If the lore I've studied was correct, no part of the dimlock can touch human skin. His and mine must be protected.* She pulled out a pair of gloves and looked to the cwel skinned bundle, nodding thoughtfully. She was ready. Responding to her gestures, the box refolded and became ordinary again.

Moving to the fire, she unwrapped the meat from the cwel skin and laid it on stones near the fire to cook slowly. The skin, she cut into two pieces. She hoped the cwel skin would serve to protect him long enough for what she needed to do.

At the fire, the man had closed his eyes. She could see he wasn't sleeping, could feel him gathering his strength for what she had to do. She sat beside him and wiped his face with a damp cloth.

"Are you ready?" Again, a nod. "I have to turn you…" But he was already rolling onto his left shoulder, exposing the lock on the collar. Like the collar itself, the lock was a dull grey.

"We begin," she murmured. She sprinkled a bit of powder on the lock and he stiffened.

"*Yenwar, heneth,*" she whispered and inserted the pick into the lock, easing it in, turning it gently, twisting, until the lock opened. The simplest task was done and the lock was nestled on part of the cwel skin.

"The lock is open, but the collar has embedded itself. Each medallion holds a spell that the key would have released and each will have to be dealt with. Are you strong enough to continue?" She saw him take a deep breath and exhale. "Then we go on."

The thin blade was now in one gloved hand while the other held a cwel skin to the collar, knowing it would burn if she touched it and renew his pain if it touched him. She dusted the dimlock with powdered herbs then inserted the blade at the edge of the first medallion and began to push it slowly under the metal. He stiffened at once, his eyes tightly shut, and a tremor passed through his body.

"Be steady." She put a hand on his shoulder briefly. She pushed the knife farther and the first medallion came free, dangling from the link that held it to the lock. Link and medallion were tucked in with the lock. "Not as deep as I feared," she murmured, "a good sign."

One by one, Brillar loosened the progressively larger medallions of the dimlock collar, cutting and tearing flesh as she did so. There were only two near the lock, but each time one was removed, the man shuddered, the tremor each time slightly more violent. Blood seeped from each wound. When she reached his shoulder, Brillar rolled the mage onto his back and stopped. She cast a light spell, then a stronger one to deal with his pain, but they didn't seem to be effective.

"The dimlock again. Spells will not be much use." She gave him more water, drank some herself, and rinsed the blood from her gloves.

"Rest a moment," she told him, but he opened his eyes warily. "Resting eyes are closed," she said sternly, and felt an echo of humor as he shut them again. Remembering the tubers she still carried, she shoved them into the ashes of the fire, adjusted the spit and the meat Pilik had roasting, and then added more wood. The smell of roasting meat distracted her only a moment.

Brillar took up her delicate work again. Around them, the forest had darkened, but sight and firelight were enough. Link by link, the chain came free and medallions rested on the cwel skin. With each removal, the man's tremors grew stronger.

"I'm at the center pendant." She made sure the medallions were well rolled up and tied in the cwel skin. "Rest a while, then I'll need to roll you to your right side." A sweaty hand grabbed her wrist. "I need rest as well. This is not an archer's skill." His hold relaxed and she took a moment to cut some meat from the roast, eating hurriedly. A somewhat underdone tuber completed a hasty meal.

"Ready?" In answer, he rolled to his right. "Very well then." She sprinkled more herbs on the links, the medallions, and slid the knife under the first, as always, feeling his tremor as she removed it and slid it onto another part of the cwel skin. Again, she rolled him to his back as she reached the shoulder, then continued her bloody work. She took a moment to wash the flesh as she removed these medallions, sickened by the damage they had done, and dusted them with powdered herbs. Herbs, at least, would ease the pain where spells could not. She set a cup of water to heat near the fire.

As she removed the remainder of the medallions, his breathing became light and fast, the tremors longer. It was well into the night when she reached the pendent, the last and most powerful part of the dimlock. The rest were well secured.

Brillar stopped. Taking some herbs from their pouch, she crushed them between her palms. The air around them seemed to freshen, the fire to brighten. She dropped the herbs in the cup at the fire. As she had hoped, they swirled and turned orange in the warm water. She picked the cup up gingerly. Turning, she saw his eyes were open and staring.

"You'll need to drink this," she said, but his hand was already reaching for the cup. "No, you may spill it." She held the cup to his lips and he drank deeply then lay back down.

"The pendant will be the worst. You know that. Take a minute for the herbs to do their work."

"Yes," came his hoarse words, "you've done well thus far." The words were almost condescending even though, once the collar had been locked, he could not have removed it or even touched it with a hand.

"Many thanks," she muttered to herself, a bit vexed, "perhaps this knife should slip. Ready?" she said aloud. She could see him steel himself for what would come, his body tightened, then he nodded. She had to admire the courage behind the simple nod.

Letting the cwel skins and their deadly contents hang well-wrapped on his chest, Brillar scattered more herbs on the pendant. His body shuddered as her knife slid under the pendant, and he gasped in pain, the first sound he had made as she cut away the dimlock. Her highest spell against pain, cast quickly as he gasped, seemed to make no difference to him.

This time, the blade needed to go deep and deeper still. With each new cut, his shuddering grew worse and she had to wait for it to subside before she could go on. Fresh blood reddened the area around the medallion, running across thin ribs. She slid the blade to the left, cutting around the edge of the pendant. His breath came in short gasps. She cut through the last of the flesh and prized the pendant out, cradling it on a hastily snatched piece of the cwel skin before it could touch him again.

Her patient seized, back arched in agony as the last of the dimlock came free, a reaction to his release from its dark spells. He thrashed arms and legs violently, nearly throwing himself into the fire. Brillar threw herself on his legs, holding them until the seizure eased.

As suddenly as it had come, the fit left him. His body relaxed, sagged, all its strength drained.

Brillar moved to check his heart and saw his pulse beating weakly in his neck.

"Not dead then," she said aloud, exhaling sharply. She took out more herbs, added them to fresh water and began to wash her patient, cleaning away the blood and wiping away accumulated dirt from his imprisonment. Exhausted, she drew in mana and cast spells against her own exhaustion. Spells for healing him would have to wait. A full healing on someone as wasted as her patient was, would take time. She moved away and opened the foldbox. The entire dimlock, she wrapped more tightly in the cwel skin, retying it with more strips of leather from the box, and stowing it safely away. Now she removed her cloak, blankets and some herbs for the morning. Looking to her patient, she found him still quiet and covered him with a blanket. She stopped to eat some more of the cwel and a fully cooked, pale tuber. Trog had piled branches nearby and she added wood to the fire.

A nicker from one of the horses caught her attention, and she went to where they were tethered.

"I see I'm to draw water for you as well," she told them and took their empty buckets to the spring. "Too dark for more, friends," she told them and went back to the fire.

Now, kneeling by him near the fire, she took time to inspect her patient. He was haggard, his face grey with exhaustion and lined with pain. A ragged beard covered half his face and his hair was lank and dirty.

Certainly a Master and not young. That is to be expected. No one skilled enough to warrant a dimlock could be young. Still, he seems strong and must have been healthy. A good face and he's un-greyed. Brillar's thoughts began to wander. What she had done, the hours it had taken, had been more tiring than a dozen archery competitions. Recognizing her own fatigue, she wrapped herself in the cloak, leaned against a log, and drifted into a light sleep.

*** 2 ***

Birds were singing, and she woke with a start, quickly realizing she must have slept well into the day. The fire had burned to ashes and her patient still slept. Standing, she stretched to relieve cramped muscles and went to check on him, finding that his pulse was stronger. Taking a stick, she stirred the fire and was rewarded with live coals. She added more small branches and watched them come alight. The rest of the previous day's kill was well-cooked, and she sliced some from it to eat as she worked. With daylight, she was able to search the cart and found some men's clothing, a kettle, cups, a bit of food and some pots, under rough sacking. The post with his blood on it, she wrenched off and threw in the fire. Then she filled the deep kettle and set it to boil, adding the rest of the meat. Still ravenous from the night's work, she dug a warm tuber from the ashes and ate it, following it with gulps of spring water. She put water, herbs, and cwel meat into the kettle to cook. Near the spring's pool, she refreshed herself, then washed and returned to the fire.

"Good morning," she greeted her patient when she saw his eyes open on her return. "Turn down that blanket and let's see what needs be done."

When he complied, her eyes widened, evoking a chuckle from the man.

"You named me 'mage' and you're still surprised?" His voice was weak and tired.

Brillar knelt and examined his chest. His bruises were fading and minor cuts had healed, but the wounds from the dimlock were still ugly and there was something odd about them. He pulled up the blanket as if chilled.

"Yes," he said hoarsely, "they'll heal slowly and will need your help." Wounds from a dimlock, she remembered, took time to heal and were impervious to even the strongest healing spells.

"I'm only amazed that you had the strength to draw in enough mana to perform any self-healing." She dipped a cup into the kettle and added more herbs. "Drink. It will warm you. I have to tend to the horses."

She fetched more water and, finding a rope in the cart, encircled a section of the clearing as a grazing area, making sure the stream from the spring ran through it. In daylight, she inspected the trio she would have to lead to fresh grass. The largest, a chestnut stallion, pulled on his lead, nickering and showing her the whites of his eyes. The others, a fine grey mare and a roan cart horse, responded to his distrust with their own.

Breathing a sigh, Brillar closed her eyes and relaxed her body. She reached out to the animals with friendship, soothing their fears. When she opened her eyes, all three had approached, ears pricked and attentive. She let the stallion nuzzle her hand, then brushed his forelock, finding a charm tied there. Feeling its darkness, she removed the charm, throwing it on a rock and breaking it with her heel. The stallion's head went up at once and he whinnied his distress but responded to her waves of soothing. When they were all calm, she untied the leads and took them to the new pasture. Satisfied, she returned to the fire to find her patient shuddering.

"That drink was to warm you, not freeze you," she said. She put her hand on his forehead. "Fever. I'm sorry, I should have guessed with the wounds from the dimlock. And then your exertion to heal scratches!"

"Don't scold," he shivered in response.

"Don't speak!" she scolded. Pulling down the blanket, she inspected the wounds and smelled them. The odor nauseated her. "Infection. Be as still as you can."

She added her cloak to his blanket. "I'll need more herbs. A few moments only." Opening the fold box, she took out healing herbs and a small orb. Closing it, she went back to her patient.

She crushed the herbs into a cup of water. Holding the orb above it, she chanted the arcane words then breathed over the cup. As she did so, the water and leaves blended and thickened, becoming a light green salve; its glow spoke of its power. Taking a clean cloth, she dipped it into the ointment and began to press it lightly into the infected wounds, still chanting.

His body stiffened and he clenched his teeth as his breathing became labored. Still, she tended the raw flesh, first on his chest then his shoulders and back. As she reached the last of the wounds, his breathing eased but she continued until all the salve was gone. A few words with the orb and she dispelled the fever. His body relaxed and he slept.

Sitting back on her heels, she inspected him again, shaking her head at his thinness. His shrunken flesh was a reminder of her own hunger and a glance at the sky told her it was already past midday. Trail rations and slices of meat had to suffice as they could be eaten as she worked.

"Sleep is healing in itself," she murmured, "but the waking must be working." There was fuel to gather for the fire, more water to carry, the cart to tend to. Then there was the matter of more food. The tubers in the cart, she cleaned and cut and put into the kettle to cook with the meat. She searched the area around the camp for herbs. When she returned to add them to the pot, he was snoring.

Gently, to keep from waking him, she touched his forehead. "Fever broken already? The Sisters would be proud," she said quietly and chuckled to herself.

'More time,' Sister Rodenis had insisted. 'You need more time with us.' But Brillar had been impatient and left her sister Alliana to her studies with the Sisters.

She shook her head at the memory. Now, the sky was darkening as she took a cup of stew for herself, adding more fuel to the fire and water to the kettle.

Checking her patient, she began to think that sleeping looked like a fine idea. She stretched her far-sight to the limit and sensed no danger. The stallion responded from the pasture with a whinny and she smiled a bit. *As I thought, the stallion is his. Let him keep watch then.* She stretched out by the fire and slept. A light rain fell overnight, waking her, and she put a lid on the kettle and added wood to the fire. Twitching rain off her cloak and checking her patient, she went back to sleep.

Sleep is indeed a healer, Brillar thought as she woke. A glance at the sky said she had slept well into the morning. Her patient was still asleep but she could see he had a strong pulse. The blanket over him was damp and she removed it, covering him to the waist with her cloak so she could tend to the wounds left by the dimlock. She made more of the healing salve and he slept through its application, although he twitched a bit and moaned when she touched the place where the pendent had lain. It had cut him near to the bone and the flesh around it was red and raw despite her salve. She hung the blanket to dry. One edge of the cloak he lay on had been near the fire and was dry, the other was damp, but it was too soon to shift him from his resting place.

Brillar checked the soup, which had bubbled down to the consistency of stew while she slept. She scooped some out and enjoyed its rich flavor. *Not the usual way to break a fast, but good enough,* she thought. Her patient, however, would need broth. She added more water to the kettle then checked the horses which came to her without caution. *Time,* she thought, *to see if he'll take some soup.*

This proved harder than it sounded. She had to raise him up a bit, more than half asleep, and give him short sips. Still, she was able to get soup into him before he lapsed into a deeper sleep. She spent the rest of the day tending to the fire, the food, the horses. The blanket dried quickly in the spring sun, and she retrieved her cloak, recovering him with the blanket and applying more of the salve. Deciding he wouldn't wake, she also tended the other cuts and scrapes that he had partly healed with a spell. Her healing spells were stronger, but even spells sapped some of the patient's strength as his body responded to them, so she used the salve liberally. He did not wake.

"A healing sleep is long and deep," she recited from her lessons quietly. "Perhaps he'll be ready to speak in the morning."

A farmer passed by on foot in the afternoon, heading toward Denwis. He looked at her curiously as he passed, but she turned her back, wanting no company. Trail rations and some soup were the evening meal. Brillar added more water to the soup and wood to the fire and settled in for the night.

This time she woke early, stretching stiffly. She washed and refreshed herself then put more wood on the fire and water in the soup. Her patient came awake as she finished some trail rations and water. Time for some answers if he was able.

"Can you sit to eat?" He nodded, and she helped him sit, astonished as he tried to stand, shakily.

He looked at her ruefully. "Necessaries," he croaked. She made him sit long enough to find a stout stick he could use as a cane. He nodded then took himself behind a tree. His ragged clothes barely covered him. Coming back, he nearly fell and she had to assist him. Settling him near the fire, she handed him a cup of soup.

He sipped it, savoring its rich flavor, chewing bits of meat and vegetables. He took several strong pulls on the broth and stretched it out for more. She refilled his cup, watching him drink, feeling him gather his strength. She stretched out on her cloak, taking an attitude of ease.

"Now," he said finally, "it is time for answers." Brown eyes stared at her, probing. He took a long pull on the cup. Sick as he was, she could feel his power and sat up slowly, smiling.

"Indeed," she returned, resisting him, "answers." Green eyes stared back at him. "You first."

Her reply caught him in mid-swallow and he sputtered, coughing, then chuckled. "A strong answer. But first, might I have more of that wonderful soup?" His voice was querulous.

She filled his cup and waited as he sipped and ate.

"I am Garnelden, called Elden, Mage of the Four Powers, with First Standing in three." That raised her eyebrows. Even her mother held only two Firsts and she was an Elder.

"Not many reach such heights, and yet there you were strapped to a cart wearing a dimlock," she responded quietly.

He hung his head sheepishly, lank brown hair falling over his face. "I was taken unawares."

"A Mage of the Four Powers? Unawares?" She stirred the fire and added a branch casually.

He cleared his throat. "Drink was involved."

Brillar gave him a slight smile. "And a woman, I'd wager."

"Two, in fact," he admitted grudgingly. "But your name?"

"Brillar of Laurenfell, student of Life only. Daughter of Lady Darwallen of the Life Sisterhood and Sir Prendar."

"Well met then, Brillar of Laurenfell." Brown eyes stayed on her steadily.

"And to you," she responded politely. "And so, Mage of the Four Powers, how did a woman or two manage to get their hands on a dimlock collar and why? The one I killed was no woman."

He looked at her sharply. "I thought I felt death, even in my state. Was it Pilik?" When she nodded, he continued, "Bounty hunter. He paid the women."

"So, a bounty? If it's great enough, I may stop feeding you," she said jokingly.

"Is 20,000 in gold enough?" He seemed almost wary now as she sat back in reaction.

That much in gold was enough for a long and rich life of leisure for more than one family. Then she laughed. "Enough for some, but blood money doesn't interest me." She refilled his cup again. "And the collar?"

"They had it from the man who set the bounty." He stared into his cup, sad, withdrawn.

She considered more questions but put them aside and stood up. "Enough tales for now. Do you feel strong enough to wash?"

His lips twitched upward. "Am I a bit rank, then?"

"A bit, and still too weak for more casting, so don't argue with me on that. There were some clothes in the cart, so I'll bring water there. The spring is farther and there's no need for you to walk that far." She had to help him, supporting one arm while he leaned on his stick. He sank down on the end of the cart with a sigh of relief, already weary with the exertion as she took the jug for water and poured it slowly over his arms and down his legs. He rubbed them with sacking as she went for more water.

On her second trip from the spring, the stallion was with Garnelden.

"It seems I was so rank that even Jez would have no part of me." He smiled as she poured water on his back below the dimlock wounds. Then he asked for one last jug, and she turned her back politely so he could finish washing. With a final rinse, Garnelden declared himself clean enough for clothing and dressed in the things from the cart, rough, ill-fitting clothes but no boots. He stroked the stallion's long cheek. "Go back to graze and keep good watch for us." The stallion eyed her but returned to the pasture.

"My thanks for finding the charm that bound him." She tilted her head, questioning. "There must have been one; without it, he would have tried to kill to free me and been killed in return. We've been together a long time, Jez and I."

Ignoring his thanks, Brillar nodded at him approvingly. "You clean up well," she told him, although the clothes hung on him.

"I've lost some weight, it seems." He pushed himself up, holding the cart, and she helped him back to the fire.

She had him sit a moment while she removed the bloody cloak, set it aside and spread a blanket on the ground. Once he was settled with a second blanket over him, she sat back and waited. A man will talk or not. Waiting was best. Garnelden was able to help himself to more soup. Tension and relief came from him in alternate waves.

"They took me at West Riversgate. That was on the sixth day of Tebil, during the festival." He looked at her inquiringly.

"Seventeen days." To herself, she thought, *How is he even alive?*

He shuddered. His words came out haltingly. "Once the dimlock was fastened, I lost track of day and night; both were one; the Light was gone." He seemed to shrink into himself. "I ate and drank, I think, when they thought or cared to feed me. Everywhere was the same. There was only the pain, the separation. The separation was worse than the pain." He stopped and put a hand to his face.

It was Brillar's turn to shudder. Not fully trained in any of the Powers, she could feel mana always. Not to feel it, to be separated from it, seemed to her like a small death. She rubbed her legs, feeling a chill.

"I'm sorry," he said, looking up. Brown eyes were full of concern.

She shook her head. "No. No, I am just glad I took the way of the bow and not the Powers. Well, not to the point of someone gifting me with a dimlock."

"Ah, yes, the dimlock. How did you know that it wasn't warranted? I might have killed you as soon as you removed it."

She pursed her lips, amused. "You couldn't have killed a butterfly when I removed it, but my knife was ready." He nodded sadly. She smiled at him in encouragement. "As for the dimlock, it's wrapped in a hide and well stored. I don't have the power to destroy it."

"Few, if any, know how," he said, then waited for the rest of her answer.

"Two things then. The dimlock held you, but its power was focused inward. Still, even before I was attacked, something was wrong here. I felt something, a darkness; I thought it was some sort of strange animal. But it was gone as soon as Pilik died. Even Trog carried none of it. Then, when I searched you, the only thing that seemed wrong was the dimlock. From you, there was a faint Light." She reached out, searching. "It's grown stronger now that the collar is gone."

Garnelden nodded approvingly. "In my state, I was the 'animal' you felt. Good that you weren't slack in all your lessons."

She chuckled. "Not all or you could be dead now."

His face turned dark and troubled. "Between a dimlock and death..." Garnelden sighed, leaned back and rested his head on a log. The day was getting late but blue sky could still be seen through green-clad branches and the breeze was gentle.

"If I had any thoughts in the last days," he said, half to himself, "they were that I would never see the sky again." He closed his eyes and soon drifted into sleep.

Brillar watched him, a bit amused. Between eating and sleeping, he seemed to have healed sufficiently during the day, but she still had things to do. She added more water and trail rations to the pot and put more wood on the fire. Better to keep it burning, although she now thought that Jez would indeed wake them if anything came near. She went to check on the animals. Her bow and knife, as always, she kept close by her.

Night came slowly and she enjoyed its advance. She gathered her cloak around herself. *Strange*, she thought, *to feel so content in the wild. Well, half-wild, just off the world's track.* The last of the day birds flew through the darkening sky to their nests and a night bird hooted in the distance. She lay back, warm in her cloak, watched the stars appear and slept.

*** 3 ***

A noise woke her and she bolted upright, knife in hand under her cloak. Garnelden was taking some of the last of the stew from the pot, scraping the bottom as he did.

"I didn't mean to wake you, not so rudely," he said as he settled back on the blanket while she stood and stretched.

"There's still some left for you." She nodded and helped herself to what remained in the pot. They ate in silence.

"I'll need to hunt today after I tend those wounds. Healing spells don't touch them and you are in no condition." He looked at her quickly. "Yes, I said no condition to perform self-healing or for me to cast to heal you. You know it saps the body of strength. For a while, you need to be an ordinary person with ordinary cuts and bruises. I have salves for them and teas for you. Rest, food, and no exertion," she said firmly.

"I will obey the healer." He made his voice meek and contrite and she laughed.

"When was a Mage of the Four Powers ever meek?" She was rewarded with a slight smile.

"Then, good healer, I will sit by the fire like an old uncle and wait while you hunt." He leaned back and closed his eyes. She shook her head at him, opened her foldbox for a sack then went off to the horses.

The grey mare was the focus of her soothing spell and came to her promptly. A piece of rope attached to her halter as reins was enough and they set off back to the field where she had taken the cwel. Leaving the mare, she made a short stalk through the field, flushing a covey of linic. The fat birds scattered, but she was able to down one before they found the trees. Another half hour, and she took an unwary cwel. Checking the ground around the second kill, she found two types of tubers and put them in the sack. *More than enough,* she thought and went back to the mare.

When she returned to the camp, she found Jez by a sleeping Garnelden and returned him and the mare to the roped enclosure, changing its configuration a bit to include fresh grass. At the fire, she cleaned her kills, cutting the cwel for stew and leaving the linic for roasting. She took the kettle and the jug for water. Sliced cwel and cleaned sliced tubers went into the kettle, herbs and water into a cup for tea. Garnelden needed liquids as well as food for healing.

Satisfied that everything was done for the moment, she fastened a few skewers for the linic and set them to cook with herbs, then leaned back and let her mind wander as she listened to spring birds in the trees.

"I was dreaming of food," came his voice, stirring her from her reverie, "and I see why." Garnelden was sitting up, reaching for a skewer. He looked at her, questioning.

"It should be done, although the stew will take more time."

Satisfied, he began to pick the meat from the skewer and eat. "By the Light, you are a fine cook," he exclaimed, closing his eyes in bliss as she laughed.

"Hunger is a good sauce, my father would say," she replied.

"No truly, the sauce perfect."

She handed him a cup of herbal tea. "You need liquids as well; drink that and then some water." She handed him more linic and took some for herself.

"The mare went well for you?" he asked between mouthfuls.

"A lovely animal. Is she yours as well?"

He shook his head. "I have no idea where she came from. For all I know, Pilik," he nearly spat the name, "owned her, or he could have stolen the animal. He must have ridden hard to take me at Riversgate." West and East Riversgate were trading towns where a large river emptied into Clee Lake, the largest of the northern lakes.

"Ridden from?" She knew there must be more of this story.

"It doesn't matter. I tried to mix my trail. He could have picked it up anywhere."

Not ready to speak, then, she thought. *A dimlock would make anyone cautious and there is still the bounty.* Aloud, "Now then, I need to tend to those wounds." Working quickly, she made more salve. This time, he was able to sit up straight to let her apply it but still shuddered at it touched the lesions.

"My spells don't seem to prevent the pain here." She spoke quietly as she worked, moving his hair off his neck.

"The curse of the dimlock," his voice was grim, "is more than just its hold."

"I don't know very much about them. There is a key, I'm told, although I was able to pick the lock. I would have thought it should be harder to open without the key."

He gave a short laugh with no humor in it. "Seeing a mage in a dimlock, who would want to get close enough to pick the lock? Opening the lock could release a monster." His hand was suddenly on her wrist and he twisted to look at her. "Thank you for your courage!" Startled briefly at his intensity, she stopped, flustered, then dipped the cloth in salve. He let go of her wrist to let her go on with her work.

"There's a bit of salve left. I'll put some on the other injuries." There was a large gash in his side that took some attention and small scores on his feet.

"It looks as though you were dragged at some point?"

He shook his head. "I have no idea. I don't suppose they cared much about my condition. I remember being in pain..."

She could feel his agitation, even fear. "No worries about that now," she said, trying to soothe him but his hand was on her arm now and there was desperation in his eyes and voice.

"Don't let them take me again?" His tone was tense and pleading. She sent out wave after wave of soothing, calming and felt his hand relax.

"You need to sleep. Food and sleep." She had no spell for sleep, but her waves of soothing were enough. He was still very ill.

"Sleep. Jez is here, my bow is here. You are protected." He leaned back, shivering, and she covered him then gave him a cup of broth. He drank and closed his eyes. When she looked up, the stallion had joined them. She added some wood to the fire and sat back, shaking her head.

Did I just offer to kill to defend a man I don't know? she thought. *I certainly don't think I would let him be taken again, he walks in the Light, that I'm sure of, so any who try to take him... he'll be able to defend himself soon enough.* She looked at Garnelden, asleep, evidently trusting her. *What, by all that is Good, am I doing?* She went off to gather more branches to stockpile for the fire.

That afternoon, they were greeted by a lone horseman, and Brillar waved him toward the spring. "My uncle is ill," she told the man, "but please water your animal."

"Good that he has someone to tend him," the man replied courteously. Garnelden had wrapped himself in the blanket and turned his back to the fire.

"Thank you. He does get grumpy with the tending, though." She laughed lightly and turned back to the fire.

"Good day to you then," the man said as he left them.

Garnelden rolled to face her. "Grumpy?"

"Just conversation," she replied mildly, but he scowled at her, then looked around.

"You've been busy while I slept." He was looking at the pile of branches.

"We'll need to stay here for several more days. So says the healer." She looked at him with mock ferocity.

"Then I will rest, eat and sleep, and try not to be grumpy," he replied with a half-smile.

Just before sundown, a small group of farmers passed them on foot, but they were in a hurry and exchanged only brief greetings. The next day, Brillar took the mare out again to hunt and returned with more birds and tubers.

"You must have a good hand with that bow," Garnelden said admiringly.

"Ah, you should see me at the spring games. I can't outshoot for distance with the longbow, but my short bow skill hasn't been matched in years." She smiled at the memory.

"And your teacher?"

"My father. I outshoot him as well. And my brothers. They used to tease me about it, but not any longer. I wonder if they have improved much. I was home about three months ago and could still beat them." She chuckled.

"Ho, travelers," was heard from the road as a carter came into view and stopped. She glanced at Garnelden, who nodded, then pulled the blanket around him and turned a bit from the fire.

"The traveler is welcome," she shouted and the man came forward. She stood as he approached, bow in her hand.

"What then? A fine fire you've here, and by the look of things, ye'll be here a bit?" He grinned at her and a quick spell found nothing in him but goodwill.

"My uncle has been ill and needs the rest," she told him as she looked him over. An older man, clean-shaven and with the muscles built by years of farming. His clothes spoke of some success in his labors, he wore no homespun and his boots looked almost new.

"Aye? Then I'll not stay but to water the horse and fill a jug." He gestured toward his cart which was well-loaded but covered. "Have ye vegetables and fruits then? I could sell you something; fruit is good for the sick."

"Water your animal and then show me what you have. I'd be happy to buy something." Brillar nodded.

"Lendros is me name, wait while I fill this bucket." He went off to the spring.

"Fine animals ye have there, most fine," he remarked when he returned. "Now then, me wares." He pulled back the ragged cover, revealing vegetables and fresh berries. "Eight for a copper and ye can mix 'em, and a copper for the three nets of berries."

Brillar picked out some vegetables and handed the man the coppers from her purse. "And I thank ye," Lendros waved as he remounted the cart and clicked his reins at his horse.

Garnelden rolled back to face the fire and sat up. A net of berries went into his outstretched hand.

"These seem fresh picked," he remarked, taking one of the berries as she cleaned vegetables for the stew.

"Hmm," was all she could say. Her mouth was full of berries.

They spent the next few days companionably as Garnelden renewed his strength. He was weak both from the dimlock and starvation. Every day, Brillar took the grey mare to the open fields to hunt and gather. It was a rich field and she had no trouble keeping the stew pot filled.

There were no more carters, but there was suddenly plenty of traffic on the road. Twice, a group of horsemen, then three groups of farmers on foot, off to help harvest spring vegetables. They all called a greeting and were welcomed. Horses and men watered at the spring. Asked why they were camped with the town so near, Brillar answered that her "uncle" had taken ill quite suddenly and they could go no farther. They were discreet with their own questions, but there was no news of a missing man or men, no news of an outcry of any kind. *At least not yet,* she thought. Her patient, however, seemed almost alarmed. Had he expected an outcry?

Garnelden still spent a great deal of time sleeping, eating, then sleeping again. During his waking spells, Garnelden turned their talk away from his troubles with the bounty hunters, unwilling to discuss it any further. They talked quietly of the Brotherhood and her training at the Sisterhood. The Houses were akin, although skills in War magic were never taught in the Houses of the Sisters. Her home of Laurenfell was near the Great House of the Sisterhood.

"I've traveled through that area. Lovely farms there." He was now wearing an old scarf from her foldbox around his neck, to prevent questions about the scars there. He laughed when she told him about Sister Rodenis' insistence that she continue her training, saying he deemed her skills good enough for anywhere in the settled lands.

"I have wandered the settled lands for nearly two years," she said in response. He smiled at that. Younger mages often 'walked-about' testing and increasing their skills, usually doing some good in the process.

"Now," she continued with determination, "I want more. I've heard many a tale of the Wild and mean to make my way there." That brought him upright and staring, but he said nothing. He had spent time in the Wild.

The nights usually brought some spring rains but they were light and easily dealt with. Finally, on a morning that was clear and bright, Brillar judged Garnelden strong enough to ride in the cart, which he resented.

"I have a fine horse! Why should I ride like a carter?"

"Because, *Uncle*, until you are stronger, you can rest a bit in the cart. After all, tongues will wag and we've told travelers you were ill," she said firmly. "And we need to keep up the appearance of being two average travelers when we arrive at an inn."

"An inn! My purse!" He started suddenly. He'd given no thought to his belongings as they camped.

"I wondered about that. I found a heavy purse on Pilik. The gold is yours?" she asked.

"Gold and some silver." She removed the purse from her belt and tossed it to him.

"Some of the silver, I gave to Trog to keep him quiet. As for the rest, the gold is there and the balance of the silver."

He looked at her quizzically and tied the pouch on a piece of rope he was using as a belt.

"You trust me then?" she asked lightly.

He was silent a moment, then answered softly, "You could have taken everything, including the horses and my life. I owe you my life. Yes, I trust you; and I will pay at the inn."

Brillar blushed and turned to douse the fire to hide her embarrassment. Such compliments were rare and valued. Whatever came, she would hold that to her.

"I found a pool downhill of the spring. If you will keep watch, I think I need a good bath before we go," was all she said.

There was still the sacking from the cart, and a cleansing spell would suffice for her clothes. She could have cleaned her body with an easy Creature spell, one of the few she knew, but Brillar preferred a plunge in the cool water. She let out her braid and her hair floated free around her. A quick bath, a cleansing spell for her clothes, the sacking to dry her and she was redressed. Re-braiding her wet hair, she returned to the clearing where she found that he had harnessed the roan to the wagon.

"Too much exertion and you will weaken. And after all my care." She clucked her tongue at him and he grinned, his first true smile since they had met.

"Are you a mother hen or my niece?" he asked cheerfully. "I promise to ride in the cart bed if you can handle the reins." He handed them to her with a bow.

His good humor buoyed her and she laughed in response. "Well then, *Uncle*, we should be off."

He had looped a rope around the neck of the grey and tied it to the cart. The stallion, he assured her, would follow where he went. "Jez was bred and born at the Great House. I was there when he was foaled eight years ago. I helped him to his feet and held him to his mother. He used to follow me like a puppy when I was teaching the younger students." He shook his head. "He was as much a rascal as some of them were but trained better than they did." He laughed, stroked the stallion's long face and was nuzzled in return.

Brillar watched with a bit of jealousy. Still, it was her younger brother Terol who had a true way with animals. She climbed aboard the cart as he settled in the back and clucked at the roan which moved obediently to the track. It was full morning and the air was sweet under the trees as they set off. Spring leaves were everywhere and birds were calling for mates. A fine day for travel and the road was easy.

"Now, Uncle, a story for the road," she insisted. "And it had best be a good story for a woman and her 'uncle' to be on the road together, or I will be taken as more than a niece. Who are we?"

Together, they concocted a story to ward off any inquisitive innkeeper or, if they were not questioned too closely, a sheriff's man, although they knew that the charade would not be enough if they stayed in any village for long. Too many people could recognize "Uncle Elden"— they had settled on the short form of his name for his niece— as a mage and someone from the Sisterhood might know Brillar. Some time for restocking supplies, new boots and clothes for Elden, for he carried no foldbox, and the two would separate. When she asked him about the foldbox, he shook his head and left the question unanswered.

"I know who set the bounty on me," Uncle Elden said at one point, "but before we meet, I need to recover what is mine in West Riversgate. There may be more people here and there, seeking the bounty."

"You are a well-wanted man then," was her comment. "Perhaps I should stay with you just to watch your back. And your drinking."

"Hrmph," was his short reply.

Together, they decided that when they left the first town, they would drive the horse and cart to the next and sell them. The mare, she would keep. She had refused Garnelden's offer of gold.

"I won't take money for doing what was right," she insisted. "It caused me neither harm nor delay and there may come a day when I need the help of a Mage of the Four Powers." There had been laughter behind her words but they made him thoughtful.

"What do you plan to do then?" he asked. They were crossing a small stream and had stopped to let the horses drink. Brillar hopped down from the cart, knelt at the stream, and began splashing water on her face.

"When I left the Sisters, I had no plan, just a desire to be out in the world, to be away from study. Now, I've worn out two pairs of boots, walking. With no plan, I've killed a man and rescued a mage."

She shook water from her hands and stood. "Still, I haven't seen an orc, a fire sprite, or even a harpy, and the Wild holds all those. Who knows? Tomorrow might be more interesting."

He laughed at that, thinking her both serious and naïve. He had seen everything she mentioned and more, but not usually near settled lands. Somehow the idea of her wandering into the true Wilds unsettled him. Finding himself unsettled left him more unsettled. Surely, he, Garnelden, Mage of the Four Powers, didn't care what happened to this youngling? He tried to shake off the thought. He had more pressing problems. There had been no word of a call-to-arms from any of the travelers who had stopped at the spring. Had Polsen failed to deliver his message? If so, he would have to face the matter alone. He pushed the thought aside.

"The town can't be far ahead," he said, to dismiss the feeling of unease. "I can feel open land."

She climbed back into the cart and stretched out with far-sight. "True enough. Let's hope there's an inn soon. Riding in this cart has worried my bones."

Less than a mile brought them to open farmland. The fields here were well-plowed and rich, and the scent of warm earth filled the air. Some of the crops were already tall, others just beginning to grow. The sun was welcome after the cool of the forest. A few men and women in the fields who stood to stretch their backs saw them and gave friendly waves which they returned. Carters were always welcome as they brought both goods and news. Some people closer to the road looked at their horses with appreciation.

"A fine pair a horses you have in tow there," said a man who had just come into the road from a field. "If ye be looking to sell one, the blacksmith in town does a trade in horses."

From the bed of the cart, Elden laughed. "He wouldn't be a brother or cousin of yours, now would he?" Brillar stopped the cart. The farmer seemed inclined to talk and news would be welcome.

Looking down, the farmer kicked at a clod of dirt in the road with a well-worn boot. "Well now, family is important here abouts." He looked up and grinned. "And a man who don't support family, 'tisn't much of a man." He was ruddy from the sun, with light eyes and sandy hair.

His rough good humor had Elden and Brillar smiling.

"If we asked about an inn in the village, would you send us to the best or to the one owned by your cousin," Elden offered good-naturedly.

Smiling back at them, the farmer replied, "There is only one and 'tis my brother-in-law runs it. My sister does the cooking and the food is from my farm. I was headed there now…" he paused.

"Well met then, friend," said Elden. "Climb aboard and I'll buy you a pint at the finest of the town's inns."

Nes ("Me name is Nester, but folks' calls me Nes") teased their brief story from them. "Illness on the trail, a bad thing," he said. "Good you had your niece with you." He was a country farmer in rough clothes and dirty from the fields but good company. Seeing him riding in the cart brought more waves and hellos from the people they passed.

"And there's the inn. Berl keeps a good barrel of ale of his own making, there's a barn for the horses and a room?" He looked at Brillar speculatively.

"Rooms," she turned and answered him. "My uncle snores."

That remark kept Nes in laughter until they stopped at the inn door. A sign proclaimed it—not very originally—the *Red Rooster Inn* in faded red paint on dirty white. Looking at it, they hoped that it was cleaner inside. Still, the building was of local stone, the windows had clean glass in them, and the shutters on the upper floor were well hung.

"The only rooster you'll find is 'in' the stew pot." Nes laughed at his own witticism.

"As if I would cook such a fine rooster," said a full-bodied woman coming outside. "Only hens for my stews." She had been cooking and was wearing short boots, a skirt to her knees, white apron, and a faded blue shirt rolled to the elbows. A smattering of flour attested to her occupation. She appeared to be around thirty, her face open and kind, and her dark hair was pulled back neatly and tied at the nape of her neck.

"Welcome, worthies," she said with a brief dip. She stared, first at Elden's bare feet and then at the bow over Brillar's shoulder and shouted for the stable boy.

Following her glance, Brillar spoke up. "We came through a river where perhaps we should have looked for a bridge. My uncle's boots and clothes dumped from the cart along with our trade goods.

We were hoping to replace the clothing here? He's used to better than his old clothing."

She exchanged a glance with the woman that said, 'Men. What can you do?' and they both smiled.

"There's a tailor in town and a boot maker if you have coin?" She called again for the stable boy.

"No worries then," said Elden and stepped down from the cart. "A few pints to ease our travels, dinner and beds for our weary bones." He opened his purse and took two silver coins. The woman's eyes grew round as she accepted them.

"Then this way, worthies, this way, and I'll have my husband draw the ale." She held the door open for them.

"Three pints," Elden said, "as your brother will be joining us."

"Berl, we have guests," she called as they entered the inn; she headed for the rear of the building.

The travelers were surprised at the interior. A plank floor, tables and benches sanded smooth and oil lamps for the evening. For a country inn, it had a solid look. There was a fireplace well-stocked with wood and one wall held a map of the territory.

"She had curtains on the windows, but one of the lads was in his cups of an evening and set one alight. Now she has to do without, for Berl thinks they might burn down the inn, as if stone could burn," Nes explained, chuckling. "She was a good sister, Hana was, and a good woman she's become."

"That she is," said a man coming over with three pints of ale. "And how did you manage to get them to buy you a pint, Nes?" he asked with affectionate humor.

"But we insisted," Elden put in immediately. "After all, he showed us the best inn in the village." Berl roared with laughter and slapped him on the shoulder, making him wince.

"Careful, my uncle has just recovered from an illness," Brillar spoke up.

"Beggin' your pardon then," said Berl, concern in his voice. He was taller than Elden but stockier. Light brown hair was close cut and a clean towel hung from his belt.

"No harm done," answered Elden. He sipped his ale. "A fine ale. Nes says you do your own brewing."

"That I do, and none better for many miles. And no inns, either." He laughed at his joke. "I had the boy take the horses and cart to the barn. They'll be well cared for." He went back to the bar for plates.

Nes stood; he had fairly gulped his ale. "I'll need to be going. Only one pint for me or my wife will fetch me one with her broom." They thanked Nes as he hurried out the door.

More ale from the bar and chicken stew from the kitchen appeared quickly, along with fresh bread and churned butter. After lunch, Brillar wanted her 'uncle' to rest, but Berl had called two men from the town, a tailor and a cobbler. Elden went off with them with stern instructions to return quickly and rest. Brillar went to the barn to be sure the horses were well cared for.

After ensuring that they had fresh food and water, Brillar spent some time with them, letting them become easy in her presence, reaching out to them with friendship and soothing. Returning to the inn, she was told that her uncle had come back and gone to his room for rest. Rest seemed a fine idea, but she took hers near the stable, stretched on sweet-smelling hay near the horses and watching clouds. At some point, she fell into a relaxed sleep.

Voices woke her. "There she is, well and fine." It was Berl's voice.

"Many thanks," she heard her uncle reply. She stood and stretched, brushed at the hay, then glancing around, and threw it off with a spell.

"Uncle," she greeted him, "did you rest well?"

"I did that, but food is almost ready and you were nowhere to be found." He glared at her.

"I apologize. It was such a fine day, I must have fallen asleep in the sun." She glanced at his shod feet.

"An old pair of boots the man had in his shop. Now, if you would join me, I will buy you an ale, to clear the straw dust from your throat." They went in through the back door of the inn and past the kitchen, where wonderful aromas rose from the stove, taking a table in a corner where they could see everyone enter. Brillar could feel Elden reach toward everyone, testing them lightly, and wasn't surprised to find herself subject to the same scrutiny. When she looked at him, he whispered, "Sorry. Habit." She just smiled.

The inn began to fill with townsfolk as mealtime neared, but they managed to call for a pint before it got busy. A few curious glances came their way. Both tailor and bootmaker stopped in for a pint and assured Elden that all was beginning as he had asked. Their supper, for Elden had offered a bit extra for something more than stew, was roasted duck with tubers fried with onion and herbs. It made a fine feast after their meals of linic and cwel on the trail. Elden washed his down with more ale, but Brillar chose a cider that Hana suggested.

The oil lamps were soon lit and Brillar, seeing Elden's face in the fresh light, motioned Hana over. "I judge it time for us both to get some rest now." Hana led them upstairs, where Brillar found a small but reasonable room with a chair, a stand with ewer and bowl, window, and a sturdy bed.

"The mattresses and pillows are feather stuffed," Hana hastened to tell her. "You won't see any finer in the territory."

"They will be welcome, Mistress Hana, after days on the ground," said Elden gallantly, bowing over her hand and making her blush. "You are a kind hostess and a fine cook. A good evening to you."

Unused to such courtesies, Hana reddened further and hurried away.

"And a good evening to you too, Uncle," Brillar said wryly. He winked in return and retired to his room.

In her room, she dropped her pack but went down the back stair to the necessary and then to the stable before returning and splashing water on her face. Wearily, she sat on the bed and found that the feather mattress was just as Hana had promised. *Not that I couldn't sleep on rocks,* she thought as she pulled off her boots and stripped to her scants. The pillow was also full of feathers and the blanket was soft.

"And a good evening to me as well," she murmured to herself and fell into a deeper sleep than she had enjoyed in many days.

***

In the next week, Elden, as he was now known to all, fleshed out. Breakfast at the inn was a massive affair, with fresh bread, eggs, sausage and bacon, hotcakes and fruits. Explaining that they would need to stay a few days more while the tailor and cobbler made up his clothes, Elden handed over more pieces of silver for the inn, much to the delight of the innkeeper. He also put some coppers in the hands of the stable boy, knowing that stable hands were paid little.

Every morning after they had eaten, Brillar tended to the wounds left by the dimlock. Under her careful hands, they had healed nicely and she treated them with little or no pain to him. The skin had pulled together well, particularly on the back of Elden's neck which had taken the least damage. "You'll carry scars so keep them covered from casual eyes. Best be ready with a reason for them if there's an asking, especially by a wench." She was still applying salve, but he had slapped at her hand at that.

They spent nearly a week in the village waiting for clothing and boots. The tailor, noting the loaned boots, loaned Elden some patched clothing on the second day. Brillar and her uncle walked the streets that day, stretching out for any dark signs and finding none. Elden spent more time with both tailor and bootmaker, who promised that they would hurry with their makings.

Foringil had two streets with blacksmith and harness maker at the end farthest from the inn. A plank boardwalk lined one side of both streets, attesting to a town of some prosperity. Where the roads crossed, there was a neat, cobbled plaza. A well-ordered town and clean since a night soil collector, paid by the village, removed waste in the early morning. Despite his trade, he was amiably greeted by the villagers. Shops with porches covering the walk stretched from the inn. They took up again after they crossed the street and continued down the road toward the harness maker then stopped, leaving a space between town and smith. The street was wider than in some towns, with several water troughs and hitching posts for horses. The cross street held mainly richer townsfolk, those who owned fields but didn't work them, and merchants.

After the second day, Brillar split her time between archery practice and the stable, joining her uncle for breakfast and dinner. She found that the village fletcher was a good craftsman and replenished her supply of arrows. At first, a small group of children had gathered when she took out her bow, but soon a few of the men and older lads joined her practice. Some were fine archers, but she held back on showing her true skill. They were, after all, their hosts and companions at the inn. Asked about her ability with the bow, she joked that she had grown up with brothers.

At the stable, Brillar spent time with the grey mare, learning her ways, letting her become easy with her. While the horses were well-tended, she took some time with caring for her. It was obvious that she had not been washed or curried for some time, and Brillar did both, making her true coat appear from under trail dust.

"She's finer than I thought," came Elden's voice one morning as she brushed the mare yet again. "A light coat and fine dappling."

"She has turned out to be a beauty, haven't you, pet?" she responded, stroking the mare's long cheek and being nuzzled in return.

"And you've done well with Jez; he seldom lets others approach him," he returned. The chestnut's coat fairly glistened in the sun despite the dust in the corral. "Even the cart horse looks healthier."

"Many thanks, Uncle. But perhaps you would like to take over some of these duties if you feel up to the task? I promised Berl I would hunt for the kitchen."

"You've left me little to do," he chided. "But perhaps I should give Jez some exercise?"

"If you keep it brief. No good undoing what I have done," she responded with a smile.

She turned and looked him up and down. The truth was he looked quite well even in patched and borrowed clothes. His shoulder-length brown hair was clean and curled slightly. Hana had insisted on trimming his hair and beard with her shears and the result suited him. His brown eyes were dark but clear alongside his strong nose. She had suggested he keep the beard he had grown over several weeks to hide his features. "Why trim away what time has already made?" she said, and he had agreed. It would keep any other bounty hunters from recognizing his face instantly. That, and a mustache almost hid his generous mouth and even teeth. He had put on weight but was still lean and well-muscled. A hand and more taller than she, he made a fine-looking "uncle."

He caught the intensity in her gaze and decided that she was fair game. He liked what he saw. She was tall for a woman, slender, even graceful, but there was steel in her. Under her dark red-brown hair, deep green eyes looked out from beneath curved brows. She had fair skin, evenly darkened by the sun, and high cheekbones. A straight nose, a serious mouth, but a woman's lips above a firm chin. He had suggested she put some spare clothes in a pack before they arrived in town. "So the foldbox won't draw attention." Today, she was dressed in dark green leggings and a lighter green shirt. Dressed for hunting.

They suddenly became aware of mutual scrutiny, and each turned aside, her to the mare, him to Jez.

"Yes, well, to the hunt then. And a short ride for you, Uncle," she admonished.

Lowering her head, the mare accepted the bitless bridle; she wore no saddle. Brillar took her bow and quiver from the mounting box and used it to mount the mare.

Elden chucked. "I expected you to simply scramble aboard."

"What, and risk a twist to my arm? I hunt today, Uncle." She squeezed the mare with her knees and headed out toward the fields and woods beyond.

A fine pair they make, thought Elden, looking after her. He felt a twinge of worry as they disappeared, knowing she was serious about going into the Wild; it was so easy to die there. How did this youngling manage to disturb him so? He shook his head and took down a borrowed hackamore and saddle. When he pulled himself onto the chestnut, he felt a twinge in his chest and shoulder. He patted Jez on the neck as the chestnut tossed his head impatiently. "Perhaps my niece was right. We should keep this a short and easy ride." He set off around the inn and down the town's wide street, urging Jez into his walking gait, smooth and easy, but good exercise for them both.

***

Brillar headed across the fields and into the woods, following a small track. The morning was clear, the sun not yet overly warm, and the trees were bright with new leaves. Several times she heard small game move away from them but kept on, crossing a small stream where she and the mare enjoyed its clear waters. "We must find a name for you," she said, patting the muscular neck. Vaulting back onto the mare, which would have pleased Elden, she continued for another mile until she came to a clearing.

Now she stopped, stretched out with far-sense looking for deer, and dismounted telling the mare to stay where she was. A tangle of brush near the clearing caught her attention. She counted five signs there at perhaps a hundred paces and to the left. Checking the direction of the wind, she started her approach. Four were drowsing, one more alert. She moved slowly, stealthily, bringing the distance down over an hour. At twelve paces, she rose slowly, bow ready. As she had expected, one animal rose, stirring the others. Now all were on their feet, only a second to make a choice… her arrow was true, catching a yearling buck and striking deeply. He staggered a few feet and fell while the others fled. A flock of birds, surprised by the noise, took to the air as she started toward the fallen animal, seeing that it was well fed. She whistled for the mare and began to clean her kill.

The ride back to the inn took less than an hour, and Hana was still preparing lunch when she arrived. The chestnut was back in the corral and nickered to the mare. Hearing her arrive, Berl came out the back door of the inn.

"Well, lass, a fine kill that 'twill be tender. Hana, come see what our archer has found for us," he called. He hefted the deer down from the mare. Brillar handed her over to the stable boy, Enk, with instructions to wash her down thoroughly.

Hana looked admiringly at the deer, proclaiming that she would be sure to prepare it with some fine herbs.

"And you must be hungry," she added, "what with all that time in the forest and this fine work. Come in, for lunch is near ready, and you can have something to ease your hunger and slake your thirst. How you found such a fine young buck when all our hunters come back empty-handed?" She shook her head.

"Indeed, a fine kill," added Elden as he joined them, winking at her because he knew full well how she 'found' the deer.

Brillar followed Hana to the kitchen and stopped to wash in a bucket kept for that purpose. Neither uncle nor niece used what they knew of spells in the town unless they were sure no one watched. "Now you go and sit in the great room, and Berl will fetch you an ale. Such heavy work for such a lass," she had scolded.

Elden joined her in the great room as she sat sipping her ale. "An ale and some lunch, then perhaps you'll minister to me?" he asked.

Brillar sputtered into her ale. "Overdid it? Well, I did warn you."

"It was such a fine day, and Jez hadn't been out. He fairly ran away with me," was the somewhat embarrassed answer.

"Ran away with you? And thank you, Hana," she said as stew and bread for them appeared from the kitchen.

"Oh, we had a good gallop, and now I need some of your fine salves. But first," he lowered his voice, "there was some news before you got back. News of an unidentified man found in a shallow grave with an arrow in his chest. Steady," he added when she stiffened, "drink your ale and smile."

Brillar smiled and sipped and nodded. "What else?"

"There may be a sheriff's man in town to talk to the villagers."

After a thoughtful lunch, she stood and stretched. "I think a walk would do me good. Coming, Uncle?" she asked. "It will walk out some of the stiffness from your gallop." She could hear Berl chuckle at the bar.

"A good thought. After you." He nodded to Berl as they stood.

Uncle and niece left the inn and turned toward the farmlands.

***

Hana watched them go from the kitchen door at the rear of the bar and headed back to the kitchen as Berl dipped a tankard in water and rinsed it. "Do you think them two be more than uncle and niece," he called to her.

Hana stopped to smack him with a towel. "You watch your thoughts and words, Berl. Those two are as kind and honest a pair as we have seen in many a day," and she stalked back to do her baking.

"I was only wondering," he called after her.

"Then wonder about something else," she called back.

He went back to his washing. "I was only wondering," he muttered.

***

Brillar and Garnelden strolled out towards the fields and stopped under a towering tree left as a cool place where farmers and idlers could enjoy the day. No one else was there.

"About the arrow?" Elden raised an eyebrow.

"I removed the shaft with my fletching and burned it. No one will mark it. Do they think they know when he died?" She watched birds over the fields, her mind on Pilik.

"As I heard it, scavengers had been after the body. No one has mentioned a time."

"Well, that's in our favor then." She was clearly worried.

"Besides, niece, we were together when it happened."

"True enough, but our small story may not stand up under questioning."

One of the local farmers waved to them as he went toward town.

"We should walk." They resumed their stroll down a well-packed road; the light rains hadn't disturbed the soil.

Elden was thoughtful, searching for a lost memory, but shook his head. "I don't think Pilik went through any towns after Riversgate, but I can't be sure. Someone might remember a cart with me, perhaps, covered in the back. He wouldn't have left me exposed in a town."

"Carts are common enough, and the roan looks much different now, what with good food, good care, and nothing to do."

"True enough, but we are supposed to be merchants, traders. What was our stock that was lost in the stream? What towns did we pass through? What innkeepers might remember us?"

Deep in thought, they walked back to the inn to find a bundle waiting for Elden. "From the tailor," said Berl, "he has more for you but wanted you to have this now." Elden took it to the stairs leading to his room, watching as his 'niece' exchanged curtsies with the innkeeper.

The *Red Rooster* was busy that afternoon preparing for an evening crowd. The next day was traditionally one of rest, and the townsfolk prepared for it in cheerful style. Men carried extra tables and benches outside; Hana had hired two local girls to help her serve while Enk turned venison on a spit behind the inn. A small troop of players had stopped just outside of town and were to perform the next day.

The atmosphere was relaxed and festive until one of the sheriff's men arrived at the door in the early afternoon while Brillar and Elden sat watching the excitement over pints of cider. The deputy greeted Berl and Hana cheerfully and accepted a half-pint of ale to wash away the dust. He was a dark-haired man of average height, with something of a belly that he constrained with a sword belt. Leather armor was settled on his shoulders.

"Have you heard the news then?" he asked the innkeeper.

"A man found dead? Aye, we've heard." Berl went on with his washing, knowing the inn would fill soon. Beside him, Elden could feel Brillar tense and begin to stand.

"Found dead with an arrow so deep in his chest, it struck his backbone. No belt, no money, no weapon," was the reply as his eyes wandered around the inn.

"Robbed then?" asked Berl, running a cloth on the bar.

At the table, Brill felt Elden's hand on her leg, cautioning, holding her still.

"Most likely. But we heard a tale of a red-haired archer," the deputy continued. "One with a strong bow, for the arrow would have gone clear through him if unstopped by bone."

Berl laughed. "An archer with that might, here? Are you daft? Such an archer would be on a castle wall or guarding a manor house."

The deputy laughed with him. "True enough. Have you travelers then?" He looked toward the table where they sat, listening to the exchange with Berl as any stranger might.

"Elden is my name, a merchant," said Elden, standing, "and this is my niece, Brillar, who learns our trade. I was taken ill on the track, and we're resting here for a few days." Elden held out his hand in greeting, and the man took it as Brillar stood and dropped a slight curtsey. The deputy barely glanced at her red hair.

"Well then, I'd best be off. If I press, I can reach the next town by evenfall." With a slight nod, he left the inn.

"An ale for me," Elden called to Berl, "and a half-pint, I think, for my niece." Brillar had gratefully sunk back onto the bench as the deputy left the inn, although her back remained straight.

Delivering the ale, Berl glanced at her. "We'll say nothing about that fine deer you took this morning," he said quietly. "If a man is dead, 'tis like he deserved killing." With a nod to her relieved face, he went about his business.

"A good man, that, and you had best learn to guard yourself more carefully, niece," Elden said softly.

"A good man indeed," she responded, exhaling a breath she didn't know she had been holding. She took a strong pull on the ale, then sputtered and coughed. Elden looked at her quizzically.

"That 'good man' thought I needed something stronger than ale," she said, looking toward the bar where Berl stood washing a tankard and smiling. "I'm not used to strong drink."

Elden sniffed the tankard and chuckled. "Time to learn then."

She glared at him.

"Or perhaps not." He made a sudden decision and realized it had been in his mind for some time. "I'm still missing that salve, and there's time before Hana has supper ready."

*** 4 ***

When they reached her room and the foldbox, Elden removed the scarf and turned down his shirt.

"Tell me where this hurts," Brillar instructed as she pressed lightly, then more firmly, on the wounds left by the dimlock. He stiffened only once at the place where the pendent had sunk near to his bone.

"They're mending very well," she said, applying more salve. When she finished, he shrugged on his shirt, stood, and replaced the scarf as she closed the foldbox.

"And now, good niece, it is your turn to sit," his voice was quiet but commanding. She blinked in surprise but sat obediently.

"You are young, Brillar of Laurenfell, and have much to learn. You almost lost us in the great room." She started to speak, and he silenced her with a cautioning gesture.

"You did well to respond to my touch, and the curtsey was well-played, but you need further schooling. I have decided to take on that schooling as your reward for my life." She blinked in astonishment. "Yes, yes, I know this is a reward unlooked-for, and you are probably unworthy of it," at this, her face tightened, "but if I let you go stumbling into the Wild in your sad state, you will likely get yourself killed in a week. As I see it, the world is more interesting with you in it than you dead on some deserted mountain." He stopped.

"Why you ungrateful, pompous, overbearing—" she sputtered to a stop.

"Exactly," he said cheerfully. "Now, I need to see what the tailor has made for me, and you need to get ready for supper." He left her quickly while she was still sputtering, closing the door behind himself.

Muttering to herself at the man's impertinence, Brillar took out fresh clothing, although it was made for the trail, and changed quickly. A knock came at her door, and she opened it to find her uncle well dressed in dark grey pants and an over-shirt of lighter matching grey with deep blue stitching.

"Shall we go down to dinner?" He offered her his arm. Still astonished and now speechless, she took the offered arm and allowed him to escort her to the great room.

The *Rooster* was lively that night. Dinner was boiled and roasted tubers with herbs, fresh bread, and slices of roast venison. Hana had added her herbs to tenderize the fresh meat, and the result was delicious. By now, many of the townsfolk had met both Brillar and Elden and greeted them with an open comradery. Among the first to arrive was the bootmaker, carrying new boots for Elden by the uppers.

"Give them a try," he encouraged, "I think you'll find them sturdy and comfortable." Elden did as he was asked, and the boots were a perfect fit. With dark brown leather uppers and sturdy soles, the boots were made for walking the trails and riding both.

"I thank you, Cobbler Morglain. And here is the remainder of your fee, plus a bit more for such a fine job and so quickly."

Morglain stared as four silver coins were placed in his palm. "And thanks to you, Elden. Berl keeps a bit o' brandy for special occasions." At this, Brillar grimaced slightly. "Ah, the lass does no' like brandy then? Berl, two brandies here if you please." Elden let the cobbler pay for the brandy. The coins he had given over were almost twice the promised payment.

They were interrupted by the arrival of the tailor who held a wrapped bundle. He was a bit out of breath. "It was the last stitching needed to be done," he panted, "I had thought to catch you before you came down."

"Nothing to worry you," Elden replied. "Now my niece can make a grand entrance."

Hebrel, the tailor, handed the bundle to an astonished Brillar who stood and raised a questioning eyebrow at her uncle.

"Ahem," he began. "What with the festivities and now the players come to town, I thought you might like something a bit more… suitable?"

"It laces before, not behind, you'll need no help w'that," said Hebrel, nodding at her.

"Look how she stands and stares," chuckled Morglain.

"Come now, lass, go see if my measure was right." Hebrel shooed her toward the stairs.

Brillar fled up the stairs to her room in consternation, followed by their laughter. Closing the door, she leaned against it and recovered her breath. Moving to the bed, she opened the bundle, and a dark green dress fell onto it. She felt the soft cloth and fingered the stitched design on the bodice. It was a modest dress coming to her collarbone, with long sleeves and a full skirt. It did indeed lace up from the front.

The dress amazed her. Elden must have ordered it along with his clothes for it to have been made so beautifully and quickly. She stripped down to her scants and pulled it over her head, settling and lacing it before she looked in the small, cracked mirror in the room. What she saw delighted her. She twirled around, and the skirt, which reached just below her knees, flared for dancing. She opened the foldbox quickly and took out some pins for her hair. Swiftly coiling her braid around her head, she inserted the pins. Taking the glass, she smiled at the result, closed the foldbox, and headed for the door.

At the head of the stairs, she suddenly paused, self-conscious, then straightened her shoulders and, head up, descended to the great room.

At their table, three heads turned in her direction, and the men stood. Seeing that, other heads turned, and applause began. Flushing, and giving a wave for them to cease, she crossed to the table and sat down, reaching for her cup.

"Who would have guessed that a dress could make such a change?" said Elden, and the others nodded.

"From a lass to a lady," added Morglain, raising his tankard as did the others, toasting her.

Brillar sat and sipped from her tankard to hide her embarrassment. "Enough," she said, making the men chuckle. "I thank you, Master Hebrel, for your fine work. Especially seeing that you had only your eyes and not a model for your stitching."

It was Hebrel's turn to redden. This was the first time anyone had named him "Master" in his craft.

"Master Hebrel," they chorused, raising tankards.

"Wait a moment," said Morglain, eyes widening, "If we name him "Master," no one will be able to afford to buy from him." All four dissolved into laughter.

The inn was filling rapidly. Farmers and their wives, clean and dressed in their better clothes, farmhands, merchants with their wives, elders and older children crammed into the inn and sat outside waiting for service. The town dogs gathered, waiting for whatever might drop to the dust, and a brindled cat watched from a windowsill. It was a fine spring evening with the sun low in the sky. A lute player and a juggler from the traveling players arrived to entertain, and the party became merry. The juggler remained outside as the inn was too low-roofed for his art and took what coppers were offered to him. The lute player took up station on a chair by the unlit fireplace and began to strum his instrument.

Berl and Hana bustled through the inn with the serving girls, and even Enk, cleaned up for the evening, was pressed into service carrying ale and filling empty cups. One of the townsmen produced a fiddle and struck up a tune while the lutist ate a hurried plate. Some of the men coaxed their wives onto a small, cleared area to dance, and Elden finally held out his hand to Brillar.

"Let's see if that dress swirls well in a dance," he said. Hebrel's wife had arrived, a slender woman in a blue dress with delicate lace down the sleeves. They were up and dancing and were then going to sit with friends.

Brillar took Elden's hand as the fiddler started into a lively tune. A bow and curtsey, and they were off. Elden proved a fine dancer and whirled her around and through the other dancers with ease. When the dance ended, they returned to the table where Brillar put out her hand to Morglain, who was still alone.

"A man who makes such fine boots can surely dance," she said, catching her breath quickly. In truth, she wanted no more dancing with Garnelden, his brown eyes had never left her, and there was no laughter in them.

"I'll squash your toes," he protested as she pulled him upright.

"And they will heal." She laughed as she took him into the crowd. He did indeed tread on her toes, but only once, and she sat him back down as one of the town archers grabbed her hand and swung her away.

Morglain found a new dance partner, a widow, someone told them. She did not seem to mind having her toes trod on, and the two sat back down with Brillar and her uncle when the singing began. The lutist, refreshed, took his place at the cold hearth and began a well-known ballad. He had a rich tenor voice, and the crowd stilled to listen to the song. He moved on into a love song that had some of the younger women in bright tears, then swung into a lively tune, inviting the crowd to join the chorus. The exchange of singing and dancing went on for hours. Some of those inside the tavern left for home as the sun set, and some of those outside joined the dancers in the *Rooster*.

Exhausted, for someone had claimed her for every dance, Brillar bid the company goodnight and went to her room, locking her door when she entered. *A lock would not stop my good uncle, but it might deter that sprightly archer,* she thought. *A fine party. I have not danced like that in well over a year.* She unlaced the dress and pulled it off, hanging it as neatly as she could before casting a cleansing spell to rid it of any dust and odor. *So lovely and how kind of him,* she thought as she stretched out on the bed. She slept at once and didn't stir until morning, even when the 'sprightly archer' tried the lock.

It was well past dawn when she woke and dressed. She splashed water on her face then unwound her braid, letting her hair fall down her back. Dressing quickly, she went down the narrow backstair and visited the necessary. Elden was already in the great room and stood as she entered after splashing her hands in the bucket outside the kitchen.

"A bright good morning to you, niece," he said. "Hana will be out in a minute with food, but she left a cup of fresh juice for you."

Brillar sipped the juice with pleasure, savoring its slight tartness. "And a fine good morning to you, Uncle," she returned. "But what's that in your cup?" The scent was strong.

Berl hastened over with a cup of the hot brew. "Something new. I got it from a trader who said that hot water should be strained through the powder for a stimulating drink in the morning. Your uncle and I found it tasty, and it really opened our eyes. They call it corin."

Elden nodded approvingly, and she sipped, pursing her lips at the somewhat bitter flavor. "Ah," said Berl, "Hana likes a bit of sweeting in hers." He came back with some sugar commonly used for Hana's baking and a spoon.

Brillar spooned, stirred, and sipped. "The taste is much improved," she nodded at Berl as Hana came up with her breakfast.

"It does open the eyes," Hana added. "Something I needed. It was a long night, but I got in a dance or two with Berl at the close. We can still dance, love, can we not?" She gazed fondly at her husband, who bussed her cheek. Brillar tilted her head at Hana, sensing something, reached out, and was thoughtful.

"Away with you now and back to work," she responded to the kiss, blushing, "such cleaning there is after such a night and the players later in the day." Both went back to their tasks, leaving Brillar and Elden alone in the room.

She applied herself to breakfast. "Many thanks for the dress," she began.

"It was a pleasure to see you in it," he said quietly, "Besides, I can't let my new apprentice…" She sputtered into her corin. "My new apprentice," he went on strongly, "be seen dressed for the hunt at a party."

"Nor do I recall accepting your offer," she replied softly, "dress or no."

"What? Refuse an apprenticeship with a Mage of the Four Powers? I have never made such an offer to any and, while I admit that I only have second standing in Life Magic, which is where your skills seem to lie, I still have much to teach." Brown eyes were fixed on her.

She tried to ignore him, but much to her surprise, she found herself considering the offer.

Taking a slice of bread from her plate, he continued, "It would not be all one-sided, you know. There are things in the Wild that resist magic. They can be weakened by a mage but killed only by steel."

"Perhaps, then, you should make your offer to a swordsman, not an archer," she said primly.

"None seem to be available," he rejoined.

"None available?! So I'm available, am I?" Her response was indignant.

His hand went to hers warmly. "No one else has shown such courage nor saved my life. I think it was more than chance brought us together. I would have my niece with me and none other."

Flustered, she withdrew her hand and sipped the corin. "What, then, am I to pay for this apprenticeship?" The custom was for the apprentice to pay the Master.

"You have already paid more than any other could. Your company and your bow are all that are needed," was the quiet reply.

Brillar lowered her head. It seemed to her that something in the world had just shifted and her answer would make it stable again—her answer.

"Then," she said quietly, "on my honor, I will bind myself to you as your apprentice for one year. If by the end of the year, one of us has not killed the other, we shall see."

Elden roared with laughter. "A fine answer," he said when he caught his breath. He continued to chuckle as she rose from the table.

"The horses need tending," she said tartly, "if you would care to join me, Uncle."

"That I will. And we will give them a fine grooming because," he let his voice drop and deepen, "I will teach you an easy spell, suitable to your skill level." Brillar poked him in the arm. "A spell that will tease out both dust and any insects there may be in their coats."

The Creature spell was within her reach but took some practice. The words were easy, the seeing more difficult.

"You must see and reach to the skin and not beyond. See what's there, the dust, the life."

Finding the life was the easier task, akin to far-sight but more intense. The dust was more difficult. What Enk thought to see them "grooming," their hands barely moving, her concentration evident, made him shake his head. *N'er get the job done that way,* he thought. But he felt self-conscious in their presence and said nothing.

Brillar had mastered the spell and the reaching by lunch, but with a headache as her reward.

"With practice, my dear niece, you will have your animal cleaned in a few minutes. I am satisfied," said her instructor.

"I'll want more corin with lunch, or I won't be awake to watch the players," was her weary response. "I hope that great tub of Hana's is full as well. I feel ready for a proper washing."

There was indeed a tub full of clean hot water and a towel laid out for her. It was a convenience the inn offered weekly to travelers. Brillar unbraided her hair, soaped, then climbed into the tub to rinse and soak. A brief soaking because she knew Hana and Berl were waiting for the same tub and that fresh water was on the stove. A quick spell cleaned her clothes. She climbed out, toweled, and dressed.

Hana had laid out a cold lunch; Garnelden had waited for her before eating. Covered tankards held corin, and she gulped some of hers. She could feel the headache fade away as she reached for bread and meat. Some fresh fruits had been added to the table to be enjoyed after lunch. She stabbed a slice of meat with her belt knife, only to have her hand slapped away by Elden. She looked at him in astonishment.

"Another lesson, niece, this one in manners. A belt knife is a fine thing but a fork," he produced two tined instruments, "is for gentlefolk."

"A fork."

"A refinement from the west that I think will sweep eastward," he replied. "Used for transferring meat and vegetables from plate to mouth, thusly." He stabbed a small bite of meat from his plate, put it in his mouth, and chewed. "It also leaves the hands clean and free of grease. Which means," he lowered his voice, "less chance of a sword or bow slipping if it's needed quickly. Now, you." He handed her the second fork.

"May I at least *cut* my meat with a knife?" she asked, and he nodded.

She transferred some meat to her plate. Elden took her hand to show her the proper holding of the fork, and she managed to take meat from plate to mouth with no trouble. "Again, practice is everything," he said encouragingly.

An archer has deft hands, and she had become skilled with the fork by the end of the meal. "Must I use it for the fruit as well?" she asked.

In response, he took an apple and bit into it. "This is the only way to eat such fine fruit even if it was cellared since the fall."

Taking one for herself, she laughed and went up to rest and change before they went out to watch the players. Finishing the apple, she rinsed and dried her hands, then turned to the green dress. It looked even lovelier to her than it had in the evening. Stripping off her work clothes, she opened the foldbox, taking out a small vial of perfume forgotten the previous evening in her flustered state. Now she dabbed it on her shoulders. A cream softened her hands. Then, taking a comb from the box, she tugged the knots from her hair and tied it up, fastening it with an ornamental pin. Satisfied, she closed the box and slid the dress over her head, enjoying the feel of the fabric.

"Let's see how my uncle likes this," she thought and headed down the stairs. She stopped at the sight of him because the tailor had done himself proud with her uncle's clothes. Evidently, there had been more deliveries, and he now wore a deep blue shirt over his grey trousers. A black belt that must have been ordered from the harness maker held the shirt at his waist.

She stared, then said, "The tailor has fitted you well, it seems. Are you all finery, or has something been made for traveling?"

"Travel clothing is nearly ready, but at present, we seem a pair well suited for watching the players," was all he could answer as her scent reached him. He offered his arm, which she accepted with a nod. They strolled out of the inn and were met with hellos and waves from others headed toward the show, all were dressed in their best.

The players had set up their stage, the bed of a flat wagon, near the tree just outside the village. Rough boards supplied by the villagers formed the seating. The juggler was already hard at work entertaining the crowd, and the lutist played a bright tune from the stage. A curtain behind the stage hid the players from sight. Elden paid for their seats from his purse, and they sat off to one side near the last row of seats. "We shall see many performances," he whispered, "but the village sees few players."

At a vigorous drum roll, the crowd settled, and a player stepped out to pronounce the prologue. The play was to be a comedy, set in an ancient town with strange customs. The audience applauded at once, for comedies were well-loved, and 'strange customs' meant that there would be some wildness to the scenes. He bowed at their applause and exited the stage.

Three players, two men and a woman in yellow, emerged from behind the curtain and stepped onto the stage. The men were quarreling over her shoes, and she was pretending disfavor when Elden stiffened.

Her hand went to his. "Uncle," she whispered, "you are practically broadcasting displeasure."

He took a deep breath and calmed at once. "The woman, she was one of the two at West Riversgate."

Now she understood his alarm. "Be still. We have to wait .Are you sure?"

He nodded, took another breath, and relaxed further. "We wait."

The play, which set the villagers roaring, seemed too long to them both, although they smiled and forced laughter to seem one with the crowd. The comedy was over at last, and the villagers drifted to their homes or stayed, chatting in small groups.

Brillar and Elden took station under the tree with his back to the stage as the players tore down the curtain. "Do you think the beard will suffice," he asked anxiously, "it wouldn't do for me to be recognized quickly."

Brillar nodded. "The beard hides you very well," she assured him. "Wait, I see her, separate from the others."

"See if you can bring her over; perhaps she would join us for dinner?"

Brillar strolled casually toward the woman who was still in her yellow costume. Brillar's carriage proclaimed her more than an ordinary villager, and the actress dropped a small curtsey as she arrived.

"My uncle and I enjoyed the comedy; it was well played. He's resting in the shade and asks if you would care to join us for wine and a meal at the inn."

The offer of a free meal and wine was enticement enough, and the actress, who gave her name as Jenel, went to change from her costume before joining them at the tree, now dressed in a light blue. Elden offered an arm to each woman, and they walked to the inn, seating themselves in a corner near the stairs. "I am sure that a player as lovely as you would be swarmed with admirers, and we prefer a quiet supper. Then perhaps you might recite a few lines?" Jenel preened at the compliments and nodded.

Hana had prepared a light soup then sliced herbed venison with good red wine instead of ale. Elden and Brillar demonstrated the use of forks as a refinement, and Jenel, believing herself refined, insisted on trying one.

"Yes," she agreed with feigned sophistication, "so much more genteel. I will have some made for the company."

The meal completed, Elden lifted his wine and said quietly, "A toast to our new friend Jenel," she fluttered at this, "who, I think, had another name when we met at West Riversgate." At the last words, his voice dropped, and he met her eyes steadily for the first time. She stared at him closely and then with recognition. She tried to rise, but his hand on her arm was steel. She tried to speak, but a quick arcane word stopped her voice.

"Now, my sweet Jenel, I think you and I need a private word." He rose, pulling her upright, and steered her toward the stairs and up them, toward his room. She went, unresisting.

Hana had just served the few guests; there were not many who could afford to eat in the inn two days in a row. Now, on her way back to the kitchen, she gathered up their plates and winked. Brillar simply rolled her eyes, and they both laughed.

On her way past the bar, Hana whispered to Berl, "I said they were uncle and niece. He's taken a player to his room." Berl's eyes widened a bit. "Aye, the fancy one in yellow. Fine sport they will have," she said as she went back to the kitchen.

Brillar waited a while, enjoying another glass of wine, then went up the stairs and rapped gently at Elden's door. He opened it and had her enter quickly. Jenel was sitting on the chair, wild-eyed and helpless. Elden was evidently letting her speak, but only in whispers. She looked at Brillar with pleading eyes.

"Please, mistress," she begged hoarsely, "make him stop. I've told all I know. Pilik paid me and another."

With a wave of his hand, Elden silenced her, and her eyes bulged slightly.

Brillar looked at her without sympathy. "What has she said?"

"Little more than that. Pilik gave her drugged scents. She wore the first perfume that lulled me, while the second woman wore a stronger scent that dulled me further. I was already well in my cups, so I didn't notice what was placed in the drink they gave me. When I woke, I was trapped." His voice was grim, harsh, with barely controlled anger. He looked at Jenel without pity.

"She knows more, but there's a block on her memory. It will take some time." Jenel shook her head, clearly terrified. "You had best go back to your room and block your ears. If there are sounds, they will be like some harsh lovemaking; some like it harsh."

Jenel shook her head again, and her eyes were now wide with panic. What she had endured in the space of less than half an hour was clearly enough for her, but Brillar, remembering the dimlock scars, simply nodded and left them alone. She went downstairs and took a glass of cider, used the necessary, then went up to retire. She murmured a brief spell, undressed, and went to bed. Whatever sounds came, she never heard them.

*** 5 ***

In the morning, Brillar dressed quickly and found her uncle already in the great room with, to her surprise, Jenel at his side smiling at him. He gave his niece a quick wink and kissed Jenel's cheek. "Time for you to be off, my dove," he said jovially. The woman smiled again, nodded at them both, and went out the door obediently.

"What on earth?" Brill began quietly.

"Ah, breakfast," he interrupted, "and more of that fine corin. Such a great host you are, Berl, and what an excellent cook you married." He seemed pleased with himself and the whole world, and she grinned to herself, remembering her father's expansive mood the day after he arrived home from travels.

She almost giggled but restrained herself. "You seem in a fine mood, m'lord Uncle," she teased, feeling that was expected.

"Now then, girl," he admonished, "none of your impudence. Eat and drink and keep to yourself."

Which she did, laughing internally and impatient for the real day to begin.

"I think the horses could use some exercise," he said when they had drunk the last of the corin. "Join me in a ride?"

"With pleasure, Uncle," she responded. Nodding to their hosts, they went out the back door of the inn to the stable. It took no time to get the horses into borrowed saddles and bridled. Brillar took her bow and quiver, "Just in case," she said and swung up on the mare.

"Thought of a name for her yet?" he asked.

"I've decided on Bright. Her eyes are bright and a fine feature," she responded, and the mare twitched an ear back, catching the sound.

"A race then, to the other side of the field," he shouted and dug his heels into Jez.

Bright leaped after them, almost unsettling her rider. Leaning forward, she shouted into the mare's ear, "A horse is supposed to wait for a command," and laughed into the wind.

Jez was too far ahead to be caught and Elden had flung himself from the horse to be seated on a log when they arrived.

"What kept you?" he asked innocently.

"An honest race someday?" she replied, hopping down. "But first, you have a story to tell and perhaps two."

"I have that." He settled himself more firmly, taking a deep breath of the spring air. "In case you worried, I left no marks on her."

"I had no such worries." She sat and leaned against a rock.

"Well, then. Her name is not Jenel; that's her stage name. When I met her first, she called herself Eldana and she worked for a smaller company. Her time in the pleasure house was staged by Pilik, who approached her with a proposition after one of her performances. He had, he said, a rich patron in Lands-end who needed a favor. She met with the man and described him."

"And you know him?"

"To my misfortune, yes. But let me finish the story. The man, Harrolen, offered her gold for her work. He gave her the perfumes and the drug for the wine and asked her to engage another woman to help her in what he called a jest at my expense. He put a block on her memory and made Pilik the only one who would come to mind if she was questioned. Removing it took some time." He frowned. "I dislike such methods, even when I have to use them."

"And this morning?"

"Ah. When I had what I needed, I eased her mind so she slept. While she was sleeping, I blocked what had happened and added the memory of such a pleasant night with me that she insisted on more this morning. What could I do?"

Brillar drew back, tilted her head a moment and burst out laughing. After a moment, he joined her. She laughed until tears ran down her cheeks. Pointing at him, she continued laughing, "Then that ruse this morning, not so much a ruse."

He slapped her hand away. "After all I've dealt with, a few moments of play..." he left the statement hanging. "Besides that, you locked your door," he accused.

Brillar continued to chuckle. "I locked it against an archer. As if a lock could stop you."

"Except that knowing it was locked was all the lock needed."

She eyed him and nodded. "Well and good," she replied, "for I have a fine uncle and am apprenticed to a fine teacher. For now, that is all I need and all I want."

"Well said. That is what you shall have, niece. Now we had best get the horses back to the stable. Does Bright have a fifth gait?"

"We shall soon see. You ride ahead a bit and we'll follow."

They were quickly astride their mounts and Jez set off at his walking pace. "Can we match that, Bright?" Brillar whispered in the mare's ear, then gave her a squeeze. To her delight, the mare moved smoothly into what some called the traveler's pace and caught up with Jez.

"So much better than bouncing around in a trot," she called, passing him.

Both man and horse were surprised as Bright continued to pull ahead. Slower in the gallop, she was faster at the walking pace.

At the stable, Brillar slid from the mare and leaned against a post. "What kept you?" she asked innocently, and Elden responded with laughter. They continued to chuckle as they wiped down their mounts.

"A fine morning. Do you suppose Hana would provide an apple apiece for these wonderful horses?"

Hana could and did, and the horses munched them gratefully.

"Mistress Hana," Garnelden said when they went to the great room and settled in for lunch, "I am sorry to say that this will be our last night at your fine inn."

Hana just stared. Then, "Well, you've been good lodgers," she said, "and we will miss you."

"Who will we miss?" asked Berl, bringing ale to the table.

"Good host, we must be going," Brillar put in. "My uncle, as you may have guessed, is well mended." This brought a snicker from Berl and a slap on his arm from Hana. "The horses are rested and we need to be on our way on the morrow."

"If we go to West Riversgate, how many days do you think by cart?" Elden asked.

"With the cart, perhaps twenty," Berl answered.

"And to Land-end?"

"Land-end! No, that's not a place for two honest traders, not now. Most avoid it. I would nae send you there. Something dark has happened to the town, they say," Berl replied.

"But if we had a need?" Elden pressed.

"By cart then, a week, perhaps ten days. Some of the roads be rough and the people have recently been unfriendly."

"Well, then, we will take your advice. I thought I heard of some fine pottery nearby?"

"Aye, that would be in Eafel," Hana responded. "Near enough, and fine enough pottery for trading."

"Eafel it is then, and our thanks to you," said Brillar. She and her uncle had finished their lunch while they chatted, then they stood. "Dinner and breakfast and then we'll be off. I think, Uncle, that we should see to the cart and have a talk with the harness maker about a few things."

The harness maker's apprentice was quick to serve them. He had hackamores of the type they wanted, more sturdy rope and a few odds and ends for the trail. Elden tipped the lad a copper for his help, knowing that apprentices usually had little pocket money. They bought dried meat and fruit for the trail and some plates to eat from. Cups were good enough for stew, but plates served better at times. They also stopped at the tailor's shop and received a bundle of travel clothes for Elden, paying for them in silver.

Before supper, they had a moment of quiet conversation.

"So we're bound for Eafel?" she questioned.

"To Eafel and then beyond. I think that we should perhaps keep up the behavior of merchants, fill the cart with pottery and go on from Eafel." At her surprise, he said, "There may be others looking for bounty. A merchant teaching his niece the road will be less suspect than one alone or two on horses. We need time before Riversgate, time for me to plan and for you to take instruction."

When she raised an eyebrow, he went on, "There are some things of mine there that I would like to reclaim. We'll probably find them in shops or already sold. I had a foldbox, left in my room at an inn when I went out for the evening. The innkeeper probably tried to sell it or threw it away when it wouldn't open. I would like it back." He smiled grimly.

She nodded thoughtfully at that. "A hard thing to lose. Yours is charmed?"

"It is. If I can get within a mile, I'll find it."

"A mile! A few hundred feet for me to pick up the charm. I suppose the maker never thought I would be apart from it."

Elden grinned. "Remember, a First in Item spells, although I didn't make the foldbox, and I sometimes need to leave it behind. I can help you learn some spells for Item, handy ones at that. However, I think your time is better spent mastering more of what you've already learned."

At the stable, they inspected the cart and found that Enk had made a few repairs and washed it down. More coppers left Elden's purse in thanks. They packed what they had purchased and tied it all down securely.

Supper that evening was a fine affair. The news that two well-liked travelers were leaving brought many to the inn. Berl opened a new keg of ale and made a good profit on it.

"Good friends," said Elden, standing, "we are off in the morning, so we must make an early night. We look forward to a speedy return, for such a fine inn deserves another stay." There were cheers at that, and they went up the stairs to their beds.

Before dawn, there was a tap at her door. Elden was there already dressed for travel. She hurried to join him, dressing for the road with what she didn't need in the foldbox at her belt. She put a silver coin on the bed where Hana would be sure to find it and went down to the necessary then breakfast. Hana was used to early rising.

"You are well dressed for travel," she said, seeing Elden in his new clothing. The tailor had made him a fine blue long shirt suited for the road and dark breeches of soft hide. "Are you sure you can't stay a while longer?" Hana asked as she served them.

"Good hostess, we have stayed this long only so that my uncle could recover his strength," answered Brillar.

"Well then," and Hana almost sniffled, "I've put an old basket in your cart with a few things to ease your journey."

"Many thanks," said Brillar, standing and giving the woman a hug. Then, remembering something she had heard in the village, that Hana was barren, surely belied by her sense of the woman, she whispered, "The child you have hoped for is within, a fine boy."

Hana looked at her in astonishment.

"I have some foresight in these matters, you'll know soon."

Dabbing at her eyes, Hana fled to the kitchen.

Elden stared at her.

"She would guess in another month, and it made a good parting gift," Brillar said, shrugging.

"As did the coin you left on the bed."

"What? Am I to have no privacy then? Perhaps I should travel alone." She glared at him but had to smile when he began to chuckle.

They left the inn through the back door and found Hana, Berl, and Enk waiting. The roan was hitched to the cart and everything was ready.

Berl rushed over to her. "Is't true then?" he asked anxiously, for the pair had been twelve years married and had no children.

"Aye, 'tis true," she replied, and Berl surprised them—and probably himself—by bursting into tears and running back into the inn.

Hana blinked back tears as well. "I'd best see to him, good travels then," she said and turned away quickly.

Elden and Brillar climbed aboard the cart and bid Enk farewell. Jez and Bright knew to follow the cart and they started off for Eafel.

The morning was bright for all that it had rained the night before, leaving the track a bit muddy.

"No matter," said Elden when she mentioned it, "we can always lighten the cart by riding the horses and leading Hob." They had given him a simple name for a simple animal.

The road to Eafel led back past the clearing where they had met and Elden stopped there to water the horses. Brillar stepped down from the cart and stood looking out over the clearing, the spring, and the remains of the fire. The blood that had been there had been washed away by the rains. Sensing her mood, Elden came up behind her silently. When she lowered her head, he put a hand on her arm. "You grew a bit here," he said quietly.

"I've killed for food, but never a man, not until here." There were unshed tears in her voice. "I tell myself it had to be done. I *know* it had to be done. Then, when I saw you tied to the cart…" Her voice hardened. "There are indeed times when a man needs killing," she said, echoing Berl. She turned abruptly and climbed back onto the cart. "If you will, Uncle, we should be on our way."

He clambered up beside her and clucked the reins. Much to her surprise, he began singing in an acceptable baritone and, after a look back at their old camp, she joined in. The day seemed brighter with song and lightened her mood. They reached the crossroad and turned toward Eafel.

At noon, they stopped and inspected the basket Hana had laid for them. To their delight, there was fresh bread thickly buttered, venison, cold tubers and a flask of Berl's fine ale. There were even some bruised apples for the horses and fresh ones for them.

"After such a feast, a nap would be pleasant, but we've a town to find," said Elden.

When the track turned too muddy for the cart, they hopped on their horses and led Hob, reaching Eafel just as the sun was setting. They were taking care to appear ordinary. Brillar's foldbox was stored in her pack and they allowed themselves to show the strain of the road.

In front of the inn, they were scraping the mud from their boots when the owner came out to greet them. "Ah, good travelers, welcome to *The Rose*. What will you be needing, for you look to have come a long way?"

"Only from Foringil, but the track was muddy and Hob was stubborn," Elden answered. "If you have room in the stable for everything? And a place where my niece and I can remove some of the road?"

"That we do, and my wife will thank you. Many a traveler has muddied what she just cleaned." He led them to the stable himself and showed them where to pump water for washing. Once the horses were well taken care of and their boots were cleaned of mud, Brillar and Elden went back to the great room for ale.

"Now, good folk, what will you need? Ah, lass, you look fair worn out. Ale, a meal and a soft bed?" The little innkeeper's head was bobbing as he questioned and they had to smile as they thanked him.

"All three, good host. We'll only be here for the night. We mean to buy some of your fine pottery for trade down the road."

His ale was not as good as Berl's but the supper laid for them was satisfying and the rooms adequate. The pair kept to themselves since their stay would be short. After breaking their fast, they looked at local pottery and found some they thought might be suited to "traders" such as themselves.

"We had something like this," confided Brillar, "for daily use at Laurenfell."

They haggled over the price, something expected, and loaded the cart, declaring themselves off to Healdsten, some two or three days away.

"There be a house of the Brotherhood halfway," said the potter. "Mayhap you can stop a while there."

They thanked him and set off on the road, which had dried and was suited for riding in the cart. "The Brotherhood usually welcomes guests and I imagine you have high standing," she said as they set off.

"No," he replied, looking grim. "I've avoided the Brotherhood since Land-end. I've no wish to bring trouble on my Brothers."

She waited. When they had cleared the town and were back on the road, he began to speak slowly. "I trained first in the War Powers. I was young and hotheaded. My Brother and friend Harrolen and I went across the sea with Lord Celbex. He initially recruited us to fight against orcs. We fought behind a shield wall and saved the lives of many soldiers as we cleared the orcs. Harrolen used blades on them and laughed at the blood; I struck them with stone. At the celebration after the battle, it changed. Celbex rewarded us with the gold he had promised but told us that some of his farmers had been slow with their taxes and that he wanted us to teach them to submit to their lord. 'A lesson in obedience' he called it, that would keep the rest of his tenants biddable. Harrolen agreed readily, but I only pretended to agree. Harrolen had reveled in the blood of orcs, I can still hear his laughter during the battle. He drank and toasted when told that two small groups of homes were to be set alight and everyone killed. I drank and toasted to save myself but stole away that night to warn the farmers. They helped me to the coast and into a boat. The last I had heard of Harrolen, he was still there and still killing. I came back home, although it was some time before I went back to different studies with a cooler head and forgot about him. Well over a decade has passed with no word of him. Until recently." He was quiet for a while.

"During Wyth, there was news of a powerful mage who had taken over the city of Lands-end. The mage's name was unknown to the Brotherhood, so I was asked to investigate and report back. The town swarmed with soldiers, but I went through the gate in disguise. The city folk were like mice trying to hide from prowling cats. I saw two soldiers pull a woman from her market booth, screaming, and take her into an alley. No one moved to stop them." He paused again. She was chilled by the story.

"It's not so much magic he rules with but fear and strength of men. Except for killing the lord who ruled and his family, I doubt much magic had to be used except in demonstration. I bought drinks at a tavern and learned something of what had happened. A richly dressed man proclaiming himself a lord came by ship. He gained an invitation to the ruling house and came out the new lord of the city. It seems he had men on the ship and set them loose on the citizens. A second ship arrived with more soldiers, and the taking was complete." He was briefly silent. "I was fortunate. I felt soldiers approaching, left the tavern through a high window in the kitchen and was over the wall before I was seen. I was unseen, but I had recognized Harrolen. He may have had to go to the tavern himself, but I'm sure he knew me. I sent word to the Brotherhood and tried to disappear." He was pensive.

"Those with true talent are rare, but people hear of the Brotherhood and think of great and powerful spells of destruction. In fact, most of the students study Item magic or Creature, more useful skills. Those who study for War have different paths. They die young with an arrow through the neck, retire young and rich, or find that, although the spells are exhilarating, they dislike the smell and taste of blood and want no part of killing. Some return to the Brotherhood for study in other schools, some have gone into isolation; others have died at their own hands or despaired and gone mad. Each living member pays a yearly sum for those who need care. There are few true War mages outside the Elder teachers in the Great House, fewer still of the First Rank, and we are widely scattered. There are too few to take such a town by storm, not when it's defended by a mage as skilled as Harrolen must be and surrounded by men-at-arms. One of my Brothers was to have sent a message to the Brotherhood and the king, but there has been no word of movement; no army gathering."

His story took most of the morning, and she had kept still, aware of what the telling had cost him; she could feel his remorse. Coming to a stream, they stopped to water the horses and dine on trail rations and apples. The day was pleasant enough, and the stream sang as it danced on the rocks, but his mood was dark. There were plowed fields on both sides of the road, and some were already greening with new sprouts while others had standing crops probably planted in the fall.

"Now, good niece," he said with a sigh as they finished lunch, "reach out and tell me what you see."

She had not expected a lesson but did as she was told. Relaxing, she closed her eyes only to be pinched on the arm. She looked at him, surprised.

"Eyes open," he commanded. "If you close your eyes, you can be taken unawares."

Obediently, she relaxed her shoulders, preparing to try, and heard, "No, no. Anyone with eyes would see you change your posture. Try again."

Sitting up straight, she cast a glance around, trying to look unconcerned, then reached out. Open-eyed, her range was only fifty paces. She told him so.

"Again. A deep breath from the belly, no one could fault you for breathing, and this time actually *try*."

She glared at him, took a deep breath from her belly, and pushed herself.

"More that time. Perhaps eighty paces. What did you see?"

"Cwel, to our right and behind the rocks. Birds. Little more than that."

The lesson continued for nearly an hour and left Brillar exhausted. She handed him Hob's reins, curled up as best she could among the sacks of pottery, and closed her eyes. The sun was setting when she opened them again.

"Since you have rested," was the greeting, and she could tell his mood had brightened, "you can light a fire and set the camp in true apprentice fashion. But first, what do you see?"

She groaned inwardly but obeyed. Open-eyed, she reached out.

"And work as you do it," he commanded.

A deep breath as she reached for some dead wood. "Water nearby, cows to the left where tomorrow's road lies," stretching farther, "and a farmhouse. All is quiet and without danger," she finished.

He hid his surprise at how well she did while gathering firewood. She lit the fire and put the kettle on to boil with some dried meat and tubers, then laid out their blankets. The horses were not tethered but grazed nearby.

"Something comes," she said suddenly.

"And?" He didn't seem concerned.

"A dog, probably from the farm; he seems friendly."

"Well done, niece. Yes, I see him. Probably came to sniff us out and found no danger."

"Hmm," she mused, "it seems I am the only one in danger—from a headache."

"What?" he queried.

"Nothing, Uncle. I think your meal is ready."

*** 6 ***

The morning included more lessons, even as she did the chores he assigned. They shouted a hello at the farmhouse they passed and were greeted in turn. Even on the road, there were more lessons. Lunch gave her brief respite with her bow after she 'saw' several cwel in a field and went off to hunt. The fresh meat made a pleasing change from trail rations and dried fruit.

Since healing was her greatest skill, he asked about her lessons and was surprised to discover that she was well taught in the healing of others but had neglected spells for self-healing.

"Are you daft?" he almost shouted after he found her deficient. "You expected to go into the Wild one day with a level two skill *in Self-Healing!*"

She stared then lowered her head, shamefaced, and sputtered nonsense in answer. After that, he took pains to jostle her, pushing her off the cart so that she fell painfully. Her skill improved quickly as a result, but lessons slowed their travel. Still, headaches disappeared, as did riding sores and aches from riding on the cart or being pushed from it.

Although she tried to keep alert for more 'lessons' in healing, he caught her unaware as she was climbing into the cart after a stop to water the horses. Unbalanced, she fell against a rock beside the road and was sickened to hear a 'snap' in her right arm.

Elden was at her side at once as she cradled her arm and looked at him wordlessly. "Together then," he said, "you have the spell; I'll guide it." Feeling slightly nauseous, she cast a spell against the pain and began the arcane words of healing, matched by the slightly different spell he spoke almost silently. She could feel him guide her to the ends of the bones and then monitor her drawing of the two ends of the bones together, sealing small tears in the muscles as she went. Even with his guidance, the repair took some time, and he insisted she eat and drink before they continued on the road. He did the same. "You know that casting takes strength and not just from mana; casting and the healing itself draw from the body as well."

She nodded and ate, smiling to herself. She had said much the same to him when they first met. They rested a while, then she tested her fingers, made a fist, and bent her wrist. Relaxing, she smiled.

As if the lesson had been more significant than she realized, Brillar began to heal herself without even thinking. Despite the bruising, the days were pleasant, and the lessons became easier. He might not have named himself a master in the Life arts, but Elden knew healing spells very well. Asked about it, he replied grimly, "Wars are good teachers. I had plenty of practice in healing myself in my time over the sea. Neither Harrolen nor I had trained much in healing others. We were young and centered on ourselves. Men who could have been saved died around us, something that never seemed to bother Harrolen but which affected me deeply. He seemed to have no trouble sleeping while I sometimes needed more than wine to be at ease and sleep. I slowly grew to dislike the man I thought of as a true friend and wondered why I left the Brotherhood with so little teaching. It was years before I returned to the House for training, but then I made sure that some of that training was in Life magic, from a Sister who stayed with us for a while to train in Creature spells and our own healer."

There was traffic on the road, a few other carts laden with goods, flocks of sheep, and small herds of cows being moved from one pasture to another. Friendly greetings came from rough farmers and their lads, and the dogs that sometimes accompanied the flocks gave friendly barks as they worked. Their slow pace meant that even Hob was easily used and well-rested.

One afternoon, there was a deep rumble of thunder that brought a nicker from Jez. Looking behind them, they could see that the sky had darkened there while the sky was blue ahead.

"We'll need shelter," said Elden, clucking at Hob to move faster. "What do you see ahead?"

She stretched ahead as far as her sight would allow. "Plowed fields, nothing more," she replied.

"Far-sight will need more work, then," he replied, and the thunder came louder from behind them. "There's a farmstead down the glen, perhaps two miles." He slapped the reins, and Hob moved off at a trot.

Trot or no, the rain caught them before they reached the farmhouse. A barking dog greeted them, and Elden jumped from the cart as the door to the home opened. The man who stepped out was of medium height and stocky, but his hair and beard were white, and he leaned on a crutch. "Daughter," he shouted, "where is that grandson of mine? We'll need help here."

A lad of about thirteen came running around the side of the house. "I saw them, Gran'," he said, "the cows are fenced, and the horse is in the barn." The boy was out of breath and his grandfather patted him on the shoulder, "Good lad to have all that done before the storm. Now have we room in the barn for three more and a cart?"

The boy grinned, knowing the answer as his mother came into the room, wiping her hands on an apron. "Who is that out there in the rain?" she asked. The rain was now beating down hard, and a flash of lightning had shown her a hunched figure on the cart. "Come in," she shouted above the wind and thunder, "come in before you drown."

Brillar hopped down and did as she was asked, shivering from the rain. "You stand by the fire while they tend to the animals," the woman told her. Behind her, the door closed as her son and Elden headed for the barn.

Her father stayed behind with them, pointing at his foot. "I'm not much good in all this, not right now," he said ruefully as his daughter helped him to a chair.

A glance told Brillar all she needed. "It's broken, then?" The foot was heavily wrapped in torn strips of cloth.

"Aye. We've a nasty bull likes a bit of play; he stepped down hard," said the farmer, sitting heavily on a chair. Brillar smiled to herself, seeing a way to repay them for the kindness already shown.

"I have some skill in healing," she said, "if you could raise the foot on a stool so I can examine it?"

A bit surprised, the woman went to the kitchen, returning with a footstool. Brillar raised the foot gently. "Do you have a cup of hot water for my herbs? What I need to do may be painful for…" She turned to the man.

"Moreg," he said, settling back.

"For Moreg." She smiled and began to open the foldbox. There was a slam at the rear of the house, and the boy came in.

"Merchant Elden said he would stay a moment with the horses, then come in… what is that?" The glow from the foldbox had stopped him short.

"Rob, our guest is a healer. She carries her medicines in this. Now sit and try to be still as she works," said his grandfather.

A cup of hot water arrived from the kitchen, and Brillar tossed some herbs in it, speaking quietly over the cup.

"Is that a spell? Are you a mage?" Rob asked, but a look from his grandfather stopped him.

Brillar smiled. "Yes, that is a spell, and I am accounted a mage in some skills as well as a healer," she indulged the boy while giving his grandfather the cup.

"Drink it all," she directed him, "it will taste sweet." Moreg was quick to comply. She heard the rear door again, and Elden came in, drenched to the skin, stopping at what he saw. Brillar motioned him to the fire to dry.

Looking at Moreg, she saw that his eyelids were half-closed. What she had given him was not for pain but for rest. She began to unwind the bindings on his foot, using spells for the pain, and he barely stirred.

Relaxing, she looked deep into the bruised and swollen foot, finding three small broken bones. Bending closer, she moved her hand over the breaks murmuring spells, drawing them together. Moreg winced then settled. Feeling the muscles and tendons, she mended their twists. Moreg twitched and shook a bit, then relaxed. Putting her hands on either side of the foot, concentrating, Brillar drew dark blood from the foot, easing the swelling. The blood fell on the bindings, which she tossed into the fire.

Sitting back, she found that Rob's mother had come in while she was working and smiled at the woman's astonished look. "He'll have to keep off that foot for two more days and be well fed." The woman blinked and nodded. "I'll give you more herbs for him to aid the healing, but his foot will be sore. If you have more cloth?" The woman nodded again, went to the kitchen, and returned with cloth strips. "The binding will remind him not to put his foot down." Brillar smiled as she worked.

Outside, the storm raged, but Brillar had taken little notice. Now she started at the crack of thunder and shot Elden a worried glance.

"The animals are tended, but we had best sleep with them for their comfort," he said as she handed herbs to Rob's mother and closed the foldbox.

"You must have something to eat with us first, something to warm you." She hustled them into the kitchen, away from her sleeping father. "I am Lahna. I have a pot on the fire." She said little else but gave them bowls and spoons, then cups of cider.

"From our own press," Rob told them and was hushed. Lahna was evidently unused to company, especially not a healer, suddenly appearing when they needed one.

After they thanked Lahna for the meal, Brillar and Elden took a lantern and dashed across the mud at the rear yard of the house to the barn where happy nickers came from their animals. The rain was coming down in torrents, and thunder was loud overhead. They could hear the cows, restive in the storm, outside in an enclosure. Brillar reached out to the horses, soothing them, then to the cows, quieting them as well.

Seeing her concentration, Elden nodded. "You have some skill with animals then," he said as he smiled at her. While she worked, he had piled straw on the barn floor, covering it with saddle blankets he had found in the barn.

She opened her foldbox again and took out dry blankets.

"I was surprised to see you open that," he pointed to the foldbox, "in front of the family."

"Necessary," she shrugged. "It seemed to me that the boy and grandfather were the only men in the house. Without proper healing, Moreg would have taken months to mend or pushed himself and never mended. It seemed the only thing to do. I think that a coin or two, properly placed, will keep them from talking too much about this night. And they can use the coins."

There was a sudden loud crash of thunder, making her jump, but there was no complaint from the horses or cows.

"Perhaps you should cast a soothing spell on yourself?"

Brillar glared at him and spread her blanket. They were settled and had extinguished the lantern when she said into the darkness, "When I was a child, there was a violent storm, the worst, elders said, in living memory. A tree crashed down on the house. If I'd been in my bed, I would have been killed, but I'd crept downstairs to find a treat in the kitchen. When I ran back up the stairs, my parents were screaming my name in the ruin of my room. They had never been so glad to find me out of bed."

She rolled in her blanket, shut her ears, and slept, while Elden blinked into the dark, wondering what other surprises this 'apprentice' had in store for him.

The rain stopped during the night, and Rob came out to collect them, with, "Mother says you have to have breakfast with us before you set off." As they were gathering their blankets, he went on, "Gran' is much better this morning and says his foot feels almost like new. Did you hear the storm? And the cows were so quiet; they're never quiet during a storm, but they hardly made a sound last night."

He kept up the chatter as they crossed the farmyard but ceased when his mother called to him. "I hope he hasn't been a bother. There are eggs for your breakfast and fresh bread." She bustled about the kitchen while they ate.

Moreg came in, leaning on his grandson. "My lady healer, I cannot thank you enough," he began, "I had a thought that I would never walk proper again."

Brillar looked at him sternly. "Have you heard my instructions? No weight on that foot for two days."

"S'all right, Gran', I can care for the cows until you're mended." The boy sat down and made a hasty breakfast, "And I am off now and will see to all while you sit there."

Everyone smiled after him as he rushed from the kitchen. "He's a good lad, a good lad," said his grandsire.

Elden stood. "We have to be on our way; many thanks to you for sheltering us from the storm."

Both adults asked them to stay one more day because the track was muddy and their way would be slow, but Brillar replied, "My uncle has that look in his eye, so we must be off."

Elden, with Rob's assistance, had Hob hitched to the cart in quick order, and he gave the boy a copper for his help. Before leaving the kitchen, Brillar put a silver coin on the shelf with the herbs she was leaving for Moreg, sure it would be found, then joined Elden in the cart. They left with happy waves from the farm family.

"It seems to me," she said thoughtfully, "that Hob could have been hitched more quickly without the boy's help."

"It seems to me," he replied, "that my apprentice will soon run out of coins if she leaves them behind so often." But his apprentice only smiled quietly.

The day went slowly and they had only gone on for two hours when they began to wish they had stayed at the farm. Hob fought with the mud, so they took to riding and leading him or leaning on the wheel to push it forward. Some of the way was flooded to their knees, and the fields around them had a soggy, ruined look.

They had struggled up a small rise when Elden called a halt, looking around them at the road and fields. The storm that that swept through had left clear skies and bright sun in its wake. The rise was dry and it seemed to him that the road would be better in the morning.

"No farther today," he said, much to her relief. "And no magic," he added, feeling her ready to cast a cleansing spell.

Her answer was a deep sigh.

"We are ordinary travelers. How would it look if we were clean when everyone else is covered with mud?" he admonished her.

"Yes, yes, I understand. Ordinary travelers. May this 'ordinary traveler' at least use water to clean her 'ordinary' face?"

He looked at her closely. There were splashes of mud everywhere on her face. As he watched, she removed a small blob from her right eyebrow, shaking it from her hand to the ground. He smothered laughter.

"You fare no better," she said tartly. "Or do you always let mud dangle that way from your beard?"

His hand found the mud and removed it. "Water and a cloth then," he said, and she hurried to comply.

At the bottom of the rise, was a pool of cleanish water which she dipped out, washing her face as best she could. More water, and her neck was nearly clean. Nothing could be done with her hair, so she washed her hands, rinsed the cloth, dipped water for Elden, and went back to the cart, where she found him picking dirt from his beard.

"Well, you look ordinary enough; water for your face." She handed him cup and cloth.

"Good that we covered the merchandise with something waterproof, or we would have a true mess." He had unhitched Hob, who lowered his head in misery. He was covered with mud from hooves to belly and was clearly unhappy.

Shaking her head, Brillar led him down the hill and splashed him with water. Elden followed to assist.

"Jez and Bright had an easier time of it, walking where they wished. Still, they'll need grooming later. Poor Hob! Days of easy travel and now this. And my poor apprentice, a morning of struggle and now an afternoon of lessons!"

She almost groaned but turned it into a deep sigh. "As the Master wishes," she said, and he looked at her sharply.

"First then, and before we eat, mend Hob's aching muscles."

As she did, Hob, clearly relieved, looked around him and walked off to graze on the hillside.

"Well done, and quickly."

"Quickly, because I'm hungry after this morning's work and want some food." Then, "A carter and a horseman. Both from ahead of us on the road."

"Yes, but no darkness. They will probably want what we found, a place above the waters," Elden responded, pleased that she had continued to check their surroundings even though she was tired.

The horseman arrived first, calling out, "Ho, travelers," as he approached.

"The traveler is welcome," Elden shouted in reply.

The rider and his mount, mud-covered and slow, mounted the rise as Brillar busied herself with trail rations.

"A miserable day for travel," the rider said, sliding from his gelding.

"We're done for the day and will camp here the night," Elden replied. "I'm Elden; I travel with my niece Brillar, who is learning the merchants' trade."

"Warick," replied the rider, "headed to Laurenfell to visit my father, who is at the House of Healing there."

Elden was pleased that Brillar made no sign of knowing the town. He glanced down the hill to see that the carter was bogged down in the mud again.

"Perhaps we should lend a hand?" he asked Warick, who nodded. The men went down the hill and slogged through the mud. Brillar watched as they pushed the cart while the carter led the struggling horse through the mire.

Movement caught her eye to the left, where there were small hummocks in the field. Reaching out, she found a sodden cwel perched on one. Taking her bow, she made a short stalk, downing the animal. Returning to high ground, she found the cart already there, the men laughing at the mud they carried. She cleaned the kill and returned to the now more cheerful camp.

"Your niece is an archer, then," Warick said admiringly.

She gave him a brief smile. "There's some fairly clean water downhill," she said, pointing, "if you want to remove some mud." She had washed mud and blood from her hands before rejoining them.

"That will be wasted unless we can start a fire," said the carter, introducing himself as Round Tobin, for he was a man of some size. "I think I have some dry sticks in the cart. A good thing to carry in the spring when the rains start."

Elden and Warick searched the hillock for branches then cut some from a small shade tree. There were enough for a fire, and the cwel went on to roast, then the men went to 'remove the countryside and return it to its proper place,' as Tobin had said, laughing.

As the day went on, Round Tobin produced some fruit from his cart and shared it around. He was a man full of stories and laughter; everyone enjoyed his company, although Elden and Brillar shared few stories. Warick seemed tense and kept glancing at the sky.

"You expect more rain?" asked Tobin, "I can tell you that last night's storm will have cleared the rain for many days."

Warick shook his head. "A messenger came for me saying my father was very ill and had been taken for healing. My mother asked me to hurry, now the weather has delayed me. I'm afraid I may be too late."

The group sobered at that, but Brillar stood. "I need to check on the horses," was all she said, but Elden saw her meaning and nodded.

There was little talk after the meat and rations had been shared around with more fruit; everyone had been exhausted by the day's struggles. Round Tobin was snoring as the rest finished their fruit, then they all wrapped in blankets and found places to sleep as soon as they could, Brillar under the cart, Elden next to her, and Warick under a small tree. No one tried to shift Tobin from his resting place.

As they settled, Elden whispered, "The gelding?"

"Warick will find him well-rested on the morrow," was the answer. "And Tobin's cart horse as well."

She heard his chuckle then settled down to sleep.

The morning was fair and bright when they woke to find that Warick had already left them, "He was very anxious to be off," Round Tobin told them, "and his horse seemed fresh."

They parted with the carter after many good wishes all around and some of Tobin's fruit for their travels.

*** 7 ***

The road was much improved after a night of clear weather, but there were still some areas where going was heavy. At times they walked, to lighten Hob's load. Lessons continued, with spells in Item magic, which Brillar found difficult for some reason.

"See the edges of the cloth as the broken ends of a bone and knit them in the same way," Elden encouraged, but while bones had seemed easy for her, Brillar found cloth difficult.

"There are too many threads," she insisted.

"There are no threads in leather, yet you can't mend that either," he scolded, and she scowled at him.

"It feels to me like thread, even in leather. Skin is much easier." That brought a sigh from her uncle.

The lessons in far-sight proved easier, and she had stretched her sense considerably. It still gave her headaches, but she banished them quickly.

The next day was even brighter and the road drier so they made good time. They stopped for the night by a quick stream swollen by the rains but with a dry bank. The horses had an easy time finding good grass and the camp was easy to set up. Then, as she was gathering firewood, Brillar suddenly cried out in pain and gasped to find one of her own arrows deeply embedded in her thigh.

Elden walked to her, bow in hand, as she twisted in pain on the ground, a hand at the bloody wound. Harsh sounds were all she could utter; the wound was agonizing and oozing blood.

"Level 6," he said, seemingly unconcerned with her agony. "You know the words. Stop the bleeding! Reach inside the wound. *Speak the words*," he commanded.

The words came out through clenched teeth as she probed the wound with her mind. The bleeding slowed and slowed again. She gritted her teeth, her chest tight, taking short gasps for air.

"Better," he said calmly. She threw her head back and glared at him. "Forget me," he said.

"Would… I could," came out between gasps.

"The bleeding has stopped; now ease the pain; let it fall away." He waited a moment.

She sucked in mana; it was already depleted with her exertion.

He paused again, then said, "Now, the difficult part. Break off the fletching and push the arrow through."

"Are you *insane*?" The pain had eased further, giving her a moment for speech.

"You know how to do it for others; now learn to do it for yourself." He was infuriatingly calm.

She glared as she reached with her unbloodied hand to steady her leg, using the bloodied one to break the shaft. The new wave of pain was brief, quickly stopped by a spell. She surprised him by pushing the arrow deeper without further instructions from him, although she uttered more spells; then, she grasped the arrowhead with her hand as it emerged. A quick pull and the arrowhead and shaft slid free from her leg. She writhed a bit in pain and stilled it quickly.

"I am apprenticed… to… a madman," she managed to get out.

"Now, reach into the wound and secure the small bleeding."

How can he be so composed? she wondered. She could feel that he was following her every move and withholding aid.

"Now the torn flesh and muscle, slowly. We are not threatened, so take your time."

"I am the only one threatened," she muttered as she spoke the words while seeing each bit as she healed and fused it. Her breathing became much calmer, and she began to relax. Still more healing.

"Now the last, the outer flesh," he said.

The entry wound closed first; the exit wound followed. Brillar lay back shaking; she was exhausted and drenched in sweat. More than half an hour had been spent in the 'lesson,' most of it in pain. He waited; then, judging her sufficiently recovered to return to the camp, reached out and offered a hand. She batted it away, furious. Without looking at him, she rolled herself onto all fours and struggled upright, swaying. She cast a spell for strength.

The camp was only a few paces away, but those paces went slowly. Her leg was stiff and aching, although she knew she could ease that in a few moments. She reached out for more mana, feeling it flow into her, renewing her, uttered a few more words, then collapsed by the fire.

Elden sat down casually, with effortless grace, as if nothing had happened.

"Did you think, my good apprentice, that a spell of that power could be truly learned by practicing words? Or perhaps you thought you would learn it in battle when time was important?"

She gave no answer, knowing he was right.

"And there is still water to be fetched," he added, leaning back and looking contented.

Scowling, she fetched the water, then, smiling impishly, sent the entire bucketful down on his head, leaving him sputtering until a spell made it vanish and dried his clothes.

"I seem to have slipped," were her innocent words. "I will, of course, fetch more." She still limped slightly, but the prank made her smile. Behind her, she could hear him laughing. She felt something move at her leg and found her leggings mended and the blood gone. Perhaps a lesson or two more in Item magic might be a good thing.

In the morning, the last of the ache in her leg was gone, but she still glared at him when she mounted the cart.

"A lesson well learned?" he asked.

"Well learned," she agreed grudgingly. "How were you taught?"

"Much the same way, but with a sword," came the reply, "and took much the same retribution, although it was a small rain of pebbles."

At this, they both laughed and started the cart.

"Didn't know I had skill with the bow, did you?" he asked merrily as they set off to more laughter. Noon was an easy meal. Her Master, as she now fully admitted him to be, even fetched firewood. His minor scratches, she healed quickly.

"From what the potter said, I think we will reach Healdsten in an hour. Our time on the road has been well-spent," he commented, dousing the fire. "Then we will see if we can make a profit on the load. Paying for this lot has left me with a light purse."

She burst out laughing, and he stared.

"Uncle, I wore out two pairs of boots with walking and stayed in many an inn. A foldbox can hold more than herbs and hairpins."

"Money? And you have let me spend my coin with no thought to the lightness of my purse," he replied, making his voice petulant, which fooled her not in the least.

"Have no fear. I just know that a man prefers his own coin. A moment only, and I will refill your light purse." Brillar opened the foldbox and took out some silver and two gold coins.

"By the Light," Elden exclaimed, "I have found a rich apprentice!"

She laughed. "Wherever I traveled, there has usually been the need for a skilled healer. From the wealthy, I accepted a coin or two, from others, a place to sleep and a hot meal," she explained. "The merchant whose son broke his leg in three places was very grateful; it was already partly healed and twisted." They remounted the cart and set off.

Their road now led between fine herds of cattle, sheep, and horses. It was good land for grazing but a bit boulder-strewn for farming. They passed a few cottages near the road with small stone-marked gardens in cleared areas near them. Children came to gates to wave or played with toys near doors. It appeared that carters were often seen on the road and not feared.

As Elden had predicted, Healdsten soon appeared and looked to be a more prosperous town than Eafel. Still, like all good country towns, this one had an inn at the entry road. A planked walk in front of the inn and a roof over the door proclaimed the inn to be as substantial as the town.

Elden called, and a man came to the door wiping his hands on a towel. Like most innkeepers, he was stout, aproned, and smiling. Elden's lips twitched into a smile. After all, who would trust a skinny innkeeper? That the man and his clothes were clean and neat also spoke well of the inn.

"Good afternoon, good folk," he greeted them, "and welcome to the *Sword and Shield*, the finest inn and rooms in Healdsten."

"I wonder," uncle whispered to niece, "if there is another."

"Welcome, welcome, you will need stabling for the horses, of course, and a place for the cart." He whistled for the stable boy who was already nearly there because he had seen their approach from the rear of the inn.

"Ah, there you are, lad. Be ready to assist these fine merchants." Glancing at Brillar, he said, "You'll not need a bow at our inn, mistress, for we have a sheriff's man here who keeps order. And we have a good tub for washing as you seem to have found some mud on the road."

"You have not named a price," remarked Elden, unmoving. "We will need rooms, supper, and a good breakfast, for we hope to sell our goods and move on quickly."

The innkeeper looked them over a bit. "Four coppers for each room, three for each meal, two for each horse, one for watching the cart," He began to count on his fingers. "A silver and seven in all, worthies."

"And would two silvers find us with better overall?" asked Brillar. "The trail was long and refreshment scarce."

At the sound of two silver coins, the man's eyes widened. "Aye, mistress, and a bottle of wine with your supper." She handed over the coins.

"Wife," he shouted, and they jumped from the cart, handing Hob's reins to the stable boy, "we have company."

Elden had a few words with the stable boy, handed him a copper, and joined her at the inn.

The lower portion of the inn was stone, but two stories made of wood stretched above. Ceilings were low and heavily timbered. The walls, plastered and whitewashed, suggested a well-run establishment, and the innkeeper had hung prize animal heads as decoration. The cold fireplace was massive and spoke of many a merry winter festival at the inn.

The innkeeper came out with two pints of cider, "To wash away the dust," he said, lingering. "Harkort, is my name; my wife is Salma. If you have a need, just call, and one will answer." He paused, waiting.

"Elden, merchant, and this is my niece Brillar. I've been teaching her the trade." He saluted Harkort with his tankard.

"Well met, then, well met. And what are your wares then, for I know all the sellers in town, and a fine town it is I can tell you? We've nine hundred or more here, yes, nine hundred, and some respectable homes for those who have coin. Why, there is a fine, cobbled plaza in the center of the town and good shops around it on cobbled streets. Then down the roads, you can find those who make—workers in leather and cloth, gold and silver. Fruit sellers, fishmongers, we even have a fuller and a dyer of cloth, although they be a fair pace from town—the smell, you know."

It seemed that Harkort would go on forever, so Elden put in, "Is there anyone likely to buy good Eafel pottery?"

"Well, then, do you plan to stay the night only and want to make a quick sale, or will you stay and set up a stall on market day."

"A quick sale would suit us and back on the road in the morning," Brillar spoke up.

Harkort thought about it. "I'll confer wi' me wife, a moment only."

He returned with her as they finished their ale and Salma opened the conversation. "My brother has a stand on market day and could likely sell what you have. I sent our lass to fetch him."

Her brother, Kenlen, appeared at the door, a bit breathless, and Elden took him around to the cart to show the wares while Salma took Brillar to a room where she could 'wash off the countryside,' she was told. It was a simple affair, an overhead tub of cold water that could be opened to flow down as the washer scrubbed. Still, they were trying to seem 'ordinary', and Brillar used it at once.

She had finished and redressed when Elden returned, looking pleased. "Sixty in silver," he remarked as he sat to sip the last of his cider. "Kenlen seemed to think that he could sell it for a nice profit and can store what he doesn't sell quickly."

"Did he suggest wares for us to buy? Perhaps from another member of the family?"

Elden glanced at her. "In fact, niece, when he heard we were heading to West Riversgate, he suggested silverwork. The silversmith in town has a good trade there, making ornaments for ladies of the town. He moved here when he married a local lass from a good family. I am told that, although he makes less money here, he prefers it to a larger town. Carters are said to have reported a good profit from his work."

Elden took himself for a quick wash, then dressed, and they sought out Reblin, the silversmith. Together, they picked out several dozen intricate pieces at a good price. Elden lingered a bit in the shop while Brillar walked the plaza and bought two unusual pieces of fruit.

"Uncle," she called, tossing him one as he came from the shop. "What did you learn?"

"His old master had been sorry to lose him. He gave me the names of several people who might be interested in his pieces." Then, quietly and with command, "What do you see?"

In a respectable town with a sheriff's man in place, they had both relaxed, perhaps a bit too much. She continued walking and reached out. "So many people."

"Sort them," was his harsh whisper.

At the command, she glanced at him, then refocused on the town. "Brightness, children at lessons, housewives." She almost stopped walking. "Behind us, some darkness, three men, drink, I think they may have noticed us, our coin and purchases."

"I think we should go and take our supper, then retire. Well done, niece, if a bit slow. Supper then sleep, with our weapons at hand."

She had felt fleeting pleasure at the "well done" and rankled at "a bit slow." Supper with wine sounded acceptable to her as the fruit had improved her appetite rather than dulled it. They kept their walk easy and casual until they reached the inn. She could feel one man following them and told Elden in a whisper, getting his nodded agreement.

Their supper was indeed better than the standard fare they saw around them. Salma had prepared a roast hen in savory herbs, fresh vegetables, warm bread, and custard for dessert. Harkort brought an open bottle of wine to the table and poured it into tall glasses. Their meal brought good-natured comments from the other folk at the tables, but none seemed to begrudge them their food since, like good merchants, they had cheery smiles and 'hellos' for all.

Brillar sipped appreciatively at the wine and then took several swallows. "He keeps a fine vintage for the weary," she said, looking at her uncle, who had barely begun his wine while her glass was half empty.

"A very fine vintage," he replied, too quietly, "although another lesson is in order, as you did not inspect the wine." Guiltily, she reached out to the drink, testing it, and finding something wrong.

"More of the roast hen for you, niece, and bread to soak up the wine, for I don't recall teaching you that cleansing spell yet."

Brillar forked more hen into her mouth. "In fact," her uncle added, "it might be well to finish the bottle and appear to have succumbed to whatever is in the wine. I'll cleanse it later."

He took a deep draught of the wine, encouraging her with a nod, raising his glass in a toast. "To a fine inn," he said to the applause of the company, and tankards were raised all around.

As they ate their custard, Brillar could feel the heavy effect of whatever had been in the wine. She staggered a little on rising and was steadied by her unsteady uncle. Salma rushed to them and held her other arm as she guided them to their rooms. Brillar managed to reach her bed and threw herself on it. Once safely in his room with the door closed, Elden spoke quietly, cleaning himself and then Brillar, of both wine and sleeping potion. In the next room, she was suddenly wide awake and alert. Finding their rooms joined by a locked door, she rapped quietly and joined him when he opened it.

They spoke in low voices. "How long do you think?" she whispered.

"There's still some light. After midnight, when the inn is empty," he replied. "You can sleep a bit with your blade beside you. I'll keep watch."

"There was no darkness here," she said, confused.

"Someone else is at fault here, not Harkort. Perhaps the wine dealer is in league with the robbers. We shall see tonight or in the morning."

She went back through the door, and he closed it. There was a candle in the room, and she shuttered it. Its light might be needed. Armed, she stretched out, not on the bed, but on a chair after crushing a pillow and blanket on the bed into something like a sleeping form. Her purse, boots, and cloak, she left in plain sight on a small table by the bed. Confident in her uncle's watch, she managed to doze a bit.

He woke her sharply and she tightened her grip on her dagger. There were footsteps in the hall, and she stole from the chair to station herself behind the door. She heard keys in both locks and smiled grimly. The thieves were about to get a surprise. The man in her room crept stealthily to her purse and cloak on the table, took the purse, turned, and headed back toward the door.

In one movement, she un-shuttered the candle and slammed the door with her foot. Startled, the man dropped her things. "Stand down," she barked, showing the knife. In the next room, she could hear noises. Unarmed but faced with what he thought was a mere woman, the thief lunged at her.

Brillar dropped the candle, sidestepped his lunge, and slashed his arm. The knife bit deep, and he screamed. Next door, she heard a crash then Elden was in her room, stamping at the candle.

"Do you mean to set the inn alight?" he demanded.

"I was busy," was her steady reply, pointing at the bleeding man. There was a rush of footsteps in the hall and bright lanterns.

"By the bright sky." It was Harkort, followed by a serving-man. "What is this commotion? What's all this here?"

"Thieves," replied Elden, "come to take what they could in the night and leave us dead." The servant was dispatched for the sheriff's man.

"Not dead," said the thief from the floor where he was holding his wounded arm and rocking. "I carried no weapon."

Elden threw a short sword on the floor. "Not you, perhaps, but your friend was ready to kill."

"I didn't know," he pleaded.

Salma was heard on the stairs, a robe wrapped around her nightclothes and another lantern brighter than the first in her hand. Harkort went to Elden's room and came back, shaking his head. "A fine blow was struck there," he said, chuckling. "He'll sleep into the day and wake sore."

Salma just stood, aghast. "That this should happen in our inn," she cried as other guests, wakened from their sleep, came to see what had happened.

Elden went to her and put an arm on her shoulder. Brillar could feel his comfort flow to her. "My good lady," he said soothingly, "these are none of your guests." Her soothing joined his and extended to the other guests. "It's obvious that they came by stealth and stole the keys. This is none of your doing, and the speed," he emphasized, "at which your husband came in response!" He chuckled. "Why, I have never seen such concern for guests."

At his kind words and the kinder quiet spells, she calmed just as the sheriff's man came up the stairs, sword in hand and ready.

"What's here?" he demanded of the assembled company.

"Theft here," responded Brillar, taking up her purse from where the thief had dropped it, "and perhaps more in the next room."

"Send for a healer," he commanded the servant. "And have someone send up a mop and bucket," he called after the lad.

"I'm Thorstes," he told Brillar with a slight bow, "the sheriff's man here." He looked at the wounded man. "You've a fine hand with a dagger," he said, looking her over in surprise.

"Better with a bow," said Elden, coming back to the room. "Harkort supplied some rope, and we've tied the other for you."

Both robbers wore rough, brown homespun and well-worn boots. They looked akin, and the injured one confirmed the other thief was his brother.

Thorstes gathered the short sword and a knife from the other man. "Best see if anything is missing," he said to Elden, who assured him that everything was in place and accounted for.

"I heard him come in and used my fist before he could act," said Elden, flexing his hand. Brillar was surprised to see that it was actually bruised.

The serving lad arrived with a healer and two men who helped Thorstes with his unconscious prisoner. Brillar felt sudden darkness and straightened, staring. Elden nodded to her. As the men took the prisoners downstairs, Elden had a quick word with Thorstes as she listened. The others had returned to their beds.

"That man in the dark red shirt, do you know him?" he asked, "I think we saw him with the other two earlier in town when we were buying silver."

"All three are new to me," Thorstes replied. "You can be sure that inquiries will be made and answers found." He nodded to them both and left.

Salma bustled up again with a mop and a maid to do the cleaning. "Such doings in my respectable inn," she fumed, rattling some new keys. "You'll not want those rooms now," she insisted. They gathered their things and followed her up the second set of stairs. "I think you will find these suitable," she said, opening two doors. "We keep them for the lords who sometimes happen by." She quickly had candles lit. They showed larger and better rooms than those below.

"You do us too much service," Elden said with smiling grace and a slight bow, leaving her flustered. "But it's late and we're tired. We'll see you in the morning." Salma dropped a curtsey and fled.

"Well," said Elden as he looked around, "a fine reward for doing away with ruffians. Sleep well, niece." He entered his room and closed the door. Setting her things down and undressing, Brillar flopped on the bed and squirmed comfortably in its warmth.

Let's hope the local healer hasn't my skill, was her last thought.

Her new accommodations had heavy curtains at the windows, and Brillar was alarmed when she opened them. She'd slept late. Muttering a cleansing spell, she opened the door and found an ewer and basin in the corridor. She carried them into the room, washed her face and hands, then, finding a mirror, she shook out and combed her hair before rebraiding it. When she finally went down to the necessary and breakfast, she found Elden in conversation with a group of locals.

"Good morrow, Brillar," he called and beckoned her over. There was bread, honey, and jam on the table. She greeted her uncle hastily before taking a bite of bread and jam. He laughed heartily. "My niece seems to have developed an appetite after her night's work," he told the group, laughing again.

"And how is that bruised hand this morning?" she asked with a bit of a smile. "Still sore?" He flexed his hand as the group laughed at his discomfort.

"Perhaps I should see the healer," he mused.

"She's busy with thy niece's work," came a voice from the crowd which roared in response.

Salma bustled up with a laden tray. "Now you've had your news and told it. Be off and let the lass eat," she told the crowd.

They disbursed, leaving Salma to say, "Now then, you seem well this morning, and here's a fine breakfast and corin for you." She bustled off.

Brillar sipped the hot brew, added honey and smiled, then applied herself to breakfast while Elden told the morning's tale; the sheriff's man had already come and gone.

"All three were in on the game," he began, "one to tamper with the wine, the others to do the robbing. The healer is dealing with the one you sliced; you cut him to the bone." She nodded. "Your friend, Thorstes, has them in a locked cell. He wanted us to wait for the judging," he looked at her, "at least he wanted *you* to wait." She scowled at him around a bit of sausage. "But I told him we must be on the road. There are enough to tell the tale. I also had Salma's serving girl go around with some coppers and buy us food for the road. All is packed and readied for us."

"You *have* been busy," was all she said and went back to the room for her few things there.

Salma and Harkort came out to bid them goodbye. "We hope you won't be holding all this against us or passing word about it on the road." There was pleading in Harkort's voice.

"Not a word," Elden promised. He clicked the reins, and they started off, Jez and Bright following.

*** 8 ***

Now the days tended to full summer. Eager to reclaim his property, Elden kept them moving and increased Brillar's lessons. Her Life skills and her sight improved rapidly, and he gave her a few lessons in Item magic, basics only. She had the cleansing spell but had gone no further. He continued to try to teach her to mend cloth, but that was slow going. He switched to a spell for repairing metal armor which she proclaimed, 'as easy as knitting bone.' No more arrows flew at her, although he threatened. Her arrows kept them well fed on cwel and linic hen. They reached the outskirts of West Riversgate in only a week.

In their last few days, the road had widened to accommodate increased travelers, mounted, with carts, or on foot. Once, a fine carriage happened on them, guarded by men-at-arms, and they had pulled to the side of the road to let it pass. They'd traveled the southern route and didn't need the bridge that spanned the river.

As they drew close, Elden grinned. "I have it!" he said excitedly. "Closer, and I'll be able to pinpoint the location!"

West Riversgate was an imposing town with a fine stone wall and several gates. As they approached one, a guard motioned them to take themselves to the merchant gate, and they went, uncomplaining, first looping ropes around Jez and Bright to declare ownership and to keep the horses close to the cart. The merchant's gate was narrower than the first, but they passed through easily onto a cobbled street that widened after the gate. Houses and shops lined the streets. A butcher and fishmonger had open stalls near the wall and were doing a good business. The smell of fresh bread mixed with other town scents. Children, young or freed from their lessons, were everywhere. A small boy, pushed by an older child, fell, hitting his arm on stone and crying. Without thinking, Brillar reached out, mended the sprain, and eased him.

"Have a care, niece," said Elden, "a display may bring attention."

"And you," she said sharply, for she had felt him reaching out for his foldbox.

"I said it was here," he whispered to her gleefully. "It seems the innkeeper kept it, or at least the charm is in that direction." The streets had been well laid out, and Elden found his old inn easily. "Yes! It's here."

They pulled up to the portico where he hopped out to hold Hob's reins. "Niece, go in and ask for lodging and a barn. I don't want to be seen too quickly." Nodding, brushing trail dust off her clothes, she entered the inn and stopped.

The inn was high ceilinged and well furnished. Cloths covered some of the tables while sconces adorned the walls held lamps. The bar was long and curved and seemed to be one piece of polished wood. The stair to the right had a heavily carved balustrade, and the walls were hung with paintings. If Elden had been trying to hide here, he was having a pleasant time of it. The innkeeper, a heavy balding man, came over with a slight sneer at her clothing. Opening her purse, she stopped his sneer by handing over four pieces of silver and saying in an imperious voice, "My uncle and I require two of your better rooms and stabling for a cart and three horses. The horses," she fixed him with a stern eye, "are to be well cared for, as they are fine animals."

Taking another look at the silver in his hand, for few visitors handed their coins over without some haggling, he swallowed and stammered, "Of course, mistress. At once." He turned away, calling for a servant to see to the animals, then, "Refreshment, mistress?"

"Wine for two travelers, good wine, if you please." She heard Elden come in behind her with their trade goods and take a seat.

"A lovely, quiet place you picked for your hideaway," she murmured to him, but his attention was on a glass box with a plate above it.

"Look near the fireplace," he whispered, "but show nothing."

She glanced around casually. To the left of the fireplace, she saw a glass case and knew its contents at once. A sign above said, "One copper to try this curiosity, one silver if you can open it."

"So," she said quietly, "he's found a way to make money from it."

"And quite the time they've had with it. Dented!" Elden replied with dismay.

The innkeeper returned with the wine, placing the beautifully ornamented glasses in front of them. The silvers had evidently done their work well. The man was practically groveling.

"My man has taken horses and cart to the stable. Perhaps you would like to see your rooms when you finish the wine? Supper will be two more hours." Brillar nodded. "My lass is heating water and will bring it to your rooms."

They sipped their wine, calling when they finished. Several tables had filled as they drank, and it seemed a good time to make themselves more comfortable for the evening. The rooms they were led to were not as fine as their last, but better than most. Both enjoyed the hot water, although cleansing spells were faster.

Elden had left her at the door with, "Now, niece, I think it's time to refine ourselves for supper."

Brillar had taken time to survey the room. There was a soft chair and the mattress was down-filled. *Good rest there,* she thought before opening the foldbox and taking out the green dress and a pair of light shoes she had forgotten. She refreshed them with a few words. The wall held a long mirror, and she enjoyed the first full view of herself in the dress. She let down her hair and brushed it to a deep sheen then added two small braids to pull it from her face. She fixed one side with an ornament and looked at herself again, thinking that her uncle had never seen her hair except in a braid. She was just finished applying scent when there was a knock on the door. Closing and storing the foldbox, she opened it, stepping back and straightening. He glanced, then looked more keenly. She raised an eyebrow.

"Well, who would have guessed so fine a lady would come from under so much trail dust?" he commented. He looked quite dashing himself, dressed in the greys the tailor had made, with a knife and purse at his belt. "But," he took something from a pocket, showed it to her, then removed her ornament and fixed the new one in her hair.

"When?" she asked.

"While you were buying fruit."

She blushed slightly, turned, and put her ornament on the table. "It's lovely, many thanks, Uncle," she told him as she looked into the glass.

He offered his arm. "Shall we go down?" He led her to the steps. There were stares when they reached the bend and a landing.

The innkeeper rushed to meet them. "My lady," he gushed, but she silenced him with a wave.

"We wish to travel quietly," she whispered as he showed them to a fine table then rushed off for wine.

There were more stares, then the conversations began around them again. One of the townswomen looked at her and sniffed, thinking her no niece, although the innkeeper had obviously announced them as related. Brillar tapped on her glass when the wine was served, gathering attention.

"My uncle and I are merchants now traveling in silver ornaments and pins. I see you've noticed the one in my hair. If you have an interest in our merchandise, perhaps you will ask after we have supped." She sat with an easy grace.

"I thought we were going to gather no attention," he muttered.

"I will not be thought a harlot. Besides, I know someone who will try his luck for a copper later and may be able to open that curiosity." She smiled at him wickedly.

Several men and ladies did come over after they dined, to admire her pin, and Elden went up the stairs with several of the gentlemen, telling her that they were making a satisfactory profit.

The inn grew lively and they stayed after supper and sipped wine, waiting. Finally, a student called to the innkeeper. "Good man, what's that in the glass?"

"Oh, a curiosity that, a fine curiosity. You can see it is meant to be opened, but none can open it. It's well made and heavier than it looks. You can use only your hands to try it—someone has dented it already—and you have five minutes to take your chance."

Intrigued, the young man handed over a copper and received the foldbox. He turned it over and over, puzzling. He shook it, tried to open its sides, then its ends. He attempted to pry it open to the laughter of his friends. Finally, the innkeeper took it while the others at the table laughed.

"You try it then," he told his friends. Taking up the challenge, two more of the students twisted the curiosity with no luck. There were no more takers and the innkeeper was taking it back toward its box when Elden spoke up.

"I would like a try if you please," he said, handing over a copper and receiving what he had sought.

Elden seemed to study the box for several minutes while the crowd stared, amused, and a few bets were placed. Finally, responding to its owner's touch and a deft movement of his thumbs, the box popped open. Several people nearby moved forward to see how he had done it. He lifted one edge, holding the box high so everyone could see that he had won, then snapped it closed as the innkeeper came with his coin.

"Such a fine toy," he said, as the man stared from him to the now sealed box. "Keep your silver and I will keep this."

The crowd cheered at seeing the inn-man beaten; many a copper had been lost trying to open the box.

The inn-man stammered, wanting to keep the silver but loathe to lose the coppers.

"Perhaps," Elden said in a loud voice, "we can discuss a price in a place more private, as I would certainly like to buy this." The two left but several of the locals came to keep Brillar company in his absence. They all had questions about how he managed to open the box, but she feigned ignorance.

The innkeeper led Elden to a small storage room. "That box has been a fine draw for my inn," he complained, "surely worth more than a silver coin."

"Is it worth your life then?" came the menacing response. "Because I will have what is mine." Elden's dagger was suddenly in his hand as he grabbed the front of the man's shirt, holding him.

The inn-man stared at him closely. "No, you can't be, not possible. There was word that you were dead," he whispered, his voice fearful.

"Very possible," hissed Elden, "and it was you who sent me out to that pleasure house where they took me." His dagger was at the man's throat.

"I-I… it is a fine establishment, I was told. I mean, it was when I visited. Truly." The knife never relaxed.

Eldred probed and found only truth in the man's words. He moved the knife away from the man's throat. "Now, we shall go out together, you and I, and tell the crowd that I gave you three silvers for this." He fixed it on his belt. "Then you will make a list of anything else that might have been 'mislaid,' and if it's worth my time, I may collect it; I see one of my surcoats there on a shelf."

"Whatever I have that was yours will be returned, but some has been sold, some given away," the innkeeper was fairly gibbering in relief.

"Then smile, good friend, and we go out together."

Which they did, with Elden calling, "A fine bargain I've made and ale or wine for all present, on my coin, although we must retire." More cheers followed.

Brillar stood and went with him up the stairs to his room.

"Now you will see," he said, laughing, "what a year's making will do." He had no secrets from his niece/apprentice; the foldbox opened and reopened under his hands. When it nearly filled the room, she stared, dazzled, running her hand over fur, brocade, and silk. Pouches held gold coins and herbs lined a shelf.

"That hat is yours, really?" She smiled impishly.

"Well, in some places, fur and feathers are well suited to impress." He stopped as she gave a merry laugh.

"By the heavens. I have found myself a rich Master." She laughed then left him for her own room so he could take what he needed and refold the box.

Brillar slept comfortably and left the bed reluctantly. When she went down for breakfast, she found that Elden had already gone out. She ordered more corin and waited until he came in.

"For me, good niece? Thank you, I am a bit thirsty." He helped himself to the brew and turned a lip. "Sugared!"

"Well, it was mine, Uncle Elden." She beckoned for more for him. "What news of the day?"

"The innkeeper and I have had a brief conversation in my room. What he had of my things, he has returned. It seems that Reblin's old master was here last night after we retired and has made an offer on our other items. There is nothing to hold us here longer. I stopped at the harness maker and bought us two good saddles; the time has come for us to go."

"I also learned," he added, taking a swallow, "that there is a small teaching house of the Sisterhood just a few miles on across the river." He raised a brow. "I thought you might like to send word to your family?"

"A fine idea, good uncle," she replied, pleased with his thoughtfulness. "I'll gather my things and be down shortly."

It took only a moment for both to be ready for the day. The innkeeper, perhaps wary of Elden's temper, did not come out to bid them farewell. Instead, he sent the stable boy with horses and cart. On the way to the merchant's gate, they shopped a bit, adding tubers, dried meats, and fresh fruit to the cart. Traffic on the road to the bridge was light, but they had to wait there for a drover to bring his cattle across from the far bank.

"Did you find Jenel's partner?" Brillar inquired as they crossed the bridge and started down the road.

"I never looked," he replied. "Probably just some courtesan hired for the evening and long gone. Let's have one of those small melons I saw in the cart; a day as fine as this makes a man hungry." When she reached for the melon, he gave her a shove, tumbling her into the dirt, and worse, the cattle had passed along the road.

"I can't have you forget your lessons now, can I?" he said, laughing as she picked herself up and murmured the healing spells she had learned to ease her pains.

"That would have bruised," she said accusingly as she climbed onto the seat next to him, fully aware that she smelled rank. He sniffed and turned away.

"What you have done, *you* undo," she said neatly. Her clothes were suddenly clean, but she refused to speak to him again until they saw the house of the Sisterhood down a treed lane. They turned left into the lane, enjoying the cool under the trees. She looked at it and sighed, full of memories.

A Sister came out onto the porch of the clean white structure to meet them. Windows lined the walls, some open to admit the morning air.

Brillar stepped down from the cart and made the traditional greeting of the Sisterhood. Surprised, the Sister returned it.

"I am Brillar," she announced. "Daughter of Darwallen of the Life Sisterhood in Laurenfell."

"Good Sister," she was answered, "come in, visit and rest with us a while."

"I apologize, but we're in a hurry. I only came to ask that you send word to my parents that I am well and in good company. Oh, and to make a gift to your house of this cart and Hob. He's been a fine animal for us, and I know you'll treat him well."

Garnelden was already saddling the Jez and Bright and transferring their purchases to saddle packs.

"I see," said the Sister, glancing at Elden's foldbox, "that my report to your parents will be truthful." The heads of curious children had appeared in the Sister's classroom. Without looking, she said, "Back to your studies," and they disappeared amid giggles. She smiled warmly.

"My lady Brillar?" Elden had the horses ready.

"May your travels be safe," said the Sister, waving her out.

"May your students be less trouble than I was at that age," Brillar answered with a laugh.

They put their horses into the traveler's pace and made time to the road and onward, following the Carlin River that flowed through West and East Riversgate. Now, in full summer, the heat of the sun was brutal on their mounts even with their easy gait. They rode in the early morning only and rested in whatever shade they could find as the sun rose higher.

'Rested' was a relative word. The horses rested, certainly, and the first day, they were well-watered at a pool the river had formed on its way to the lake, but Elden continued Brillar's lessons.

"Swords and arrows are easy," he explained. "Armor is the best defense against them, although archers are usually in the back ranks."

"I've heard we sometimes hide behind shield barriers?"

"A good thing too, as arrows fly both ways. Still, there are other ways to die in a battle or just a nasty fight. How is your defense against magic?" Without waiting for a reply, he sent a weak bolt of lightning against her, but she cast it aside.

"You're becoming predictable, Elden," she remarked.

A frost bolt, much stronger than the lightning, left her chilled to the bone. A word from between chattering teeth, and she was warm again. "I think, Master, that I could use a lesson or two."

He responded with a smile. "Perhaps after lunch."

She had hunted early in the day and close to camp, bringing down linic hens that were already roasting at the fire but not quite ready to eat.

"A swim then?" She stood and stripped down to her scants, heading to the water. "Coming?"

Reluctantly, he stood and followed, pausing to take off his boots. Brillar was already in the water. The river had carved a deep pool beneath some shade trees, but the water was warm enough. Elden rolled up his pants and waded.

"What's this? The water is fine for swimming, Elden," she said, splashing him. She had, for the most part, given up calling him 'uncle.'"

"There is something, perhaps, I should explain." He stopped.

"You can't *swim*?" she asked, guessing his answer. She was treading water in the middle of the pool.

"Indeed, I lack the skill." Elden looked somewhat sheepish.

"Not from fear of the water?" Brillar had learned to swim as a small child and loved the water.

"Only from lack of teaching and experience, I assure you," he responded, miffed.

"Then remove your finery," she replied, going to stand in shallow water, "and I'll be the teacher for a while."

Elden proved an apt pupil. A bit of instruction in an easy stroke, a bit of sputtering, and he could move clumsily through the water. The aroma of fully cooked hen pulled them from the pool, and he cast to dry their clothing so they could re-dress.

As they ate, she asked formally, "Master, you seemed in a rush to get to Lands-end; now we travel more slowly."

"We have hill country to cross, which can be dangerous. I want the horses rested."

She accepted the answer but felt something else behind the words. Sometimes she saw his lips move soundlessly and wondered what words there would be if they were spoken aloud. Elden's silent mutterings were his review of spell, dispel and counter-spell, spells of War and Creature magic, spells he believed he would need in Lands-end.

*** 9 ***

Another day of easy travel and they entered hill country, sometimes needing to lead the horses through narrow paths. Still, it was beautiful. Her travels had not taken her through the hills, and her eyes were constantly finding something new, which she would immediately point out. The first day was full of such sights.

"Elden, look at that waterfall! The height of it and how narrow it is." The fall was a hundred feet in height or more.

"Arrow Falls is its name. We're headed to Old Man Rock. No, don't ask me about the name; you'll know soon enough."

"How lovely the flowers are here, and the scent! What are they called?" Elden, who had traveled the hill country, had a hard time keeping up with her questions.

The wind in the hill country could be chilly at night. Elden helped gather enough firewood to keep a fire going all night. "There are wild things here in the hill country, some with sharp teeth. No proper wolves, but dogs gone wild can be dangerous. Tonight, we dine on dried rations and fruit. I want no scent of cooking meat to draw them."

They wrapped themselves in blankets and woke by turns to keep the fire burning.

Their second day led them up and down hills and once up along a narrow trail above a deep defile. Going was slow and there was little time to talk.

On the third day, they came out near a waterfall, and she stopped, pointing. "Old Man Rock," she said. "Now I understand. He has a fine chin on him."

Elden smiled, indulgent, but waiting.

She stiffened. "There are men behind us." She reached further, "And to the right but at a good distance."

"And?"

"No darkness in them. Concern perhaps?

"Well done. They're hillmen. They keep small crofts and even market areas here, although not true towns. They'll have someone follow us to make sure we mean no harm, but it's unlikely they'll come much closer than they are. A cautious folk, hillmen, but not unkind to strangers."

"By your tone, you've met them."

Elden smiled. "I have passed through the hills many times. We're on friendly terms, the hill folk and I. We may even see their flocks from time to time; they produce fine wool in the hills."

Past Old Man Rock, it was only another day to come out of the hills. The hillmen evidently thought them no danger as they began to see flocks of sheep and the occasional shepherd with his dog.

As they left the hills, they filled water skins at a small stream. The river was behind them now as it flowed west. There would be water for the horses here and there, but Elden wanted to ensure their drinking water.

"Two more days, and we will be near enough to Lands-end. The town is set up above the sea with a cove at its base. We'll see it in the distance."

They ate cold rations that night and dried fruit side by small fire. They spoke little; there were no lessons. Elden was tense, and she could feel his worry. He had not told his apprentice that he planned to leave her behind on the last day. He knew she wasn't ready for what he had to face and wanted to forestall the arguments he knew his decision would bring. He also knew he could leave her in a binding spell, with the horses for protection, long enough for his business to be completed, but he thought of the idea with deep displeasure. While he hoped to come from Lands-end alive, he was uncertain of the outcome. He continued to review his War spells and protections but, if Harrolen had been using them constantly overseas… *Life is always uncertain,* he thought, watching his apprentice sleep.

There had been no sign or rumor of the army he had expected his message, sent through Polsen, would raise. No sign of the Brotherhood gathered to deal with one of their own gone rogue. He was nearly sure that no message had been sent and feared that his friend might be dead.

Have all my choices been wrong? I tried to draw them from the Brotherhood to give them time, but suppose I was wrong; suppose he only wants my *life. Stupid to think I was safe in West Riversgate, although I discerned no darkness there. Light, I was so tired!* His recriminations were cut short when something brushed his shoulder. He reached up to stroke Jez. "I know, I know. I'm sorry I worried you." The stallion pushed his shoulder. "Yes, I'll sleep now. Nothing else to do with you keeping such good watch."

They were both more alert for trouble the next day, even though the fields were still prosperous and well-tended. They were a good thirty miles from Lands-end when they stopped for lunch. They had only trail rations and dried fruit, filling but hardly tasty.

"Elden, if we are to have something substantial for supper, I'll need to hunt. There were birds earlier, roused as we passed. A short ride, a brief stalk, and a better meal tonight."

"We're too close," he said firmly.

"Close, yes, but there hasn't yet been any darkness, nothing to mar to the last few days. Besides, the birds are behind us, so I'll need to ride away from the town."

"You're restless?"

"You've taken us miles out of our way; no farmhouses, few people to report they have seen riders, yes, I'm restless. And hungry." Her tone was insistent.

Elden stretched out with his far-sense, feeling a prickle here and there but nothing to worry him. Still, he worried. "Mark our place and mind your distance," he cautioned.

"Just when have I been lost?" she asked sweetly.

"Be off then."

They had unsaddled the horses, but she needed no saddle with Bright. Taking her bow, she looked at him, "Nap and dream of a fine supper." She put her heels to Bright and they were off.

***

Brillar doubled back on their track for miles, to where she had seen birds in the distance. She crossed an open field and went through a short, wooded patch. She had gone over three miles from the road when she felt something, darkness moving quickly and from the road behind her. She urged Bright into a canter, reaching forward.

At the camp, Elden was suddenly on his feet. "Brillar," he breathed.

Bright was in a gallop now, moving through an open field heading away from the road and the camp. More horses and men came from the right. She expected spells but none came. She was moving

Bright to the left when a group of horsemen came from the wood on that side, their horses fresh. She urged Bright back to the right but was cut off. Murmuring a spell for the mare, she was rewarded with a fresh burst of speed, but two more men appeared, cutting her off, one swinging a rope. A few strides more and the rope found her, wrenching her backward and hurling her to the ground. She struck her head on a rock, skidding, bow lost. Barely conscious, she was aware of a man bending over her, then there was nothing.

"The horse," one of the men said as Bright galloped off.

"Forget the horse; we have what we came for," was the reply. Brillar was thrown over the man's horse, unconscious, and carried off.

***

At camp, Elden reached out, searching, finding only small signs and patches of darkness but nothing from his apprentice. He waited, pacing, uncertain, for an hour before Bright, heavily lathered and wild-eyed, joined them.

"Brillar," he said, choking as he leaned against Bright before he could fall. There was nothing to do; it was nearly dusk, and Bright was exhausted. All he could do was wait for the morning.

***

The men who had taken Brillar had horses set in relays toward Lands-end. When she started to rouse, something harsh was poured into her mouth. She tried to spit it out, but her jaw was clamped shut until she swallowed the bitter drink. Two changes of horses and they clattered through the dark gate at Lands-end and to the home of their lord. Lord Harrolen.

"Confine her," he told them, "and have her drink this." He handed them a flask. The men nodded and carried her to a cell, shackling her wrists, and forcing another potion down her throat.

Harrolen took an easy supper; Elden took none. He rubbed Bright down, giving her a small drink, then walking her. He brushed her coat and let her drink her fill. *It would not do,* he thought to himself, *for Brillar to find her mare weak and muscle strained. And we have a lot of ground to cover in the morning.*

When Harrolen had dined, he went to Brillar's cell, where guards were posted. "She drank?" he asked.

"As you said," came the uncomfortable reply.

Harrolen looked at the man sharply. "It's necessary. He must come alone." The man nodded reluctantly.

Harrolen took a lantern into the cell. The walls were damp, redolent of mold. For a moment, he studied his prisoner as she lay on stale, musty hay, then he took out a small flask and shook it. A K'ish potion. He bent down, forced Brillar's mouth open and emptied the contents, making sure it was swallowed. He stepped back to wait for it to take effect.

His men had already told him what they knew of the story. When no word came from Pilik, he had sent others to search and found Trog. A few silver coins and the man had told them everything they needed to know about Pilik's death and the archer who had killed him. Now he had her foldbox with the crest of the Sisterhood that marked her as a mage from the Life School. He knew she must have removed the dimlock, but that scarcely interested him. No, he needed to understand why she was still with Garnelden and if he would come for her. "Now," he said, as she roused, "I think we should have a talk." He sat on a small bench his men had placed in the cell for him.

The drug was powerful; the blow to her head had left her sick and dizzy, so she had little will to resist. The first drugs had been used to keep her unconscious, and the last sapped her strength even as it woke her. She tried to fight the questions but couldn't find enough Control. Mana slipped away as it was called, not even leaving enough for her to cast a cleansing spell. The brief session left her drained, exhausted.

Satisfied at last that he knew all he would get with the small methods he had used, sure that he knew all he needed, Harrolen forced another K'ish potion through her lips and left her slumped on the straw. He had paid the guild of the K'ish extremely well for the potions and for the charms that blocked her use of spells. It would take time enough for her to waken, time enough.

Now he will come, thought Harrolen. *Now, he will kill to save his apprentice.*

***

Elden began before first light and covered the ground to Lands-end at a gallop, strengthening both Jez and Bright when they needed it. He took the horses to within a half-mile of the gate. He had seen no one. He removed their bridles and unsaddled them, stroking Jez affectionately on the cheek then doing the same with Bright.

"You know the way," he told Jez, who had been bred and born at a house of the Brotherhood. "Take Bright home with you." He gave the chestnut a slap on the hindquarters and, shoulders hunched, filled with regret and foreboding, turned away toward the town. A few strides, then he straightened and quickened his pace. Whatever waited, he had to be ready.

The town gate swung open as Elden approached, although he neither heard nor saw anyone. It stayed open as he went through and down the cobbled street.

So he doesn't expect me to flee, he thought grimly.

The street was utterly, disconcertingly quiet. Nothing seemed to move. Rats had all appeared to have found their holes; even the people he could sense were disturbingly still. The streets widened; his path ahead was clear. He walked by quiet shops and homes, knowing his way, and stopped at a wide plaza.

Drawing a breath, he stepped into the open, unprotected, half expecting a dozen arrows, but there was nothing. A few paces more, and he stopped in front of a broad, short stairway. Harrolen, dressed in the simple clothing of a Brother, appeared at the top of the stairs and descended two steps to face him.

Elden glared up at him. "Where is she?" he demanded, his voice harsh.

At Harrolen's gesture, a guard appeared on his right, dragging Brillar in shackles, an archer by her side. Elden stiffened.

"She's unhurt thus far, only drugged," Harrolen answered the unasked question. "Although taking her may have caused some bruises." Elden scowled at him at that, his face tightening. "Still, I will release her as soon as we have finished our business."

"And what guarantee—" Elden began.

"You have no guarantees," was the shouted reply. "You deserve no guarantees. And," he menaced, "I could always tell them to kill her now. Or perhaps they should take their pleasure first?"

At the threat, Elden took a step forward. Archers appeared instantly.

"Another step, and you both die," Harrolen said callously.

Elden took a deep breath and exhaled slowly. "My life for hers then." The words came out more calmly than they were felt.

"I don't want your life!" was the screamed answer, and Harrolen was suddenly trembling violently. He collapsed on a step. "I want no more lives." The shuddering words sounded as if they were said through tears.

Elden tried to take it in. The rightful home of the rightful lord, now dead, behind Harrolen. The dozen archers he could see and the others he knew were behind him. A crying man on the stairs? Perplexed, Elden ventured loudly, "Then why are we here?"

"Because you left me!" was the screamed answer as Harrolen shot upright, still shaking. "Twice, you left me! Yes, yes, you think I'm mad. But cunning enough to bring you here, once sent by the Brotherhood," the words were spat out, "and now by lure."

Elden took several steps back. Madmen are dangerous, and this man was clearly mad.

Harrolen advanced no closer. "Brother," now Elden could see tears, "you left us, abandoned Parday and me, to Lord Celbex over the sea."

"What are you saying? Yes, I left you," he sneered the words, despite the danger. "You loved killing so much; you took such joy in it. When he said we should clear villages, you laughed with him, and I escaped that night. If that was a leaving, then I left you."

There was mad laughter in answer. "You fool! Didn't you know we were watched? Listened to? Followed? I joined in with the laughter and the drinking, not knowing what you planned. Thinking we would plan together to run for the sea, all three of us. And you left us to him. After you were gone, they took my Parday! Took her and my unborn child, hid them away. I saw them only when it was permitted and under heavy guard. I killed for him to save my son! To watch him grow when I was allowed to see him. And there was no escape. There were two guards with me day and night, her death and his if I tried to leave them!"

Elden felt a chill, a shock of disbelief. He shook his head. Had he left them to that? To grief and agony?

Harrolen was pacing now, ranting, "What I have suffered… the blood of men and their wives… of children, yes, of children. Soldiers raping women and girls, tortures, and I had to smile. I had to drink the blood wine that I would vomit out in secret after all were in a stupor, the blood wine, wine mixed with the blood of children," he sobbed, seeming near collapse, "blood only my death can wash away."

"And the family here?" asked Elden, wondering if they were alive after all. He was now wildly uncertain.

"A ruse! They're on my ship; I grew rich while I protected us, becoming a minor lord in my own right. My son holds those lands now and Celbex is dead. My wife is gone, lost to years of suffering, and there must be a balancing of the scales *here and now*. These men around you," he gestured to them. "when I die, they will have a share in my ships and my riches." He gestured again, and the archers stepped back, lowering their bows and setting them on the ground. The guard holding Brillar set keys to her shackles, but she remained where she had been left, barely aware. "These men were selected to look hard and frightening. The few who touched people in the town were punished."

Elden stood transfixed. "A hoax? A wild hoax? Then why not reveal yourself to the Brotherhood, to your friends?"

"And let you off so easily? No, no, there had to be more, a balance for me, for her. I won't be shut away as mad. There *will* be more. I can't remove the blood of the innocents," he rubbed his hands on his arms, "but the Brother who kills me will bear its stain! That is *your* punishment." He was trembling again, fighting to remain standing. *"You,* you who left me. *You* will bear its stain."

"You wanted me alive then?" Now Elden was angry and shouting. "You gave a *dimlock* to your bounty hunter! You would have had me *dead* for all it mattered to you."

Through fog and pain, Brillar heard shouting and the words "dimlock" and "dead." She began to gather strength wordlessly, without moving, breathing in deeply, fighting the pain in her body, the fog in her mind.

"It was only to be used if needed," was the shouted reply. "I expected them to take you sooner and *closer*. I suspected that you wouldn't come willingly to kill a Brother, even one such as I have become."

"I would not," Elden shouted back. "I've not killed in many years. I want no killing!"

"That one," Harrolen gestured toward Brillar, "*has* killed, and for your aid. That much, I had from her."

Elden stiffened again. "She was attacked by your man. The kill was in self-defense."

"As you say, Brother. No matter, it's time for you to do a kindness for a member of the Brotherhood. I will not defend myself." He came down one step.

Elden stepped back again and tripped, falling to one knee before recovering.

Brillar saw him fall through swollen eyes, closed them, and drew in more strength, reaching almost unperceptively for what the archer had left behind, drawing it toward her.

"You will *kill now*!" Harrolen screamed.

"You have archers," Elden began.

"They are *innocent!*" another scream, "the *blood* must be on a *Brother's hand.*"

Brillar, hearing the screamed words, readied, drawing in more strength, praying to the Light that they wouldn't notice.

"You *will* kill me; you must," Harrolen ranted. He sent a sudden bolt of lightning at Elden, who was forced back but turned it aside. A second bolt, this one of fire, singed his clothes but was turned before there could be more.

Hearing the screaming, smelling the smoke from the spells, knowing their attention was on each other, Brillar made one great effort, pulling bow and arrow to her hand, drawing in strength as she could. A deep cold blanketed the room briefly and was gone. She was nearly ready…

Harrolen howled again, filled with anger and frustration, "It must be your hand!"

"Not my hand, Brother." Elden stepped back finally, submitting, eyes closed, spreading his low-held arms at his sides, knowing it could mean two deaths.

Seeing him through a haze, Brillar pulled herself to one knee, drew the bow, and let fly.

Harrolen crumpled to the ground silently, an arrow deep in his neck, as Brillar wavered and collapsed on the stones.

Opening his eyes at the sounds of the falling bodies, Elden stared, first at his Brother, then at Brillar. He rushed to her, already chanting the few words of healing he knew she must need. As he reached and gathered her, a man stepped out toward them, hands raised in friendship.

"He knew he would die here today, by some means. I'm his lieutenant. His instructions were clear. You're free to go. Horses are being brought to the plaza, or there's a cart if she can't ride."

At Elden's first spells, Brillar had strengthened a little, and now she could faintly hear the arcane words whispered in a string. She stirred a bit.

"A cart, I think, and many thanks," replied Elden, blinking rapidly, still bewildered. The lieutenant left without a word.

"Is," she choked and swallowed. "Is—"

"It was a true arrow, fast and true." He nodded, tears in his eyes.

"Then," he could barely hear her, "you must be alive." She sagged in his arms.

Part II

None who have killed man can return to us.
Law of the Sisterhood

Symbol of the Sisterhood
Teachers of Healing, Life, and Item Magic

*** 10 ***

Harrolen was dead. His lieutenant and men wrapped him in rich cloth and prepared to carry him to his ship.

Elden could hear the men moving around him, someone shouting orders. He could even hear the sound of a cart being brought to the plaza, but he couldn't seem to move, couldn't seem to think clearly. He knelt with Brillar where she had fallen, muttering spells, drawing in mana as he needed it. With all that he could do, her face was still swollen and pale.

Finally, he felt a hand on his shoulder and looked up at Harrolen's lieutenant. "Her cart is ready. We'll take our lord back home by ship; that was his final wish." At Elden's uncomprehending look, the man nodded. "You are free to go, truly. You are in no danger from us." The man smiled. "You must wonder what happened to your messenger. He and his family were taken, but they have been released."

Edlen looked at him uncomprehendingly.

"You should know that he is a good friend and true. He offered to kill our lord for you." The lieutenant gave him a final grim smile and turned away.

Elden tried to rise, still holding his apprentice, and staggered. A hand was under his arm at once and he managed the few steps to the cart, placing Brillar on piled blankets in the back, noticing that her foldbox was there. He looked around, confused; the plaza was full of people all standing quietly. They parted as he moved to the horse's head, taking the bridle and moving forward.

"She killed him then," someone ventured, and he nodded. There was an odd stillness about the crowd. Harrolen had taught them to fear his power, the power of a madman seeking death, and their fear for his soldiers lingered even as those faithful men gathered to take his body away. He had kept the town in thrall, and they knew and resented it. Elden could sense their anger, their confusion. The crowd parted and he walked toward the gate with the horse's hooves and the cart's wheels making the only sounds.

Elden had only gone a few hundred yards past the gate when he lost Control and broke down, sobbing for his lost Brother, for Polsen, and for his apprentice who might also be lost. How long he knelt in the dust, he didn't know, but there was a sudden nudge at his shoulder and a soft snuffling at his face.

Elden looked up wearily at Jez, with Bright by his side. He stroked the stallion's long face with astonishment and rose unsteadily.

"You were told… you were sent," he began and was nudged again, "and I am glad you didn't go." He struggled to his feet and wrapped his arms around the strong neck, finding renewal in the familiar.

He went to the rear of the cart. Brillar was resting comfortably but unconscious on a pile of blankets; he covered her lightly. Food, water, and other items had been placed in the cart. He took a cup, filled it and held it to her lips. She squirmed away until he splashed a bit on her mouth, then she drank greedily, choking a little, then sank back. Elden reached out again with what he knew of healing others and found only the unknown. This was not a simple bruise or break; potions had been used, and he knew nothing about them. He went back to the cart horse and led it back to where he had left the saddles and bridles.

"A great shame on you, Jez, you disobedient brat," he scolded, putting the saddles and bridles in the cart. He had to shift Brillar a bit to do that and she moaned. She was pale; the skin around her eyes and lips held a greenish tinge that he feared and could not reach. He gave her more water and drank a cup himself while sitting on the back of the cart. Looking through what had been stowed there, he found something more satisfying—several bottles of wine. Removing a cork, he poured himself a cup, then a second, and suddenly found himself laughing. He had gone to Lands-end expecting to die, half expecting Brillar to die with him, and they were alive. The thought made him giddy; then he sobered. She was alive *for now* but so badly used that he feared for the future.

The best place for her now, for both of us, is Laurenfell, he thought. *She needs more healing than I can give and the Great House of the Sisterhood is there. They'll have the healing she needs; they must know about potions and poisons there.* He turned the cart to the southwest.

It was a three-day journey to Laurenfell and the House of Life. His skills in the healing arts continued to be insufficient for her and

Brillar remained lethargic; she could take only water. Her fall, the many potions, all different and used carelessly, had all taken their toll. The greenish tinge he had first noticed had spread, creeping along veins in her face and now in hands and feet. For most of the journey, he trotted at the horse's head, afraid to let go of the cart's reins, worried about the road and how much it would jar her. He had nothing but what was in the cart and ate when he remembered to eat, usually at dawn and when it was too dark to see the road ahead and judge its condition.

He was consumed with dread; whatever she had been given, the drugs had clearly poisoned her. What people thought as he hurried the cart horse forward, he didn't care. He answered none of their hails. When the road was suitable, he climbed aboard the cart, urging the horse into a faster pace. He covered the distance more quickly than he expected and with little sleep.

On the afternoon of the third day, he came upon a farmer near the edge of a town and asked its name.

"Laurenfell," was the answer, and Elden closed his eyes, swaying with relief. He felt a steadying hand on his arm and opened his eyes.

"And the home of the Lady Darwallen?" he insisted.

The farmer pointed to the east, "Ah, the Laurenfell House. A few hundred paces is all. And do you need help, then?" Elden shook his head and dragged the horse forward.

The massive house of quarried stone was close to the town, set in a grove of trees by a lake. A long tree-lined lane led to it, and his approach did not go unnoticed. He barely glanced at the lake, concentrating on reaching the house. The dogs that came out to bark at a stranger quieted quickly, finding him no danger.

As he came to the broad steps, a servant came out to greet him, bowing slightly at such a rough and dust-covered guest but politely asking his need.

"I am Garnelden," he hoarsely answered the polite inquiry. "I bring the Lady Brillar to her mother and the Sisters for healing."

Astonished, the serving-man glanced into the cart and rushed back into the house, calling out wildly that it was Brillar, injured, shouting for Darwallen, but it was Prendar who bolted from the house and down the stairs first.

"My daughter?" he questioned, demanded.

"In the cart, Lord Prendar," was the unsteady reply. He held the cart horse's reins for support, casting another spell for strength.

A red-haired woman came flying down the steps as Prendar gently lifted his daughter. Brillar stirred as he did and called for Elden, then seemed to focus.

"Father?"

He carried her inside, followed closely by his wife. Elden turned away, but a young woman he hadn't noticed came up beside him, laying a hand on his arm. "Come inside. There must be a tale here. I'm Alliana, and with my sister, there is always a tale." She was not smiling.

Obediently, he followed her in, aware of his dusty clothes and muddy boots but too tired to care. The house was in a frenzy. Servants rushed about, one to fetch another healing Sister, one to find the sons of the house, others to the storerooms for herbs. In the kitchen, there was a great noise of pots being brought down. Through all this, Brillar's sister led him calmly, taking him to sit in a quiet room where she closed the door and offered him a glass of brandy.

"We have stronger in the house if you prefer," she said and sat down, composed, waiting for him to speak. She was dressed for summer, in a blue shift that matched her eyes. Her hair, like her father's, was a soft yellow. He took her in briefly, noting similarities to her sister, and drank the brandy gratefully, then leaned forward on his arms, drained.

"I think the story should wait for everyone," he said finally but straightened when a youth brandishing a short sword flung open the door.

"If you have harmed Brillar—" he began and was interrupted.

"Terol! Stop at once," said his sister. "He did her no harm; he brought her home!" The lad looked confused but hesitated.

"I was just about to get the story, although he is correct; everyone should hear the story from him. Sit and have a brandy or go and see her for yourself." She turned to Garnelden. "Please excuse my brother; he has always been fonder of my sister than of me," Alliana said with an indulgent nod to Terol.

Embarrassed, Terol muttered, "Untrue, and you know it." He left in consternation.

"A moment, please, while I have a room readied for you and the animals cared for." She went to the door with easy grace and called to a servant. "Our guest will be staying for a while. Please have the animals and cart taken care of."

Elden looked at her admiringly, to remain so calm when all else was a frenzy. She was slender like her sister and composed, but there was a softness to her, and he saw no hint of the steel he had found in his apprentice. She poured him another brandy.

"Supper, I think, will be later than usual as the story of Brillar's return has, I am sure, already spread. We have a fine bathhouse should you care to freshen yourself."

Well, he thought, *time to see if this one can be startled.*

"No need, thank you," he said, uttering spells that cleaned both himself and his clothes.

Surprised, and then laughing, she responded, "Leave it to my sister to bring home a mage or to be brought home by one."

The door opened once more, but quietly, and Darwallen entered, distressed but composed. "Thank you for bringing my daughter home. Sister Rodenis is with her. We were fortunate; she was visiting us when you arrived and was quick to attend Brillar. She's unconscious," Darwallen bit her lip, "but if you'd like to see her?"

Standing quickly, he put the brandy glass in Alliana's hand and followed Darwallen to a room on the main floor of the house. It all passed in a blur for him until the door to the sickroom was opened.

Brillar was lying on a small soft bed, with an older healing Sister to one side. The Sister was passing an orb over her patient, murmuring cleansing spells and spells to draw out poisons; dark oily stains were spreading beneath her patient. Elden had never heard the incantations before.

"That," said Darwallen quietly, "is Sister Rodenis. Her skills are above any in the Sisterhood. My daughter was poisoned, she thinks, by a combination of potions that might have otherwise cleared quickly. They were worsened by a heavy blow to her head."

He nodded, unshed tears welling in his eyes. They stepped outside and closed the door softly. He leaned against the wall, eyes closed, and she waited for him to compose himself. "I didn't have the spells, the herbs. All I could do was give her water. I thought we would… come too late."

She took his arm. "But you're here, the Great House is here, and Rodenis will heal her if any can." He only nodded.

There were already people in the halls and others were arriving. Darwallen spoke quietly to everyone as they passed. Alliana rescued Garnelden, taking him back to the windowed sitting room with its blue and white decorations, asking him to stay just a few moments. He leaned against the cushions wearily and closed his eyes, falling asleep at once.

An hour later, Darwallen woke him apologetically. "Supper is ready. I came to escort you. It's a hasty meal, I'm afraid. We have some guests. Again, I apologize. Half the town has already heard that you brought," she stopped and took a deep breath, "brought our daughter home."

She led him to the great hall where Garnelden found supper and wine laid out for the household, neighbors, friends, and Sisters of the local house who had all heard the news of Brillar's return and her condition.

Prendar, obviously relieved, immediately greeted Elden and handed him a cup of wine. "We will dine first," he said, and the assembled group grumbled. "And no grumbling!" he barked at them. Elden could see Darwallen hide a smile.

"There is a story to be told and the man must be fortified for telling it," he said, commandingly waving at the company. Planked tables had been hastily assembled with benches for seating. Servants passed food to everyone and refilled cups.

The meal was devoured quickly since everyone wanted the story more than food. Servants, all fond of Brillar, left the plates where they were to stand along the wall. Her childhood maid/companion was weeping softly; others were sniffling.

"First, a toast to the man who has restored a daughter of this House to it and her family." They all raised their glasses and drank.

"Now, if you please, enlighten us with the story," he said to Garnelden. There was a brief rustling as they settled in.

Elden took a deep breath and stood, drawing on his knowledge of court etiquette. He felt better than he had in days. "I am Garnelden of Torennwood, Mage of the Four Powers with First Standing in Three," he began formally, at which the assembled started in with questions.

They were silenced by Prendar's, "Let the man speak!"

"If Brillar's life has been saved, it's because she saved mine first after I was unjustly taken." He opened his collar slightly, revealing the scars left by the dimlock. Darwallen, recognizing what the wounds must be from, began to rise, staring, for no one survived a dimlock. She was gently reseated by her husband.

It was a long story, even with what Elden omitted, and full dark when he finished. Darwallen, in tears, went to Elden with an embrace, pronouncing him a member of the House, to cheers. Prendar, Terol, and Brolin, Brillar's elder brother, shook his hand in gratitude. The others in the hall would have had him shaking hands and answering questions until after midnight, but Prendar clapped his hands.

"Good Sisters, friends, guests, family; Sister Rodenis has announced that Brillar will be asleep for some time. I ask that everyone depart quietly and give us a few days to recover from our shock. Our guest must be tired after such a difficult day. Terol, if you would escort him?" The lad took him out of the hall.

"Are you truly called Garnelden? I was told my sister said 'Elden' when Father lifted her, and the Four Powers, how long was the study?" Terol's words gushed out, and he barely waited for answers.

"Terol," Alliana was suddenly beside them, "our father said *lead,* not *pester.* I will lead him while you take yourself to the stable and make sure that the horses are well taken care of there."

"The stallion is Jez, the mare, Bright; their stalls should be close together," said Elden catching his sleeve. Terol hurried off down the broad hall.

"He always hurries," said Alliana with a tolerant smile. She took Eldon up the stairs and through well-lit corridors, finally opening the door to a large, windowed room with a high, soft bed, a table with glasses and brandy, several plush chairs, and a desk. He thanked her wearily as she closed the door, then removed his boots and clothes. Dousing the lamp, he fell into the bed twitching the soft covers over himself.

We are both alive, was his last thought.

*** 11 ***

The house was quiet in the morning, respecting the rest Brillar needed. Elden looked at himself in the mirror and decided that it was time to remove the beard he had grown. He had often used the spell, but not on such a thick growth, and decided a mirror was needed. A small door near the bed proved to be an indoor necessary, complete with chair, ewer, water, mirror and other items. He refreshed himself, then stared at his face and began the spell, managing to clean away the whiskered growth without incident. He ran a comb through his hair. Clean-shaven, he was surprised to see how pale his jaw was. *Soon mended,* he thought.

Back in the main room, he opened the foldbox and removed the grey clothing with trim that Brillar had admired. Dressing quickly, he found his way to the stairs and descended.

Darwallen met him at the bottom of the stairs; she had sensed he was awake. She was casually dressed in a white blouse and skirt. She raised an eyebrow at his cleaned face. "Well met a second time," she smiled, "rest has made you a new man."

Despite himself, Elden flushed.

"We are at breakfast. Come with me." The family dining area was as bright as the sitting room, white walls trimmed in blue and hung with paintings, the crest of the Sisterhood on one wall above a side table. Prendar rose when he entered and waved him to a seat as a servant brought in a platter heaped with sliced fruits.

Breakfast was a leisurely affair, although a bit hushed. Rodenis had been with Brillar all night but joined them before they were halfway through the meal. She was dressed in a robe of pale blue and ate with a hearty appetite. It had been a long night, but she seemed lively and talkative.

"Sister Idelia is with her. She is nearly free of the poisons and I have begun to mend her head. She must have cracked it somehow." She bit into bread spread with honey.

Elden stiffened, his face tight, his eyes dark with anger. A light hand on his arm soothed him. "She will heal now," said Darwallen, "and be safe."

"She will stay safe as well," added Prendar, "and finish her studies if I have to nail her feet to the floor." There were chuckles all around at that, and Elden thought that the trick might have already been tried.

"Few things escape me," said Brillar's mother, "but *she* did. Walking off with whatever she could stuff in the foldbox."

"Running off," interrupted Terol, "why did you think she practiced so much? To run in the races at the spring tournaments?" There was more laughter at that, and Brolin roughed Terol's blond hair. Terol was a slender lad of sixteen, and the family seemed used to his interruptions. His grey eyes and straight nose matched his sire's.

"Running then," said her mother. "Master Mage, if I may have a word?" she asked when breakfast was finished.

He went with her to the sitting room he and Alliana had used. Through the window, he could see the lake and wondered briefly if that was where his apprentice learned to swim.

"Darwallen," he began as they sat down and was stopped with a gesture.

"I am called Darwa by friends and family. Sometimes even less." She smiled. Looking at her, he could see Brillar. The hair and green eyes were there, and her daughter had her mother's firm chin. The steel must have come from her father.

He smiled in return. "Darwa then. You know I didn't tell the whole truth last night?" She nodded. Her serenity was remarkable, and he hated what he would have to tell her.

"My meeting with your daughter was not quite as I told it. I was not merely 'found.' She approached the men who had taken me and had to kill one of them; he attacked her before we had even met."

Darwallen paled; she clenched her hands in her lap, dropping her eyes to them. Her daughter? Taking a man's life? A tear appeared on her cheek and she brushed it away.

"You're sure of this? You know what happened?" Her voice was pained.

"I was held by the dimlock, but what I saw later was evidence of the truth, and the man who took me… there are no words for him or what he would have done to her." A moment passed as he let her compose herself. "I'm sorry. I know the position of the House of Life on the matter."

"Yes, well. We won't discuss that further. Not now." She sighed. "But the dimlock. I've heard of its use and recognized the scars from drawings, but I've never heard any sure stories of someone who was released from one. Not until after an execution. You say my daughter removed it?" A nod. "And knew somehow that it *should* be removed." She stared at him, searching him, and he put up no defense. Satisfied, she relaxed a bit. "She saw all that through the dimlock?" When Elden reddened, she added, "I didn't mean to embarrass you." He shook his head.

"Now, if I could see the scars the collar left? My skill is healing."

Elden nodded again and opened his shirt for her. She held back the cloth and examined the marks, first the nape of his neck, then round the shoulders to the deep scar where the pendant had been. She touched it lightly, her face grim at the extent of what he had suffered.

"How long?" she asked.

"Seventeen days," he replied, resettling his shirt.

Darwallen turned pale and sat quickly. "So long," she murmured to herself. "Brillar removed such a thing? Alone and unaided?"

"She did, or I wouldn't be alive. I was barely that when she began," he replied.

"This is a story for Sister Rodenis after she rests. To think that Brillar had the skill, that *anyone* had the skill, to remove a dimlock except the keeper of its key! And seventeen days! From the scars, it was sunk deep. Would you be kind enough to show the result to Rodenis?"

Nodding, he smiled, and she rose.

"There's something more."

Darwallen took her seat again.

Elden stood and poured one brandy, handing it to her. She looked surprised but took the glass.

"One more thing I withheld. It wasn't a townsman who killed Harrolen. Brillar drew in enough strength at the end to wield a bow."

Darwallen did indeed need the brandy. Elden tried to soothe her and was rebuffed. They sat quietly for several minutes. Fortified,

Darwallen finally stood and straightened as there was a soft rap at the door. Alliana was there and said, "She wakes and asks for you."

Darwallen brightened. "No, Mother, begging your pardon. She asks for Elden." Darwallen raised an eyebrow at that but acquiesced, gesturing him to follow Alliana, which he did, somewhat red-faced.

"Mother, she'll want you soon as well," Alliana assured her mother.

The two led Elden back to the sickroom, but he entered alone. Like the other rooms in the house, it was brightly painted and had a large window. There was a chair by the bed. Sister Idelia was nearby, ready to help as needed. Brillar stirred as he sat; he could see her color was better; the green veins had almost faded from her face.

Turning her head, Brillar gave him something of a smile. "You *are* alive then. And you managed to find your way here?" Her voice was dry and she reached out a thin hand. She had shrunk so on their journey.

"I did. I came as fast as I could since my healing was not all you needed."

"Rodenis has seen to all that. She and Idelia say that now I need rest and feeding. I seem to have faded a bit."

"That's easily mended. But I should send your mother in. She was a bit put out that you spoke my name before hers." He patted her hand, stood, and went to the door. "You should know that your father has threatened to nail your feet to the floor," he said and was rewarded with a weak laugh. Courteously, he held the door open for Darwa, and Alliana watched as her mother took her daughter in her arms, then closed it softly.

He met Prendar in the hallway. "Now, if I may have a word?"

Elden nodded.

"Perhaps under the trees."

Elden was led across a green lawn to a wide bench near the lake. Prendar was dressed for riding, in a rich, dark blue shirt, short breeches, and black boots. He was above average in height and a bit stocky but looked strong and fit. Grey eyes stabbed at Elden; his face was stern. He gestured for Elden to sit while he stood, arms folded for a moment. Finally deciding, he said bluntly, "Besides her obvious troubles, what other *harm* has my daughter taken?" His voice was firm.

"None from me," was the quiet answer. "As for others, she did lock her door against a 'sprightly archer' of a night."

This brought a gruff laugh from Brillar's father. "She always led the village lads on a short leash. Headstrong and always into something, that one; more trouble than her brothers."

Elden took a breath and shifted uneasily. "I named myself Mage and didn't want to upset Darwa, but Brillar has bound herself as my apprentice for a year."

"What do you say?" Prendar demanded.

"I made the offer; she made the bargain." He kept his voice composed.

Prendar began to pace. "Go and change that finery," he said abruptly. "I assume you can ride since the two animals you brought in were saddle horses and there were saddles in the cart. You're strong enough to ride?" Elden nodded. "And there is something else there that you should see when you're changed."

A bit bewildered. Elden hurried to change, surprised when he located his room without trouble.

As he came down, Alliana smiled and said, "I see you and Father have had a talk? The stable is that way," she said, gesturing.

Jez was giving the stable boy trouble with the saddling, but the horse quieted when Elden arrived. He saddled the stallion, then Prendar took him to the cart.

"Pull back all the blankets and tell me what you find," he ordered.

Elden did as he was told and gasped. There were ten bars of gold in the cart, well covered in thick quilts and blankets. He gaped! Open-mouthed, he turned to Prendar and was clapped on the shoulder.

"I take it you knew nothing about this then," he said firmly.

Still open-mouthed, Elden could only shake his head.

"If you wish, I'll have Terol and Brolin take it to our storeroom."

A nod was all Elden could manage and Prendar sent a stable boy for his sons.

"Let's see then if you can stay in the saddle after such a shock." Prendar mounted his dun gelding while Elden mounted Jez. Prendar put his horse into an easy trot which was matched by Jez's walking pace. He nodded approvingly, then clicked his horse into a canter and led the way across a fallowed field. He put the roan over a hedge and a fence and cantered down a long track. He reined up at a small brook and both dismounted.

"You ride well enough for a mage," he said approvingly.

"Even a mage has the need now and then," was the steady reply. Elden was all but holding his breath, feeling that he knew something of what the man would ask, already forming his answer.

Prendar dropped his horse's reins and paced a bit. Pacing was his usual when he confronted the unusual. He stopped. "It seems to me from your foldbox, I know of them, what with three mages in the house, that you had some wealth before that gold." Elden waited. "Now you're even wealthier. There are good fields here, good land for horses. The stallion and mare are well suited." He raised his eyebrows.

Elden waited.

"Speak up, man; what are your intentions?"

Elden had half-expected the question. He had brought Brillar home to Laurenfell. True, he was older than she was, but such pairings were not unusual. There was an obvious connection between them. Brillar had spoken his name when lifted from the cart before she called on her father. Later, she called for him before calling for her mother. He had pondered the matter a bit himself. It was now to declare for good or for ill.

He looked away over the fields, then brown eyes met grey levelly. "I have an apprentice," he said evenly, "one who, at present, wishes only to learn. What is in the future is for both to say, not one." At Prendar's slight scowl, he continued, "I made the offer because your daughter, whom you named headstrong, all but told me she was headed for the Wild." There was a slight gasp. "Completely unprepared. A year's binding and she may lose all taste for me, if she has any, and for the Wild, even if we never venture there," he finished to allay the man's concerns.

"Hmm. A sound answer. The horses are ready. A quieter ride back to the house? Lunch should be ready by then."

They remounted and rode off slowly. Prendar gestured to fields and woodlands, talking about his holdings and his dealings as a merchant. He pointed out the wall of the old town and the tower of the Sisterhood in the distance as they went. Now that the looming question of his intentions had been satisfied, it was a pleasant ride.

Lunch was served at a long bench under the trees, surrounded by flower beds and shrubs. Servants fetched and carried, glasses of wine were raised and Elden was bombarded with questions from Terol, who appeared ready to run off to the Wild himself. He had, it seemed, developed a case of hero worship for the mage who had brought his sister back to them. If it hadn't been for stern glances at Terol from his father, Elden would not have been able to feed himself. Rodenis had joined them for lunch, saying her patient had taken broth and was sleeping again under Idelia's watchful eye. Rodenis was grey-haired, with pale blue eyes and a well-lined face that spoke of both care and laughter. She raised a brow at Elden when they finished, and both excused themselves, going to a now-familiar room.

Without a word, he turned down his shirt. She examined the scars then touched them lightly, examining them with a practiced eye.

"My student did this? Removed a dimlock? Alone and unaided?" She didn't know she was echoing Darwa's words and he nodded. "Hmpf. Here, I was sure she never listened. Wild, that one." He smiled at that.

"She opened the lock with a pick? I knew her fingers were deft, despite all that archery." She shook her head. "The pendent hung here?" She touched the deep scar on his chest and he nodded again. Like many Elders, she had a tendency to speak both to herself and for her patient.

"At least she remembered to carry the herbs and instruments in her foldbox, and an orb perhaps. Hmm. Powders as well, I see. You carry other scars, less recent, which could be removed. The scars of the dimlock cannot be removed, not even with my skill."

She helped herself to a brandy, eyes sparkling with good humor. "You told the story last night, I hear, and it was retold to me. The man who used the drugs on her or had them used had little skill with such things. Those were certainly of K'ish making." She scowled at the name. "The combination would have killed if you hadn't brought her here." Elden lowered his head and could only nod.

Rodenis went on, "I have known Brillar all her life. I taught her or tried to. But a dimlock! I'll search the records, of course, but I don't remember a record of the removal of a dimlock except by its key." She eyed him as Darwa had, probing; he stiffened at the depth of her search but opened his mind and allowed it. Her probing reminded him of Tribaje. "A key which was only used after an execution. The Light must have guided her, for it seems that she made the right decision." She released him and he shook himself.

"Now, though, there is something else I see in my student, a shift in her, something different that I cannot quite discern. It troubles me." Her eyes were on him steadily as he adjusted his shirt.

Sensing that Darwallen would permit it if asked, he said quietly, "She has killed two men, both in defense."

Like Darwallen, Rodenis stiffened and sipped her brandy. She nodded with understanding. "What is done is done," she said, "it cannot be undone nor, I think, should we wish it undone. Not if a dimlock was involved and used unjustly. Now I will see if my patient can take some more soup."

She went calmly from the room, leaving him there to review the morning.

•

*** 12 ***

When she woke up, Brillar did take soup but only as broth, then slept again. She came awake at intervals without regard for day or night. A Sister was always with her and the kitchen kept broth ready at all hours. Sometimes Alliana would sit with her, holding her hand quietly. Darwallen was in such distress whenever she came from the sickroom that Prendar finally asked her to stay away. Rodenis supported the idea then refused Prendar entry. "The distress you feel when you see her affects your daughter as it does you and your wife. Alliana seems the only presence that is calming. From her, there is only light, girlish chatter. Girlish chatter from Alliana! She hides her concern very well with her chatter. First time I have ever heard anything like it from her. Always a quiet one, that girl, serious about her studies, and never any chatter."

In the next few days, the family received numerous visitors, all concerned about Brillar's health. Some left small gifts, soups, sweets, flowers that brightened her room, a music box, wind chimes, a soft scarf. Most, those who had been unable to hear the story of her homecoming, also wanted to know more of what had happened.

To escape the visitors, Elden often took Jez out in the mornings, sometimes accompanied by Prendar, sometimes by Terol, on Bright. Prendar insisted on taking him through Laurenfell with Brolin as added company. The town was beautifully laid out with wide streets in a grid pattern that stretched to the west.

"The seat of the Sisterhood is here," Brolin explained when he walked with them, past shops and homes built of local materials. "It's an old town but was well-planned and built, first in wood and now in stone. No need for the old wall now that the town has grown. The healing hall, dormitories, guest houses, it was natural for there to be a clean and organized town here."

"I was brought here for healing after the Coastal Raids," Prendar put in, and Brolin was silent. His father seldom talked about his time defending against the raids, but he seemed willing to tell Elden what happened. "We called it that so that people wouldn't be alarmed." He glanced at his son. "I'm sure you heard the stories while you were in service. Shall we sit?"

They took seats outside a tavern and called for cider. The day was warm, the sky touched by small clouds here and there. Elden admired the tables set in the courtyard; the carving and care the wood had received over the years had left them with a dark patina lanced by flecks of lighter wood.

"More than twenty-five years ago, sea raiders had landed in force, thousands of them and more coming. They had taken Lands-end and Tramka Shores before there could be any real defense. Messages were sent to the Brotherhood and the king, but we were able to gather forces here. You've been at war, Elden?"

Elden nodded. "Across the sea and against orcs, not men."

"Then you have some idea about it. I led the attack to take back Lands-end. We succeeded but at such a loss in soldiers and people from the town." He stopped and called for cider to be replaced by ale. "I was in the healing hall for some time, recovering. That, Brolin, is how I met your mother." He clapped his son on the shoulder. "She led me on quite the chase, too, before she agreed to marry me." He smiled at the memory. "And I would chase her again if it came to that, but back to the story. Danyar was generous. The owner of Laurenfell House was widowed in the fighting and childless. She was glad to part with the house so she could move back to Auden Shore. I bought the house and miles of land around it then expanded the house for my bride. Of course, I was an only son and inherited money and land from my family, all invested in trade and mining." He smiled at Brolin. "You, my boy, will have a good start in life."

Brolin nudged his father and pointed. Across the plaza, was a group of teenaged students, all brightly dressed. Their teacher had gone into a shop, telling them to wait for her.

"Like beautiful birds, aren't they? 'Little Sisters,' students of the Sisterhood from the healing hall and Life Sisterhood," he told Elden.

The students were huddled together and seemed to be whispering excitedly. After what appeared to be some prodding, one left the group and headed toward the table, glancing back at her friends nervously.

"Here we go," Brolin said, smiling into his ale.

The girl, in her early teens and dressed in pale yellow, approached and dropped a curtsey at their table.

"Lord Prendar?" She looked nervously back at her friends.

Prendar pretended severity. "Speak up, child, speak up."

Eyes wide, she looked from him to Elden. "And are you Brother Garnelden?"

He nodded at her, trying to hide a smile.

"I... we..." She looked over her shoulder again.

"Child?" Prendar insisted.

She took a deep breath. "We just wanted to say we're glad that the Lady Brillar is back and thank you, Brother Garnelden, for bringing her home." She dropped another curtsey and fled. Their teacher came out of the shop, scolding and herded them away.

Elden turned to his friends, eyes dancing. "Perhaps we should only come out at night when they are well tucked away."

Brolin laughed. "Then, you'd have to contend with the other students, older students, and their teachers."

"You never seemed to mind having them around, did you, boy?" His father laughed, and Brolin flushed. "A bold one, that little one in yellow; something for your brother to think about. They all want to get a look at you, Elden, so be careful. But you, son, now that you're back, the older students will have an eye for you, so you take care as well."

"You were away?" Elden asked.

"Service with the king for two years. Nothing, really. A few bandits here and there, aiding the sheriff's men when they needed it. Now that I'm back, Da has given me land of my own, and I mean to settle down properly."

"And who have you settled on?" his father wanted to know, but Brolin just smiled.

"Wouldn't be fair to tell you before she was asked, now would it?"

"Hmm," Prendar started. "I know one who was asked while you were away," that got his father a sharp look, "and said 'no' to a handsome offer. Better be quick."

Brolin had walked out with several young women, students at the Sisterhood and from the town, for years. Now that he was back, he seemed to have settled on the quiet, intelligent daughter of a local merchant. She was well-known to the family, a slender, serious woman with brown hair and blue eyes who smiled a great deal but laughed little. Both families were waiting for word of a proposal.

"Ride out with me to my farm?" Brolin asked Elden in order to change the subject; marriage was on his mind, but not ready to be discussed. "Tomorrow, perhaps? And we'd better go; I see another flock of students." The men settled the bill and headed out of the town.

Except for his first short visit with Brillar, Elden had also been banned from the sickroom even though his apprentice asked for him. Everyone now had to content themselves with reports from Alliana, the Sisters who sat with her, and the cooks who reported how much broth she drank when she was awake.

Broth was all Brillar was permitted for nearly a week, but it was fortified more each day and she regained strength on it quickly, although her waking and sleeping confused her. When she asked her sister why her other family members and Elden never visited, an excuse was always given. There had been a visit, but she had been sleeping, or the family had taken Elden to the village, everyone was asleep, or her mother had been called away to attend a birth. Because she was weak and easily confused, she would sleep again and ask the same questions when she woke. Finally, she was alert enough to see that lies were being told. She insisted that someone, anyone else, come visit her. It was her mother who finally came in with a fine soup, rich with minced linic and ground tubers.

After that, Elden was also allowed to visit her and watched strength return quickly. Two more days passed until he entered her room with two bowls of hearty stew. She sat plumped up on pillows and made short work of the stew he had brought, complaining that there was no wine.

"Neither Rodenis nor my mother will allow me anything to drink but teas, well brewed with herbs, water, and juices," she fussed.

"I have juice here," he said, "if you're thirsty." She made a face at him but accepted the glass.

"It seems I am always thirsty," she said peevishly.

He gathered the bowls and empty glass.

"So soon?" she asked.

"The good Sisters and your mother are very strict with me." He smiled and took his leave. It seemed to him that she was asleep before he closed the door.

Two days later found Brillar insisting that fresh air and sun would be revitalizing. When told to wait, she threatened to go outside without help even if she had to crawl. Acquiescing, her brother solved the matter by carrying her to a bench on a terrace. She was there, surrounded by blankets and pillows, sipping yet another glass of fruit juice, when Elden and her father returned from an early ride. They were greeted with a wave.

Darwa appeared with a tray of fruit and more juice; she had seen the riders approach. She set them on a low table near her daughter.

"Is this a good idea?" asked her father, jumping down from his horse. Elden followed suit.

"She threatened to make her own way, so Brolin carried her out before going to visit his young lady," answered his wife. "In fact, the sun will do her good."

"Really? 'In fact, the sun will do her good?' To listen to anyone here, people would think me an aged grandmother," Brill remarked tartly. Elden hid a smile. "Now, you will all sit down, have something to eat, and give me all the news," she told them firmly as she snagged a piece of fruit.

"Are you sure you want to hear everything?" asked her father with a laugh.

They all settled down to enjoy her outing. The tall doors to the house were open, the sun bright on the pale grey and white stones of the terrace. Elden smiled as he watched the family together. He had composed a letter for the Brotherhood summarizing what had happened at Lands-end and sent it off with a messenger. What the reply would be, he didn't know, but for now, he was content.

The news was delivered over fruit and juices. Crops were doing well in the south fields. The new bull was prepared to prove his strength when the cows were ready. Yes, someone was exercising Bright for her.

Bread and meat were brought out by servants so the group could continue to enjoy the sun. Before they were half-finished with lunch, Brillar leaned back and closed her eyes.

"I'll stay with her," said Darwallen, seeing Sister Rodenis come up the walk. "You men take the rest of your meal indoors, and quietly."

"Insisted, didn't she?" Rodenis sniffed as she joined Darwallen. "Headstrong. Always was, and her walkabout hasn't changed her." She examined Brillar by eye. "Well then, she should spend more time out of doors now. Fresh air, good food, and rest."

Darwallen pushed a plate toward her friend, and they enjoyed the sun and food together.

The days settled into a routine, with Elden accepted as a member of the family. He visited the healing hall where he learned that a young man named Warick had arrived in time to say goodbye to his father and comfort his mother. She lived nearby so he paid his condolences but found her well-attended by her daughter and son-in-law.

He also spent more time in the town, taking a glass at the tavern with Prendar several times, but always late in the evening. The older students and even some of the Sisters had suddenly taken an interest in a glass of cider at the tavern in the evening. Fortunately, they were required to be back in their dormitories quite early. Prendar found their interest in Elden amusing.

"A tavern does a man good," Prendar told him, "especially after the students have gone away." Elden and Brillar's father had become easy in each other's company. There were jokes at the tavern and sometimes a fiddler in the evening. Elden began to feel more comfortable than he had in years. Brolin went with them once but had other things to attend to; Terol often went with them but was only allowed cider.

Rides with Prendar were both energetic and soothing. The older man enjoyed a hunt and the dun jumped very well, but he also enjoyed the quiet, shady lanes. He had stopped pointing out prime land, much to Elden's relief. On days when Prendar was busy, Terol would sometimes insist on riding with him.

Terol, at sixteen, was a likable youth, and Elden began to tell him stories of his travels to keep the boy from asking constant questions. Questions did come, of course, but they were more directed. As best he could, Elden influenced him toward the settled life. Terol was too old to train in any serious Power but had a deft way with horses and other animals. He had an idea for taming linic and keeping them as food birds that Prendar had dismissed. Now Elden spoke with the boy's father, who began to see it as a way to keep the lad close to home.

The best part of the day came after the rides. After weeks of convalescence, Brillar was walking daily and had been out to see

Bright. When she was told of the treasure that had been in the cart, she was shocked.

"The gold in the cart must belong to someone else," she insisted, but he shook his head and took her to sit on a bench.

"When we left Lands-end, the lieutenant told me a cart had been prepared for you. I'd forgotten what he said. I think Harrolen meant it for any..." He stopped, aware of her distress. He put his arm around her, comforting her, and she leaned against him as she thought it through, then straightened.

"Then it's ours, yours and mine equally," she said. "I said once that blood money didn't interest me. It is truer now. Sister Rodenis will have a bar, my siblings a bar each when they come of age or marry, and a bar to my father for some of that fine bloodstock he always talks about but never buys. There, I'm done with what is mine." She would hear no more about it.

Brillar was delighted when told she could leave the sickroom and move to her own room on the second floor but insisted that the room be cleaned of childhood things first, leaving that to Alliana and her mother. They cleaned the room but left her books. That night, Brillar slept in her own bed, well aware that Elden was just down the hall.

After the move, Brillar's health improved rapidly. In days, she was insisting on long, not short, walks, which grew longer every day. She also began to swim in the lake on warm days, usually in the company of Terol and her sister, often joined by Elden. Even Darwa and Prendar swam with them; she was a graceful swimmer but Prendar tended to lumber through the water. Elden's swimming improved to "acceptable" and he enjoyed the time with all of them. Sometimes Brillar received old friends. Young women she had grown up with often cast admiring glances at Elden and there was good-natured speculation about the pair.

One morning after exercising Jez, Elden returned to the house to find her outside with a new bow, longer than the one she usually carried. Terol had set up a target for them and was practicing with her. Leaving Jez at the stable, he strode up behind them tight-faced as she let fly.

"Exactly what are you doing?" he demanded, taking her by the arm.

"Elden, I'm sorry," Terol began, but he waved the lad aside.

"This is none of your doing," he said, but Terol quickly took himself away.

"I said, what are you doing?" he asked Brillar roughly.

"Why, I'm just breaking in this fine new bow, or was, until you interrupted us," she replied evenly enough, although there was a flash of warning in the green eyes. "My muscles need strengthening; Rodenis had no quarrel with it."

"Was she even asked?" he growled in reply.

"She told me to gain the strength I needed. She made no mention of how. And my brother needs some instruction. Didn't I tell you I could outshoot all the archers at the spring games?"

Something seemed to shift around him; Elden closed his eyes a moment, sensing defeat. "Do I fetch the arrows that miss the target for you, or should I get Terol for that?" he sighed resignedly.

"Garnelden!" she responded, pretending shock, "do you think for a moment that I will *miss* the target?" She nocked and loosed another arrow which hit with a satisfying, 'thunk.'

Looking at the target, he shook his head. "You do need practice. You won't hit a linic that way." She only laughed and nocked again.

Seeing Terol close, but not too close, Elden waved him over. "If you have a third bow, perhaps we can all practice."

The morning went pleasantly for them. Noon under the trees, found Sister Rodenis at the house for lunch. She sat down next to Brillar.

"Not here to check on me, I hope?" Brillar asked, reaching for another roasted tuber.

"Hmph, not with that appetite. I hear you've taken up the bow again?" Rodenis took a sip of fruit juice.

"Well, it does keep me standing in one place," she said with a smile, "unless you want me to practice for the races at the spring tournament?"

"No, I think that can wait for a while." Rodenis looked piercingly at her student, smiled, then turned to speak to a neighbor who had joined them for lunch.

I wonder what that's all about, Brillar thought as she took more fruit juice.

Rodenis was at the house daily and not just to see her patient. She and Brillar's mother were good friends and they often had long talks as they walked through the grounds. There was a great deal of activity at the Great House and in the town. Guesthouses had been opened, and Sisters were arriving from the teaching houses. Elden saw several Brothers he knew in the tavern one evening, called for a conference they told him. He was thanked so frequently for his work at Lands-end that he began to avoid his Brothers. Some had brought wives and older children 'to give them a holiday,' was all they would tell him. He was suspicious but was occupied with other things.

Laurenfell House was not just the family home; it included cottages for servants, stables, storage houses for trade goods, barns, and a mill. Now that she was stronger, Brillar insisted on visiting everything and everyone. Elden usually went with her to ensure she rested when he sensed she was tired. He was also helping Terol with his idea of taming linic. Terol had quickly discovered that snares and traps often left the birds in such a panic that they died but that a mage could call and soothe the birds so that they were easily gathered. He now had a small flock of the more easily tamed birds and Elden was sometimes called on for assistance.

The days went by pleasantly until Rodenis appeared one afternoon just after lunch, as Brillar and her mother were relaxing near the lake.

"Not come to check on me again." Brillar smiled as Rodenis joined them.

The woman looked very serious. "Younger Sister," Rodenis began, and Brillar straightened at her tone. "Younger Sister," she went on formally, "I have come to ask a favor of you as a member of the Sisterhood, although one who should have stayed and learned more."

Glancing at her mother, who seemed tense, she composed herself, replying formally, "What I am asked, I shall do if I can."

"You have the dimlock collar in your possession?" Rodenis asked quietly.

"The dimlock? I have it, and it's safe." Now she knew why her mother was tense and felt apprehensive.

"Then, as your teacher and head of the Order, I have this formal request. I want you to bring the dimlock to the Great House, where you will display it for everyone. You will bring everything you used to remove it and explain in detail how it was done. All this, you will do as reward for the training you had and as your duty to the House that trained you."

Brillar sat back in her chair and looked at her mother.

"She told me what she was going to ask." Darwa stared at the grass. "I wanted to forbid it. You've come back to health so well and the strain of the telling..." She let her words hang in the air.

"I am Brillar's healer. Would I have asked if I didn't already feel that she was ready? No, no, I would never have asked," Rodenis insisted. "And the Sisterhood must know, the Brothers as well. I have searched all the records. There are certain and sound references to the use of the dimlock collar, and all of those refer to someone on whom it was justly used. Someone who was later executed for crimes of some sort."

Seeing shock in their faces, she continued, "Not in over two hundred years, has there been such a need or such a use. It was believed that all the dimlock collars had been destroyed and no more made. We must know if this is one from former years or something newly made. If one survived or if someone new has found the making of such an evil thing, then we must be made aware. A dimlock was never to be owned by an individual, only by a Great House. How did one man come into possession of one? Was it recently made?" She shook her head. "Too many questions remain."

Brillar drew a deep breath and exhaled in a sigh. "Then, of course, I'll come. When have you planned for this?"

"Tomorrow, after everyone has had lunch."

"So soon?" Her voice held a hint of panic, but Rodenis only nodded. She had known the answer would be 'yes' and knew that the answer should be followed by action quickly.

"Yes, tomorrow. Only the older students will be allowed at the assembly. Sisters have been arriving for several days from other houses, Brothers as well."

Brillar looked up sharply. Elden had told her there were Brothers in Laurenfell for a "conference" and now she knew what the meeting was really about.

A sound, half laugh and half choke, came from Brillar. "I am well and truly trapped. If you will excuse me, I'll begin to prepare. Elder Sister," she said to her mother formally, "if you will assist me?"

"A word with your father and brother first? I think Elden should be far away from us this afternoon. There's a three-day horse market at Mevrin that I know your father wants to visit to see if he can find something there with your generous gift. A good distance and it will keep them all occupied."

*** 13 ***

Once the men were away, they went to the stable, where Brillar found a pair of heavy gloves, then to the kitchen for hot water in an ewer, a basin, a silver bowl, a small brush used for cleaning pots, and a silver tray. At her mother's glance, she said, "The dimlock can't touch flesh or even, I think, something made of earth. Pottery won't do for it. Just a feeling." She shrugged. They took everything to a spare room. Brillar fetched the foldbox then bolted the door and poured the water into the silver bowl at a desk.

"Be ready with cleansing spells," she said as she opened the foldbox. Her mother nodded. "Not for the collar, for the room; there's bound to be an odor. And healing spells as well, in case it touches me. Open the windows, please, then stand well away."

First, she took a knife and scissors from the foldbox. When she was ready, Brillar put on gloves and took the cwel skin, cut the straps, and dumped it into the hot water. The stench that arose was quickly dispelled but not before Brillar stood back, holding her breath. She could feel her mother steady her. Slowly, she pulled the cwel skin from the collar. It resisted, and she cut it away with the knife, dropping all the bits into the basin. The work was time-consuming and the gloves awkward but necessary. Even through them, she could feel the pulse of the collar.

Bit by bit, the dimlock was separated from the cwel skin. Darwa freshened her daughter when she felt it was needed. It was nearly two hours before it was all completed, but there was still the dimlock itself to be cleaned. Brillar picked away at the bits of flesh there, trying desperately to forget it was Elden's flesh. More than once, she was sure she would vomit, but her mother healed the feeling quickly. Once, a slight awkward movement allowed a link of the collar to touch her arm; she cried out, but a healing spell was cast at once.

***

Miles away at the horse market, Prendar was watching with delight as an owner put a black mare through her paces. Elden was tense and uneasy but didn't know why.

"A fine mare, that," Prendar said quietly. "Only three, well trained and ready for a stud."

Elden started to answer, then paled, grabbed Prendar's arm, and would have fallen if the older man hadn't supported him. Still, he sank to his knees before Prendar could straighten him, calling Terol to his side.

"Help him to the tavern, boy, while I speak to this man. I think he's had too much dust and sun."

Elden was helped to his feet. Terol managed to get him to the inn, where he sank to a chair and dropped his head into his hands. Terol came back with a tankard of ale, but Elden only shook his head and whispered something the lad couldn't hear.

***

When the collar was finally cleaned, Brillar lifted it from the water and laid it on the silver tray. Before they could finish, she asked her mother to take away the basin and its filthy contents, then bring fresh water, new gloves, and another large platter of pure silver.

While she waited, Brillar went to the window and took huge gulps of clean air. She felt wilted, exhausted. A knock reported her mother's return with water and a servant carrying the silver tray. The servant was asked to wait in case anything else was needed.

Fresh water went into the basin, and Brillar, now in new gloves, sat and scrubbed the collar with the brush, removing everything that remained on it. The brush was quickly used up by the touch of the collar. "See how it eats the boar hairs," she murmured to her mother.

Finally, the collar was cleaned. Brillar laid it on the silver tray, placing the second tray over it. From the foldbox, she removed a few lengths of leather and tied the two trays together then stood back. Her mother was quickly behind her and she relaxed into her comforting arms.

"To think," her mother whispered, "you had to take *that* from a man."

The tears that had been unshed welled up in Brillar's eyes. She turned to face Darwa and let herself be comforted by the warm embrace, aware that her mother, too, was crying. Finally, she pulled away, wiping her eyes on her sleeve.. Looking at her daughter's drawn face, Darwa ordered her to bed for a short nap before dinner. Brillar went willingly while her mother safeguarded the trays and had the servant clean the room.

When she woke, Brillar could smell cooking and knew she must have overslept. She used the refresher then uttered cleansing spells. Ruefully, she looked at the mark on her left arm where the dimlock had touched it and shook her head. *So light a touch and so quickly healed, yet I may carry it forever,* she thought and carefully chose a white blouse trimmed in green, with long sleeves, and a full matching skirt. She tied a green sash around the over-blouse, added slippers, and considered herself ready for company.

"You and your mother were hidden away this afternoon," Elden said as he met her in the hall, offering his arm. He had clothing suited for many occasions in the foldbox, but Brolin had insisted that he have something made in town. Tonight, he was dressed in a deep blue shirt with brocade trim and dark blue trousers over his boots.

"You look well turned out, m'lord Elden," she said, avoiding the implied question.

"Had you forgotten? Your parents have guests for dinner, two families, including the family of that young lady Brolin fancies, and there's to be dancing after dinner."

"No, I *had* forgotten. I should change, or Brolin will be embarrassed!" Extracting herself from his arm, she rushed back to her room, hastily pulling out a light blue brocade gown with long sleeves she thought would suit and tying up her hair.

Elden was waiting and gave her an admiring glance before saying sternly, "We're called for," and offering his arm.

Despite her tiring afternoon, Brillar was able to enjoy the gathering. Before she left, such dinner parties had been common at Laurenfell. Several of the servants played instruments and were always glad to accept the extra coins that inevitably followed their performances.

Dinner, wines, and desserts, were eaten slowly with the new forks Elden had introduced. There was easy conversation and gossip. There were many glances at Elden then Brillar because she had unwittingly chosen a blue gown that was a complement to what he wore.

When dinner was over, the servants struck up a tune, a slow one suited to dancing after dining. Faster tunes would come later. Terol claimed her for the first dance, saying he needed practice, Brolin partnered Mairen, and Elden held out his hand to Alliana. More wine was served between dance sets as the players took a moment for themselves. Partners were exchanged. Prendar escorted both his daughters through a dance, remarking, "Who do you think taught them to dance so beautifully?" to laughter in the company. Elden partnered his apprentice several times in slower dances then took her out onto the floor for a lively twirling dance.

As they danced through the tune, their arms went up, and her sleeve, which had loosened with all the dancing, slipped down over her left arm. He started and recovered. As the dance ended in a bow and curtsey, Elden took her arm, lightly, it seemed to others, but with steel, and steered her out into the garden. Darwa turned her head and followed them with her eyes.

"Exactly what have you been doing?" he demanded, eyes flashing, "I know that mark." She quickly pulled her sleeve down. "No, the damage is done." Taking her left arm, he pushed the sleeve back again. "This afternoon?"

For once, she was not defiant, only calm. "You asked where we were, my mother and I. We were cleaning the dimlock."

His knees buckled, and he sat heavily on a bench.

"She was with me. I was in no danger," she said soothingly.

"What do you call that mark if not danger?" he replied tensely, eyes angry.

"I call it a chance contact, quickly healed, although I will admit it scarred," came her steady reply. "Rodenis has as much as demanded my presence at the Sisterhood tomorrow, where I will tell what I know about the dimlock and how it was removed. You will not attend." Her voice was firm.

He sat shaking his head, rubbing his arms as if chilled. He was unable to find his voice.

"Master," her voice was a whisper, "my presence is requested, required, demanded. I cannot refuse." She turned and left him there, said goodnight to everyone at the party, and went to her room.

When he was able to stand, Elden went out to the stable and was greeted by Jez. He took a bucket and carried fresh water for Jez and Bright. Finding some apples, he gave one to each animal, then opened the box stall and went in to Jez. Taking a brush, he began to groom the stallion's already shining skin, not using any spell, just merely brushing. Jez nipped at him and nuzzled his leg. "All is well," he said, leaning against the strong body. "All is well."

"All is not well," he heard from the half-door, "or you would not be here."

It was Darwallen who had felt his distress but given him time to deal with it in his own way. He continued to brush Jez.

"How could you let her come close to such a thing or agree to what was asked?" There was suffering in his voice.

"Oh," she replied lightly, "then you haven't met my daughter Brillar?"

He leaned against Jez. "She is a great deal of trouble, your daughter Brillar." A tear fell on straw.

"She has done for you," came the quiet response, "what no one, for Rodenis has searched back over a thousand years of records, and *no one* has ever removed a dimlock except the one who owned the key. The story must be told. Come back in when you're ready."

A stable boy found Elden in the morning, curled on the straw, still asleep. He moved away quietly and went to the house for his master.

Prendar went to the stable to find Elden stirring. "Too much wine then," he said loudly, "and I thought mages could handle their drink." He pulled Elden upright and brushed him off.

"The cook found something new from one of my traders; corin, it's called and it will wake you. We all need waking after a party. You had best change first, though."

Prendar pushed Elden up the back stairs. When he was calm and fresh in clean clothes, he went down for breakfast. Brillar was already missing, but he said nothing.

"Corin for our guest," Brolin called, "he looks a bit pale." Elden accepted the good-natured joking about his night in the stable amicably.

"I think a ride would do me good," Elden said when they were all finished. "Perhaps Terol will take Bright? She looks as if she needs some exercise. And food," he added hastily, "for a ride, a hunt perhaps, then lunch out in the fields? I do need some refreshing," he said, adding to himself, 'and to be away from here today.' Like it or not, Brillar had a duty to the Great House. He understood duty.

His idea was quickly agreed to and Prendar called to the kitchen for lunch to be packed. "A large lunch, for we'll be hungry. We'll ride to the east; there are some new farms out that way but also game. Bows for the game and none of those mage's tricks. A fair hunt, a fair kill, and some fine dining for the next few days."

There was a flurry of activity in the kitchen and stable before they were ready. "That cold meat will do, some of the fresh breads and new butter. Sweet rolls, fruit, and wine, and don't forget the cups."

The lead cook shook her head. "Whatever my lady Brillar wanted with that fresh chicken skill this morning, I will never know. Bird 'twill be tougher cooked without the skin."

*** 14 ***

Brillar was not at the Great House. She was still in her room, taking the morning to prepare what she would say and how. She had another pair of thick gloves, knowing it would have to be handled, a dark cloth, and a silver jewelry stand. Finally, she put on the green dress and pin Elden had bought for her and was ready. When the bell rang at noon, her mother, who had spent an anxious morning quietly talking with Rodenis, joined her. Mother and daughter went to the empty meeting hall and waited for the assembly to begin.

It was a short wait. Everyone who had been able to gather ate quickly and filed in to find a place to sit where they could see easily. The front rows had been reserved for the senior Sisters and the Brothers who had come to see this relic. The tiered hall filled quickly; people pushed together to give others room to sit. Behind the dais where she had put the trays, gloves, and stand, was the crest of the Sisterhood. As she looked out over the company, Brillar almost smiled at its colorful nature, even though she worried about what was to come. The Brothers, fond of darker colors, blended their dark blues, deep reds, and purples with the bright colors of the Sisters, most of whom preferred the colors of sunlight and flowers. Pinks, light greens, peach, yellows were everywhere. Their familiar colors relaxed her. Finally, younger Sisters, not allowed in the hall, closed the doors.

Rodenis, in pale green, stood, and everyone was quiet. "We know why we are here. Begin," was all she said and re-took her seat.

Brillar stood. She'd prepared a way to display the dimlock. Now, she put on gloves, cut the thongs on the silver tray, and put the dimlock on the silver stand—her mother's and made for a necklace. Brillar had placed the dark cloth behind it, and the dimlock seemed to pulse with menace.

Miles away in a field, Elden brought Jez up sharply. "Brillar!" he breathed, then shook himself and turned back to the hunt.

There were mutters from the assembly. She let them look at it for a few moments, then began the story of how she had found

Garnelden bound by the dimlock and searched him to see if he was lawfully held. She held up the pick and told what herbs and spell she had used on the lock. Holding up orb, powders, knife, everything that she had used to remove it, she explained how and when each was used. She explained how she wrapped each link of the dimlock in cwel skin to keep it from touching them. She stopped and answered questions at each point.

When she came to removing the pendant and Garnelden's response, she stopped and bowed her head, overcome. The company was silent while she calmed herself. She added her forgetfulness that there might be an infection and fever and explained how it was cured. She told them about the profound healing sleep it had taken for him to gain strength. She told them about the herbs she used in stews to strengthen him. Then she stopped.

"This, I had yesterday," she said, baring her arm, showing the crescent scar there, "after the merest touch of a link and with a healing mage ready with a spell." There was a stir in the assembly. "Now watch."

She re-gloved and removed the dimlock from the stand, replacing it with the chicken skin, then she put the dimlock on the skin. A stench came from the skin, and she removed the dimlock quickly, revealing that the skin was already marked by it. The collar, she placed back on the silver tray.

"The dimlock has only one purpose: To separate mage from mana and the world, sending him into a half-life, leaving him unable to cast a spell, unable to touch what burns him. Only another person can remove it. I removed it using the skills the Sisters taught me here and a cwel skin to protect us both, then I wrapped it and kept it in the foldbox. Now I ask that it be destroyed, for it is wholly and utterly evil." She took her seat and sighed deeply, relaxing her shoulders.

There was silence when she sat, then everyone one was standing, clapping, shouting. Rodenis stood and took the dais, hands in the air to quiet the crowd.

"Silence!" Her voice carried over the din, but it was still some time before all settled. "All students are dismissed; yes, the senior students as well." There was some grumbling, but they all filed from the hall. The teachers, scholars, and elders remained seated. Once the hall was cleared of students, Rodenis announced, "Discussion may now begin."

First, they formed a line to get a closer look at the dimlock, probing it as it lay on silver. "Why silver?" was asked again and answered more than once. Healers asked to see the mark on her arm, so Brillar left it uncovered. Healing spells were offered, many strange to her, but the mark remained. Brothers probed the dimlock with muttered spells and were repulsed. "No," she said, many times, "I don't know how it was made."

Rodenis was asked for the lore she had discovered. She had the texts in the hall and scholars from both Houses pored over them. There was information on the locking of the collar and its removal with a key but nothing on its making or unmaking. Some proposed that perhaps there had only ever been one such collar made long ago and the process forgotten, then the collar reused. That idea had some deep in thought. A Brother was dispatched to their Great House to have the more elderly scholars there review all the writings they had.

Brillar finally sealed the dimlock between the two silver trays. She handed them to an astonished Rodenis.

"I've kept it safe only because no one knew about it. Now everyone knows. I can't take it up again; it's for other hands now."

Rodenis nodded agreement and left unaccompanied. "No one else should see where I put it," she stated firmly.

As soon as the dimlock left the hall, Brillar felt something lift from her that she hadn't known was there. Her eyes went to her mother who was waiting quietly. As a Senior Sister, she had never left the room. Suddenly, she began to laugh gladly, almost giddy, and her mother laughed with her. The others in the hall looked toward the sudden sounds and smiled.

Brillar breathed deeply and exhaled. "I hadn't known how dark it was until it was gone. Senior Healer?" Her mother nodded. "Is it close to supper? I'm suddenly hungry." There was more laughter at this. "If everyone will excuse us?" Brillar and her mother walked home, her dark green gown and her mother's ocean blue shifting in the twilight.

The men had been back for some time and were enjoying wine on a terrace when they arrived. Elden looked at his glass and refused to raise his eyes.

"Welcome home, sweet," said Prendar, kissing his wife, "and don't the two of you look wonderful. Your afternoon must have agreed with you." The women just glanced at each other and took wine from a tray.

"How was the hunt?" Darwa asked.

"Wait until you taste the linic hens," Terol put in excitedly. "I took a cwel at a distance. I almost missed because Bright seemed to stumble a moment when Elden reined Jez in." that got Elden a sharp glance, "but I hit him well, didn't I, Father?"

"A fine shot, fine. But now I hear the cook calling." He put his arm over his son's shoulder as they went in.

Dinner started with a bowl of light chicken soup. "Cook said you took a chicken skin with you this morning."

Brillar nearly choked on her soup.

"Something Rodenis wanted," Darwa put in, getting a look from Elden. "Nothing important."

To delay further discussion of her day, Brillar went directly to her room after dinner, leaving Elden to her mother.

"A word, Elden?" she asked when her daughter had left the table. They went to the sitting room where she poured a brandy for each of them and recounted the afternoon's happenings.

"So they think that there may have been only one dimlock all this time? Over two thousand years, set aside, hidden, then re-found and used?"

"There isn't any record of how to make them," she answered, "and I would think that a skill like that would be recorded somewhere."

"And a destruction," Elden added darkly.

They finished their brandy and said no more that night.

***

The discussions in the Great House continued for well over a week. Finally, a messenger arrived and went into conference with Rodenis and the Elder Brothers. Three days later, a carriage arrived, carrying an elderly scholar and a parchment. Brillar and Darwallen were summoned, and Darwa asked her husband to make sure that Elden was away from the house. He was puzzled but had been married to a mage for a long time and simply nodded his compliance.

Mother and daughter walked to the Great House. As was now her custom, Brillar dressed in green. Rodenis greeted them and led them to a small meeting room where they were introduced to Brother

Chefin, a bent, grey-haired Brother who had been teaching for over seventy years.

"I believe I have found the answer," the old man began, eyes sparkling, "and such a simple answer it is, and so easy, no one would have thought it. Oh, what a fine time I had in locating it, I can tell you. The parchment is decayed, torn, and the question had never been asked or we would have known so quickly, but it's all here for anyone who can read it." He coughed. "Dusty in those vaults." A senior Brother handed him a glass of watered wine. "Dusty everywhere down there and we need to get these old parchments copied before we lose them. Now, where was I?"

"The dimlock, Brother?" his friend prompted him.

"Ah yes, the dimlock. A nasty thing." He spread a parchment on a table. "It is all here, oh no, not the making. That is surely lost, for there are few parchments left older than this, no, no, this is its destruction. You see, first a list of herbs to be spread." Everyone bent close.

"I can't read it," complained Rodenis.

"I can read some words," spoke up an Elder Brother. "I studied with Brother Chefin. Still, Chefin, if you would."

"The problem begins and ends here," he said as he marked the page with a finger. "First the herbs to be spread on it, 'by one who knows it well.' That, I think, is a person who has had contact with it? Then it says, '…it is to be salted a…' do you see?"

"I take the meaning to be that it is to be hidden? Salted away?" asked one of the Brothers.

"I admit there is much lost, dimmed, a hole in the parchment, but the final faint words, 'can… be… dest… yed."

He looked around at the silent company. "Salt!" he shouted. "Not 'it shall be salted away,' as in a hidden place, but that 'it shall be salted,' herbs first then salt!"

"Salt?" came the question from many lips.

"Salt!" he replied. "Oh, there are the other things, the herbs to be powered and spread, I said that, didn't I? Then silver to be used, but most certainly, salt."

"Herbs, which herbs?" The herbalist was in the room, and Chefin read out a list.

"At once." And she went off as more of the group gathered around to get a better look at the parchment. The room was full of questions and discussions.

"I am told," said Chefin, going to Brillar, "that you sheltered it in silver. Well done, well done. We must talk, you and I. However did you think of silver?"

Before she could answer, the herbalist came back with her powders and a Sister came up with a cask of salt.

"I think this is best done now and in the courtyard," said Rodenis, "if you will go there while I fetch the dimlock?" The courtyard was paved with heavy stone and dotted with stone tables and benches. Students and younger sisters were sent away and told to stay away. Senior Sisters were directed to stay with them. Rodenis set the trays on a stone table and cut the bindings, lifting off the top tray and setting it aside.

Brother Chefin leaned closer, staring. "No one I have ever met has seen such a sight, well, except those here. If I am right, no one will ever see one again."

Brillar whispered to her mother, "They were away?" and received a nod.

"You, you," he beckoned to Brillar, "you took it, you know more about it than the rest of us." Brillar stepped forward reluctantly, shuddering. He handed her gloves. "I think this is for you to do." He gave her an encouraging pat on the arm. The others stepped back. Brillar looked desperately at Rodenis and her mother, but the senior Sister only shook her head.

"Pile salt deeply on the empty tray," Chefin commanded. She was shaking so hard that she emptied half the cask onto the silver and spread it by hand.

"It appeared to me that the herbs were to be spread directly on the collar," he said and handed her a deep cup where the herbs had been combined. "First, sprinkle half the herbs on the salt." He wait until she completed the task.

"Now, place the collar on the salt, cover it with the rest of the herbs, then smother it in salt."

She was loathe to get close to the dimlock again but did as she was told. As she set the collar on the herbs, it began to turn color, filling the air with a cloud of dark, choking smoke.

"Now!" Chefin shouted.

Brillar spread the rest of the herbs on the collar. It hissed and spat; acrid smoke curled from it. She felt weak and couldn't see clearly.

"The salt!" a voice said, and she shook the rest of the salt on the dimlock, covering it. The smoke was in her eyes, her nose, her stomach heaved, she was falling toward the dimlock as it twisted in the salt like something alive and in pain. Hands grabbed her roughly and threw her to the stones to vomit. Her arm was on fire. Grabbing the scar, she screamed, "Elden!" and could hear an echo of his distant screams. They tore at her as her arm burned, and the thing in the salt hissed and writhed. That was all she knew.

*** 15 ***

She was in a quiet room, a cloth on her head, something was being pressed to her lips, and she drank. "Elden." She jerked upright, was pushed down, and quieted with a soothing spell.

"In the next room and being tended. They say he screamed he was on fire then dropped like a stone in the field. They brought him right here."

She blinked and looked around, recognizing a small room in the House of Healing.

The cup was pressed to her lips again. "Is it gone then, destroyed?"

"Completely gone," said her mother, coming in quietly dressed in the light blue often worn by healers. "What have you been told?"

"She's only just awake," the healing Sister said gently. "She knows Elden is here."

Darwa nodded. "And I've been tending him for two days."

"Two days? I've been here two days?" She struggled to get up and was pushed back.

"You were very close when it was destroyed. The blow was powerful." Her mother's hand was on her forehead, cool and soothing, scented with herbs.

Brillar struggled to push herself up, and her mother tucked a pillow behind her. "I need feeding now and not just broth but rich stew; otherwise I'll roll out of this bed or die in the trying."

Her healer left, nodding to Darwallen. "I'd thought as much." She smiled at her daughter. "Something has already been prepared."

Alliana came in with stew and Darwallen left. "I am to spoon it into your mouth or tie your arms," she said, eyes twinkling. Brillar allowed the spooning and drank from a cup her sister held. As she ate, she noted that her green dress was hanging on a hook and smiled at it.

Alliana wrinkled her nose. "I'm glad I wasn't there. Do you know how many times I had to cast a cleansing spell on that garment to rid it of the stink?" She stuffed another spoonful of stew in Brillar's mouth without giving her a chance to answer. "And you soiled it," she scolded. "When it was handed to me, I thought I would soil it at well." More stew. "Only a few had been allowed in the courtyard, but some of the students were crowded at the windows. Not all of them made it to basins. What a time we had cleaning up after them." A cup to her sister's lips, then more stew. "Nearly everyone in the courtyard was ill, even that scholarly Brother Chefin. He had to be carried to a healing room and, I am told, is a terrible patient. But I brought you something," her voice dropped to a whisper, "knowing how you dislike herbal teas." She stood and threw the rest of the tea out the window. She refilled the cup from a small flask. "One of Father's favorite wines," and she held the cup to her sister's lips then took a sip herself and refilled the cup. Both began to smile. When Brillar opened her mouth to speak, Alliana stuffed it with more stew.

"Remember when Father said I was too young for wine and you doused me with brandy to show he was right?" Brillar could only nod. More wine followed the stew. "I thought I would die, now here I am, stuffing you and giving you wine. There, finished." She drank the last of the wine. "I promised to leave once you had eaten. You're now to sleep again; I think they added something to the tea."

"Alliana," Brillar took her sister's hand, "come again and bring me news about Elden."

Her sister smiled and took her leave, to be replaced by a healing Sister in blue and white who sniffed the air. "Wine, or I have not lived these thirty years." She removed the pillows. "You will sleep now. Wine in a sickroom." But Brillar was already sleeping.

The next morning, Brillar got out bed when the Sister removed her breakfast tray. Too unsteady to fully dress, she wrapped a robe around her gown and was at the door when the Sister returned. She held the door open and insisted loudly, "I'm going to see Elden."

At the noise in the hall, her mother came out and clucked her tongue. "A moment only, then," and helped her daughter into Elden's room. He was unconscious and pale, his scars angry on his chest. She could see something dark hovering around him.

She looked at her own scar, which was still painful. She took a chair by his side and her mother left them alone in the room.

"Master, what are we to do, you and I?" and she began to murmur healing spells, then placed both her hands firmly on the dimlock scars. Feeling fire but refusing to let go, she drew on all her reserves of strength, calling him back from the darkness. Sensing something from outside the door, Darwallen was inside shouting for help, sending wave after wave of mana, strength, and healing toward her daughter. Then a Senior Healer was there, then Rodenis, with others outside lending support, strength, being fed mana by the newly arrived as they depleted themselves and took a moment to draw in more. The younger students could feel some of what was happening and clung to each other. Time seemed to stop, then, finally, Brillar sagged forward on Elden's chest, and he stirred, a slight turn of his head.

They carried Brillar back to her bed. An orb was brought, then another, as Sisters spoke words of healing, strength, and soothing over both of them throughout the night.

Neither woke again for another day. Some of the Sisters, exhausted by their efforts, were put to bed in the healing hall. Others fell into their own beds and were tended by older students. The Brothers who had remained at the House could do nothing to help except with simple tasks, but none would leave. They visited Brother Chefin; they tended horses, cooked food, tried to help with lessons, played simple games with the younger students.

At Laurenfell, the mood was somber. Darwallen and Alliana were at the Great House most of the time. News traveled to and from their home and the House of Healing. Visitors came and went all day and Brothers joined them at dinner, trying to cheer them with stories of their craft and things they had seen.

"Having her here and ill, is worse than having her on walkabout and not knowing where she was," Prendar remarked that evening. No one answered.

The second morning, Brillar suddenly sat up and asked for breakfast, much to everyone's astonishment. Her sister brought her a tray and was asked for more.

"I feel very light-headed," Brillar announced, "and I think I need something else."

In the next room, Elden also woke, took broth then rolled on his side and fell into a healthy sleep.

That afternoon, after she had lunch, her father was allowed to visit. "This must stop," he said firmly. "Are you to be sick then well, then suddenly sick again?"

She could only laugh. "That is for the morrow," she said. Then, seeing his face, she said, "Tell me the news. Is someone exercising Bright? How are the new crops?" These, she knew, were easy topics for him and they talked for a few minutes until a Sister shooed him out. Brillar immediately asked for more food, because "all that talk of crops has made me hungry." Alliana came in as she was eating to sit with her and marveled at her appetite.

"You've surprised us, and not just with your appetite. You haven't asked about Elden." Alliana sounded concerned.

"I haven't asked because I know. He's well and sleeping. He can be nothing else." Her eyes held a far-away look, then she smiled at Alliana. "He'll be hungry when he wakes up, so make sure there's stew."

When Elden woke in the evening, there was stew. From that moment, he gained strength rapidly, surprising all the healers in the House. Brillar, who had been sent home with instructions to rest, visited him daily, always in the green dress.

"It's gone then?" was the first thing he asked when she visited. He had been told but wanted it from her.

"Utterly destroyed, I'm told, eaten away by the herbs and salt and taking a silver tray with it; Brother Chafin's instructions were complete. It was…" she stopped. "It was like something alive under the herbs and the salt. They tell me I was falling toward it and had to be pulled away, thrown on the stones." She shook her head.

"We need to talk about something else, anything else," she said, and he nodded, then closed his eyes.

She told him about the new black mare that her father had bought at the horse fair and the other animals he was considering. "The mare is a fine animal; I'm glad he bought her. And he wants to know if you'll let Jez stand at stud?"

He nodded, grateful for small things, glad that he was alive and she was there with him.

The second day, he was walking with her in the hall of the healing house, laughing at her news about Jez's enthusiasm and success with the black mare.

On the third day, he was sent back to Laurenfell to complete his recovery.

Rodenis and the healing Sisters were astonished at the pair. "Up and walking outside? A swim in the lake? No one recovers that quickly," she could be heard to mutter.

A simple week after they went back to Laurenfell, both insisted on a short ride, although Prendar and Terol rode out with them to ensure that the ride was short. The rides quickly grew longer.

Archery practice on the broad lawn began again, with Brillar consistently outshooting her brothers, father, and Elden. Even Darwallen came out with a bow one day and had everyone laughing at her first shots. She gave up quickly. "Too much time at healing, not enough with the bow," she complained.

The days passed comfortably.

In the evenings… in the evenings, Brillar retired early but not to sleep. She had found an old book with her things and was now practicing arcane words—words of Deception—and feeling their power grow. She began using the spells to conceal her intentions, intentions that did not include staying at Laurenfell.

Elden and Brillar were soon riding out together without companions, but with stern warnings to keep at the traveler's pace and the time short. Brillar proved amazingly biddable at the suggestions, which everyone should have found suspicious. Still, they increased the length of their rides daily, sometimes taking lunch with them. Sometimes Terol or Brolin accompanied them and she remained compliant as her strength and Elden's grew.

Hers grew, in fact, more quickly than she let anyone know. Her skill at Deception had increased as she practiced privately. Her parents were certainly taken in.

"A fine pair," Prendar remarked to his wife one morning, "a fine pair."

"He does seem to have steadied her," was the reply. "They certainly need no providing for." When her husband looked at her, she just smiled back. "If that's their intention."

Brolin, the eldest at one year over Brillar's age, had told his parents that Mairen's family had been asked and that they had been pleased to give their consent. The families conferred and the wedding was planned at Laurenfell. The house was in a flurry of preparation.

A week after the proposal, on a fine autumn morning, with the sun still warm, Brillar and Elden saddled their horses. "I need to get away from all this fuss," she had announced at breakfast.

They were away before the plates were cleared and were ten miles south before Brillar urged Bright into a gallop, leaving a startled Elden behind for a moment. He covered the distance easily and brought Jez close.

"Slow that animal," he shouted into the wind and was surprised when she did.

"Do you want to undo all the good that's been done?" he demanded. Laughing, she put Bright back into the traveler's pace and moved southward again. He urged Jez to keep up with her then reached out. "What do you think you're doing?" he demanded, reaching for her reins, which she twitched away.

"Whatever do you mean?"

He moved Jez ahead of her, blocking her way. "You know exactly what I mean," he growled. "I can feel my foldbox charm here, now that I've looked, muted but here, and we're too far from the house for me to find it unless you have it with you." He grabbed Bright's reins.

"Why, Uncle…"

"No 'uncles' from you. Hand it over," he demanded.

"That I will, when we camp for the night, as far from Laurenfell as we can ride in a day."

"Of all the idiotic, headstrong, addlepated… you mean it, don't you?"

She looked at him soberly and sighed. "Behind us, is a wedding, and no, it's not that I want to miss it, but it prickles, everyone rushing here and there." She dropped her Deception and let him really see her. "As you see, even you can be fooled if you are unwary. I knew that." He glared at her, not dropping the reins.

"Master," that unsettled him, "I bound myself to you for a year and it's passing without even a lesson in weeks. There are the Wilds to be seen, explored. If I go back now, they will trap us into something; I can feel it."

"You were too ill for lessons," was all he could reply, "and far too ill for the Wilds. Then there was the dimlock."

"Then we'll make the most of the day and the next few days, hunt and rest until you decide we're well enough to go on. I left a gift for my brother and his bride. They'll know they are thought of even without our presence."

"I could bind you," he began and stopped.

"Yes, you could cast and bind; you could force me back if that's what you want. But I will not be bound without a Defense."

Green eyes glared at him, resolute, daring him to begin the words. Beaten, he dropped the reins and turned Jez to the south and the Wilds beyond. Behind him, he could feel her smiling as she followed.

It was mid-afternoon when Rodenis arrived at the house for a visit and was told that Brillar and Elden were not back from their ride. She took a seat with the family by the lake.

"Brillar took food with her, so they've probably stopped for lunch. The rides have been good for them both, and they should be back shortly," Prendar explained.

Brolin galloped up on a lathered horse and slid off, running to his parents. "This was just delivered," he said, panting, as he held out a note.

"Dearest Elder Brother," it began. "I am truly sorry that we will miss your wedding, but we offer you one bar of gold from the cart so you can begin your lives in ease. Please tell my beloved parents," at this, her mother lowered her head, "that I am bound to Garnelden as apprentice for one year and the year is already more than a quarter flown. I can wait no longer. We will send word when we can. Your loving sister, Brillar."

"Send horsemen after them," Prendar ordered. "She was to stay here. She was to rejoin the Sisterhood, complete her training, become a healer like her mother."

"Send no one," Rodenis interrupted vehemently. "The moment for her to continue her studies with us has passed." Her voice was stern, severe. Prendar stared at her, questioning. "She has twice killed men. No one can rejoin us after such acts. That is the Law."

Shocked, Prendar sank into a chair and covered his face with his hands. Darwallen dropped to his side, comforting him. "I didn't have the heart to tell you, not so soon. Not when we hoped they would stay."

He raised his head, "As I," he said quietly, "had no heart to tell you she was bound as his apprentice."

They sat in silence for some time.

To the south, Brillar and Elden were still in well-settled lands when he called a halt for the evening. "There's no sense tiring the horses or ourselves any further," he said firmly. They had eaten only trail rations earlier. "When you planned all this, did you make any plan for food?"

"A moment only," was the reply, "and we dine." Brillar opened her foldbox and took out sliced meats, bread, fruit, and a bottle of wine. Plates and cups appeared with them, along with blankets for the night. His foldbox was produced and handed over. Meat piled high on fine bread was an easy meal, although they spent it in silence.

Elden looked around them. They had settled beside a pond so the horses could enjoy fresh water. The sky was darkening. "Jez will keep watch. The night's warm with no fire needed." When she didn't answer, he looked over to find her fast asleep. Covering her with a blanket, he lay back on his own and wondered how he had managed to saddle himself with such a headstrong apprentice. He was still wondering when stars appeared.

***

At Laurenfell, wedding preparations had momentarily ceased, and the house was quiet. On a bench under the open sky, husband and wife also watched the stars appear.

"He's a good man," said Darwa, "he'll protect her."

"You think then that any of this was his doing?" He was staring into the sky.

"This," she replied with a small smile, "was certainly all our daughter."

***

There were scattered towns in the southern areas, but they weren't tempted by them. The fields they passed through were rich with game, fruit trees, and the occasional tuber.

"Besides, I walked these roads and healed many people in need inside the towns and at the farms." Now, away from Laurenfell, she chatted freely. "There were times I stayed at an inn for days in the far south, near the Wilds, when the local people had no skilled healer, receiving my bed and meals as my fee. In a town, I sometimes taught the local healer more about herbs and even some light spells. Sometimes I slept in the open, sometimes in a barn. But I did send word that I was well; no need to cause worry at home."

"Not until now," he muttered.

At noon, when they ate and rested, Elden took up his duties as Master, concentrating on Item spells that she would find useful. She wanted no part of War spells but was willing to consider some in Creature.

"For war," she told him, "I have a bow, although I think it unlikely that my Master would take me into a war."

He growled.

"But no Creature spells to call animals; they are unsporting. I have no wish to lower the strength of a cwel or linic so I can make an easy kill. Those spells of renewal and revitalization could be useful, though."

In the end, they concentrated on Item spells for increasing the protection of their armor. Elden did insist that they spend time in a town where a leather worker fashioned the armor favored by archers for her. As it was, it provided scant protection but was very flexible. They also had the man fashion two newer and better packs for them, although Elden would not tell her why. He had produced a sword from his foldbox and began wearing it.

While they waited, Brillar visited a local shopkeeper. She had been in the town before as a healer and had found a seven-year-old girl with a talent for helping hurt animals. She had sent word back to the Great House about the girl and now found her parents pleased with the result.

"Sister Idelia came and talked with our daughter and walked out with her. When they came back, she asked if Hebba could go to the Great House for training! We miss her, of course, but on her last visit, she was already so different, stronger, more grown-up. Imagine, our daughter at the House of Healing." Brillar congratulated the pair and left a silver coin where they would find it as a token from the Sisterhood.

Once they left the town, Elden insisted that she wear the leather to increase its flexibility. In the evenings, he had her practice increasing its resistance. She found all this tiring and the armor too warm; they were far enough south that it wasn't yet autumn.

One afternoon as she wore the spell-strengthened armor, he dropped behind her and slapped at her with his sword, nearly knocking her off Bright. The armor held.

"That bruised," she said accusingly, but he laughed as she cast a healing spell. "And you startled Bright."

"The testing was necessary. Very soon now, we enter the Wild."

Brillar stirred with excitement.

"We enter the Wild and send the horses back to your father."

"Send them back?" She reined Bright in sharply.

"Two things. In the Wild, it's better to go on foot and with as little noise as possible. It's also wise not to draw attention to wealth, and these two," he patted Jez, "would draw many."

Brillar was silent the rest of the afternoon. "I'll miss them," was all she said that evening. Turning her back on him, she rolled herself in her blanket. Elden studiously ignored the soft sounds he knew were choked sobs. In the morning, she gave no hint of her distress and listened closely to everything he had to say.

"The Wild isn't called that just because it is unsettled; in fact, there are huts here and there, although the people in them are apt to move abruptly when worried by animals or threatened in other ways. Then there are the Rovers, bands of men and their families wilder than the hillmen, to the north because the land is wilder. They can be more dangerous than the animals of the Wild, although the men and women Brother Verian and I met seemed kind enough."

He would make a statement like that and leave her to think about it for a while, then answer any questions she had.

"There are things living in caves and some that tunnel under the ground. If a hut is built or people linger too long, a hole can open under them, swallowing some or all. Camping near rocks can disturb things that are venomous, so they have to be cleared before we can camp. There are unpredictable welling-up of magic in the Wild, and no one has been able to clear them. The things they produce are always dangerous."

More silence as she considered it, then more questions.

"There are mountains in the Wild and harpies that can take a child or kill an adult. Then there are the birds that attack travelers in a flock, aiming first at the eyes then joining in for the kill." The days went on with lessons and instruction. She often hunted, keeping them fed with linic and cwel without unsporting spells.

One morning he announced, "Game can either be scarce in the Wild or will be found in great herds that would likely trample us if we tried to take an animal. Today, we hunt together, something large, and dry the meat."

He had her reach out until she found a herd of wellis, those fine animals whose hides leather workers prize for boots. They dismounted and approached downwind. It was a long stalk, and the buck she chose took two arrows before dropping. She had glared at him when he suggested spells.

"A fine choice," was Elden's compliment, "and I will do the cleaning." He reached out for Jez and both horses came to them.

Brillar had taken the wellis near a stream where the herd had been drinking. Looking around, she saw a stand of saplings and cut some for a drying frame. Lashing it together quickly, she said, "Excuse me, Master." That brought a sharp glance. "But perhaps we should camp here?"

Nodding, he agreed.

Firewood for drying the meat was gathered quickly and a second drying frame made. She produced herbs for the meat, which they both sliced and hung over the fire to dry and smoke. It was a tiring day.

"It seems to me," she began as they ate some of the meat they had roasted over the fire, "that there should be a spell for drying meat."

"Oh, there is, I've just forgotten it," he answered, a remark that had them both laughing.

They kept the fire going all night, taking turns sleeping, feeding the fire and turning the meat. It was another day before they had finished and put the meat away. Now the reason for the packs became evident.

"We use the packs as much as possible, since we don't know when or if we'll meet strangers. No need to call attention to the foldboxes; those go in the packs. We're simply two explorers venturing into the Wild in search of treasure since there is plenty to be found if you survive long enough to take it back to settled lands. I found some when I was with Verian."

"People do come back from the Wild with wealth then? I had heard tales, but no one had actually said, 'this I did and this I won,' at least not when I was listening."

"The rare golem that shatters sometimes drops a gem or two. Some are worth keeping. Giant rats will gather bright objects from the dead, and blood kites will take a ring or two from an unwary traveler to their nests, after they kill the traveler, of course. Still," he said, having noticed her shudder at the mention of rats, "few bother with danger of that sort."

"Thank you for that. I take it that the kites nest together?"

"They nest close, but not too close, and on the sides of cliffs. They do flock together. One of a pair is always with the young. Other kites are not particular when looking for an easy meal."

The land had been changing slowly as they rode south, drier, the soil sandier, and grass was scarce. Now they were in scrubland, where the trees were smaller and there was more brush. They hadn't seen a farm in two days and there wasn't enough grass for cattle.

They were halfway through a morning when Elden drew up and pointed to a small cabin. "We'll stop there a moment." He called out the traditional greeting and was answered.

An older man, dressed in the simple clothing of a hunter but with a breast patch proclaiming him a Brother, came out to greet them.

"Well met then, Brother Garnelden," he said in recognition. "And the lady?" He raised an eyebrow at Brillar.

"My apprentice." The Brother's wide eyes went back to Elden. "Yes, yes, Thilian. I know I said I would never have an apprentice, but that was a long time ago."

Brillar had dismounted.

"We're traveling to the Wild and would like you to have the horses taken to Laurenfell House, home of my apprentice. They know the way, but I would rather they go with someone for safety."

"I can take them myself." He smiled at Brillar. "I could do with some fresh fruit." He sobered. "There have been disturbances in the Wild in the last month. A mana pool opened very close to the border just last week. I still get some young fools who want to hunt in the wild, but they usually come out shaken if they come out at all. One family came out weeping over lost children."

"Thank you for the warning." Elden put silver coins in the man's hand. "To help with your journey. Tell Lady Darwallen that we're doing well? Don't mention the mana pools. I know most of what's dangerous and how to avoid it."

Elden stroked Jez's neck and saw Brillar saying her goodbyes to Bright. "Best tie them both until you're ready to leave. The last time I left him, he followed me anyway." He handed the reins to his Brother, spoke firmly to Jez, and looked at Brillar. The glance was all she needed. Without looking back, she stepped past Thilian's hut and into the true Wild.

*** 16 ***

"Do you know Brother Thilian well, then?" she asked as they left the cabin behind.

"Well enough. He's been here for over twenty-five years." His eyes were on the land around them.

"So long?" She was reaching out with far-sight.

"He finds the quiet life here preferable to any life in a town or even a House of the Brothers. You remember what I said about some of the Brothers skilled in War."

She was thoughtful, then, "And you? You told me you spent time in the Wild but not how much."

"There was a Brother here many years ago, a Grand Master of Item magic. When I returned from war I… let's say I found living with the Brothers difficult and went looking for him. At that time, he had been in the Wild alone, for some years. It took me some time to find him and more time to convince him that he should take me as an apprentice. He was an old man when I found him. I stayed with him for three years and became a Master in the skill, then I buried him. He had loved the Wild and wanted to stay; I gave him his final wish. What do you see?" he asked suddenly.

"Animals to the left, but no teeth to them. Something with teeth hunts them, I think, but only one hunter." She was thinking about danger coming on them so quickly.

"One in your range, three in mine. Keep the bow ready."

"Then they'll resist magic?"

"No, but your first kill in the Wild should be an easier one. Others will come later. And with more teeth." He continued to move on but away from the teeth. The ground was already different to her, much drier, although it had been changing over the last few days. They had walked several miles when she stopped.

"Elden?" she said. "Ahead, a sandpit? Something else?"

"Well done. We'll give that a wide berth. A sandworm. The sides of the pit are made slippery with small grains of sand. Little that falls in can scramble out again. Can you feel the bones?"

"Buried? Under the pit?"

He nodded. The trap of the sandworm was thirty feet wide and some fifteen deep.

"Should you happen on one unaware, deal with the worm first, then tunnel through the sand until you find solid footing." At her look, he nodded again. "Yes, I speak from experience." He could almost feel her slight smile.

"As the Master says."

"There's a small spring ahead and the water should be safe. We drink there and save what we carry. Springs are scarce and safe ones are always marked with a sign, a small star, if others have drunk from them. It's usually scratched into a rock. Still, be sure to reach out and check the water before drinking. Not that any spring is really safe; everything that lives has to drink and some have teeth."

The pair stopped and drank, then moved off to eat trail rations. The land around the spring still carried some of the rich grass of the settled lands, but most of what she could see ahead was drier and sparser.

"In the morning, it's best to decide where we stop at noon. In the afternoon, we'll mark a place for the night. Now, apprentice, keep this in mind at all times. If we have to fight more than one, we do so side-by-side if we can back on rock or steep hill, and back-to-back if we're in the open." At her raised eyebrow, he continued, "If we're caught in the open, surrounded, I'll cast ring spells of some sort and need you close or you are likely to be hit by one. If we are attacked from above, the spell will be a dome. Whatever happens, be ready. Those spells drain mana quickly. If I'm depleted before the attackers are driven off, the word is 'Refresh' and you'll have to defend us both as I draw in more mana. My commands will be short, simply 'Back' or 'Side' as there is likely to be little time. Keep your quiver well stocked."

"Still," he continued, seeing her solemn expression, "we're close to the border and I don't expect such an attack yet. Now," he said, pointing into the distance, "that rise and rocks? We spend the night there."

As they continued, he pointed out the various plants he knew, some with toxic thorns, others with edible tubers, still others with small insects in them that would sting or bite if disturbed. "Most things in the Wild have a defense," he explained. "They aren't gentled like the plants on farms." Some of the tubers she collected for their meal, other plants she avoided as instructed.

The only time Brillar chanced to glance back, the settled lands were far behind them. Around them spread the Wild, wide and harsh, flat with small hillocks, mountains in the distance, and plants that were green only at the base and dun or tan above. The sun baked them and sudden gusts of wind stirred dust. Things that were trees in settled lands were stunted here from lack of water.

Once, she asked, "Is that fruit?" and pointed to a squat tree that seemed to have small red balls hanging from it. Elden picked up a stone and threw it at the tree. The "fruit" erupted into insects that circled a bit, then resettled.

"There is no fruit for us in the Wild," he said sternly, "and little else. Tubers, and if we're fortunate, a kind of ground melon near a spring, although animals enjoy those when they ripen and are not likely to leave any for travelers."

Twice, they stopped and changed direction, once, to circle around three sandworm traps close together, and once, when he decided they were too near to dire wolves. "They hunt in packs. Two will usually harry the game, tiring it while others wait to make the kill. Best to take out the first pair and wait for the others to close in. Running from them is a dead man's game."

When they stopped for the night, Elden took some time checking the rocks and boulders for occupants, insisting that Brillar do the same. When they located anything dangerous, a quick spell dispatched it. He allowed them a fire, to roast some of the tubers, and they warmed herbs in water.

"After today's lessons, I think I'll find sleep difficult."

"SIDE," he shouted, and she scrambled up, bow ready.

"Well learned," came from where he was seated, and she sank back down. "You moved before you looked to see what I was doing."

"I have been knocked from a cart, pierced by my own arrow, and nearly unhorsed by a blow from a sword," came the weary reply. "A barked word from you and I will move, and quickly."

Elden chuckled. "Well said. But you'll sleep because I'll set a watch for the night." He opened a pouch and took out what appeared to be a small bug. Tapping it three times, he set it on a rock above them. "A Ward. If anything approaches, the noise it will make could wake the dead." He stirred the fire. "But that is for tomorrow."

He folded himself in a blanket, seeming to have no cares. Brillar did likewise, but it was some time before she slept, warning bug or no.

She came awake just after dawn. The fire had burned down and he was already adding small branches. The Ward was back in his pouch. A brief warming cup, trail rations, and they set off again.

"Today's lesson is to name back what you learned yesterday," Elden began. He was surprised when she made no mistakes, even finding tubers he hadn't seen. There were no 'fruit trees' for her to throw rocks into, but they did stop at a sandworm trap where a small animal was struggling up the side only to fall back.

"Watch. Better a known enemy than one unknown." They watched until the exhausted animal, something like a cwel, fell to the bottom. What appeared to be feelers, found it, then a dry head appeared, a mouth gaped, and the animal was pulled under the sand. Brillar shivered. He took her arm and pulled her away. He had chosen their noon camp and it was still some distance away.

"Elden. Under the ground and ahead to the left."

"Well done, we'll move around it; they don't like footsteps above them. Murks, they're called and they live in darkness under the ground. They eat tubers and roots. If you are starving, and only then, they can be eaten, for the taste is foul, although there are creatures that dig them up and eat them."

"BACK," came the command, and she nocked an arrow as she took her place. "They're moving fast." He felt her stiffen and ready the bow. "Dire wolves, perhaps those we sensed on the first day, now joined into a full pack. They're starving or tired, or they would have tried to chase us down first."

Elden spoke and gestured as the pack gathered around them; a ring of fire kept them back. He heard her bow and the dying yelp of a wolf behind him. Snarling, a dozen more moved closer and were met with fire and arrows. Snarls and whimpers came from several wounded wolves, then the remainder jumped forward. A ring of blades sprang from Elden's hands and he shouted, "Refresh," to the sound of her bow as he pulled in more mana, then sent out directed fire. The rest of the wolves, only four left unwounded, ran off yelping.

He turned to find his apprentice standing calmly. Reaction, he knew, would come later. "There are two wounded that won't live," he said and sent spells into both. "Never leave the wounded to suffer. Not even your enemy."

She nodded, then pulled arrows from five animals. "I thought I counted six arrows."

"Easy enough to miscount the first few times in a battle." Now she shuddered, and he went to her, holding her against him.

"And this is a common enough reaction." He felt her nod against his chest. When she took a deep trembling breath, he released her. "Well enough?" he asked.

"Yes, well enough," she returned.

"Now then, there is a ritual you need to learn. One claw from each wolf." She stared. He held up a great hairy paw, pointing. "There is one claw up behind the others that curves as it grows. One curve for each year. Four curves on this animal." With his knife, he cut it free. "Take the others from your kills. The paw on the left only. Some have tried to claim extra kills by taking both, but the curl is different." She went obediently about her task, trying to think of it as cleaning a kill meant for dinner, but still a little repulsed. She collected four more claws.

"By rights, at least two of these were slowed by fire," she said, calm but somewhat repulsed.

"It's the kill that matters."

"You take no claws from your kills?" she asked.

"If I need to, I'll wear the claws I have already." At her look, he smiled. "A foldbox can carry many things besides silly hats." She gave him a smile for that. Glancing up, he added, "Carrion eaters are coming; we need to hurry."

They moved off at a trot, making good time even with detours around 'fruit trees' and reached their noon camp in the early afternoon. Their stop was brief since the night's camp was still some way off. A good pace and they reached it as night fell. Elden set the Ward as Brillar gathered twigs for a small fire. With his belt knife, Elden showed her how to scrape the claws then set them in the ashes for final cleaning.

"Tradition," he said when asked why a cleansing spell wasn't used. "Brother Verian taught me and I need to teach you the same tradition." She could only agree.

The sky darkened as they completed the task and a wash of stars appeared in a clear sky. Brillar stared upward, transfixed by their number and their clarity. The moons hadn't risen, but starlight alone was enough to bathe the land in a silver glow. He followed her gaze, first at the sky, then at the stark beauty of the Wild.

"Verian and I used to lie and watch the sky at night." His voice was soft, muted. "You see that bright star to the right? The light is slightly blue?" She murmured a 'yes.' "The 'False Home Star,' Verian called it. Easy to find, due to the color. Follow a line up and to the left, and there is a star that never changes position. The 'True Star', he called it. Find it, and you will be able to find your way." They lay back on blankets and watched the sky until sleep took them.

In the morning, Elden opened his foldbox and took out a leather thong, tying the claws to it. "For your pouch." She accepted it without a word. He had spent time in the Wild and she was sure there was a reason for what he was doing.

They spent the next few days easily. There were no more attacks, although they were alert for them. They did skirt several areas where Elden, with his better-developed senses, thought he felt some darkness. They moved steadily southward and to the east toward some low hills.

"Good hunting there," was all he would say when she asked.

One early morning, Elden brought them to a halt near some low rock-strewn hills.

"Something odd," she began.

"You see it? Now reach out and tell me what you find." He waited, always a patient teacher.

Eyes open and glancing around them, she reached out, tensed, tried again. "Something moving? No, not really moving… bubbling? Things living but not alive?"

"A well of mana and magic. It does bubble up and move, and things spring up from it. Things living but not alive. They'll resist most magic. The best I can do is weaken them for you. As I told you, the wells come up unpredictably and are highly unstable. This one," he reached out, "is probably only a few hours old. We were lucky to find one so soon."

"And?" was her pointed question.

"And I thought I'd give you experience with the creatures spawning here. These are golems, although other things can spawn, including sprites." She brightened at that; sprites were something that had drawn her to the Wild. "You seldom find golems even when you're looking for them. Stay out of their reach; they're quicker than they look. Aim for the area between their jointed rocks; it's where they are weakest. A tall rock outcropping is a fine perch, a tree they'll knock over quickly. I'll weaken them, make them vulnerable but from a safe place." That brought a stare. "Oh, and don't get too close to them. They are currently in something of a sleep. Too close before you're ready, and they may wake up and try to smash you."

"Many thanks, *Master*," she said when he finished. "How much time do you need to find this 'safe place' of yours?"

"Around the hill, and you'll see everything. These golems will look like piles of rock but shimmer slightly. You fire first, then I'll drain or weaken what you hit."

"Shimmering rocks and him in a safe place. A fine day this is," she muttered to herself as she began the stalk around the hill, bow at the ready.

"Those rocks should be high enough for your stand," Elden said, gesturing, "and only a moment for me to find a good spot to cast on them. Oh, and keep them occupied? Once I cast on one, it may come for me instead of you."

He moved to her left and took station higher up on a hill. Slinging the bow, Brillar climbed the rocks he had indicated, searching for handholds as quietly as possible.

Atop the rocks, she knelt and readied an arrow. The "shimmering rocks" were well within bowshot. As her first arrow struck its mark, the 'rocks' twisted and moved into something shaped like a man made of stone but many times the height of a man. A second pile also surged upright.

"Drained," came the yell from behind her as she loosed again. With each hit, the creature made a shuddering, grinding sound. A third arrow, then a fourth, and the creature crumpled.

"The second is well-drained and vulnerable," came Elden's shout. It was moving past her perch toward him when her first arrow hit and it turned toward her rocks. The creature's arm struck at her, shaking her perch, and she had to steady herself. The second arrow found some vital spot and it crumpled.

"Another down the valley," he yelled, and this time she could see a faint glimmer as his spell hit the creature. Three arrows dispatched it and she stood.

"No more in my sight," she shouted.

"Nor in mine," he replied, coming down from safety as she scrambled off the rock.

"Well done, my fine archer, well done; the golems were well struck. It's hard to decide if they have vital spots except for where the rocks are joined," Elden called as he approached. Nearing, he added, "There may be a time when we need to do something like this. It was good practice for you. Now, let's see what we can find among the shards."

Most of the kills, if they could be called that, had disappeared. Watching Elden, she bent over, running her hand over the short scrub and dirt, striking something hard then holding it up into the sun, amazed. He had moved to the second golem.

"Elden?" She turned to him, holding up her hand where a diamond the size of a small egg glimmered and shown in her hand.

"On your first kill? Look at the size of it! Fit for a king's crown, that." He came over and took the gem. "Best check the third." He held the gem up to the light, shaking his head.

"Just these," she said on her return, holding out her hand. Three small gems glittered there, and he could only stare.

"I have seen many things in the Wild, but these? On your first kills? The first has no flaws!" He examined the smaller gems. "A bad flaw in one, the others are perfect. And on your first kill." He shook his head again. "Stow them; we should move off."

She put them in a belt pouch as he began to move. "On her first kill," she could hear him muttering as he began a smooth trot, and she grinned as she followed.

They pushed hard for the rest of the day, eating rations as they moved. When he finally called a halt, Brillar was exhausted despite the spells she cast. When the Ward was set and the fire lit, Elden put his hand out for the gems, looking at them in the firelight.

"If you will now, please explain?" she asked.

"As I said, there are welling up of mana and magic creatures all over these hills, although diamond golems such as we found are very, very rare. Even without my spells, you would have downed them, but it was faster with spells. They are what draw some into the Wild.

We could leave the Wild now—no, let me finish—return to Laurenfell or any other settled place, and want for nothing. Of course, that was true before we set out for the Wild."

He handed her the gems. "Put the three good gems in the foldbox and the flawed one in a belt pouch. And from now on, wear the wolf claws."

She tilted her head at him in an unspoken question as she did so.

"Rovers could be camped nearby. They can be bargained with, and the claws we will both wear," he had taken out a long necklace of claws, "will suggest that we are to be left alone."

"If we're not?" She watched him in the firelight.

"Then we shall see. The foldboxes mark us, so they're best kept stowed in our packs."

"A moment," Brillar said and opened the foldbox, removing herbs and powders, then closed it and stowed it.

"These will show me a healer," she said. "I imagine even Rovers need the occasional healer?"

"They have their own, but who knows their skill? Always good to be prepared." He settled back. "Rovers have their own customs," Elden explained. "And they vary widely. The Rovers I met when I was a student with Verian were quiet enough, even friendly. One group of families camped near us for a while, and they were good neighbors, but we're deeper in the Wild than I ever ventured."

They spent three quiet days moving through the Wild, although both now wore leather armor even when sleeping. They had found several springs, but one had been surrounded by animal bones, suggesting it was unhealthy or that something nearby was waiting for the unwary. They were in the low hills now, and the mountains in the distance could be seen in more detail. The ground was less dry, the trees a bit taller, suggesting water nearby.

One morning, she woke to a hand on her arm.

"Make ready," he whispered. "They're just outside the range of the Ward." He scooped it up quickly as she prepared her bow.

"And now?"

He could feel her tension. Tension, but not fear. *More interesting every day, this apprentice of mine,* he mused. "Now, we wait. They'll be watching, and they must know we're awake. If we more off, we're easily surrounded. We stay, keep our backs to the rocks and wait." Elden settled back down.

They waited. It was nearly noon when he said, "Do you see them? Rise slowly, bow ready, and make sure the claws can be seen." She did as she was told as more than a dozen men came towards them, well-spaced, their own weapons ready.

One stepped forward. "You are in our territory," he said, his accent harsh but understandable.

"We meant no intrusion," said Elden, spreading his arms, holding them low in a gesture meant to project harmlessness. "We merely came to take our chance in the Wild as many have."

The man gave a gruff laugh and was echoed by those closest to him. "With a lass?"

"The lass," replied Elden politely, "wears an odd necklace for a woman, don't you think?"

Another laugh greeted that. "Claws can be given," the leader started, but stopped as an arrow hissed into the ground at his feet. Another arrow was already nocked and ready.

"And a 'lass' can collect what she wears," came Brillar's quiet retort. "Or perhaps you would like another demonstration?"

"Calmly, woman," said Elden sternly, then, to the Rover, "She's a bit headstrong as you can see."

"What is one bow against many?" the Rover replied, although he did look at the arrow less than a finger's breadth from his foot.

"Two dead, before I fall, and you first," she snapped at him.

"Woman, QUIET," Elden shouted at her, sensing something she hadn't. He gestured and smiled ruefully at the Rover. "She has taken some taming."

At that, the man roared with laughter and there were echoes all around. "Then you have your hands full. I suggest you give her the flat of your sword now and again to season her."

Brillar's aim had never left the man's heart. "So Rovers must 'season' their women to keep them?" Her voice was full of scorn.

That brought her a stern look. Then a forced laugh at Elden's problem. "Are you sure she's worth the trouble? Perhaps we should take her off your hands." There was more rough laughter.

"Many thanks for the offer, but I have some time invested in her and would hate to have to begin again." Elden's hand came up and pushed her bow down, although it went reluctantly. "Besides, she's a healer of some skill and useful… at times." Now there was a warning for her in his voice.

There was more laughter, but one of the men left his place and crossed to whisper in the leader's ear, gesturing at Brillar.

"My friend reminds me that his son took a bad fall from some rocks. His eldest boy, although not yet of man height. If your 'healer' can keep her bow tucked away?"

Brillar held the bow down and relaxed her stance, then nodded.

"Blindfold them," came the command, and a man started forward.

The bow was up at once, aim steady. "If I am to be trusted with healing, I will see where I walk," she said firmly.

Elden simply shrugged at the leader, who laughed even more.

"Well said, for a woman, well said," he replied, but there was a sneer in his voice. "Put down the bow then and follow *if you can.*" The last words were a challenge. With a gesture, he gathered his men and started off at a run.

Elden groaned and took off, with her trailing.

*** 17 ***

The Rovers ran at a steady pace; if Elden and Brillar hadn't been hardened, they would have fallen behind. "And that," puffed Elden, "would never do," as he muttered spells to renew them as they ran.

It was two hours before they reached an encampment by the only running water they had seen. Elden's spells meant they arrived only slightly out of breath.

"These travelers are welcome among us," the leader called out as the camp stirred. Children came out to stare or hold their mother's legs and peek at them while dogs barked at them from tethers. Men stood as they passed, most dressed in short leggings of animal hide and sandals. Some were bare-chested; others wore sleeveless shirts of cloth or leather. All carried belt knives, but other weapons were evident—swords, long and short, spears and the occasional ax. The leader gestured to the camp as several armed men stepped forward.

"They take no harm here. Obis," he called, and the man came up, "take them to your son."

Obis appeared to be in his thirties, strongly built, with dark eyes and a steady gaze. His arms and chest were heavily tattooed. He led them up a slight hill next to the stream. The camp was in a gently sloping valley. Rovers were camped on both sides of the stream, which was no wider than two paces across but seemed to have a steady flow. The tents nearest the water seemed better than those behind them. All were a good size, however, broad and deep, made of varied materials. Doors and some walls were made of blankets, thick and thin, some whole and some patched. Skins covered the tops of the tents, which were pitched with long branches of a wood Brillar hadn't seen before. Most had flaps at the side facing the stream. There were small fires in front of some of the tents. Glancing around, she could see that cooking seemed to be done at a large, communal fire where an oversized kettle was hung alongside a spit of roasting meat. Women tended the fire and the kettle, and she could see a second fire some distance from the first.

The Rovers seemed a clean people. Brillar had expected a rank odor when she saw the size of the camp, but these people evidently moved away from the tents when they needed to relieve themselves. The clothing she saw around her was dusty but not ragged. In all, she counted more than forty tents around the stream and one farther away. Behind her, there was some activity. When she glanced back, she could see men putting up a small tent set away from the others. A look at Elden, and he said, "A guest tent, I imagine. Away from the others but close enough that they can keep an eye on us."

Obis led them to a large tent, pulled back the flap, and secured it. A woman in her late twenties stood up as they entered, a second knelt by a boy of perhaps eleven who lay motionless on his bedding.

"She's a healer," Obis told them as Brillar moved to the boy's side, thrusting her bow at Elden.

"Our healer," he said, gesturing to the woman who had stood, "much good she has done him." He pushed the woman out of the tent. "And my wife," he gestured to the kneeling woman who looked at Brillar with anxious eyes.

"More light," Brillar told them, "and clean water." To the woman, but quietly, "What herbs do you have?" Seeing them, she shook her head and removed her pack.

"I said *light*; remove the top of the tent if you have to." Obis and Elden scrambled to the task.

Brillar ran her hands over the boy. His body was hot with fever, his breathing harsh, but he was still as she probed. "Ribs, internal injury, his head, how long has it been?"

"Two days." There were tears in his mother's voice.

"Two cups of hot water for herbs. Now!" she snapped when no one moved. She looked at Elden and shook her head.

"It can't be helped. I have to open it." He clenched his jaw but nodded.

Brillar dumped her pack quickly and pulled out the foldbox. A crowd that included the leader had gathered, but she opened the box, pulling out her orb and more herbs. She could hear muttering and astonishment from the small crowd. Cups of hot water were set down near her as she closed the box. She crushed the herbs and moved the orb over them, then set the cups aside.

To his credit, Obis pushed everyone away. "Move back, be still, let the healing be done." A few words from the leader were more helpful. "Everybody, MOVE," he bellowed. They moved.

In the light, Brillar now moved the orb over the boy's chest, muttering spells. Up and down the boy's body, went her hand and the orb, searching for damaged bones and organs. She dipped her fingers in one of the cups of herbs and painted them over his chest and upper belly, still speaking spells. The boy moved slightly and made a small noise in his throat. Still, she moved the orb, holding it over one place, then another. The boy moved his head, and she turned him on his side so he could vomit weakly.

"Hold him like that," she told his mother, "there'll be more."

Now she painted the boy's back with the heated herbs and moved the orb. The boy vomited, again and again; those left nearby moved away at the stench until only the boy's mother remained. Feeling her need, Elden moved away from the crowd and muttered under his breath, renewing her.

Setting the orb down, Brillar took more herbs, rubbed them between her hands then moistened them in with herbal water from a cup.

"Now his head." She smeared the herbs on the bruise at the back of the boy's head, murmuring spells. The deep bruise, swollen and purple, oozed out rank, clotted blood. Brillar took up the orb and spoke spells over his head.

The boy's eyes fluttered, and his mother's hand went to his cheek. "I fell," he said, "tell Da… sorry." His eyes closed in sleep, not in pain. Beside him, his mother looked at Brillar, who nodded. His mother's face crumpled into tears.

Obis was instantly in the tent, his knife in his hand, ready to kill if his son was dead, but he only heard, "He lives, he lives," in choking sobs from his wife.

"We'll need cleaning here and at once," were Brillar's directions. "Water and sweet herbs to clear the air, clean cloths, something for his head."

Someone thrust a rolled blanket into her hands and she placed the boy's head on it gently. "He is to have nothing but herbal teas and broths until I say he is ready." There were nods from husband and wife. Obis looked dumbfounded, stricken. "All others are to be kept away, no excitement for him." More nods. "Your name?" she asked the mother gently.

"Obiswife," was the reply.

"Obiswife? Do you have another name?" she asked quietly. Wife looked at husband, and he nodded.

"Norrel," was the soft answer.

"Well then, Norrel, you should rest now. A few hours," she said kindly, "I'll need to watch him."

As they spoke, the woman who had stood when she first entered the tent had come in and cleaned what she could. A girl also joined them, carrying a boiling pot of sweet herbs. Setting it down, she fanned it with a large feather, sweeping the scent through the area.

The first woman looked astonished and sputtered the question, "Then he will live?"

Brillar smiled at her. "He will. Another day, and he would have been beyond anyone's skill." The woman looked at her sharply, but Brillar kept a steady smile. "You did very well to keep him alive for two days."

The woman flustered at that but said nothing. "Will you keep watch with me while Norrel sleeps?" The woman looked surprised but nodded. The breach that could have occurred between the two women was prevented in the next few hours. The woman, who insisted her name was "Widowanlis," kept nodding.

"I have heard that there are great schools for healers," she said, "away from the Wild, but none born here leave the Wild."

Brillar kept assuring her that she had done well. "Perhaps you can show me the herbs you use here, and we can see what to make of them." That was readily agreed to.

Exhausted, Norrel slept for six hours and woke with a start. "My son," were her first words.

"Better and resting," was the reply.

It was full dark when Brillar took herself away, going out to a fire where food was being prepared and eaten.

Without knowing, or, for that matter, caring, she went right to the principle fire where people were slicing meat from a roast and cut a piece of meat from the spitted animal, creating a stir. Glancing around, she located Elden and went to sit with him, noticing as she did, that the circle contained only men.

Too late to worry about that, she thought and took a bite of the meat.

"Since when does a woman sit with us?" shouted one of the group, standing as he spoke.

"Since she healed my son," said Obis, also standing, staring the first man down. "Norrel and I," there was another stir, "Norrel and I are forever in her debt. Who would speak otherwise?" He glared at the assembled men.

"I lead here," came a third voice, "and let no one forget it." The man they had identified as the leader of the Rovers stood. "Unless there is a challenge." His tone was severe. The other men took their seats.

"These people are outsiders, unused to our ways. The woman has done us a service. Obis' son will live. For tonight, she sits with us. Tomorrow, is for the dawn." He sat back down.

Brillar began to shift. Elden steadied her, his hand on her arm was enough, and stood slowly, first looking at the headman for permission.

"My woman meant no offense, for we are strangers here. If there are more who need healing, that also is for the dawn. For now, I ask permission for us to withdraw and rest."

"Well said. You have our leave," was the reply.

Elden dragged Brillar up by the elbow to some muted laughter and led her off to an area a short distance from the tents. He had retrieved her pack and spread blankets under a hastily made tent erected for them by the Rovers.

She had barely passed from the firelight, Elden still holding her elbow, when she wrenched it away from him, muttering. He could only wait for the inevitable, which came as they reached their tent, some distance from the fire.

"'My woman' you say? 'My woman'? And, *my lord,* will you now beat me with the flat of your sword? 'My woman' indeed. To be treated this way? Denied a place at the fire? 'My woman'?" She was in high dudgeon, but she kept her voice controlled.

"If my lady Brillar would remember where we are and who those people are out there, and continue to *keep her voice down*, I think all will be well. I hadn't expected you out so soon, or I would have warned you. The local wives did, however, make some provision for you here." He pulled a cloth off a basket, showing her fruits, tender roasted meat, flatbread with honey, and a flask of wine.

"A woman brought it all to the tent earlier. The wine is a bit harsh, but it should suffice. You've had a difficult day. The customs of these Rovers are nothing like the ones I'm familiar with, and I didn't have time to warn you about them."

Seeing what was provided, Brillar was somewhat mollified. The meat was still warm, the wine a bit harsh but more warming, the bread and honey, perfect. Fresh fruit was a real treat because they had nothing but dried fruit in their packs.

"I thought you said there were no fruit trees in the Wild," she questioned, keeping her voice down.

"None that I ever saw," he replied. "But then I've never seen all of the Wild. We kept to a small area, Brother Verian and I. Even the Rovers haven't seen all there is. These Rovers keep their woman obedient to the men. You need to be careful. As to the rest of the Wild," idly, he took a piece of fruit, "they've been telling me stories of a great expanse of sand to the southwest, with dunes that seem to have marched inward from the sea. And huge areas of stone where nothing grows and you have to carry all the water you need because there are no springs or pools anywhere. There is no shade there, and the sun is so intense that thirst will overtake you in a day."

"I want no great areas of stone, but the sea? That would be a sight." Brillar stretched, yawned, and lay back on a blanket. She was asleep in minutes.

It's a good thing, he thought, as he covered her with a blanket, *that she didn't hear the sport that was made of her before she came to the fire. Or what I had to answer in order to be accepted.* He stretched out and fell quickly asleep.

He woke in the morning to find her already at Obis' tent, checking on his son, and went out with some of the men to hunt, although he decided to withhold his true skills.

At Obis' tent, the boy was still asleep, but his breathing was even and rhythmic, and his face, which had been ashen, held some color. His head, when she probed it, was mending.

"He won't die then, lady?" another of the family's children, perhaps age seven, asked her.

She smiled, reached out, and stroked the child's cheek. "No, he won't die. He will be around to pester you for a long time," she teased.

The little girl just nodded solemnly, then reached for her and planted a kiss on her cheek. "Thank you, lady," she said and ran off, leaving the healer warmed by her gesture.

Norrel came in with hot water and a cloth. "May I wash him?" she asked.

"His legs and arms perhaps, but I would leave the rest for another day." Brillar sat back as the woman began wiping the boy's legs carefully.

"Did you really go to the men's fire last night? I heard it from others but… did you really go?"

"I really went," Brillar replied, checking the boy's signs as his mother worked.

There was wonder in Norrel's voice. "Women have been beaten for even going *near* the men's fire after dark. Did he beat you? Your man Elden?"

"As if he would dare," she replied tartly.

Norrel sat down sharply, taking a deep breath, letting the words come out in a rush. "Then it's true? That there are other ways? I worry about Ralla. She's already promised, and I don't like the choice the elders made, but I have no voice. I don't wish anyone for myself but Obis, but the pairings they sometimes make, and the girls so young…" She came to a sudden halt, embarrassed. "Truly, there are other ways?" she asked, recovering her breath.

"Many other ways," Brillar assured her and settled back, satisfied that her patient was in a healthy sleep. "My home is to the north. Families there sometimes encourage certain of their older children to make a selection, but no one is forced. Before we left…" She stopped a moment, remembering her family and the wedding they had missed. "Before we left, my elder brother, who had cast an eye on many fine young women, finally made his decision and asked for the hand of one. I knew her, studious and with a strong mind. She may have helped him make his 'decision' because I think she had settled on him long before he knew it."

"So a woman can make a choice?"

"She can make half the choice and hope the other chooses her in return." The exchange left Norrel thoughtful.

Widowanlis came to the tent later in the morning, standing stiffly outside the tent.

"Your pardon, but if you could help me?"

Brillar stood at once. "Any help you need will be given freely."

Widowanlis relaxed visibly. "It's my gran'ther. He can barely walk. Can you help him?" Her question was timid, but Brillar gestured for her to lead the way. The widow took her to a small tent, perhaps twelve feet square, behind the tents at the stream.

The man she found lying on a padded cot was thin and grey-haired.

"Gran'ther? I've brought the new healer," the woman said loudly, knowing he was hard of hearing.

Brillar knelt to look at the man, whose joints were swollen and barely flexible. A quick examination, a probing, and a few words, then she stood and stepped aside to speak to Widowanlis.

"We call it joint ill. It afflicts elders everywhere. There is no cure, but there are brews that will ease the swelling and the pain. First, we give him what I carry, then, if you'll help me, I may be able to find local herbs that will be of value."

Widowanlis quickly brewed a tea with Brillar's herbs and made sure her grandfather drank all of it. "Rest now, gran'ther. We go to collect herbs." The man had barely spoken while Brillar was present. Now he just grunted at his granddaughter.

Widowanlis gathered a sack then called to an unoccupied young man to accompany them. At Brillar's look, she said, "Women don't gather without a protector."

They went upstream, away from the encampment, keeping an eye on the ground as the man watched for danger. As far as Brillar could tell, the women here never touched weapons. Widowanlis pointed out the herbs she used. Each time they found a plant that was new to her, Brillar reached deep into it, probing leaves, flowers, and roots. Several that she thought would be helpful were new to her companion. Some, she dug up whole, handing them to Widowanlis to examine and put into a sack. Others had their leaves or flowers removed to be wrapped in cloth. She kept up a steady stream of conversation with Widowanlis, explaining the use and preparation of each plant. She also asked questions.

"Why are you called Widowanlis? Is that a proper name?"

"Until two years past, I was Anliswife," replied the woman proudly. "Anlis was a fine hunter, so strong, so brave. But a stern man. I felt his hand many a time when I didn't behave properly." Her tone was somber. "Still, it was a good pairing, although we had no children."

"And now?" She reached for a plant with a thick stem.

"I am permitted to stay with my gran'ther as I have some skill in healing, taught by the elder woman who was our healer. She died these five years ago."

"She taught you very well," Brillar said, and Widowanlis blushed. "But you said, 'permitted to stay?' I don't understand."

"There's no man to hunt for me, but I have family to care for, my gran'ther. Anlis was killed in a hunt for irex. My gran'ther was a good hunter, but he can't go out with the men any longer. If I wasn't a healer, we would be cast out, or worse." She lowered her head. "I have only a little skill with snares. We eat what we are given. That is all. To be cast out..."

Worse? Brillar was angry, but she kept it to herself and said quietly, "Isn't there a wifeless man who might wish to marry you?"

Widowanlis' voice held shock. "No one would ask me. Not after I was wed to Anlis! It's forbidden. If there had been children, another man might be permitted to take me, but I was barren. 'A woman with a child is a woman useful' say the elders. Another woman might be skilled in basket making and be useful, but a woman with a child has proved her value."

"Suppose a young woman's man is killed soon after they marry. What then?"

"Sometimes she's traded to a new band. We have a gathering every two years. If someone at the gathering wants her, she'll be traded for cloth goods, iron, or even a different woman."

"And before a gathering?"

Widowanlis glanced at their guardian, who was a dozen paces away. Still, she lowered her voice. "You saw that there was one tent set apart? A small one?" Brillar nodded.

"She is there."

"She?" Brillar dreaded the answer.

"As you say, her man was killed soon after they were joined. Until the gathering, she will be used."

"Used?" She managed to keep the horror out of her voice.

Widowanlis' voice dropped to a whisper, "Used by the men. For sport. Or by young men not yet wed."

Brillar kept her face bent toward the grasses to hide her outrage. When she felt she could control herself, she said, "She can't return to her parents? Learn a skill making her worth her keeping? Or stay with them until a gathering?"

Widowanlis' voice showed her shock. "That is not done! Once she was wed, she belonged to her husband."

Brillar sat heavily and patted the ground beside her. "Have you ever wished that things could be different?" She kept her tone light, pretending unconcern.

"They are different in your country?" asked the widow.

"Many things are different in my country," was the easy reply.

"Well," Widowanlis glanced again at their guardian, "there is a man in the village whose wife died in a wolf attack when she strayed a bit too far searching for tubers. His daughter brought the sweet herbs?" Brillar nodded. "She is young, but he has two younger. He has looked at me with pleasure, I think, and I at him." She stopped, blushing. "He's a fine man and strong. He doesn't go to the pleasure woman; he just looks at me." She blushed more deeply. "I burn for him and he for me, I think. But it is forbidden."

"Have you spoken to him? Asked him, perhaps, what he would do if there was a choice for you both?"

She shook her head vigorously. "Forbidden."

"But you've exchanged looks; you feel for each other. The children need a mother, and it seems you would be a good choice."

"They are fine children. The girl studies healing a bit with me; the others are sometimes found underfoot at my tent. I have come to care for all three."

"Perhaps if the girl or one of the younger children were to speak to their father?"

Widowanlis lowered her head.

A few moments of quiet for the woman's pain and Brillar said, "It seems to me that we have all we need if I've gathered correctly. Now I'll show you the preparations, and you can show me what you have." They nodded cheerfully at their guardian and returned to the tents where they found Norj sitting on his bed. They spent part of the afternoon preparing herbs. Some, they set to dry, roots were pounded and boiled, flowers and leaves steeped in boiling water. When the first of the new preparations were ready, they added honey and gave them to Norj.

"He'll need the tea four times a day. We should see a result in his trouble quickly."

Widowanlis nodded gratefully, then asked, "There is a child you might see? I set her arm, but if a true healer could look at her?"

Brillar smiled and nodded.

The little girl was about four. Her arm was bound by strips of cloth and fastened to her chest. She pulled away from a strange woman at first, but Brillar reached out with soothing and was rewarded with a bit of a smile. An examination showed that the bone was well set and already healing.

"You did very well; the child's arm is mending beautifully." Her words were met with a broad smile from her companion and the child's mother.

Since she had agreed to one, she found there were others to be looked after. A child with a fever, a woman with stomach pains; she went with a smile wherever Widowanlis led her then returned to check on her first patient.

"Tonight, dine with us at the women's fire. For company," said Widowanlis at last.

When she found Elden coming back from a hunt, she told him about the invitation. "Good, it will keep you out of trouble," was all he had to say.

*** 18 ***

Norrel and Widowanlis led Brillar to the fire and space was made for her at the circle. The women's fire was some distance away from the men's but much more cheerful. *Or perhaps*, she thought honestly, *it was just my presence last night.* Stew in great bowls was handed 'round with wooden spoons for utensils. There was light chatter all around the fire and she was included, although there were some references that she didn't understand. Glancing up at one point, Brillar saw another figure, set apart by a few paces, her back to the group. Seeing the direction of her glance, Widowanlis whispered, "The pleasure woman."

Brillar bent her head, shaking it angrily, then stood abruptly, placing her bowl on the ground. Leaving the fire, she strode to the girl, who looked at her in astonishment.

"Your mother wants you by the fire." There was command in her quiet voice. Taking the girl by the arm, she half led, half dragged her to the circle. Locating her mother by the expression on her face, she sat the girl firmly beside her. Brillar returned to her seat and took up eating as if nothing unusual had happened. Across the fire, an arm went around the girl, and she was pulled to her mother.

There was no more chatter that night.

The next day, Pral sat up, demanding food and complained when 'food' was only light soups.

"You, young man," said Brillar firmly, "have made a mess of your head and your insides. Light soups for two days, then soup with meat, then you can have real food."

"We mean to enforce that, Pral," said his father. He knelt to put his arms around his son, and Brillar heard him whisper, "We almost lost you." He straightened. "So you will behave!" The boy settled back meekly.

Brillar went back to Widowanlis and spent the morning teaching her more about the herbs they had gathered. Norj declared that he was feeling better and was able to step outside. "To be shut away, having to listen to all this chatter is unhealthy for a hunter," he proclaimed. He was able to hobble to another tent, where an older hunter sat on a crude bench. Behind him, the women smothered laughter.

In the afternoon, the two visited the woman who had stomach pains, finding her up from her bed and cheerful. They were back at Widowanlis tent when a woman came with a boy who had, that morning, fallen into thorn brush and taken deep scratches which his mother had already washed.

"They will fester," Widowanlis said, "without an ointment." She took a covered bowl from a shelf and applied it to the scratches. The woman sat with them and chatted for a while. When she left, Widowanlis explained how the ointment was made and how long it kept. Brillar nodded, assuring her that it looked and smelled like something she also prepared and used.

Brillar was again asked to join the women's fire and was happy to find that the 'pleasure woman' sat with her mother. That evening, instead of keeping to one place, some of the women came to push Widowanlis aside and sit next to Brillar, quietly asking questions about her home, her life there, and the bow all had heard she carried. One finally asked, "Did you really fire an arrow at Sarl?"

"The headman is Sarl? Well, not at him, but near enough to his foot to make him cautious." Those within hearing could only stare at her.

Elden looked questioningly when she came back late to the tent, but she was only thoughtful and in no mood for conversation. She fell asleep quickly.

***

Before dawn the following day, Brillar was shaken awake. "Up and quickly," urged Elden, shoving her pack and bow at her, "and move. Something's happening."

When the pair stood, they were confronted by Rovers.

"You are to leave, now," came Sarl's stern, angry voice.

"We're ready." Elden's reply was calm, but she could feel his tension.

"Without the woman," came another voice.

"She has brought disorder here. She will be punished for everyone to see," Sarl stated with finality.

Reaching out, finding only anger around them, Elden made the only answer he could, unleashing a ring spell that caught the men by surprise. The spell was dark, smoky, mixed with dancing lights, and men around them dropped like stones. He drew in more mana. A spear whizzed past them, thrown from some distance.

"Run," he shouted, and they sprinted downslope toward open land. There were five miles or more between them and the Rovers when Elden brought them to a halt. He had revitalized them several times during their flight; now he grabbed her arm, spinning her around.

"What, by all that is Good, have you been up to?" he shouted; there was fire in his voice.

"Healing," she shouted back, "I have been up to healing."

"And something more, I think, you little fool," he continued to shout.

That brought her up short. Elden had never spoken to her that way before. Taking a deep breath to calm herself, she answered, "Widowanlis and Norrel asked questions, and I answered." She was still defiant. "Norrel's daughter, Ralla, is only seven, and already promised to a bully of a boy twice her age. She asked if it was so everywhere, and I answered. Others asked and were answered as well."

Elden could only turn in a circle. "So you just *answered*? By all that stands in the Light… just answered?" He stalked away, leaving her to follow.

He set a hard pace, putting distance between them and any who might try to follow them. It was nearly dark when he stopped. She pulled up behind him, holding her side. He had offered her no help during the day and no time for comfort. She was tired, dusty, hungry, and thirsty. He gave her nothing, not even the ease of a fire. Brillar dumped her pack, which had been hastily stuffed, relieved to find everything there. She took a long pull of her water flask, finding it close to empty. Opening the foldbox, she added water to the flask then took out rations and a blanket; her other blanket had been left behind.

There had been no words between them since Elden's outburst, and for some reason, she felt lost. Neither slept well, despite the Ward.

It was the same in the morning, just silence as they sat and ate where they had slept, then, Elden said, "I should never have brought you." His voice was so low, she could hardly hear it.

"Then I would be dead already, torn apart by dire wolves." Her voice was just as quiet. "You know I would have come anyway."

"Then we are, both of us, fools."

They sat silently for a time; Elden stood and adjusted his pack. "We need to move. The spell will have held them and left them too weak to follow, but there were others." Both put on the leather armor they had placed in their packs.

He did set a hard pace but gave her support when she needed it. He even stopped and allowed her to dig some of the tubers she recognized, and she hid a smile, knowing there would be a fire that night.

That afternoon they had to push their way through brush with heavy thorns. Elden thrashed at it with a short sword, but they were still heavily scratched and bleeding, leather armor or no, when they entered an open area.

"That, I think, was the barrier marking the end of the Rover's territory. That's what I was told as we hunted, but there are other bands of Rovers. We've pushed hard, even with magic, and I think a bit of rest will do us some good."

Brillar was busy with healing spells and nodded her agreement. They were quiet as they made a fire and ate. She waited for him to say what was on both their minds.

"I knew you were troubled there," Elden finally began, "by the treatment of the women. I had few dealings with Rovers when I stayed with Brother Verian and none since. I thought the bands had similar laws, although codes of behavior would be better terms for them. In the band of Rovers I met, men and women both hunted. These Rovers were different. They may have seemed harsh to us, but this is a harsh land. You were troubled the first night; there were other things?"

As she told him about the way women were named and wed to men without their consent, he nodded. She went on to tell him of Widowanlis and how she was treated even though another man seemed ready to have her, and he nodded again. When she came to the treatment of the pleasure woman, Brillar nearly broke Control. Then she related what had happened at the women's fire, and he looked up sharply.

"She was a child," she pleaded, "grief-stricken by the loss of her husband, sent off to be used as a whore? Then traded off like a cow or a goat? No. I would do that again."

Elden stared into the fire. "I'm sorry." She looked at him quizzically. "They told me about the pleasure tent when we went out to hunt, thinking I might want to use it, seeing that I had such a… difficult woman. We should have left then, but the boy was still so ill, and I knew you wouldn't come away easily or without explanation. We're well away from them." He looked at her ruefully. "You caused quite a disturbance. Sometimes, apprentice, you are a great deal of trouble."

Somehow, that soothed her. Both slept better that night.

They had been traveling south; now Elden suggested they head a bit toward the west, staying along the thorn hedge until it stopped. The hedge was apparently fed by an underground stream that kept it alive, if not green and healthy. Keeping it to one side, gave them some protection from attack as few animals would willingly push through the barrier. Still, they moved with caution.

Lessons were few in the next few days. Constant use of far-sight, ongoing concern about attack was draining. Draining but useful.

"Elden?" She drew up.

"I see it. A mana pool to the south and farther west. Spawning." He stretched his sight. "Fire sprites."

"Sprites?" Her voice was delighted, lilting, expectant.

"Yes, I know, you've heard of them," he said wearily, "and wanted to see one. Now you will. If we keep to the hedge, they'll be aware of us, and we'll be within their range. We could step away now, move around them, but there may be other trouble. Hold out six arrows. There's an Item spell you haven't learned."

Brillar held out the arrows while Elden cast a frost spell on the arrowheads, which became white with frost.

"They're most susceptible to cold. Use those first. How many will spawn from the pool is always unpredictable. As I told you, sprites range in size. Take closer ones first, and we'll try to get past them along the hedge. We fight side by side today. Be wary. The dancing lights can be mesmerizing."

The fire sprites were quick to notice them and Brillar was slow to fire at first. They might be dangerous, but their dancing lights were as beautiful as—

"Now!" Elden shouted, and she let fly at the nearest sprite, then the next, as the first crumpled to the ground. A third fell to a frost

arrow. Beside her, Elden's hands cracked with frost as he lobbed bolts at larger sprites farther away.

"Slide along the fence," came his command as another arrow struck its target. As they moved along the fence, she used her last two frost arrows and began using those without the spell. Her targets proved more difficult to drop, taking two or three arrows to fall as Elden kept up his barrage.

"Refresh," he shouted, and she sent arrows as quickly as she could, dropping the two closest sprites before hearing his crack of frost again. The sprites were in the distance now, visible but no longer attacking. Elden urged her along the fence.

"We're out of danger from them now. They usually stay by the pool unless they sense a threat. You, apprentice, were slow with an arrow." His voice was stern.

"You were right. They were beautiful. It was hard to focus. I'm sorry." They moved farther to the west in silence. "The Item spell you cast on my arrows?" she asked finally as they continued to move along the fence.

"I did say Item is useful. There's a spell for fire as well that I think you can learn with your skill, although easy spells don't last long, and the others are beyond your reach at present. If they're needed, you will have to rely on my casting."

"Yes, Master." Her voice was almost humble, and he gave her a sharp glance.

"You," he said, "are not to be trusted when you are meek."

"I only thought that we should stop soon. I need more arrows from the foldbox."

He looked at her, concerned. "How many in the quiver?"

"I began with twenty; there are six now."

"Then we stop. Even these thorn bushes provide some shade. From now on, I want thirty arrows in the quiver at all times. If more can be safely held in the pack, place more there. How many do you carry in the foldbox?"

"I began with five hundred full arrows, and there should be close to four hundred now and perhaps five hundred more arrowheads. 'Shafts can be made, arrowheads must be carried,' was the advice of my instructor."

"Shafts can be made if there's the right type of wood. When we can, we'll replenish your supply. Perhaps a thousand mounted shafts will do." She raised her eyebrows at the number but said nothing. Dried wellis meat had to satisfy them at noon when they stopped to deal with the arrows, but as they ate, the ground began to shake. Brillar bolted to her feet.

"Down," yelled Elden, grabbing her hand and pulling her to the ground beside him. Around them, under them, the land twisted and heaved. They could hear cracking sounds near them and slid a bit to one side as the ground beside them tilted downwards. The rumbling, the shifting of the land, seemed to go on forever, tossing and bruising them. When it was finally over, Elden moved cautiously to his knees to survey what had happened, then pulled her upward.

She was unsteady as she rose to kneel beside him. "What?" she asked shakily.

"A tremblor they call it, or a quaking," Elden replied, "not that I've been near one before. Now I understand the stories I've heard." A smaller tremblor sent them to the ground again, but it was over in seconds. They rose a second time, standing to look around.

The landscape had changed. It was still scrub and dry, but there were holes in the earth and areas where the ground had been uplifted sharply. In the direction they had been traveling, a vast fissure had opened in the earth. It extended through the thorn brush behind them and out of sight to the south. One side of the crevice stood like a wall, the other tilted downward.

"Our way southwest is blocked. We'll need to go back to the east," Elden said, surveying the damage. "Let's hope this tremblor has shaken out the mana pool." He stopped.

"Thunder?" she asked. The feeling in the ground was not a new tremblor.

"Irex, look there." He pointed south and west. "There must be thousands of them. Look at them."

The irex, larger than cattle and much more dangerous, had been stampeded by the tremblor and were now rushing eastward headlong at and over the fissure in the earth some distance from them. They could hear bellows and squeals in the mad rush as some that tried to jump the breach in the ground missed their steps and fell to their deaths. Dust from the herd and the musty scent of the animals reached them.

"They wander in herds, so there must be water behind them to the west, or there wouldn't be so many. The quaking must have been worse to the west, for them to be running so madly."

The rush of animals went on for at least five minutes, then trickled to just a few animals. Finally, they vanished to the east, and Elden moved off toward the area they had vacated, urging Brillar along.

"We don't dare take one from the herd, but there are many that died as they missed the jump. 'Ware the surroundings, as this much meat will draw wolves and other scavengers." He covered the ground quickly and reached a calf that had died of a broken neck in its jump. A few quick cuts and Elden removed a hind leg from the animal as Brillar stretched her sight to the surroundings.

"Dire wolves from the south," she warned as he finished the cut. Elden hefted the meat and rushed them back to the thorn hedge.

"And from the west, although I don't know if they can cross the gash. And things from the sky." Elden stopped long enough to wash the blood from the raw meat and speak a cleansing spell, then hurried them past the thorn bushes to the east. He was grinning.

"Fresh meat tonight, and if we are safe enough, perhaps a stew," he said as they moved.

When they reached the site where they had found the sprites, there was nothing to be seen.

"The tremblor must have shifted the mana pool. It should be safe enough for us to camp here," Elden decided, setting down his burden and beginning to remove the meat. With a sigh, Brillar began her 'apprentice task' of gathering firewood and preparing the camp. She took a small kettle out of the foldbox and filled it with water. Spotting some of the plants with tubers, she dug, washed, and sliced them into the kettle. Elden seemed deep in thought.

"Is there a problem?" she asked, busy with the fire.

"We can't eat this much meat before it spoils. There's a spell that will preserve it, but I can't bring it to memory. Not the same spell I wanted for drying the wellis."

"Rest and eat first? Perhaps you'll be able to remember the spell in the morning. Could you teach me the spells for my arrows while we wait for the kettle?"

The lesson was not an easy one to master. It was hours before frost appeared on an arrow, only to disappear quickly. Spells had to be learned in levels, with skill building upon skill.

"This will take some time," she said finally.

"Imagine doing nothing but this all day and nearly every day for three years," Elden grinned, "that's how I learned."

"Before I even think about it, I will need food, and the stew, poor as it is, is ready." Bowls and spoons came out for the stew, while some of the meat was spitted to roast slowly during the night. Both gathered what firewood could be found and stacked it high. Elden set a Ward before they slept.

"The scent of roasting meat may draw something to us despite the dead irex. Be ready."

As the sun dropped, the night, as always, grew chilly and they wrapped in blankets to sleep. An alert from the Ward brought her suddenly awake near midnight. Elden had already sent a firebolt at what threatened as she nocked an arrow.

"An old wolf, from the smell of it," Elden said. "Probably too old to keep up with the pack and too stubborn to die. They're scavengers and I sent a warning bolt to tell this one to scavenge the irex."

"And now?" She stared into the night.

"It will probably avoid us. Go back to sleep."

She did but slept only lightly until dawn. She woke to find him looking pleased.

"The spell came to me in the night. The meat is preserved and will keep for at least a week, I think. There is another spell for longer use, but it still won't come to me. 'What is seldom used is soon lost,' Verian always told me. Like the bow, magic must be practiced."

They settled the camp and began the day.

"If the map I saw at the Brotherhood is correct, the mountains in the east are the greatest, although there are others." She looked at him happily. "Where there are mountains," he said sternly, "there is increased danger. Blood kites, great cats, harpies, rock falls; the dire wolves will still be with us. We will move with caution, not with haste. For now, we will continue at the edge of these thorn bushes."

Whenever they stopped for a meal or a night, Brillar continued her Item lessons. The frost and fire now stayed with the arrowheads long enough to be useful. Twice during the day, they spotted small herds of irex because the large herd had fragmented to graze. Once, they waited for a day when a large group of irex decided that there was good grass around the thorn hedge and others grazed to the south. A day of Item spells was useful. They kept far-sight alert for anything unusual.

The hedge went slightly uphill in their direction of travel. Once, it bent north and split, one section going to the north and one east.

"I think I was wrong about the brush following a natural stream. It seems that a watercourse must have been dug at some point, or the hedging would follow one track."

"There is water nearby, though," she replied. "Perhaps fresh?" Elden nodded and they walked toward the water sign cautiously, then stopped short.

"What is it?" she asked.

"Tell me what you see." She stretched her sight into the water.

"I can see something; its body is sunken in the water near a rock. The pool seems shallow, but I think it's deeper than it looks. What is it?"

Elden just shook his head. "I have never seen or heard of anything like it, but I sense it's waiting. Look how green the grass is at the side of the pool. A trap, I think, for the hungry and unwary. Whatever it is, it must be an ambush hunter, one that waits for prey that comes close and then takes it with a lunge. Well, we're not unwary. It will have to wait for something else." They returned to the hedge to move eastward.

***19 ***

It was only a day later when he stopped in mid-morning. "Rovers near the hedge and on this side of it." He sighed. "We'll have to move to the south and around them."

She reached out in the direction of the Rovers. "Elden, wait. There's something familiar here, and see them? They're wary but not angry."

"Bored with my company and lessons," he asked with a smile.

"A little closer?" she pleaded.

Another quarter mile and she stopped, reaching, then, "Widowanlis?" He stared at her, waiting. "She was the healer with the Rovers. I spent a lot of time with her. Closer, please?"

They moved cautiously along the hedge. "Can you see them?" Brillar asked anxiously.

"Perhaps five or six families, children," he replied.

A few more paces and Brillar brightened. "Widowanlis, Norris and Obis and their children. Others I think I know."

"Slowly, apprentice," he cautioned. "We'll approach where they can see us and light a fire. If someone comes out, we'll see."

They topped a slight rise, gathered some thorn twigs, and lit the fire. A child, playing near a tent, tugged at a man's leg and pointed. There was a slight commotion in the camp, then the man walked out to greet them, stopping downslope of the fire.

"Obis?" Brillar called out. She was answered by a wave. The man turned, and she heard him shout, "The healer!" excitedly.

Without waiting for Elden's word, Brillar sprinted down the hill as the woman she knew as Widowanlis rushed from the camp, waving. The two women embraced as Elden joined them and clasped Obis' arm.

"Well met," said Obis, "well met. Come, join us."

The women were already heading to the camp and they followed. There were five families gathered there.

"I am no longer Widowanlis," Brillar was told at once, "we have decided that women should keep their names." She took Brillar to a man standing quietly with the girl she remembered. "This is my husband, Forge, and I am Wanla," she said proudly.

"Welcome, healer. We have a lot to thank you for," said Forge.

Wanla took her by the hand to introduce her to all the families. Sarif and Jerrin and their daughter, Kylin, who had been the 'pleasure woman' Brillar had dragged to the women's fire, were there, as well as Obis and Norrel with Pral, Ralla, and their younger children. Now she was introduced to Inlee and Lanna, whose four-year-old Minly she had examined in the Rover camp, plus Cham and Arda, whose infant daughter, Orali, clung to her mother.

"How did this all happen?" Brillar asked.

Wanla sobered. "That is a tale for telling later. You'll stay with us? At least for the night?"

Brillar exchanged a glance with Elden, who nodded.

"We'll stay."

Wanla embraced her.

***

Obis and Forge had taken Elden aside. Obis began, "The camp is a hasty one. We left hurriedly after you were threatened. Sarl intended Brillar for the pleasure tent as punishment for what she told the women. We didn't join them and were glad when you got her away."

Elden nodded grimly, knowing Brillar would have killed with her bow, then her knife, any who tried to take her. For a second, he wondered if any Life spells could have other purposes.

"That spell you used," said Forge laughing, "had most unconscious until mid-afternoon. Then they staggered around like they were drunk when they roused. It was dusk when they were sober enough to think. By then, some of us were decided."

Sarif approached them. "A word?" and they nodded.

"We left the others with only the food we could carry easily and not much of that. If the mage could help us in a hunt?"

Elden nodded. "That I'll do and soon. There are scattered herds of irex to the west and we can take several. If we find a small group, I can call them from a distance and weaken any who charge so they can be safely killed. But for tonight," he knelt and opened his pack, which was full of meat, "Brillar carries some as well. There should be enough for everyone and we can hunt in the morning."

The men were much more at ease, seeing what was being offered them. They joined the others.

"Norrel found a small pool with no danger and the water is fresh. A spring from the hills perhaps." Brillar waved toward it then turned back to the small group of children she was amusing. She had taken out an arrow and was turning it cold with one spell, then making it flame with a second. "You said I should practice," she said, answering his scowl.

The afternoon went quickly, meat was prepared, and some tubers put into the fire to roast. When all were finished and the children put to rest, the men and women sat together at the fire. Finally, Elden said quietly, "You have a tale to tell?"

All looked at Forge to begin, and he put his arm around Wanla. "When those who fell recovered, they held a council. I had not joined them to take you, so I was not asked to sit with them."

Wanla spoke up, her voice outraged. "They came for *me*. Sarl said that I had spent time with you, too much time, and that I could no longer be trusted. They tried to drag me from my tent." She stopped, and tears ran down her cheeks.

Forge took up the story. "Her gran'ther, you helped him with herbs, got up from his bed and tried to beat the men off. The old man got in a few solid hits before someone pushed him to the ground. He didn't move." He cradled his wife. "One of the men, who had more sense or kindness, spoke up for Wanla, and the men released her so she could care for him, but he was lost."

Wanla straightened. "After that, they left me alone. Forge came to me that night." She patted his knee. "He was so brave to do that. He said that he wanted me, but that there could be no place for us with the clan." Her eyes were bright. "He asked me if there might be others who would join with us to leave the clan. In the morning, the elders took my gran'ther to the resting place for the dead. While they were gone, I went to Norrel and Obis. They were willing. Sarif and Jerrin, I was sure of after you brought Kylin to the fire. Inlee and Lanna, I knew, disliked the way men looked at their daughter and her only a child. Cham and Arda came to *me* when they saw me speaking quietly to others."

Cham took up the story. "Arda had been planned for another, an older man, but he died in a hunt. I went to Sarl with a bribe, three spearheads that I had traded pelts for. I had heard such things were done. Sarl," there was disgust in his voice, "readily agreed to the match. I gave another gift as well, to keep him to his word, a fine irex pelt from an older animal that I took alone on a hunt."

Arda spoke up shyly. "I had watched Cham. I wanted the match." She ducked her head, unused to speaking up in the presence of so many.

"I will not keep silent," said Jerrin, "I will speak my mind and the truth. Kylin was given to a fine young man only six years her elder, and we were happy, but we had also paid a bribe. We agreed to it, Sarif and I."

Sarif shook his head, looking at his wife pleadingly.

"We have left them and their ways. I will tell the truth now for all to hear." He hung his head.

"We paid a bribe that we agreed to after many long discussions. Sarl's wife was dead. There was no woman in the pleasure tent. Sarl wanted me, so the bribe was decided on. I was the bribe." There were startled gasps and movement in the group around the fire. "I will finish my tale," Jerrin said firmly. "I was the bribe. I went to Sarl's tent alone at night. If he promised our daughter to Resh, I would come again twice and once after they were wed. It is not a proud thing I did, but I did it to save my daughter. Then Resh was brought back dead just a few weeks after their marriage and my daughter," she shivered and began to rock to and fro, tears running down her cheeks, "my daughter was dragged, screaming, to the pleasure tent. And there was nothing I could do," Jerrin collapsed, weeping and rocking in the firelight.

Sarif gathered his wife in his arms. "I was a coward that day," he started.

"No, no, never a coward, just bound by might," Obis spoke up, "bound by laws made by a few for everyone."

Sarif stood, pulling Jerrin to her feet. "I will take my wife away now." She leaned against him as they went.

Everyone at the fire sat stunned by what had been said. There was nothing more to say. One by one, couples left silently for their tents while Brillar and Elden gathered blankets, set a Ward, and stretched out by the fire. Soft, muffled sobs came from her.

"They're freed now. They wished to be freed, had waited to be freed," he said into the night, quieting her with words and then with soothing spells. From the other blanket, there was a soft laugh.

"You have a lot to learn about soothing spells," she said, "but for the words, Master, my thanks."

Breakfast at the camp was cheerful even though it was only cold meat and tubers. The men were making ready for what they hoped would be a short and profitable hunt, and the women were striking the tents and packing so they could be close when the hunt was over and they were needed. Brillar was happily getting ready to join the hunt when Elden bent close.

"I wonder if it's wise?" he said. She looked at the hunters. Only two carried bows; the other three had spears. Undeterred, she went over to them.

"Would the archers care to test themselves against a woman?" she asked. Behind her, Elden shook his head and sighed.

"Pick your target," said Cham, unslinging his bow.

"That piece of thorn? A spot of black on it?" she replied, pointing.

Cham nocked an arrow, took a breath, and let fly. His arrow hit above the black. He bowed to her, and she nocked an arrow. It thudded into the branch just below his.

Inlee stared a moment, then said, "The rest will need protection as they move. I can hit an irex, but that twig?"

"Thank you, Master Inlee," Brillar said politely "for I often shoot at twigs, not having the courage to hunt irex."

Her good-natured reply had everyone smiling.

"How do you do it?" Elden whispered in her ear.

"Most men are quite susceptible to flattery," she whispered back, and they set off on the hunt.

The Rovers moved out at a trot with Elden and Brillar behind. The men moved confidently over ground that would have taken the pair half a day to cover. Elden reached out and directed their hunt toward a small group of irex. In minutes, the men in front of them suddenly fell flat at the top of a minor rise. Elden and Brillar followed suit. In front of them and downhill, was a herd of twenty or more of the animals they were looking for. As one, all heads turned to Elden.

"I can call out the ones you want," he said, and there was some discussion. The Rovers were unused to the presence of a mage who could 'call out' an animal.

"Cows with calves, I think, should be left with the herd," Cham offered. "There are four of them. For hide, the larger of the yearlings? That prime bull is near twice the size of the others and his hide could nearly make a tent, but he would be tough."

"The yearlings first then," Brillar put in, "their absence will be less felt." When heads turned toward her, she just shrugged. "I've not hunted irex, but most game animals are the same."

Elden put his mind to one of the yearlings that was already separate from the herd. They all moved backward slightly. The calling took only a few minutes, then the yearling moved around the hill and stood looking stupidly around him. Two bows twanged as one, and he fell before he could make a sound.

Two men hurried to the butchering as Elden called out another animal, which was quickly dispatched. A quiet discussion was held, and it was decided to pack the meat in hides and carry what they could back toward the earlier camp. More hunting would wait for the next day. Before they started, Elden cast a strengthening spell on each individual. They lifted heavy packs of meat with ease.

A few miles away, they met Inlee coming west with their families. The women immediately began to put up the tents, and the older children, Pral and Kylin included, began to cut branches for drying frames. Drying and smoking the meat would take several days, and they planned to take another yearling in the morning.

Another day was spent hunting for the new, small clan, but Elden could see that Brillar was chaffing at the camp activities. The clan would have to stay where it was for some time, drying meat and preparing hides. They needed to be off, although their decision caused distress, especially among the women and children.

When the morning came for them to leave, Wanla stood and spoke for everyone, calling them true friends and asking them to return someday. "We know there are no promises in the Wild, but we will hope to see you sometime again."

Elden and Brillar set off again to the east and still along the fence, moving steadily but with no hurry. In the late afternoon, Elden stopped them again. "Ahead, what can you see?" he asked.

"More Rovers, I think?" she answered him, "but no darkness…"

"Your time with the camp seems to have made a greater impression than we realized. I can see more families, and you're right, no darkness in them. Just caution."

"We should tell them where the others are," she began and was rewarded with a smile.

"That was my thought," he replied.

The camp was a cautious half hour away. Again, they stopped and lit a small fire and waited to be greeted.

"Well met, healer," came the call, and they moved toward the group. The families, Brillar was quick to recognize, were those whose women had sat beside her at the women's fire and asked questions. They stood and waited for the tale. Finally, one of the men, Qala, spoke up.

"When Obis, Forge, and the others left, Sarl decided to tighten his grip on the rest of us. As punishment for all those who had been corrupted, earlier promises of marriage were broken. He demanded that all unwed girls be brought to the men's fire and examined. Girls as young as five had to be taken by their fathers. My daughter is five years old. The children were made to drop their clothing and were examined for flaws in their arms and legs. Unwed young men were paired with some of the girls. Sarl made the pairings. He made one other change, something I think to bind the older men to him. Those men whose wives were barren or could no longer bear children could now have a second woman at their fire. He said that this was true in other camps and would now be the practice of the clan. He bound some of the older girls to his friends and gave others to those whose women were older or to men who were widowed."

"Sarl said all the bindings were now sealed and the younger girls would be wed as they came of age," a woman said angrily. "Five years old!"

"There was worse," said an older woman. "I am Solni, "she said proudly, "such my husband has always called me when we were in private." Her husband came up behind her and slipped an arm around her shoulders. "I have seven children who have lived, and four are with us. After the pairings were made, each joined man was told to bring his wife into the circle. Some had to be dragged, some were screaming. Those who screamed, Sarl slapped. They stopped quickly."

Her husband looked at her proudly. "Solni came into the circle with a straight back and a level gaze for everyone." She smiled back at him, then her face tightened.

"The archer had escaped them, Sarl said, but she had spread discontent and caused a breaking of the clan. Since she was gone, and to remind the women of their place, all women would be punished. He had canes beside him and handed them to our husbands. Those with elderly women were told to seat their wives behind them, but everyone had to watch the punishment. Widowed women, those useful to the clan, weavers, potters, and those who could sew, had to stay and be punished. Each man was to give his wife five strokes." Her voice was voice tight. "Our clothing was stripped from our backs. Sarl took one of the weavers and stripped her back. It seemed to me that he took pleasure in beating her, in hearing her scream."

Overcome, Brillar sank to her knees, her hands over her face, and began to rock in grief. "If I had known I would cause such suffering in the Wild, I would never have come."

"No… no," Solni was beside her. "It was necessary to tell you everything and the weaver is here with us." Brillar leaned against Solni whose arms went around her, comforting.

Elden looked to Qala. "There's more?"

Qala nodded. "Most of us, I think, struck lightly. In my heart, I wept as I struck and wept again in our tent as I washed Solni's back. She was fortunate, though. Two of the men, they are with us with their families, struck too lightly, and Sarl took notice. He shoved their men aside and began the punishment again." He dropped his voice, shaking his head. "I will always hear the screams" Elden put a hand to the man's shoulder and used what spells he knew to calm him. "We gathered what we could carry on drag sleds and left at night, worried what Sarl would do if he found more leaving. But now, if the healer will attend the women?"

Elden looked toward Brillar. She was on her feet and had pulled Solni's shirt up to see her back. He could read the anger in her face. A few words, and they went to the tents to deal with the injuries all the women had suffered.

"The others?" Elden's attention was pulled back to Qala. "Have you seen where the others went? We want to join them if they'll have us."

"They're to the west and camped. We hunted with them, and it will take days for them to deal with the meat and skins. If you go west along the fence, you'll find them easily." Qala went to spread the news to the others.

Elden watched Qala pensively as the others dispersed to their chores. He needed time to think; he walked out a little way from the camp and found a small, safe place to sit alone and watch the sky. Elden was nearly as dismayed as his apprentice. To calm himself, he let his mind drift, wishing he was truly alone.

When, he thought, *have I been alone since I took on this troublesome apprentice? Perhaps on a ride with Jez? I hope he is safe in a barn with Bright near him. She'll soon be in foal by him if he is allowed near her or if he can break a hole in the wall between them.* He took a stick and began to draw arcane words in the sandy soil. *Alone? When was I last alone? Jez was always company of a sort. Laurenfell and its town were full of people. When have I wanted to be alone since I took on this apprentice?* He looked back at the camp. *So much courage and so much softness. Why would I want to be alone?* He sat for some time, silent and thoughtful.

"Master?" her voice quietly interrupted, and he straightened. He could feel her stretching out with soothing, felt the anguish behind her spells. This was not over for her.

"Apprentice," he answered and stood, dusting himself off with a quick spell.

"They've all been attended to and all are able to travel. Qala's sent off a runner to let the others know more are coming if they'll be accepted. He should reach the camp tonight and be back tomorrow." Her voice was stiff with anger and pain.

"Well done."

"They want us to stay with them for the night."

Elden took a deep breath. "A fine idea. I'm sure you've had a tiring afternoon." In fact, the day was getting late, and a fire had been started at the camp.

"They have little, so I gave them the smoked wellis meat from my pack. We have plenty in your pack."

The camp that night was subdued. The women whose backs had been deeply lashed were still stiff, but a good rest, free from pain, and more healing in the morning would care for that.

Around the fire, the Rovers talked again about leaving the clan. "Only four of our children are with us," Solni began. "Our son with us is sixteen. After he witnessed the punishment, he told his father he was leaving the clan alone if need be." She looked at him proudly, and he flushed.

"I was told that night that I would marry one of the girls when she was of age. That will be three years. In three years, she may change, but I don't like her ways. And I never went to the pleasure tent." He ducked his head, and there was good-natured chuckling around the fire.

"Ah," thought Brillar, "here is one who can help Kylin heal."

"His brother is fourteen and was sent as a runner to the other camp. He was also promised that night but would have to wait for ten years for a bride. Most of the older girls were promised to much older men. Sarl stood and said that since his wife was dead, he would take the eldest to him at once. She and her family are with us. Our eldest son's wife is near birthing and unable to travel. They may join us." A sharp glance from Brillar and she responded, "No, she was too close to her time for the punishment. But our eldest daughter, she was punished. I think she would have come with us because she has been joined for five years and has no children, but there was no chance." Solni leaned against her husband.

"Her husband," he scowled, "is a brutish man and a friend of Sarl's. So many times, I have seen what he did to her and have been able to do nothing but send the healer to attend to her. She had spirit as a child and when she was wed, but it's gone now. The night the women were punished, her husband seemed to take pleasure in it, striking her to the ground bleeding, then dragging her away. He'll soon have a new woman at his fire; that was Sarl's promise. I may be able to go back by stealth and get her away." He dropped his head.

Brillar, shaken by what they had all suffered, stood suddenly, took a blanket, and left them.

Elden rose silently, waving them to stay seated, and went after her.

"I want no company," she said darkly as he approached. She gathered the blanket around her. Elden took the Ward from his belt pouch, put it down, and settled in for the night some distance from her.

*** 20 ***

Before dawn, he heard her shift and stand. He looked up. Somehow she had retrieved her bow and pack from the campfire during the night without waking him. Now she was beginning to walk southeast around the sleeping camp, settling her pack as she moved. Elden took up the Ward, snatched his things from the camp and followed her in a rush. He took up her stride behind her as she cut back to the north and re-met the thorn brush, still going east toward the mountains. Her distress was a sharp pain cutting through him.

He watched her from behind, seeing her avoid those plants that he said were dangerous, approaching then leaving a small spring without drinking, although he could sense her thirst. He knew she was reaching out with far-sight, although not matching his and finding nothing dark. And he could tell she was tired but couldn't bring herself to stop. The sun was high when he decided she had punished herself enough, overtook her, and forced her to a stop.

"A rest is called for," he announced, "with water and food." She looked at him blankly as he pushed his water flask into her hand. She looked at it dully, then drank.

"And this," Elden said, "looks like as good a place as any for some food." He pushed her down gently and sat with her. He waited until he could feel her pain ease a bit.

"Magic and healing among soft hills and green fields are not all the things in the world," he began softly, calmly. "There is much more to be learned, much more to be seen and felt. You've had some difficult lessons." He handed her some trail rations and took some for himself. "It's hard to see people treated like animals," he went on quietly, and her head came up. "I've seen it before, more times than anyone should have to see it, and have had to walk away, leave it behind me. Leave it to others to change if there was to be change. Now, here in the Wild, I have an apprentice who sees the wrong and makes it change. That is none of my instruction. There are times when the apprentice is the Master."

They sat in silence for a long time. Evening found them in the same place but busy with a fire. Tubers had been seen nearby and been dug. They were roasting in the ashes and what was left of the irex meat was on sticks above the fire being turned, again and again. They had both relaxed into the simple routine and it soothed them.

In the morning, Brillar was more her old self. Elden had decided during the night that they should move more to the south, away from the hedge and into the open. "Always remembering, Brill," the nickname surprised her, "to keep far-sight open and aware and remember my commands if we're attacked."

They moved slowly and easily to the east and south over the next few days. Several times they came across flocks of ground birds he said were called gwinth. They were an easy target for her bow since they were as tall as she was.

"What more can you tell me about the mountains, Elden?" she asked on the first afternoon. "You've said something of the dangers, but nothing of the mountains themselves."

"Verian took me into the mountains several times. I believe he loved them more than the place he called home. He had made his home in something like a cave or burrow between and under rocks, near a fresh spring. I had a terrible time finding him."

"How did you manage it then?" The story had distracted her from the mountains.

"I'd remembered a story about him and thought I had general directions. All I really wanted, the Wild and a single Master, it seemed right." He was struggling with something, and she kept silent. "I crisscrossed the area for weeks, getting closer to the mountains each time." He chuckled. "It's a good thing I had some healing skill because I learned about some of the plants the hard way. I was attacked twice by dire wolves and once by something small that came up from the ground. I learned to eat murk while I searched. Fortunately, the dufk seem to like the south. Have you seen any more sign of murk?"

"I have, but if their meat is as bad as you say, I would prefer to hunt something else."

"Well, I didn't know about the tubers at the time; it was Brother Verian who taught me about those. When I finally sensed him and got to his cave, he told me to 'get away and leave me! I want no company.' So I camped by his spring and made myself a nuisance. I hunted and was fortunate enough to bring down a dufk. It was the smell of roasting meat that brought him out one evening, saying that if I was going to hunt away all the game, I might as well join him. As I came to know him, he was a fine Master, disciplined, but willing to share a story now and then. On our trips into the mountains, we were lucky enough to come across several mana pools, and I was introduced to golem in much the same way as I introduced you, but they were lesser types. You wondered about my bow skills? I was fortunate in my later golem hunts and was able to leave the wild with more than training. Verian seemed pleased with the way I dispatched the golems. The blood kites were something else. They were farther in the mountains."

"Ahead, gwinth," she said suddenly. "Shall we stalk them, or would you prefer to select your dinner?" He could hear the smile in her voice.

"Hens," he said, "three hens with chicks. Do we need the meat?"

"We have plenty. Shall we look for the cocks or wait for another day?"

Elden stretched out his far-sight. "One male, we can get close to him in half an hour, and I'll call him. Who knows when we will get another chance at one."

They moved cautiously around the hens, careful not to disturb them, and stalked the male.

"Look at him," Brillar said in awe. "I've never seen such feathers."

"Courting plumage," was the answer. "There may be more females about." Both reached out and did find more birds, including another male, although he was farther away.

Elden called out the male who came toward them immediately, his head to one side, confused. One arrow brought him down. Brillar stroked the blue and white feathers.

"Take the plumage," she was instructed, "it's prized by everyone and easily traded."

They moved away from the other birds once their kill was cleaned and packed.

They were three miles from the kill when, "Dire wolves, tracking us," he stated.

"I see them."

"The smell of fresh meat. How many do you see?" He looked at her sharply.

"Two," was her reply. "As you said, two wolves to drive us, the others to wait for us to tire."

"Good, you remember. Your bow is ready? We can both face them; the others are far enough away."

The dire wolves came up to them, separated and snarling. They stopped thirty feet from the pair, who were waiting, and they seemed uncertain.

"That's right," he heard her say grimly "we don't run. How can you pursue us if we don't run?" The two wolves continued to snarl and sank to their bellies to move closer.

"Ready the bow on the left?"

"On your word."

"Loose!"

The arrow skimmed the wolf, slicing but not killing. Another arrow took it down. The other wolf turned and ran back a hundred paces, then sat down and howled.

"You let it go. Why?"

"One in front of us now and who knows how many others nearby… and they come. I had to be certain we would find them all, or they'd continue to hunt us. Take my back now. They'll try to encircle us." Brillar took her position at Elden's back.

"A small pack, only six, and wary," he said. When the animals were still at some distance, she felt him gather himself. An arc of fire sprang out, and she heard a wolf yelp in pain. Another arc spell and another yelp. The scent of burnt fur drifted to them.

"At this range, a fire arc won't kill, but it should be enough to drive them away. We left enough when we cleaned the gwinth to satisfy them." Another arc flew out and then a fourth and a yelp. She could sense the pack moving away from them.

"Refresh," and her bow was ready, but the wolves had moved away.

"Do you think they'll attack the gwinth hens we saw?" she asked.

"If the tales I have heard about them are true, those hens can kill an attacking wolf. They kick with nearly the strength of a horse."

Despite their satisfaction with the idea of the wolves keeping their distance, they made a larger than usual fire when they stopped that afternoon. As their meat cooked, Brillar took off her boots and stared at them.

"No wonder my left foot hurts," she said, holding up the boot and putting her finger through a hole in the sole.

"You've been walking on that?" He was frowning at her and narrowed his eyes.

"Well, I did have to heal my foot when we rested and refreshed things. I just hadn't given much thought to the boots."

"More than a month in the wild, and no thought to your boots?" Elden rubbed his forehead and sighed. "You have another pair?"

Brillar opened her foldbox and was engulfed in feathers, setting Elden to laughing. "You had best bundle those or they'll be everywhere."

Grumbling, she did as she was told, then tucked the worn boots into the box and removed newer ones.

"Show me your feet," he demanded, and she turned bare toes to him.

"So you healed this one every day?" he ran his finger down her foot, making it twitch, "and then walked on it again in the morning."

She made no reply. Elden looked her over sharply now. They cleaned their clothes and themselves daily with spells, but she had never properly learned to repair fabric. Now he insisted that she take out newer clothes, leave him to mend what he could, and turned his back. Her shirt, he declared impossible but kept it for her to practice her mending spells on. The leather armor he insisted they wear had worn large holes in it. She took out fresh.

"Now, you will try once again to mend cloth," he said, and she sighed. "Brother Verian insisted I learn the craft, and now it's for you to learn or we will arrive at… somewhere with you in rags." He had few clothes for travel and kept them well-mended. "Besides that," he said sternly, "many count this as a woman's craft."

She just groaned and was glad when the food on the fire was ready.

Even before their brief fight with the wolves, they had found that food was more readily available in the south and east than it had been earlier. Brother Verian had lived and taught Elden in the north and farther west than they were now. Water became less of a problem as well, although they avoided two more pools with ambush predators in them. Since they were curious about them, "Know what will attack," said Elden, he called one out.

"Have your bow ready, although I would rather let it slide back into the water confused than have to kill it," he explained and began the Creature spell to pull it from the water.

The head, when it emerged, was a grey-green, flat, and half-moon shaped with serrated teeth that ran from one side of the face to the other. Eyes were on short stalks. The animal did not appear armored, but they later decided that there must be bone under the unpleasant face as it seemed ridged. Behind the head, came a bulging neck, then fish-like gills and a thick body. The odor was compellingly dank.

"Enough?" he asked.

"More than sufficient," was her reply, and Elden let the animal slide back into the water. They gave the pond a wide berth. When they stopped later, they discussed the animal.

"As long as I am tall, perhaps more since we never saw the tail," Elden remarked. They had found space under a strangely shaped tree that both had inspected and found safe. Now he leaned against its smooth bark below the Ward.

"The way it strained as you compelled it, do you suppose the tail was holding on to something under the water?" He nodded. "That mouth, it must have been nearly as wide as a short bow. And the teeth! I think it could take a dufk or cwel in one bite and have room for more. A half-grown gwinth would disappear at a pond like that."

"And probably has," was the answer. "I wonder how deep the pond was; I didn't take time to judge." He stirred the fire idly.

"Well, at least the stories I heard are true. There are strange things in the Wild." Brillar wrapped herself in a blanket and lay on her side to sleep.

Elden watched her drift off as he scanned the sky and watched the stars, for he felt sure there would be more strange things to be met before he could satisfy her curiosity.

Part III

Rock creates no mana and shortens far-sight.
Teaching of the Brotherhood

Symbol of the Ǣlfain
The people of the southern forest.

*** 21 ***

Grass, as they continued easterly, had become thicker, game easier to find, and there were trees scattered over the land. Tubers were everywhere, and there were newer kinds which they tested by watching what the animals ate, then inspecting them before adding them to a meal.

Now Elden had his apprentice point out where they would stop at noon and nightfall, but he still examined their resting places and sent fire into holes to remove anything unpleasant as she refused to learn any spells in War magic.

They were halfway through a morning when he stopped and she drew up behind him. Feeling his strain, she reached out as well. Before she could see clearly, she found herself pushed behind some scrub where he joined her.

"Something comes, and quickly. Not Rovers, they're light and fast."

"Not animals," was her comment, "and no darkness."

"No darkness, but disquiet, distress, fear?" Both could feel them closer now.

"They've stopped. They sense us and are uneasy?" Then, wonderingly, "Ǣlfain, the southern foresters!"

Elden pushed at her to stay down and very slowly, with hands spread, rose to his feet. When he was fully upright, a man stepped into the open perhaps five yards away, armed with a bow. Elden caught his breath and motioned her upright. Like him, she rose slowly, leaving her bow in the dirt and holding out her arms. Two more of the men joined the first. Like Elden, she looked at them and marveled.

All three men were taller than Elden, slender and lithe. They were wearing clothes that seemed to change color in the light, almost matching the vegetation around them. All were alike in complexion, so well matched that they could have been brothers, with tanned skin and silvery hair. As they came forward, Brillar could see that their eyes were a light green or grey and their ears seemed to move independently. All carried bows. They were men, but not men. Ǣlfain.

"Good folk," said Elden, still holding his hands out to show that he was unarmed.

As one, three arrows pointed at his heart, and he stopped. Beside him, he could feel Brillar stand then freeze in place.

"What good are empty hands if they are the hands of a mage?" one said, his voice like frost.

Still not moving from his place, Elden replied, "Then point the arrows at my apprentice, and I will not move or make any threat."

Two of the archers shifted their targets.

Unused to being a target and finding herself one, Brillar spoke up tartly, "You are casual with my life, m'lord mage."

As the archers startled, Elden closed his eyes and slumped a bit. "If, for once, you could just hold your tongue—"

"I have searched them," he was interrupted, "there is no darkness in them," a second bowmen spoke up.

When he opened his eyes, Elden found the bows down and heaved a sigh.

"Good folk," he began again, "for I am told that the Ǣlfain folk of the south are such, you are far from home."

"Ǣlfain," she breathed beside him in wonder. Boldly, she took a step forward. "I am Brillar of Laurenfell. Well met, good folk." And she bowed. "If I may?" She stepped back to the scrub and bent slowly to retrieve her bow, holding it by two fingers in an outstretched hand.

"Your courtesy pleases me," replied the ǣlfe, "as I am sure it pleases us all. Our names, in our tongue, might be hard for yours. In towns, I am called Uthalef. Those with me are Yarell and Wa'olle." Each nodded in turn as his name was spoken. "Now your name, lord mage," he said, directing his eyes to Elden.

Elden recovered himself. "I am Garnelden but called Elden by those who have not loosed arrows in my direction."

"Elden, then," said Uthalef, with a slight smile, "for we loosed none. What are men doing here in the south? Those farther south do not go north across the dune sea to hunt here, and none but Rovers have ever ventured this far south."

"This is my doing," Brillar said unhesitatingly. "I wanted to see the Wild and would have stumbled and dropped my first day without Elden at my side."

Uthalef nodded. "And how does a mage come to know the Wild?"

"I was apprenticed to Brother Verian for three years. He made his home in the northern Wild." Elden kept his speech courteous.

"We knew of Verian. Not many of us travel that far north, but some wander. One of my kin told stories about him, a solitary mage of great strength, highly skilled." He glanced upward. "The sun is high. Shall we seek shade and share a meal?"

The group moved into the shade of one of the giant dome-shaped trees and sat down. Elden produced trail rations that the ǣlfec refused, although they shared their small, dried fruits.

"We do not rest long," said Yarell, "we are on Search." Uthalef looked at him sharply. "There is no darkness in them. Perhaps they have seen something useful."

Brillar, to Elden's relief, remained silent.

Uthalef looked at them both, searching. "We are forest folk," he began, "for there are great forests to the south and east. Our children are our joy and play freely under the trees and in them, always under a watchful eye. Despite that, a child, just four years old, went missing from us three weeks ago and more. The watcher was not hurt but has no memory of what happened. Whoever took the child was well prepared, as there were many trails left at the scene. All led into the Wild, where they split into still more trails. We are just one of fifteen groups that hunt for him."

"Do you know what took him or why he was taken?" Elden asked, leaning forward, his face troubled. To take an Ǣlfain child spoke of Darkness.

"There were orc signs and a sense of wights," said Yarell, "murk blood to confuse the trail, other signs that seemed to appear and disappear as if he was carried by birds."

"As to the reason for his taking, we can only guess at that. Since there was great preparation for the act, and wights were involved," he looked at Uthalef, who nodded, "most of us agree that he was taken by someone from the Order of the K'ish."

Elden straightened with shock, but Brillar was puzzled. "This Order, I haven't heard of it."

"Potion makers," Elden replied, then seeing her puzzled expression, "dark potions. Poisons, potions for seduction, control, death." She had been poisoned by K'ish potions, but no one had discussed it with her.

Uthalef nodded. "For the strongest of these potions, ǣlfain blood is required, a child's blood, pure and innocent." He watched them for their reaction.

Brillar began to speak, but Elden laid a hand on her leg for silence. "Where do the trails lead?" he asked.

"Most lead to the northwest. We search here, but without much hope. You have seen and felt nothing?"

"Nothing. No orcs, certainly no wights, but orcs often prefer mountains and we've not been through the mountains yet. We're heading toward them now."

"If the child was taken three weeks ago, are you certain he's still alive?" asked Brillar quietly.

"We would, all of us, feel his death. We have felt nothing. If he was taken for potions," he shook his head. "The taker would need his blood fresh for each potion. If the taker wishes to keep him alive, he will have to be kept by trees and growing things. Without them, he will fade quickly." He looked at his ǣlfain brothers. "What we fear is that the K'ish who holds him will take too much blood before we find him. If too much is taken, if he is dying, he will be drained of the rest so that it can be dried and made into a powder." Brillar shrank back. "Dead, he would still have value."

To prevent her from asking anything else, Elden put in, "If we can help you, we will. Our travels take us to the mountains. In the fields and forests, you move quickly. In the mountains, we are all of the same in speed."

The ǣlfec shared glances as if discussing something without words. Finally, Uthalef took something like a large Ward, swirled in yellow and blue from a belt pouch, and handed it to Elden.

"If you should find signs, tap this three times; it will rise, mark its place, find us, and lead us to you." The ǣlfec stood and the pair joined them.

"You were well met," said Yarell. "May the Light guide you."

"Swift travels to you, go with hope," Elden replied, and the ǣlfec stepped out quickly and were quickly lost in the foliage.

"If you're ready then?" Elden asked, and she nodded her reply. "How shall we travel?"

"Quickly, and toward the mountains," was her steady answer. They went directly to the east and the mountains.

There were no sandworms in the south, but they had to skirt gwinth and chicks and some unhealthy areas where each sensed darkness. Both were now well-seasoned and alternated a trot and a brisk walk. They pushed through tall grass near streams at times, following animal trails when they led in the right direction.

That night, when they camped and sat by the fire, Brillar was ready with the questions he had known were in her mind.

"There are things I didn't understand about our meeting. We reached them with far-sight easily, saw no darkness, and you stood to greet them. Yet it took time for them; we were in front of them, and it took time for them to know we meant no harm."

Elden nodded. "In the north, we only hear stories of ǣlfain. None I know of has ever visited the north. They keep to the great southern forests." He stirred the fire, sending sparks into the clear sky. "I have met some who actually knew ǣlfain in the south. Brother Verian also had information—not stories, but information—about them."

He settled back against the trunk of the umbrella tree and gazed at its twisted branches fanning out over him. "Ǣlfain, Verian told me, don't study magic. There are no mages among them. They're barely sensitive to mana but highly sensitive to life itself. How old would you say Uthalef was?"

"A little older than I am?" she answered, "perhaps thirty years old?"

He smiled into the night. "His true age is more likely closer to eight hundred years than thirty," he chuckled.

She straightened. "Eight hundred?"

"Ǣlfain live to great age unless killed in an accident or battle. Ǣlfain have gone to battle to protect what is theirs, and sometimes to defend the innocent," he added. "They can't use mana, but all that lives supports them. But you asked about their inability to sense that we meant no harm. Far-sight is driven by mana, as is the ability to separate Light from Darkness in what it finds. The one called Yarell had some of the gift to help him shift through us, or we would probably be dead."

"And these dark potions, the potion masters, what about them?"

"The Order of the K'ish is ancient, some say older than the Brotherhood. The members of the order sell their services, their products, to anyone with money enough to pay the price. Only a Master of the K'ish would attempt to use ǣlfi blood for such a purpose, and only a Master would have orcs in his service. How he would manage wights, I don't know."

"I've never heard of wights."

"Few outside the Wild have heard of them. They're undead of great power, spell casters, spells of War, and other spells that only they know and no one else wishes to learn. Flesh hangs on their bones; they can be scented on the wind."

Repulsed and disgusted, she sat a moment. "Uthalef talked about the child's body, but you interrupted before he could finish? What is it you didn't want him to say?" She watched sparks flying up.

Elden stared into the fire. "The dead ǣlfi. The potion maker would remove his organs and his eyes to dry and use for potions or to sell to others."

She stared at him, horrified, overcome.

"No part would be unused," he finished sadly.

She stood hastily, hand on her stomach, and left the fire to vomit out her meal, then returned to rinse her mouth.

"I'm sorry," he said quietly. "I know you want complete answers."

"If he's in the mountains, we'll help them find him. If he is not, then the ǣlfec will never stop searching, and we will search with them." She ate nothing else. That night, her sleep was restless. The very idea of something undead but still animated had deeply alarmed and disturbed her. In her dreams, dark forms stalked her. More than once, a loud moan or fearful whimper woke Elden. Each time, he sent a spell to soothe her. In the morning, she remembered nothing of her nightmares which worried her Master.

It was dawn when they smothered the last embers of their fire. They set out at once, eating and drinking as they loped and walked. The land rose up ahead of them, and there were times when they splashed through small streams. Trees grew taller around them but were still low compared to northern trees. They continued to wear the claw necklaces but avoided the only small group of Rovers they found with far-sight.

Except for Elden's instructions and questions, there was little to say.

"You've meet ǣlfain, what did you sense of them?" was his first question as they stopped briefly.

"They had a scent of green and forests, of things alive and growing. They felt… it sounds foolish. They felt like spring air."

"Yes, I've heard that those who have met them have spoken of the same feeling. When we search, that is part of what will lead us to a hidden child, the ǣlfi. What else?"

"Such deep sadness and loss." She shivered in the sun, remembering the K'ish.

"The ǣlfi will feel something of the same."

They spoke only briefly, only strained out with far-sense to find dangers to be avoided and any hint of an ǣlfi. They reached the foothills that afternoon and began to climb.

"Far-sight is something I learned late, but it's stretched with your teaching and all this practice," she remarked as they stopped briefly to shift small stones from boots. "In the scrubland, it seemed to fly out. Here, it seems foreshortened."

"Far-sight is mana driven. Rock creates no mana, and little here leaves its touch on rock or touches it so lightly that the mana quickly dissipates. As we climb, it will be harder to draw in mana for spells." He glanced at the sky.

They climbed then headed north and west. Little grew on the rocky slopes, and far-sight reached less far uphill than down. As they camped, there was more instruction.

"The day that we turn back to the south and east, we will mark in our minds the reach of far-sight and climb to that height. We don't want to miss anything."

The next morning, she stopped. "Elden, there are deer below us, and our supplies are running low. If there were a mage about, I would ask him to call one to us? A long stalk will slow us."

She could feel his concentration and a yearling buck came upslope with the same confused look as the irex.

"Am I to do everything?" Elden whispered; she had been so fascinated with the approach, she had neglected her bow. Nocking an arrow, she let fly, and the animal dropped. They took the meat they needed and left the rest for scavengers.

They had only gone another mile when a large rock sailed down the slope at them.

"The boulders, take cover," Elden shouted, pushing her ahead of him.

Another rock flew at them as they scrambled for safety.

"Orcs," Elden breathed, as another rock smashed into the ground near them and bounced away.

She reached out. "Only one, I think."

He nodded as a rock smashed into their covering boulders, sending debris down on them.

Time the throws. I think he has a steady supply of rocks and only needs to bend to pick them up. We need to decide on the shortest time between throws." More debris rained down. "We need to separate, make two targets." She nodded.

"The boulder to the right for you and see if you can spot him as you run." More debris. "NOW!"

Brillar scrambled to the boulder he had indicated while Elden took that moment to move left and see uphill for their attacker.

"I see him," she shouted across to Elden as a rock struck the ground near her, showering her with dirt.

"I don't. When I move to draw his attention," was the shouted reply, "you stand and fire." He saw her nod.

Elden stepped to the left and waved his arms, shouting "HO, THERE," and dove for cover as he saw a rock fly down at him and heard her bow twang.

"It fell," she called to him, and both moved forward cautiously.

"That stench," said Brillar as they reached it, "and this is the second ugliest thing I think I have ever seen." At his questioning look, she added, "The thing in the pool is still the first."

In a dead heap, she could examine the orc easily as he kept watch. Its face was broad, the eyes small below a receding skull. The nose was wide, and flaps of skin seemed to hang from its cheeks near nostril slits. Below the nose was a wide mouth with jutting teeth; its chin was thick and protruded. The rest of the body was broad and heavy with muscle. Standing on its short legs, it would have been only slightly taller than Elden.

"They are foul. Remember the odor; it may help us spot them before they send rocks down on us. This one, I think," he said, pushing at the corpse with his foot, "is only a scout. There will be more. I think we need to add one more command. Shout, 'Cover,' if you think any more rocks are headed at us."

"Are rocks all we'll have from them?" She stared at the ugly corpse.

"Rocks from a distance. For close attacks, they'll use clubs. Orcs are too clumsy for bow work." He looked at the sky. "Carrion eaters; we need to go."

"Gladly," she said, and they went back to the northwest along the hills.

*** 22 ***

Two days passed, and they saw no more orcs. Elden pointed out nests of blood kites above them on the second morning, and they took cover at once.

"We need to clear them or make them cautious, or they'll plague our way. Be ready with arrows. The plan," he went on, seeing her puzzled look, "is to burn individual nests, making them protective of their eggs and chicks. You can see each nest is occupied." The nests, some of them three feet tall and as wide, clung to the cliff face above them. She saw at least one adult bird on each nest when she peeked upward. Looking straight above them, she could see that other kites were already circling them.

"So I am to fire as they attack, and you are to make them even more interested in us than they are already?" She pointed with her bow. "Such an interesting plan," she added wryly.

"Begin!"

She fired almost straight up at the birds as he stood and flamed a low nest, then fired again as he sent out a wall of flame at clustered nests. A bird fell with an arrow through a wing as she sent another arrow at a bird that had swooped in low. This time the arrow was accurate. More flame crackled from Elden's hands, and she loosed another arrow. From behind her, she felt a bird strike her head and turned to fire at it. As it fell, she was struck again and loosed another arrow. Fire hissed as a dome of flame formed above them.

"You're hurt," Elden shouted.

"Too many at once," she shouted back over the sounds of the flaming dome he had cast to protect them, shaking blood from her eyes.

"Only a few more nests," came his shout, "and they should withdraw. Ready?"

"Ready!" As the dome faded, the birds continued to circle in the sky but none dove at them; they were growing wary of her bow. His fire bolts disintegrated nests above them. She sent two more arrows at the birds, but they were calling and retreating toward burning nests. Now he sent walls of flame at the retreating birds, killing a number of them, as her arrows began to fall short.

Finally, Elden turned as she sat back heavily, already chanting spells of self-healing he had insisted she learn on their long trip to West Riversgate. As he rested on his heels and watched, the bleeding stopped, and long stripes in her skull sealed although he saw her wince in pain more than once. He nodded, satisfied, then cast a cleansing spell to clear away blood as she drew in mana.

"So, now we know how to fight blood kites," he said, satisfied with the result.

Brillar pressed her hand to her hair. "A painful lesson is one well learned," she replied, but she was smiling crookedly. "If you think we're safe, I'll restock from the foldbox."

When she finished, Elden stood and held out a hand. She took it, and he pulled her to her feet. They took a few moments to recover what arrows and shafts they could from the dead birds, then they turned again to the northwest.

The following day, they found no sign of orcs and saw danger only once.

"A solitary hunter," Elden said as he halted them, "a great cat. Unlikely it will bother us."

"I see it. Taking its ease?" She could feel the cat on a sunny ledge.

"Likely, it's killed and eaten recently and will have no interest in us. There is another problem." He sat and pulled her down beside him.

"First, a solitary orc, likely a scout. Then, nothing. Then, blood kites blocking our way and now, a solitary cat," he said then fell silent, waiting.

"We're going in the wrong direction," she said firmly.

"I agree. Mark the length of far-sight, and we'll climb to it then go south and east."

"Three wasted days," he heard her mutter as they climbed and could only agree silently.

When they turned, they were moving away from the solitary cat and above the blood kites. Their view over the scrublands was remarkable, a clear vista that spread for fifty miles or more, but neither had an interest in what was far away and unimportant to them. Their only thought was to an ǣlfi and the time they had lost in their search. It took them only two days to come out above where the dead orc had lain. Far-sight showed them little below them but his bones.

"Now we go slowly. We are no good to the child if we die before we find him," he stated and was acknowledged with a nod.

That night, Brillar showed him an unknown skill. He would allow no fire, so she opened the foldbox and removed herbs of different kinds. She smashed them between two stones, then added strips of raw meat, folding them over with her hands, then pounding them lightly, soundlessly, until they were well mixed with the herbs.

"Half an hour and the herbs will cook them, not with heat although there will be some, but by seeping into the flesh." He shook his head. "Wait and see then." She began the process with other strips of meat. "Easy to do as much as I can now while we're waiting."

For the second making, she added some dried fruit to the mix. All he could do was watch and wait, wondering what other new skills she might have. When he ate, he had to admit that meat prepared this way was better than the thin raw strips he had envisioned as a meal.

"You may," he said as he finished, "have skills worth your keep." He saw her grin at him in the growing darkness.

The following day they took a cold breakfast, shivering in the mountain air. Both had taken cloaks from packs, to wear during the day and to use as blankets at night.

They had gone less than a quarter mile when Elden stopped them. "Water ahead, fresh and pure from the mountains above us, and we need water."

Elden kept the pace slow, suggesting there might be things nearby that could sense them. They were almost to the stream when he yelled, "Back!"

Then a shouted, "Undead," and he loosed a ring of flame that crackled outward.

"Nothing behind us," she shouted.

He responded, "Side," as another spell sprang from his hands. As she whirled to his side, she cringed, sickened, and truly afraid for the first time in their travels. She looked at the animated skeletons that were rising in front of them, bones clacking, and her stomach lurched.

Elden's fire spells shot out in waves, but she closed her eyes against the sight and smell. More fire, then, "Refresh!"

Steeling herself, she opened her eyes and let fly with an arrow. It appeared to go right through the skeleton, which came on, only falling at a third arrow when it was nearly on them. Then there was fire again, fanning out in front of them. Shaking, she took out three arrows and cast an Item spell on them. She was relieved when they burst into flame. At his next shout, she was able to take down three skeletons with three arrows. Two more flame spells, and all were down.

Even Elden sagged in relief and went quickly through a field strewn with bones. He had been too busy to notice her hesitation in the fight. Brillar stepped carefully, shaking as her foot brushed a skull. The stream they had wanted to reach was only a dozen paces away, and they crossed it before Elden stooped to drink from it as she reached out for more trouble. They filled flasks hastily and headed for an outcropping of rock near the water.

Now that they were safe, the full horror of the encounter hit her. "They just rose up from the ground? Our approach must have triggered them, and they just rose up? And so many."

"You were quick with the Item spell on the arrows. I'd heard that fire was best on the undead but never had a chance to try it before this. There was no sign, nothing; they were just suddenly there."

"I wonder if they could have been set there on purpose." He looked at her sharply, alarmed by the tremor in her voice. "Could there be more near this stream above or below or near any water or food?"

He could only shake his head. "Since we seem to be safe for the moment and the water is fresh, we should replenish what we carry in the foldboxes. If you're right, this may be our best opportunity." He opened his foldbox and went for water. On his return, he found her foldbox open, but Brillar was taking rocks from her boots. He filled her containers for her, but the boots were just a ruse. She had no intention of getting closer to the undead.

"A solitary orc, now undead. We seem to have come in the right direction." He was thoughtful. From what he remembered of stories, undead could be stopped by a fire spell, but it took actual fire to burn the bones to ash.

"Can the K'ish order them?" The skeletons filled her with dread. She could face the living, she could face flesh and blood, but undead? She shivered with revulsion, but Elden was deep in thought, trying to remember everything he had been taught about the K'ish.

"K'ish are potion makers. I suppose he might have negotiated with the orcs, but the undead? Who can speak with the dead and ask for their aid or direct them to stand between travelers and water? What could he offer them in return if someone could speak to them? Orcs perhaps, but what do undead want or need?" He shook his head, wondering if the other stories he had heard were true, stories of the Savic.

"Where are they found usually, the undead?" She splashed cold water on her face, trying to dispel her unease.

"Graveyards, so I've heard, and sometimes battlefields if the dead were left unburied."

"If we strike them down, then what? Are they quiet then?" The idea of their reanimation was revolting. She smothered a shudder. *Only bones, they're only bones,* she tried to tell herself.

"Some people say that if they are struck a second time after their original deaths, they melt away like mist, but we saw no mist rise, and we stepped over bones. Others say that the bones of each seek their fellow bones until they re-form and can attack again if disturbed."

Brillar was thoughtful. *They are only bones,* she recited to herself again, then she stood and loosed an arrow toward the bones. Around the shaft, four rose, and she gasped as she heard their bones rattle together. They stood only a moment then fell again to the ground. He gaped at her as she sat down, speechless.

She struggled to keep her voice calm. "It was something we needed to know," she said, nauseated by the idea of them. "It seemed to me that a single arrow wouldn't disturb them too much."

"A warning next time you're going to do something so rash?" was all he could manage to say.

"It might be a good idea if I loose an arrow now and then if you think we are coming into danger?" He looked at her sharply, seeing loathing in her expression, before nodding his thoughtful agreement.

Now they began to move very slowly, often having to move around large boulders. Three more times that day, she sent an arrow ahead, and they moved around two new spawns of the undead. Toward dusk, Elden shouted, "Cover!" and they sprang in different directions as rocks pounded down where they had stood.

Lying behind a boulder, he muttered to himself, "At dusk, the worst time for either of us to see," then shouted, "All well?" and heard her solid answer as rocks pounded the ground near him and struck the boulder where he was hidden.

"Can you see them?" he shouted.

"I glimpsed one when he stood to throw," she called, rolling sideways to avoid more spattering dirt and rock.

"I saw none. I'll stand and draw them, be ready!"

"Ready," was her shout.

Elden stood, sent out a bolt of swords, and dove back behind his boulder as her bow sang.

"A hit, I think," he heard her shout. There was a loud crashing as a massive rock struck his hiding space, making it shudder.

"Again, ready?"

"Go," she called, and he stood, shooting something like a fist toward their targets then diving for a different boulder.

"Whatever you sent struck one at least, and he's down. I'll move this time, and you strike, ready?"

"Go," he shouted, and she stood, yelling, and dove for a boulder closer to the orcs.

His spell of Thundering Fists shattered rock above them, and it rained down, pulling more rock with it in a small avalanche. The body of an orc fell with it, part of her arrow still visible.

"How many more?" she yelled over the noise.

"Two, at least," he said and then dove for another boulder, stood and fired as two orcs missed their throws.

To his right, he could see Brillar scramble to another site. Rocks thudded in her direction. It was becoming too dark to make out the orcs as they threw their rocks. He stood and sent lightning crackling at them, outlining them for her to see. His spell hit one who bellowed and crumpled while an arrow took the last. Cautious, they moved toward the orcs' perch, and he heard her bow. He scrambled over fallen rocks to reach her.

"You said not to leave even an enemy suffering. That one," she pointed to a lightning-scored orc, "still lived."

"They were well protected here," Elden said as he looked around him. "A wall of sorts and piles of rocks the right size for attacking strangers. I wonder if these will be missed or if they were to stay here for some time."

"Here," she said. "They had food and water." An entire stag lay outside the enclosure where several casks stood, one with a tap.

She knelt and opened it, dipping her fingers in the flow. Bringing the liquid to her lips, she smelled it and licked her fingers.

"Wine! A bit raw, but for orcs, perhaps raw is best; I see no cooking fire."

"The stag is untouched. This group hasn't eaten here. This must be a new emplacement for them," Elden remarked. "Help me roll the bodies out, and we can stay here tonight."

"Elden, what about the K'ish? If he's nearby, will he see that he's being attacked?"

"The Order confines itself to potions, I'm told. Even if he has some far-sight, it will be blocked by stone as ours is blocked."

"And if an orc escapes us and returns to him?" She looked around her into the growing darkness.

Elden was grim. "It's best that no orc escapes us." They settled in for the night. Brillar prepared more of the meat then unbraided her hair, taking a comb from the foldbox. At his curious look, she said, "I can clean it with a spell, but it was becoming ragged. Hair and bowstrings are a bad mix." She re-braided it, tucked the comb away, then let the braid swing free.

They set off slowly in the morning, now well aware that far-sight wasn't any help at sighting undead. Coming around a large heap of rock, they stepped right into a small group of skeletons, although they were quickly dispatched with fire so they could move around them. They were able to spot one group of orcs by the noise they made.

"I'd heard they are quarrelsome," Elden said in a whisper. "Let's hope the rest are the same."

They continued southeast, avoiding what they could sense or see when Brillar motioned him to stop and crouched.

"Can you smell it?" she whispered. He frowned at her. "The scent of flowers, here where there are no flowers anywhere."

Elden tested the air and turned to her with a sense of wonder.

"Flowers and a scent of spring!" he whispered, joy on his face. Then he shook his head. "So much pain," he whispered.

"The ǣlfi!" There were tears in her eyes as the child's anguish struck her. She started to stand and was pulled down.

"Not here. We have to descend and release the Summoning charm." They went back the way they had come, knowing it was clear, and began to descend. Once again, she stopped them, smelling flowers. Both reached out with far-sight, getting an idea of a small valley and water. When they had descended several hundred feet, they began to move east, stopping only when they heard the harsh laugh of an orc ahead of them. Back again over their track until neither could find any danger, and they halted, wedging themselves between two large boulders.

"We may have some time to wait," Elden said with a slight smile as he took out the Summoner. Holding it in his hand, he tapped it three times and sat back, startled. The Summoner buzzed slightly as it rose from his hand, circled them, and whizzed off into the sky. "So fast," he breathed.

"It was like an arrow from a bow," she said wonderingly, sitting beside him. "Let's hope they aren't too many days from us." They were far enough from the child that they couldn't feel his pain any longer, but they knew it was there, knew he was suffering.

*** 23 ***

All they could do was be still, sheltered between boulders, leaving them only to creep away and relieve themselves. Brillar practiced her Deception skills, rusty from lack of use but handy on the morning of their second day of hiding when a troop of orcs passed within a few arms' lengths and noticed nothing.

It was mid-morning on their third cramped day when both roused suddenly, heads up but bodies unmoving, and smiled at each other. Elden was first to move out from between the rocks to call softly, "Here." They were joined by the three ǣlfec they had met in the scrublands.

"You called us correctly," Uthalef said, joy flashing across his face, "Ǣdhahren is here!"

"Orcs and undead as well," Elden said quietly. "We didn't try to locate him exactly. There are too many sentries."

Brillar stretched a bit and groaned as she moved her cramped limbs.

"Ah, how long have you been here?" Yarell asked gently.

"Too long for my legs," she replied, stretching them in front of her.

He took a flask from his belt and handed it to her, saying, "A sip only." She sipped.

The flavors and scents mixed in the flask! Summer berries, the tang of autumn, winter's frost, and spring flowers, she could feel sunlight and hear the sound of water over rocks. In an instant, she was ready to leap up, laughing, ready for the spring races and more. Wonder spread across her face. At his glance and with a nod from Yarell, she handed the flask to Elden and watched his amazement spread to match hers.

Elden shook his head, handing the flask back to Yarell. "I've heard of ǣlfa brews," he shook his head. "Nothing prepared me for that."

Yarell took the flask and handed them small, thin wafers the size of his palm. "Ǣlfa bread. Break off a small portion."

Warned by the potency of the drink, each took a bit of the bread. Strength seemed to flow through them; the days spent cramped between boulders disappeared. Brillar closed her eyes in delight.

"More of us are coming, each summoned as you called to us," Uthalef told them in whispers. "This place held two. We should move downslope to a safer and more comfortable place. The others will have no trouble finding us."

Reaching out and finding nothing nearby, Elden led them down, stopping to have Brillar fire an arrow when he worried there might be undead in their path. "We found it a useful tactic," he told the ǣlfec. "Undead rise up suddenly when someone comes too close."

They were half a mile downslope when Elden halted them. "We found nothing down this far when we passed the first time. Far-sight is blocked by rock, and the boy must be well-sheltered behind rock, probably the canyon walls."

Buoyed by the presence of the ǣlfec and sustained by ǣlfa food and drink, they waited. Over the next two days, ǣlfec joined them in groups of three and four; twice, groups of a dozen who had met in the scrublands came at once. They distributed themselves nearby to avoid detection by any who were watching. Sixty-two ǣlfec had gathered when Uthalef declared that all who would be able to reach them quickly had arrived. He called them into council after sunset. Everyone took places on the ground near him. Ǣlfain eyes are sharp even in the dark, and their ears are keen, but Brillar and Elden sat close to Uthalef so they could see and hear clearly.

"There are more coming," Uthalef began, "but they are too distant. They have been sent for, but the land between will delay them. Sixty-two of us must take back Ǣdhahren." There were nods of agreement.

"Sixty-four of us," Elden put in quietly. He looked at the company. "Sixty-four will take back Ǣdhahren." Brillar's look, when he glanced at her, was steady.

There was silence as the Ǣlfain took in the announcement, and he felt dozens of pairs of eyes on him, but Uthalef only nodded agreement.

"Then it's done," said Uthalef. "Sixty-four of us will take him back. Those with experience in war, stay with us. The rest should sleep."

Elden gestured Brillar away, and, to his surprise, she left the council without a word.

"Before dawn," spoke up one of the ǣlfec, "we should send out the swiftest, the most stealthy, to gather what we can of the site."

"I can tell you something about it," Elden out in. "It seems to be a narrow valley, rocky; there are some trees, and there are flowers. Brillar noticed their scent; that's how we found him. When they were planted or how they're maintained, I don't know. The valley is steep and narrow at one end. We didn't get close enough to see the other end. There must be some sort of shelter, perhaps even a cave."

"Keeping Ǣdhahren in a cave would mean his quick death. A tent or hut in the open?"

"The scouts can tell us. Who will they be?" Yarell put in.

The discussion, which had been in the common tongue, shifted to Ǣlfair, leaving Elden behind although he thought he heard the number five several times. The voices were kept low, and Ǣlfair is a soothing tongue; at some point, Elden slept, to be nudged awake when the discussion changed languages again.

"We would like to know how you see your part in this Elden and Brillar's part as well."

"What arrows do you carry?" he asked.

"Blunt and sharp," was the reply.

"Blunt for the undead, sharp for the orcs, although they will fall to blunt. Fire?" Heads were shaken.

"The undead won't spawn in daylight unless threatened. Arrows first, to kill the orcs. After that, a pause while I cast spells of fire on blunt-tipped arrows. The spell will hold for perhaps ten minutes. When the orcs are down, fire arrows should take as many undead as possible. When the fire fades, the blunt arrows will continue to be useful. If Ǣdhahren is not in danger during the fighting, I can cast arc spells without revealing my position. That should cause some confusion."

"And Brillar?" There were no women among the ǣlfain warriors.

"She'll insist on joining the archers; you can be certain of that. She is also a fine healer if she can reach the wounded."

"We have to remember," Yarell spoke up, "that the undead will not remain fallen. How long it will take for them to put bone back on bone, no one knows, but never think that you can advance safely. An undead that is fallen may rise up behind you. Some should remain behind as others advance."

The discussion went on far into the night.

The five selected scouts, for Elden had been correct in his Ǣlfair, left well before dawn. Each had taken a small charm from a pouch before leaving. "Sure path," an ǣlfe said to Elden, but he had no time to ask for further details.

Uthalef divided them all into attack groups, each to follow a leader with a sure path. Brillar only nodded when placed in a rearguard, one that would strike any of the undead that should rise up as the ǣlfec advanced. She took out at least a hundred blunt-tipped arrows plus a healing orb that she secured in a pouch. Elden was in the front rank but smiled his encouragement. To their surprise, each was given a hooded cloak by an ǣlfe of the rear guard. "Our clothing shifts on its own, but you would stand out."

Several hours passed before the scouts returned. The valley was narrow on the northwest as Elden had suggested but widened and flattened at the southeast.

"There is a hut where I think Ǣdhahren is kept. There are trees and flowers around it and the entrance to a cave beyond. Orcs are everywhere, but not near the hut. Hundreds, I think."

"I saw wights with the undead before dawn, but they all sank into the earth when the sun came over the hill. There was a woman near the hut or something shaped like a woman, all in red. Unless the K'ish have women in their order, she may be there for Ǣdhahren."

"The undead, including the wights, will rise again when threatened. No one steps into the valley until all the orcs we can see are down. No one must wake the undead before we are fully ready. When we are ready, Elden will cast fire spells on as many batches of arrows as he can."

Flasks of the ǣlfa beverage were passed around, and Brillar marveled again at its flavors. She and Elden received small flasks for later use if they should tire and took them with thanks.

The small army moved forward, each following a sure path that glistened in the sun.

Now I understand, thought Elden. *It's like the Summoner or a Ward, but this shows us the safe way through danger.* He had envisioned the group having to fight its way to the ǣlfi and out again and breathed a sigh of relief. *We may, in fact, live to see the sunset,* he thought as he climbed.

The groups moved steadily but slowly up the hillside, fanning out to earlier assigned locations. Brillar had lost sight of Elden immediately after he put on his cloak but trusted the planning of the ǣlfain council. She took comfort in the idea that no human blood would be spilled that day. Having already killed orcs, she had no illusions about their humanity. Wights and other undead? They had already died at least once; 'killing' them presented no problem, but the idea of them, of being close to them, sickened her *If only they would stay killed,* she thought grimly. Her duties were clear; heal those who needed healing, 'kill' any undead that rose again after ǣlfec had passed them.

They were almost at the crest of the hill protecting the lower edge of the valley when a barrage of rocks flew toward them, bouncing and breaking apart. Orcs had been roused by an incautious movement, or perhaps they also had a Ward. Groups scattered, and bows sang back at the attackers. Orcs fell from the heights and their bellows filled the air.

Orcs are not the greatest of thinkers. Assigned to the heights, many now abandoned their places and ran down the hill, studded clubs clutched in their vast fists. As they left their sheltered positions, Ǣlfain arrows found them, and they fell, bellowing. One massive orc reached an attacker alive and swung his club, smashing the bowman's arm and spinning the ǣlfe through the air to land with a thud several paces away. Brillar, in the rear contingent, moved toward him at once, careless of the rocks that continued to rain down on them as Elden's spell of Swords ended the orc.

Ǣlfain eyes missed no movement. Each time an orc stood to throw a rock, an arrow found him. Wounded orcs were screaming defiance, pulling arrows from injuries but exposing themselves as they did so.

The group assigned to the wide end of the valley moved quickly to stop orcs there and Brillar could see Elden's spell of fists crumple four orcs at a time as she rushed to the first of the injured, the ǣlfe whose arm had been smashed. He was writhing on the ground, grunting in pain. The orc's club had punctured his shoulder in several places, and she cast a quick spell to stop the bleeding, then a spell against pain. He sagged in relief as a spray of dirt splattered them, and a rock bounced away down the hill.

"A bad break; the bone is shattered." He tried to rise, and she pushed him down, shouting, "The pain will return. You are finished for the day. See if you can make your way downslope."

There was a shout, and she looked to her left. Another fighter was down, this one with both hands on his leg, hissing in pain. She gave her first patient a stern look and moved away to treat the leg injury, but pain relief and controlling bleeding was all she had time for. Her contingent was moving toward the right, the open end of the valley. Around her, attackers were remarkably silent and she marveled at their control. The Ǣlfain were moving forward up the hill, but the only sounds were those they made as they ducked behind the scattered boulders to avoid thrown rocks or the rapid twang of their bows. She found it hard to believe how quickly they could nock and release arrows. She could hear the footfalls of orcs, but Ǣlfain moved silently.

The volleys of rock were slowing; most of the of the first wave of orcs had been effectively eliminated. Elden had cleared many of the orcs on the hilltop and was now near the top himself. Orcs were crossing the open area between the two rims of the valley. Elden slid behind the body of an orc as Uthalef joined him.

"We need to drop them before they can attack," Uthalef said urgently. He was firing at the moving orcs.

"The undead!"

"Too late," Yarell joined them and stood to loose an arrow. "They come!"

"Curse them all," Elden muttered. "Fire for your arrows!" he shouted. Yarell was ready with a handful of blunt arrows and thrust them forward. A brief word, and the arrowheads flared. Now the remainder of their attack force had joined them, and Elden was busy with spells for fire arrows, then spells to drop orcs who were sweeping across the small valley trying to reach them and falling to the Ǣlfain shafts, but there was a new problem. Wights.

The undead come in many forms, from archers and spearmen to casters of Dark magic. Now spells arced from inside the valley, and ǣlfec began to fall.

Their initial sweep from the open end of the valley had been successful against the orcs; now the fourth contingent was in the open and scrambling for cover as wights turned toward them, cold and implacable. Most moved toward the main body of attackers, and Brillar moved with them, casting spells to heal burns from fire and acid, relieve pain, darting from one fallen to another as the ǣlfe moved forward. She was rushing from a healing toward another wounded ǣlfe, when a strike from a wight narrowly missed her, hissed into the ground near to her right. "*Acid!*" She ran down and left, then fell flat as another spell hissed over her. The barrage of rocks had stopped, and she could hear cheering on the height.

"The orcs are down! Wights now."

No one was calling for a healer, but she was sure the call would come and moved to a place where she could see what was happening in the valley. A quick glance was all she needed to confirm her worst fears; the undead were everywhere, crawling over the valley. She had a brief glimpse of a tall, ragged wight who was twisting its hands, ready to cast a spell. She ducked behind a rock, squeezing her eyes shut, willing herself not to vomit.

Elden had his hands full, casting on arrows thrust at him by anxious archers while others fired ones with blunt tips into the valley. He was aware of her to his right, knew she had been casting healing spells; now she was gone.

Something splashed near her, and pain lanced up her arm. Acid! She cast a quick spell against pain, almost glad for the burn that had distracted her. The call, "Healer," came from down the hill. Two ǣlfec had fallen and scrambled down to tend them. The first was not seriously burned, and she cast a spell to relieve his pain as she ran past him, feeling, knowing that the other needed all her attention.

He had taken a full hit of something Dark, and the flesh seemed to be melting from his leg as he screamed in pain. The pain she dealt with at once, but the Darkness was creeping up his body. He stared at her, eyes wide, and she cradled his head as she cast spells for healing that she knew intuitively would have no effect. The Dark spell clung to him, the stench of rotting flesh began to reach her, and she thought feverishly, *the brew!* She fumbled for her flask and held it to his lips. The creeping Darkness, the melting, seemed to hesitate then moved on up his body, dissolving flesh until she could see the bones in his hip. She splashed the brew on him, but it had no effect. Nearly panicked, she pulled out the orb, sending wave after wave of healing spells at him. The crawling rot continued to eat away at him, but she ensured that he felt nothing and his face was calm. She watched as the flesh evaporated from his abdomen, reached his ribs… Clouding eyes met hers.

"My thanks," he whispered; his head fell to one side. Stunned, dazed, she stayed where she was until she heard someone shout, "Healer." She shook herself, laid his head down on the grass, and ran toward the voice. No more of the Black spells flew at them. She wondered briefly how many wights could cast it.

Elden was finished with the arrows. Now he drew in mana and let fly great arcs of fire, hearing bones crackle as fire struck them. Everywhere, undead were clattering to the ground, and the ǣlfe around him were shouting. Twice, he stood to aim his spells and was satisfied with the hits he gave. Then they were surging down the hill.

"The cave," someone shouted near him, "she took him into the cave." Above them, the rear guard took their places, ready to fire at any of the undead who rose up, and Uthalef's contingent swept down the hill and into the valley, firing as they ran.

"Brillar," he shouted over the sound of bone striking bone, the hiss of arrows.

"Tending the wounded," one yelled back.

"No, she comes," yelled another and he could see her racing toward them along the base of the valley's rim. Spells crackled from Elden's hands while acid, lightning, fire, and a Dark spell ranged around them.

"Healer," someone called, interrupting her rush toward the cave. He had been struck in the arm by the Dark spell and she shouted at him, "Drink, and quickly!" and saw him drink as he moved toward the cave.

"Please," she grabbed a passing ǣlfe by his arm, "the one struck by the Dark spell, we need to cut off his arm, or he dies."

Startled eyes stared at her, but he rushed to his comrade, dragging him into the cave while she stopped the pain. The ǣlfe looked at his forearm in shock as the flesh fell away and exposed bone.

His companion was quick to recognize the danger and his belt knife was at his companion's upper arm.

"Cut cleanly," the injured ǣlfe's voice came as if from a distance but he felt nothing as his arm was cut away and fell rotting to the ground. Brillar sealed the wound and he slumped to the ground, unconscious. His comrade took a place at the mouth of the cave, facing outward to fire at the undead.

*** 24 ***

Elden had watched from inside the cave; now he grabbed his apprentice and dragged her deeper into its cool darkness. At the mouth of the cave, archers were felling any wights that rose again before they could cast more spells.

Brillar pulled herself away from Elden.

"Arrows, how many?" There was no answer. She opened the foldbox hastily and dumped the remainder of her arrows behind them and received a nod; then, she stepped back into the depths of the cave where its tunnel branched.

"Leave the foldbox open; it gives some light." He had opened his own, noting the shine of a crystal in the wall as the foldbox glowed. Around them, was a small group of ǣlfec, Uthalef, among them. He glanced at her arm, and she shook her head, saying, "A small thing only."

Elden looked at her sharply.

Uthalef took out a sure path and smiled. "I'm told this will work anywhere, even underwater," he said, tapping it. The sure path rose and moved off slowly, glowing with a soft light. They followed it as the corridor branched and branched again, but the sure path seemed unfaltering. Left, right, upwards or down, the it led them. The sound of the battle raging outside became louder, and Elden stopped them suddenly.

"We've been here before, that crystal in the rock? I noted it the first time we were here. This is the first branch."

Uthalef snatched the sure path from the air. "You're certain?" His voice was strained and anxious.

"The sure path is avoiding danger, but the boy is *in* danger. We're getting no closer."

Uthalef shook his head. "I have nothing to offer. We can't remain too long; arrows can't be recovered forever."

Elden looked at Brillar. She ran her hands over her face and through her hair. "One idea only," she said. "Are any here hurt, injured?"

"Just small things," Uthalef told her.

With a quick spell, she healed her arm completely then turned to the others. "Healing must be complete, and we all need to drink." She dealt with each in turn then shook her head. "I know the words, but I've never tried them. I'll ask the orb to seek someone in pain, for Ǣdhahren must be in pain. I hope we're close enough to him and far enough from the others…" She let her words hang in the air. Holding the orb in both hands, she breathed on it and spoke the spell she hoped would bring a response. She felt the sphere vibrate in her hands and spoke again. This time it pulled her forward, away from where they now knew the entrance lay. She walked ahead of them, down, left, down, right, but always down, until the corridor began to open and a glow marked the space ahead. She tucked the orb away and drew her bow with the rest.

"Welcome, honored guests," came a hoarse voice, flat, old, like dust. "Ǣlfec and humans ready to give blood sacrifice. Welcome."

Glancing out, Uthalef whispered, "There's cover, scatter and make for it, NOW," and everyone but Elden moved as he spoke; he remained in the tunnel. Nothing came toward them. Quick looks found the chamber to be two dozen paces long and half that wide. There was light, a table, instruments, a small fire, things for brewing at the far end. Shelves lined the walls, covered with flasks and bottles; the air was heavy with fumes. A dark-cloaked shape was behind the table, and a woman in red was beside him, her hand firmly on Ǣdhahren's arm.

"Shall I call the wights, my lord?" the woman's voice was thick with menace.

Call the wights? A shiver of dread ran down Brillar's spine but her bow was steady as she pressed her back to a wall and waited. She glanced toward Elden but he took no notice. His eyes were half-closed in concentration. She looked away. There were only eight of them in the chamber and she saw that Uthalef was crouched behind a rock near the table.

"No need. We have the boy." Then he called to the ǣlfec. "An even trade perhaps and no one else need die? An ǣlfi for an ǣlfain lord? We can stop the wights so that you can leave safely. Come now, a fair trade?"

Silence hung in the murky air. Uthalef hesitated only a moment, steadying himself, then his bow and knife clattered on the stone floor as he threw them aside and stood.

"Agreed then," he said firmly, and he stepped from behind a rock, hands open.

"My lord," one of the ǣlfe shouted and was silenced by Uthalef's gesture.

"The bargain is struck," he said, his voice resolute as he stepped forward. There was laughter from the end of the chamber and the woman holding Ǣdhahren fairly cackled with delight.

Then, with all attention focused on Uthalef, Elden stepped out from the tunnel, his face dark and fierce. A bolt of lightning streamed down the hall, striking the K'ish Master, who screamed in pain before he collapsed on the table, his robe smoking. Brillar was up, and her arrow struck the woman holding Ǣdhahren as more arrows thudded into the K'ish. Uthalef rushed forward for Ǣdhahren, scooping him up and running back to them toward the tunnel, but Elden strode to the center of the hall, seemingly wrapped in fire as he sent wave after wave of flame at the potions on the table and on shelves on the walls, sterilizing the Darkness there, cleansing it with flame. Acrid smoke filled the air, choking the others as they ran for the tunnel.

Brillar was suddenly at his side, pulling his arm, screaming, "We have to go!" Fire was creeping toward him and her lungs were burning. She pulled him back to the corridor and upwards. "They have the sure path; we have to follow." There was an explosion in the chamber as they reached the tunnel and ran upward. The faint light of the sure path grew brighter. "Don't stop," she screamed, seeing that they were waiting. "We're here, go... go!"

They ran for the entrance, now their only exit, following the sure path away from fire and acrid smoke, away from certain death.

"We have him," Uthalef shouted as they reached the entrance to the cave, and the defenders scooped up arrows and stood, still firing.

"To the left, the wide part of the valley," one of the defenders yelled, and Uthalef turned left. Brillar grabbed at the one-armed ǣlfe, and another bowman helped get him up. Moving southeast, she cast spells of strength on them both, but Elden stood at the mouth of the cave, his face black with rage, throwing arcs of flame ahead of them then to the side until their way was clear. Satisfied, he sprinted to catch up with them. Above them on the hill, the archers withdrew. With nothing to fight, nothing close enough to be an animating threat, the undead began to sink, one by one, first at the west end of the valley, then in a slow advance, until all had gone back to the ground, bones fallen away.

The sure path had faltered at the entrance but now stood ahead of them. Yarell, at their rear, shouted at them when he saw the last of the undead sink back to the ground.

"A half-mile. I want no one nearer," Uthalef called out, and they plunged ahead until Elden, panting, his face still filled with fury, reached out.

"Safe," he shouted. Uthalef took him at his word. Someone spread a cloak, and he lay his charge on it then snatched the sure path out of the air. The others began to gather around them while Brillar left her patient to kneel by Ǣdhahren. Her orb was in her hand as she began spells to cleanse darkness, heal hurt and soothe pains. Minutes ticked past until, finally satisfied, she stood.

"Perhaps he should have some of that good ǣlfa brew?" she asked. She faltered and sat heavily. "And some for me as well." She took out her flask and drank deeply, feeling the day wash from her, feeling only sunlight, hearing only a breeze over a field.

"Healer," someone respectfully touched her on her shoulder. She stood; there were still wounded and she walked toward them.

"I count sixty-three," said Yarell, and she stopped. She needed to speak, and the words came slowly and with regret.

"One fell close by," and she gestured, "taken by a Dark spell that crept up his body as I watched. I hoped that… I gave him a drink and stopped the pain. He thanked me…" She covered her face, wracked with sobs.

Elden took her in his arms, trying to soothe her. "A moment," he said, holding her. "You did what you could." He stroked her hair, cast what soothing spells he knew, and waited until her sobs eased. "There are more who need you," he whispered and felt her nod.

She straightened and wiped her eyes. "Who needs aid?" Her voice was husky, but she walked toward the wounded who had been directed to sit together. Ǣlfa drink had helped many recover from lesser wounds. Now she took up the orb again, concentrating on dispelling pain, knitting up broken and smashed limbs, soothing and healing burns. Despite his poorer healing skill, Elden was able to help by cleansing wounds and soothing others. The ǣlfe who now lacked an arm, thanked her and his friend for saving his life, leaving Brillar in tears once again. Ǣlfa wafers were passed to everyone, water and ǣlfa drink from flasks. Some of the ǣlfec gathered firewood, an acknowledgment that they would have to stay there. Elden brought a kettle from his foldbox and Brillar added water to herbs for a strong healing tea with honey that was shared around to the injured, then to anyone who wanted it. Tea was brewed again and again through the afternoon and into the night. Cold ǣlfa brew was stimulating but the hot tea seemed to soothe.

Most of the ǣlfec had never been to war. Now they gathered in small groups near the fire, talking in low voices, sometimes joined by elders who gave them words of comfort. Groups shifted and re-formed. Those who had been injured early in the battle wanted to be told what had been seen and done. Sleep took some early; others didn't sleep until near dawn. Sometime in the night, Ǣdhahren stirred and cried out. Brillar was at his side quickly, to find that he had been given a sip from a flask and a piece of wafer. He looked at her curiously, then leaned against Uthalef and slept.

"What he needs most now," Uthalef told her quietly as he held the boy, "is ǣlfa food and drink and the comfort of his own people. I've sent a Summoner to our home. They'll send runners for him. But first, he needs rest." He sat back, cradling the boy in his arms, and began to sing quietly. Brillar sat down next to him, finding Elden at her side; she wrapped herself in her cloak and lay her head on his leg. Around them, ǣlfec voices joined Uthalef's song, weaving a gentle web. She fell asleep and had quiet dreams.

In the morning, Elden was gone, but there was a blanket under her head and another over her. She stood and shook herself awake, then took a sip from the ǣlfa flask and smiled. The fire still lit the dawn sky, but now she could smell roasting meat and remembered that she had eaten nothing the day before but elvish bread.

"There was some meat still in my foldbox," Elden greeted her with meat roasted on a skewer, "and a mage can be handy in a hunt."

The lines of his face, the set of his jaw told her the battle had taken its toll on him.

"Handy indeed," said Wa'olle, joining. "Three fine young stags appeared before we had gone a quarter-mile. And he spotted them with far-sense. Completely unfair." She nodded agreement.

"No one else seems to object," Elden put in, laughing. "Food is like medicine for the sick and injured as I recall."

"Injured!" Brillar moved toward the injured, still pulling meat from the skewer. She found most of the minor injuries healed. Even the large acid burns were doing well and pain relief was all that was needed. The broken limbs had been splinted after she drew the bones together. Pain relief was needed there too. The smashed arm would take more time to heal. She searched the break and surrounding tissue well to make sure the arm would be useful.

"Healer," one asked, "that Dark spell? The one that took Farendai?"

"Elden told me the wights had spells unknown to the Brotherhood. Once that Dark spell struck, it grew in his flesh, creeping up, eating him away." She stopped and closed her eyes. "Even a small injury would grow into a mortal wound."

He nodded and turned away.

That morning, they were joined by three more ǣlfen and then four in the afternoon. All dropped exhausted by the fire and slept at once. They had run without rest for several days. Brillar looked at them and sent healing spells over their legs and feet as they slept.

Elden called in more animals to keep the group fed. Elven bread was sustaining but the supply was nearly depleted. Wa'olle, who always joined him, kept up joking complaints about the unfairness of the hunt; they seemed to cheer him as much as they cheered the others.

Ǣdhahren stayed close to Uthalef, taking food and drink only from him. Whenever she was near him, Brillar sent out waves of soothing and was rewarded with small smiles.

The next day was spent in quiet conversations. Sometimes as someone passed near her, she would hear a whispered, "Healer." She turned at the first few, puzzled, then simply nodded when she heard the word. She and Elden had some time together quietly as she tried to process the battle for Ǣdhahren.

"The woman who held him, she said she would call wights? How could she do that?" Her question, spoken quietly enough, brought several ǣlfec closer to hear the answer.

Recognizing their curiosity, Elden replied more loudly, "Ah, yes, the woman with Ǣdhahren." He waited as they were joined by more ǣlfec and he waited, drawing signs in the dirt with a stick.

"What can call wights?" asked an ǣlfe, impatient to hear the answer.

"You know about the K'ish, makers of Dark potions. There are other evil masters in the realms of magic, and things not taught in the Houses of the Four Powers. It's said the K'ish may predate the Brotherhood, but I've also heard about the Savic, women who sometimes practice the Dark arts. At first, I thought they were just tales. It's said that they are known for their power to communicate with the dead and that most are harmless, living by offering to help grieving families contact someone who has died so that the family can know that the loved one is at peace. There are many imitators, women who claim to be able to make that contact only to collect money and move on. True Savic are said to be rare. Savic who practice the Dark arts are said to be rarer still. How a K'ish and a Savic met and joined together, I can only guess. It may have been his potions that bound her to him."

"And she could call the wights?" came a question.

"She could speak to the dead so, yes, she probably called the wights and the other undead. They may have been bound to serve her, or she may have promised something for their service. What that could be, I can't even guess. There are legends that say the undead wish only true death; to sink into the ground one last time and become dust. These things are beyond my knowing." Ǣlfec moved off to share what they had heard with others.

When the conversation reached Uthalef, he left Ǣdhahren with another ǣlfe and joined them. "I have also heard of the Savic," he told them quietly, "but a long time ago, and the stories are true."

"How long?" Brillar had wanted to know his true age. Grey eyes turned to her, taking her in. Brillar blushed and dropped her head. "My apologies," she said quietly.

Suddenly, Uthalef laughed. "Curiosity is natural in one so young. Five hundred years and more it was when I first heard of the Savic." She kept her head down, still blushing.

"I was on a sea voyage, for at that time, many of my people went to sea. We were low on fresh water and there was an island nearby, but the sailors refused to land, saying there was evil there. A woman called a Savic, they said, had been marooned there for her dark deeds. If a ship came too close, the sailors would hear singing, dive over the side and try to swim toward the song. Sailors say that anyone who could get to land was enslaved or killed. How long she had been there, no one knew or could say. For all I know, she could have been dead for a long time or she could have had a store of potions to extend her life. In truth, Elden seems to know more about them than I do, even if he only heard stories." He hurried back to his charge.

"Someday," Elden said quietly, "your curiosity will get you into trouble."

Brillar burst out laughing so hard, she couldn't speak. Around them, heads turned to stare. Laughter poured from her and she gasped for breath, pointing at him as he gaped at her.

When she could catch her breath, she gasped. "What more trouble is there?" she asked and dissolved into more laughter. When she was able to breathe properly, she shook her head at him. Waving a hand, she asked again, quietly, soberly, "What more trouble is there?"

*** 25 ***

That night around the fire, Uthalef stood and everyone fell silent. "Ǣdhahren is well enough to travel. In the morning, we'll fix slings for those who are unable to walk and a basket chair for him. It is time for all of us, all," and he looked at Brillar and Elden, "to go Home." He sat down to cheers.

The next morning bustled with activity. Meat for the journey, slings and a chair made, and long branches cut for them, Ǣlfec were assigned to carry the burdens in relays. Only two hours after dawn, everything was ready. A sure path for Ǣlfainhome was taken from Uthalef's belt pouch and sent upwards and the group moved out to the southeast.

"We could," Elden had told her quietly the night before, "leave them now, continue our travels?"

"And miss the opportunity to see Ǣlfainhome?"

She was answered, as she knew she would be, by his chuckle. "Few are invited as we have been. No, that will be something to see and something for tales around many a hearth."

The ǣlfain pace was slow, for although they were used to going lightly, there were the injured and those who needed to be carried. Brillar stayed close to those with injuries, making sure that healing bones were not shaken too badly by the journey. Elden was often out with a hunting party, coming back with deer and gwinth. Herbal tea with honey had become something of a favorite at night and the supply of honey dwindled quickly.

Elden solved that problem, using far-sight to find a beehive as the group went through a field of flowers sprung up where several streams ran together. It was the ǣlfec who, one told him, 'sang the bees to sleep' and took several combs. Elden watched from a safe distance, not sure he could trust their 'singing.' Still, it was effective, and bits of comb were passed around with most of the honey saved for the tea. Water was no trouble for them as they moved; streams were everywhere, flowing from the mountains.

In the second afternoon, there was a joyful meeting. Runners from Ǣlfainhome met them and were greeted with enthusiasm. They carried ǣlfa brews, breads, dried fruits, herbs, and nuts which were shared with everyone. If they were surprised to see two humans in the company, they said nothing. There was a joyous reunion for Ǣdhahren as his brother, Oubren, was among the runners. Ǣdhahren was scooped up and tossed into the air to much laughter before he could be quieted so his brother could go into discussion with Uthalef; then, he sought out Brillar and Elden.

The pair was sitting by a stream, bare toes dangling in the water. When he approached, they scrambled to their feet.

"You are well met," he greeted them with a bow. "Many thanks for your help in rescuing my brother. I will see you again at Ǣlfainhome." With another bow, he turned and went back to the company getting ready to take his brother home at once.

They looked at each other in puzzlement. "A quick greeting," Elden remarked and they sat down, feet once again in the cool water. As they watched, four of the ǣlfec, Oubren, with Ǣdhahren in a pack on his back, set off at a run toward Ǣlfainhome. Their rest was brief; all were ready for home now.

That night, Uthalef stood once again at the fire. "In the morning, we collect as much water as we can carry. We soon reach the low dunes where there is no water."

Brillar and Elden opened foldboxes in the morning, storing water in flasks. Whenever the foldboxes were opened, they collected a small crowd.

Finally, it was too much, and Wa'olle asked, "How can you carry so much weight? So much… everything."

Elden smiled at the question. "These boxes are magic-made and take months or years in the making, with Item magic. I hold a First in Item, but the making of these is a much more specialized skill. Actually, I have never completely understood what goes into their making. Where the weight goes, for example, I am unable to explain. Where the space goes was explained, but I'm not sure that I understand it. Brillar?"

"My mother also holds a First, but she was helped and guided when she made my foldbox and never explained it."

The ǣlfec waited patiently.

"Well, then," Elden began, stifling a sigh, "what we see is in three forms. The line, the flat and the height." He drew the first two on the ground then added an upright stick for the last. "These are what we can see. For a mage, there are other things we can't see. Mana has an unseen form, for example. It's everywhere, always being made. A mage can feel and gather it, store it, use it for spells. The foldbox finds other forms, other spaces that we can't see and puts our belongings there. Wherever the belongings are, perhaps the full weight is with them. The one I carry would be a little heavier if I added rocks to it, but it would still be easy to carry." Seeing puzzled looks, he smiled again. "As I said, I don't truly understand it, either."

Uthalef came over to the group. "We're ready now." All the 'students' disbursed to their places and the group started out at a quick pace. Wa'olle came up alongside them with a smile. "I am to tell Uthalef when you tire, and we will stop." Both resolved to continue with spells to strengthen and replenish and to take sips of ǣlfa brew when needed.

As they traveled, grass began to thin and streams disappeared. First, the country took on the look of northern scrubland, dry and harsh; then they began to encounter dusty sandy soil that puffed up around their feet, then true sand. Vegetation grew in short tufts then vanished. Ahead of them, was a small rise consisting entirely of sand. The wind blew it toward them, making their eyes water. At the top of the first dune, greater dunes spread out in front of them. Then the heat struck them in full force, making them gasp. Wa'olle shouted in Ǣlfair and they all stopped. The ǣlfec had already wrapped cloths around their faces and provided extra for Elden and Brillar, showing them how they should be fastened.

"Wear the cloaks you were given," Wa'olle advised. "They will protect you from the heat as our clothing protects us. We all need to drink plenty of water or we will fall ill."

The cloaks were protection, cooling them, where before, they had been warming.

"Ǣlfa weave is a mystery to me," Elden remarked, but Brillar just nodded. He sent a spell for strength to her and could feel her welcome it. There were more spells before the ǣlfec stopped.

"Are you well?" Uthalef asked them as they ate and drank, and they nodded. He looked around at the dunes. "We are anxious to return home. We often cross this expanse only at night, and we will begin again after we have eaten, to take advantage of the coolness. Can you be ready?"

"We can," Elden answered for both. As Uthalef left them, he cast waves of strength and replenishment at both of them.

Then Brillar cast healing and pain relief at their sore legs and feet after saying, "Mine are on fire." Finished, she went to check on the injured and the ǣlfec who carried the slings.

A brief rest, then Uthalef sent the sure path home aloft and they set out. The dunes were difficult to navigate. Ǣlfain went lightly, but human feet tended to sink into the sand. Twice, Brillar slid down a dune, laughing at the bottom. "Much easier than walking," she said as she brushed away sand. Elden was constantly sinking to his knees and being pulled out by Wa'olle. They were slowing the group, but there were only smiles for them from the ǣlfec.

Dawn found them still in the dunes and Uthalef pushed them onward. It was nearly noon when they slid down the last of the dunes and came to a flat, desolate expanse. A halt was called and the ǣlfec took jointed sticks from packs to make short shelters from the sun. Wa'olle and Yarell showed them how it was done, and they threw themselves onto the ground under one to sleep. When they woke, a fire had been started and they joined the assembled ǣlfec. Packed meat was roasting and Brillar and Elden were rewarded with the first of the cooked pieces, then dried fruit, nuts, breads and more ǣlfa brew. By the end of the meal, the pair were feeling as if they had been on a quiet walk in the forest.

After they finished, one of the ǣlfec began to sing softly and was joined by others. To Brillar, it sounded like a quiet wind in the trees and the splashing of bright water over rocks. When the song stopped, she shook herself to release the spell. Around her, the sun-shelters had been taken down and packs were being readied. She made a quick check of the injured, making sure that no one was in pain from the journey or the sun. She paid particular attention to the smashed arm and found that it was healing faster than she expected.

In the cool of the night, the group pushed on with a brief stop for sleep. In the morning, what had been a quiet gathering, was suddenly full of sound, ǣlfec voices in the ǣlfair tongue, bright and happy, laughing. She was pulled to her feet by Yarell, who insisted on brushing sand from her. "Today, we will be home," he said joyfully. "Ǣlfainhome is ahead and only a few hours away."

The day seemed brighter to everyone. The sure path was used but not really needed and they all stepped forward lightly. There was what seemed to be good-natured joking in ǣlfair all around the humans, with laughter and even some winks and pointing.

"What's all this about?" Elden asked their companion.

"You will know when it happens," Wa'olle said, and spoke in ǣlfair to those around them, too much laughter.

"It seems we will know when 'it' whatever it is, happens," Brillar said, laughing with them.

Two hours later, as they finished climbing a small hill, Brillar and Elden stopped abruptly, to more ǣlfain laughter.

Ahead of them, down the hill and across a green meadow, were trees, titans among trees, colossi among trees. They gaped at them; trunks as wide as houses stretched toward the sky, each tree with branches as great as a forest. Flocks of birds were lost in them. They stretched upwards until their branches were lost in the clouds. Even from a distance, heads had to tilt backward to take them in. The pair stood still, agape in wonder, spellbound by the sight. Around them, there was more laughter.

"And now you know." Yarell laughed and pulled at them. "If you don't move, we'll never reach them." He grabbed Brillar's hand, tugging her down the hill and into a run.

Shouts in ǣlfair, then, "They come," Yarell shouted.

Across the field, running toward them, were hundreds of ǣlfain, singing, all carrying flowers and foods. They were engulfed by ǣlfa, who laid flowers on the necks of all who were returning. Ǣlfen fell into the arms of their returning ǣlfec and the unwed ǣlfec were welcomed by ǣlfen. Each time the pair tried to speak their thanks, food was offered. Ǣlfic tugged at their hands. They were nearly dragged across the field then onto a bridge over rushing water and into the shade of the trees, greater in their nearness than they had been in the distance. Still, the laughter and song was around them as they walked and gazed in wonder. Ǣlfainhome.

Had it not been for the throng around them, it might have been hushed under the trees where ferns grew tall along the paths. Now the very air seemed to vibrate with the joy of the homecoming.

Ǣlfec had gone out on search, then into battle, and had now returned. As they surged ahead, they glimpsed one ǣlfen walking apart but with them, carrying no flowers. Seeing where they looked, Yarell said, "Her husband was the man who fell." There was no time for more as they walked on for miles. Side paths joined theirs and more ǣlfain watched for them and waved them on.

Finally, the path widened and became a road laid with tiles, in greens and blues. Laughter and song continued but more quietly. Eventually, the path opened onto a wide plaza set among trees and filled with ǣlfain. An ǣlfe, tall and stately, dressed in white that was trimmed with silver, stepped forward and all fell silent.

"Welcome home to each and all." There was brief cheering and he held up his hand. "Our guests must be tired. Places have been prepared for you," he said, nodding to Elden and Brillar, "with food and drink." He smiled at them sadly. "Tonight, is for ǣlfain speech and ǣlfain grief."

Yarell came for them and led them away from the crowd, with ǣlfic still following until they were shooed away. Away from the crowd, they felt the hush of the forest around them and the still air. They were led through leafy paths to a clearing where the roots of two great trees formed something like chambers, with drapery over the entrances providing some privacy. In the center of the clearing, was a wide pool suited for swimming at least a few strokes. It was formed by a brook that ran through the clearing. Twisted roots curled here and there and the air itself was like food and drink.

"You may swim if you like," Yarell said, "then take your rest." Bowing slightly, he left by the same path.

Brillar sat on the bank of the pool and dipped in her hand. "Cool but not cold, another wonder in a day of wonders."

Elden had been investigating one of the chambers. Now he came out with a tray of fruit. Brillar stood and cast a cleansing spell on herself and her clothes then stripped down to her scants.

"You clean before you bathe?" Elden asked, laughing.

"It would be a pity to sully such a pool with the dust of the trail," she replied and splashed in, finding the pool nearly to her chest. Reaching up, she unbraided her hair, letting it flow freely and began to swim. Elden lay down on the bank, one hand trailing in the water. He popped a small fruit into his mouth.

"I think I'd rather eat these than swim," he said and found himself splashed.

"What is it with you and water?" he asked and dried himself with a spell.

She pulled herself onto the bank next to him, dripping and wringing out her hair. "There are places near Laurenfell that I imagined were perfection." She found herself suddenly dry and smiled at him. "They were only shadows; dreams of perfection."

"Someone comes," Elden said. Brillar answered by slipping back into the pool.

Uthalef called a quiet greeting before coming into the glade and was welcomed. He smiled at Brillar, who had seated herself on an underwater rock. Now she came out and found herself dry again. "She drips." Elden smiled at Uthalef as Brillar dressed and seated herself.

"You have questions." Uthalef smiled again.

"She always has questions," Elden answered before she could speak.

"Only a few. In the K'ish chamber, the K'ish asked for a trade, an ǣlfain child for an ǣlfe lord?"

"I am counted as one," Uthalef replied.

Brillar blushed, completely flustered.

"I think what my apprentice means, what we both mean, is that if we have ever treated you rudely…"

Uthalef waved a hand, still smiling. "I was one of the company, a leader, but one among many. There were other ǣlfain lords with us, also unnamed. All is well."

"You would have traded yourself for Ǣdhahren, then?" Brillar went on.

"I would. As I recall, I tried to and was interrupted by lightning."

Now it was Elden's turn to be flustered, but Uthalef only laughed, then sobered. "I never really thought that he meant to keep his word. Nor did I think that any of us would leave that place alive. We owe you a great debt, all of us." He was silent for a moment, looking at the pool and the trees. All is well. Tonight, you will remain here in this glade. Nothing, I think, is lacking. Tomorrow is for the dawn. Oh, Elden, one question. I have your name, but where were you born? Lord Ǣlethee has requested it." The question answered, he stood, bowed slightly, and left as quietly as he had come.

The day was already fading; they were so deep in the trees. "An ǣlfain lord among us. I could feel his anger, his fear when he mentioned the K'ish." Brillar shook her head and was silent, then, "Now, m'lord mage, will you swim or do I push you in?"

Elden swam. They brought food out beside the pool and Brillar put her hair back in a braid. As night fell, growths on the trees began to glow, giving them exactly the light they needed.

"Ferns," Brillar said, examining one great trunk. "They grow in the bark and the roots are glowing. Another marvel."

From the direction of the plaza, they could hear ǣlfain song, this time mournful.

"Sad, but still so beautiful." She stayed with him, almost afraid to move, until the song stopped and everything was quiet except for the night birds and chirping insects, then she went to her bed. She left him lying on his back on the streambank, staring through the branches, waiting for stars in the darkling sky.

*** 26 ***

The following morning, ǣlfenec brought platters of food and beakers of fruit juices. They bowed as they left. An ǣlfen joined them after they had finished their meal, and both stood.

"I am called Nywella. May I speak with you, Brillar?"

Elden bowed politely, then left them on the bank of the pool. Brillar suddenly felt the woman's sorrow and sat down in dread.

Nywella sat beside her, nodded understanding, and reached out a hand. "All is well. He has been laid to rest with song."

Brillar shivered slightly and couldn't look at Nywella.

"I was told you were with him. May I hear the words from you?" Her voice was soft.

Brillar managed to repeat the story of her husband's death, weeping when she came to his "thank you." She wiped tears away hastily.

"I couldn't stop what was happening, nothing I knew helped him. I'm so sorry…"

"No, please, it's good that someone was with him, tried to save him, and that there was no pain. Farendai was a good husband, and I loved him. He was an ǣlfain lord, and we have children I will cherish. You've met our son, Wa'olle. I thank you for this memory of him." She rose with quiet grace and was gone.

Brillar sat, stunned, and put her face in her hands.

"What is it?" Elden asked, joining her.

"The ǣlfe who died? He was a lord, and Wa'olle is his son. No one ever told me." They sat quietly for some time.

Yarell joined them soon after Nywella left and invited them to join in a musical gathering. "Ǣlfain music is not to be missed on a summer day," he insisted, and they joined him. As always, with music, there was food and drink. The music lasted through lunch unabated as ǣlfain joined them and took up instruments and songs, then drifted away.

"It seems to me," Brillar whispered to Elden, "that everyone wants to meet us or at least see us." He nodded but only sat back to enjoy the music.

As the afternoon grew late, Uthalef joined them. "I am sorry to interrupt your afternoon, but you should make ready. There will be a great homecoming feast tonight." He walked them back to their chambers. "Someone will come again to lead you," he told them and took his farewell.

"I always find so much mystery in them. Ǣlfain music on a summer afternoon, although I think it's always summer here. Now a feast?" Brillar shook her head as he left them.

She opened her foldbox, removed the green dress, perfume, brushes and Elden's gift. They were the best she had brought with her and she frowned, thinking of the finery Elden had in his foldbox. Sitting on the bed, she loosed her braid and shook out her hair, brushing it vigorously. Two braids at the side of her face were swept up and pinned with Elden's gift. Laughing at her foolishness, she set the perfume aside, thinking how wonderful and scented everything was around her. She freshened the dress twice then looked at her arm, glad that the sleeves would cover the dimlock scar. She settled the dress carefully over her head, lacing the bodice.

She was ready when Yarell called her name softly. With a deep breath, she stepped outside and stopped. Elden wore none of his fine clothing, only the simple greys he had purchased—it seemed so long ago—when they stopped at the *Red Rooster*. She blinked back tears at his courtesy and took his offered arm.

Yarell smiled at them in approval. "If you will follow me, they are waiting."

The forest walk, its air so rich, distracted them, and neither noticed that there was a stillness around them until they came to a crowd of ǣlfain all facing toward their walkway. Everyone moved aside as the pair was led forward and then closed silently behind them.

"What is all this?" Brillar whispered to Yarell.

"You are to be honored," he whispered back, eyes glowing with pride.

Shocked, Brillar's steps faltered. "But we did nothing," she told him, but Yarell shook his head.

The crowd was behind them. The plaza they had seen earlier, was ahead, but now it was empty. Yarell found their place and moved to one side with a slight bow, motioning them to stay where they were, as the Ǣlfain Lord, Ǣlethee, stepped out on a slight dais, his lady by his side. Brillar clutched at Elden's arm with both hands, her face glowing with embarrassment.

"Brillar of Laurenfell," Ǣlethee's voice was quiet but seemed to ring in the space, "approach us."

She glanced at Elden then stepped hesitantly forward until she reached the edge of the dais. There, she dropped into a deep curtsey, holding it, uncertain.

"Come, child, rise." She heard the lady's clear voice, and rose, keeping her eyes down. She could feel ǣlfain all around them, watching.

"Brillar of Laurenfell, with this gift, we name you Ǣlfainfriend," Ǣlethee intoned. He stepped toward her, slid his hands under her hair, and secured a pendant around her neck. She shivered; the gift was warming and chilling her at once. She glanced up into steady eyes of clear grey and found herself held by them.

"Another gift we have for you," said the lady, stepping forward; Brillar managed to pull her gaze from Ǣlethee's and look at his lady as Ǣdhahren came forward with a bow held on a fine cloth. "Archer, they have named you," she offered. "We give you this ǣlfain bow. May its arrows always find their mark." Ǣdhahren held up the bow and Brillar took it, tears streaming down her cheeks as he smiled at her. Feeling herself dismissed, she backed away until she was beside Elden.

"Garnelden of Torennwood, approach us." She glanced at him as he went past her and fell to one knee.

"Garnelden of Torennwood, with this gift, we name you Ǣlfainfriend."

She watched as Lord Ǣlethee placed the necklace, seeing him shiver in response as it touched him.

"Our second gift," the lady said, and another ǣlfi came forward with a small charm. "If ever you have the need, tap this three times and follow the sure path through any danger." He took the charm and rose, backing away until he was beside her again.

Lord Ǣlethee clapped his hands, and there was suddenly music everywhere. The crowd surged around the mages, congratulating them, presenting flowers, or simply touching them in gratitude, as tables were carried into the plaza, then food and drink. Goblets were thrust into their hands, and they were led forward through bowing ǣlfain folk.

"My head is swimming," Elden managed to tell her as someone took his arm and led him to a seat near the head of the table. Whatever she was going to reply, was lost in more words of thanks.

Still bemused, they sat where they were led. Brillar, nearly breathless, drank deeply and could only stare at what surrounded them as she touched the necklace. The bow, she laid on the table, wondering at its craftsmanship.

Elden's hand was on her arm. "Ǣlfa drink," he said, eyes sparkling wickedly. "Better eat something, or we will have to carry you away."

She took a deep breath, gathering herself, and she smiled up at him. "You will have to carry me somewhere, m'lord mage, for my apprenticeship is only half complete," and she raised her cup as he dissolved into laughter.

A Note From the Author

Hello, friends. You have now (I hope) enjoyed a novel that cost less than a cup of coffee at Starbucks. And, unlike that transitory coffee, you can go back and enjoy the novel for free! What a bargain!

One last thing to do: Leave a review!

Novelists live and die on reviews, so go to Amazon.com, locate the novel, leave five stars with a brief note. A few words are just fine.

Of course, if you didn't like the novel (here the writer bursts into tears), you don't have to do anything! Nothing at all. Just close the novel, shut off your Kindle, and go have a cup of coffee.

The Sisterhood

The Sisterhood is primarily dedicated to Life magic and the healing arts, although Item magic is taught there. Older students interested in more study in the latter or who wish to get some skill in Creature magic are usually sent to the Brotherhood.

The Great House of the Sisterhood just outside of the town of Laurenfell takes advanced students from all the minor teaching houses scattered across Northern Dereff. Both girls and boys are admitted to the House, although girls usually outnumber the boys, who are often drawn to skills not taught at the House.

The House and Healing Hall are of white stone, full of windows, courtyards and light. Color is encouraged and students and staff are usually dressed in a rainbow of colors, although staff members usually prefer pastels over the bright yellows and pinks of students.

Many of the married Sisters live in the town or have homes near the school. At times, they and their families move to one of the minor houses to take up residence and duties or leave completely, to become healers in the world's villages and towns.

The Sisterhood maintains, with support from the Brotherhood, a special compound for those Brothers who, broken by war, require special care. Elders from both houses are taken in by them if their families can't provide for them. This is an extremely rare event.

The Brotherhood

The Brotherhood has, since its beginning centuries ago, specialized in teaching War magic, although Item and Creature magic are encouraged and are actually deemed more valuable than War magic. Foldboxes are made almost exclusively at the Great House by Grand Masters of Item magic.

The Great House of the Brotherhood is at Anbre-near-the-Sea, near the northern coast. Its students and staff tend to be male, although many older students from the Sisterhood who want to improve their Item magic skills and study Creature magic are often found there. The House is not as diverse in its colors as that of the Sisterhood, but it is also a place of great courtyards and bright corridors.

Like the Sisters, Brothers are often married and raise families near the Great House or are posted at smaller teaching houses in the north. Brothers needing special care are sent to the House of Restoration in Laurenfell, but they are often visited by their Brothers and family members.

***

As far as anyone knows, there are no schools for mages south of the Wilds.

Author V.L. Stuart is a journalist and author living in Costa Rica with her husband and a small, comical dog.

She is a long-time reader - usually of science fiction, historical mysteries, and epic fiction. As a teen, she cut her teeth on Heinlein and found the delightful worlds of McCaffrey as an adult. Her first genres were poetry and essays, and she won awards in both. Her 'Orb and Arrow' trilogy has been well-received by reviewers and will be available on Amazon. She recently completed 'Master of Magic,' another book set in the world of Orb and Arrow. Her work in progress is an epic fantasy, 'Warriors of the Kalahn,' which covers 900 years of Kalahn history.

As for her writing process, she is a pantser - "May all the gods bless grammarly.com. Even with an English degree, my errors are legion."

At present, she lives between two volcanoes, "But no worries, only one of them is active."

Made in the USA
Columbia, SC
20 July 2022

63749640R00152